ELIZABETH NOYES

Imperfect Bonds

Imperfect Bonds

© 2016 Elizabeth Noyes

ISBN-13: 978-1-944120-07-8
ISBN-10: 1-944120-07-6

E-book ISBN-13: 978-1-944120-10-8

This book is a work of fiction. Names, characters, places, and incidents are either products of the author's imagination or used fictitiously. Any similarity to actual people and/or events is purely coincidental.

Published by Write Integrity Press, 2631 Holly Springs Parkway, Box 35, Holly Springs, GA 30142

www.WriteIntegrity.com

Printed in the United States of America.

Dedication

To my husband, Paul, whose love, belief in my work, and unwavering encouragement have played a vital role in this crazy, maddening journey.

Acknowledgements

To all my friends, family, fans, and supporters,
I do this as much for you as for me.

To my critique partners, proofreaders, beta readers, editor,
and publisher, *thank you* cannot express how much I
appreciate each of you.

Chapter One

Thunderheads, dark as indigo, roiled over the western ridge, bruises against the tarnished silver sky. Cassie Cameron stared out the kitchen window at the churning cloud formations.

Sadeé sat on the floor at Cassie's feet, shivering.

"It's okay, girl." A quick pat of reassurance did nothing to soothe the dog's uneasiness. Whoever heard of a fraidy-cat German shepherd?

Hefting her equipment bag over one shoulder, Cassie grabbed the small cooler by its handle and set off at a trot for the barn where the family kept their personal vehicles.

Sadeé kept reluctant pace, her tail tucked firmly between her legs. Big baby. The slightest rumble of thunder usually sent her running to hide under the bed where she'd cower for hours. But here she was, braving the storm so she wouldn't get left behind.

An earthy smell filled Cassie's nostrils, the kind that heralded rain. Well, with a little bit of luck and a whole lot of hurry, they might miss the worst of the weather since their path lay in the opposite direction from the storm's track.

Lightning arced across the sky in a ragged zigzag that seemed to go on forever. After a brief count of four, thunder rumbled. Cassie stowed the cooler and equipment bag on the back seat of the Honda and opened the driver's door.

The dog voiced her unease with a pathetic mewl but jumped in and settled on the passenger seat, head lowered to her paws.

"Shhh," Cassie admonished. A firm scratch behind Sadeé's ears earned her a lick.

The wind whipped through the window as they turned south on Route 93. Long tendrils of hair swirled around her face. She should have taken time to put it up in a ponytail.

A few miles into the drive, KSRA, the local radio station, began to fade. She grabbed her purse from the floor, intending to get an update from the weather app on her cell.

No service.

"Are you kidding?" The phone made a clunking sound when she dropped it in the cup holder. "How is it NASA can take pictures of galaxies billions of light years away in space, but the eggheads can't figure out how to get cell reception in the mountains right here on Earth?"

People round these parts kept both feet firmly entrenched in the past and liked it that way. How had she forgotten? Nothing had changed here. Probably never would. "Next time, I'm bringing my iPod."

Gentle doggy snores filled the silence.

Fifty or so miles to go, most of it through a series of long desert-like basins sandwiched between the rugged peaks of the Lost River Valley Mountain Range.

With nothing to distract her, Cassie's thoughts turned to the eight weeks of summer ahead. Two months of self-imposed vacation to get through. She didn't regret, not for a moment, coming back for her brother Garrett's wedding, or agreeing to help her friend Lucy with her shoulder rehab. A respite after seven straight years of school before she started a new job had sounded beneficial. The reality was something else. Too many long, empty hours filled her days. All because of the strained relationship with her twin sister and a family that tiptoed around them.

And then there was the too-sexy-for-his-own-good deputy who seemed to think she should fall at his feet whenever he beckoned. Ha, in his dreams.

No wonder she'd jumped at this opportunity to work with one of Doc Burdette's patients. "Who said physical therapy jobs don't exist in rural America. I can see it now—Have Medicine Ball Will Travel. Just like the circuit-riding preachers of the past."

Sadeé opened her eyes and rolled them sideways to stare at Cassie.

She could survive anything for one summer, but September couldn't get here soon enough. Doctor Wilkes, the orthopedist who'd performed Lucy's shoulder surgery, had

offered an interview with his group. The thought of working for such a prestigious practice set her heart racing. She'd finally have a real job with a paycheck she earned. No more living off the dividends from the ranch's profits. Of course, it meant moving to someplace like Idaho Falls. Maybe even Pocatello or Boise. Or even out of state. Far away from the ranch and her family, but that was her dream. Right?

Beside her, Sadeé shifted on the seat.

She smiled at the snoozing animal. Her summer stay had brought her Sadeé.

The rain fell harder now and pelted her arm through the open window. She pressed the button to raise the glass. The locals called this stretch of road through the canyons No Man's Land, and for good reason—no radio, no cell phone service, no stores, no houses, no gas stations, and no people. Nothing but milkwort, sagebrush, greasewood, shadscale, dirt, and rocks.

Lots of rocks.

The only signs of civilization out here were the rough pavement, a parade of telephone poles, a few road signs, and an occasional billboard.

Midway through the first valley, the rain stopped as though someone had pressed the off button. The sky began to clear. A lone eagle soared on the air currents. Three coyotes skulked through the brush.

This place was nothing like *Hot*lanta.

She snorted at the comparison. The Beaumont Orthopedic

Group where she'd interned in Atlanta before coming home for the wedding had given Cassie a wealth of practical experience, but also some much needed savoir-faire. But at what cost? Life in the southern megalopolis had changed her, taught her caution and suspicion. Had it also made her less tolerant of rural life?

It took only a second of pondering to reject the idea. She'd had a blast in Atlanta, even after her despicable brothers had sicced an over-protective deputy on her. But Idaho was home. Would always be home.

Okay, maybe Jonas and Wade weren't despicable, but they definitely had control issues. As did Deputy Derek Naughton, hot stuff extraordinaire.

As happened all too often of late, the former Navy SEAL from Texas turned small-town Idaho police officer commandeered her thoughts. Derek had followed her to Atlanta, presumably at the behest of her brothers because she'd crossed paths with the madman who'd hurt Lucy. It didn't matter that Cassie wasn't his target. Derek took his self-appointed guardian angel role to heart.

Ha. The man had mastered the fine art of arrogance, bossiness, and seduction. There was absolutely nothing remotely angelic about Derek. He'd even had the audacity to hang out in the Beaumont Clinic's waiting room while she worked, for Pete's sake. How embarrassing. And then he'd insisted on moving into her apartment.

"Somebody's got to watch over you," he'd claimed.

And like a fool, she'd let him stay.

They'd watched television, done laundry, cooked meals, cleaned, and even grocery shopped together, just like an old married couple. She couldn't go anywhere without his size fourteen boots stepping on her shadow.

But a man who cooked and cleaned couldn't be all bad, could he?

A smile hovered on her lips. An old married couple, but without any of the side benefits. Not that Derek didn't try. He'd indicated his attraction to her over and over. She just wasn't interested.

Okay, that was a lie. Perhaps unwilling might be a better word since Mr. No Commitment made it clear after the one scorching kiss they'd shared last summer that any relationship with him had a limited shelf life.

Nope, an expiration date with Derek wasn't enough. She wanted more than a fling. For a short time, she'd thought— hoped—he might want more, too, but then they'd come home, and he'd disappeared for a month without a word.

"Got something to take care of back home in Texas," was his excuse. Now he'd returned without explanation and a ton of secrets in those naughty green eyes. And tons of criticism for her.

She shrugged. His loss. Dead-end Derek didn't fit her long term plans anyway.

Up ahead the canyon narrowed. She slowed to negotiate the pass, delighted to see the sunlight glitter on exposed threads of dolomite, quartz, and amethyst on the slopes of the mountains. How could she have forgotten the rugged beauty of this land?

Ahead in the distance, she spotted a vehicle on the northbound side of the road. A little farther and she could make out a forest green GMC pickup. A big one. Jacked high. Shiny, too, like it came straight off the showroom floor. A man knelt near the rear wheel while a second man stood off to the side. Tough place to break down.

Should she stop and offer help? The idea of a woman alone, stopping for two men out in the middle of nowhere made her balk. No doubt her new wariness came courtesy of big city life. But the unwritten law of the land out here required a person to stop. Leaving someone stranded in a desolate area often meant life or death in the old days. Maybe if she slowed, kept the doors locked, and offered to send help. Yeah, a much better idea.

Cassie hit the lock button and lowered the driver's window no more than two inches. A second thought had her reaching under the driver's seat for the assurance of the small wooden box hidden there.

When the speed dropped, Sadeé scrambled to a sitting position. Panting, ears perked, she zeroed in on the two men.

The guy changing the tire didn't bother to look up when

Cassie stopped alongside. The sleeveless undershirt he wore revealed a sinewy physique with a serpent tattoo coiled around the length of his left arm.

The other guy strutted over to her car with a smirk. His gray t-shirt strained over a beer gut, and needed a good scrubbing. Splotches of what might have been breakfast or remnants from last night's dinner stained the front.

Cassie raised her chin and spoke through the narrow window opening. "Need help?"

A ham-like forearm leaned against her window. "Well, hello, pretty lady. Thanks for stopping." Dirty Shirt had a surprisingly high voice for such a large man.

The low, menacing grumble from Sadeé accentuated the alarms already clanging in Cassie's head. She might not be a genius like her sister, Mallory, but she knew trouble when it stared her in the face. "No problem. I'll call roadside assistance for you when I get to where I'm going."

"Nah. If you could help us out, we won't need them. Maybe you could hold the lug nuts while we get the spare on. Whaddya say?" He reached for her door handle.

Was he kidding? A flat tire did not require three people to fix. Did he really think she'd fall for a line like that?

Sadeé went from sitting on the seat to lunging across Cassie's lap when Dirty Shirt yanked on the door handle. Front paws braced on the window. Teeth bared. Perfect manners gone.

Dirty Shirt jumped back and let loose a string of foul words.

"Billy, leave the girl alone," the other man shouted. He hefted the spare out of the truck bed and let it drop to the ground to bounce a few times. "We don't have time for your games."

Dirty Shirt—Billy—glared at his friend.

"Sit." Cassie tugged on the shepherd's collar and tried hard not to grin. Thunder might make Sadeé whimper, but she'd eat this guy for lunch.

Her humor fled at the sight of Billy's clenched fists and furious face.

"Cut the crap and get over here," the man with the snake tat yelled again. "You forget we got a deadline?"

"Looks like your friend has everything under control." Cassie waggled her fingers. "Good luck."

"Hold on a sec." Billy removed a ball cap that had seen better days, wiped his forehead on a sleeve, and reseated the hat in a visible effort to control his anger. Sadeé had scared him. Men viewed fear as a weakness. And Billy didn't like looking the fool. "I see you got a cooler in the back. Maybe you got something cold you could share? A man can work up a sweat out in this heat."

She'd brought several bottles of Rocks Natural Spring Water but wasn't stupid enough to lower her window to pass one through. These guys could tough it out until they reached a

store where they could buy their own. "It's empty. Sorry."

"Why are you in such a hurry to leave? What's your name, sweetheart?" His fingers clamped onto the top of the window.

"Got to go. Good luck with the tire."

Billy slammed a fist against her glass.

Sadeé snarled again.

"I got your tag number, just so you know." Billy yelled after her, adding a nasty, derogatory name. "I can find you."

Fury lit her up. Bullies used their size to intimidate and inflict fear, but Billy-boy had chosen the wrong victim today.

Several yards past their truck she stopped the car on a slight rise and grabbed her cell phone. Opening the camera app, she lowered her window and leaned out. *Click.* A quick picture captured the profiles of the two men.

They looked up in surprise.

Click. Click. She added a frontal view and a clear picture of the truck and its license plate.

"Hey," the guy working the flat tire shouted. He shook his fist.

"You can't do that." Billy sprinted toward her.

She didn't wait for him. With head shots and their license number safely stored, Billy's veiled threat held no power.

Once Sadeé settled down again, Cassie pushed the encounter with the two goons from her mind. She refused to let those two lowlifes spoil the rest of her day. Her thoughts turned instead to her new patient, Coot Harbins, an older man with a farm to run. Doc said he might not be inclined to pursue physical therapy, even if it came to him.

The miles passed in a daze until sometime later, a flash in the rearview mirror—sunlight on chrome—caught her eye. Another traveler at last. Other than Billy and his bud, this was the only vehicle she'd seen.

Another glance in the mirror a few minutes later showed the blip had drawn a lot closer. She checked her speedometer. Nobody paid attention to the speed limits, especially out here where the road never curved, but this guy seemed bent on breaking the sound barrier.

Squinting, she could just make out the dark shape of a truck. Not one of those miniature toy-sized pickups like her sister drove, either.

With an eye on the rearview mirror, she almost missed the road sign that flashed by on the right. Trail Creek Road. The turnoff to Harbins farm. Two more miles.

The vehicle behind her drew closer and closer.

She could make out details now. A jacked up GMC. Dark green. Why would Billy and his friend chase after her? They'd been heading north. And the tattooed guy had mentioned a deadline.

Her imagination took flight, envisioning every heinous crime ever printed in the newspapers. She pressed harder on the accelerator and ignored the rattles her car made. The little town of Mackay lay only a few miles beyond the turnoff. Should she head there instead? They had a police department. If she could find it.

The gap between the vehicles closed even more until she could make out the features of the driver and passenger: Billy and his friend.

Fear left her mouth dry. "C'mon." She had the gas pedal pressed to the floor, knowing her Honda V-6 couldn't outrun the Sierra 2500 hemi. Her heart pounded like a million-man march. At this rate, they'd catch her before she even made it to Trail Creek Road, much less to town.

A mile screamed by. The truck gained until it was almost kissing her bumper.

"Not good. Not good." The two words spilled from her lips in a chant.

Movement in the side-view mirror drew her eye. The green truck had moved into the oncoming lane and was inching up alongside her. Less than a foot separated the two vehicles.

On instinct, she jerked the wheel left.

The driver braked and swerved, but not in time to avoid the scrape of metal on metal.

Cassie never let up on the accelerator.

Sadeé stumbled against the door before righting her stance.

"Down, Sadeé. Stay," Cassie yelled. She made a mental promise to look into some kind of safety restraint for the dog when they got out of this mess. If they got out of it.

The dog obeyed.

Trail Creek Road came into sight. They'd be on her in a blink when she slowed for the turn. Better than making a run for town. She couldn't keep this up all the way into Mackay.

The green truck surged forward.

Oh, Lord, here they come again. What if they had a gun?

A hard yank on the wheel moved the Honda to straddle the center line. She weaved back and forth a few feet each way to keep them at bay.

The guy in the undershirt didn't back off this time. He zipped over onto the shoulder and gunned it.

Her turn drew closer … closer …. "Please let this work."

Waiting until the last possible moment, Cassie slammed on the brakes and prayed Sadeé wouldn't be hurt.

The green truck flew past like a stone from a slingshot.

The Honda slewed sideways. Tires screamed. The smell of burning rubber filled the air, but she made the turn.

The momentum threw Sadeé onto the floorboard. She yelped but scrambled back onto the seat.

Amazing, her cell phone didn't fly out of the cup holder. She grabbed it. Still no service. "Aaagh."

Was it the pictures? Is that why they came after her like this?

Reaching down, she retrieved the wooden box from under the seat and set it on the center console. A quick one-handed snick opened the case. Her brother, Garrett, had chosen the

Smith & Wesson .38 special for her smaller hand. Locked and loaded, all she had to do was point and squeeze.

Her sweaty palms lost their grip on the steering wheel for a second when she turned at the *Welcome to Harbins Farm, Quality Seed Potatoes* sign.

The long dirt road ran between lush potato fields for perhaps a quarter mile. A white clapboard farmhouse sat at the far end like a shining beacon. She glanced in the rearview mirror again and inhaled a harsh breath.

The green truck turned onto the lane behind her.

Chapter Two

Rattled. That was a good way to describe her reaction. Cassie's hands shook so badly, the car almost sailed into the sea of purple potato blossoms bordering both sides of the road. Nothing had ever looked as wonderful as the sprawling, two-story farmhouse ahead. She still couldn't believe her pursuers just gave up and left. One moment they'd turned onto the drive behind her, and the next time she looked … poof. Gone.

A heavy sigh released some of the tension, but her heart still thumped like an overeager beaver's tail. "Sometimes prayers are answered," she murmured to Sadeé.

The Harbins would have a land line. She should report the incident to the Mackay police.

And tell them what? That a foolish young woman driving alone through No Man's Land stopped to help two strange men with a flat tire? That the men made her uneasy, one had cussed at her, and then they'd chased her?

Yeah, that would go over well. Now that she thought about it, the two men had made no actual threat. She'd hit their truck, not the other way around. At least she had their pictures. The cops could run the truck's license plate.

When she rolled to a stop in front of the big farmhouse, Cassie tucked the gun back under the seat and stroked her dog. Once sure her legs wouldn't collapse, she got out and checked the damage to the side of her car. A green smear marred the quarter panel.

She rubbed it with her thumb. A scuff. Nothing a little rubbing compound and some elbow grease wouldn't fix.

The front door of the farmhouse squeaked open. An older gentleman with a thinning crown of salt-and-pepper hair hobbled down the front steps. The red plaid shirt under faded denim overalls proclaimed him a farmer, but the pronounced limp assured her this was Coot Harbins come to greet her.

Sadeé jumped from the car to stand in front of Cassie. No growls this time, no undue hostility, just watchful as the man advanced.

"Well, hello there, young lady," he called out. "You must be the physical terrorist Doc Burdette sent." The twinkle in his rheumy blue eyes took the bite out of the teasing insult. Deep-seated laugh lines in a face like leather gave testament to his jovial nature. "Mighty fierce dog you got there."

After a few moments of consideration, Sadeé wagged her tail and ran off to sniff around the property.

"Physical terrorist, huh?" Schooling her lips to stave off a smile took some effort, but Cassie managed it. And slapped a hand over her heart for good measure. "I'm wounded. We physical therapists are so misunderstood. And unappreciated.

Hello, Mr. Harbins. I'm Cassie Cameron. The four-legged one over there is Sadeé." She nodded toward the dog that now inspected an ancient swing set.

The old farmer's face broke into a sunny smile. "Pleased to meet you, Miss Cassie. C'mon inside and meet my wife, Belinda. She's got lemonade and a tray of cookies for us. I'll set a bowl of water on the back steps for your Sadie. She won't wander off, will she?"

"It's Suh-DEE," she corrected. "And no, she'll stick close by."

Sadeé was such an enigma. She'd shown up in Hastings Bluff a few days after Garrett and TJ's wedding, tired and hungry, but otherwise in excellent health. Well-groomed, too, with a rabies vaccination tag and a bone-shaped name tag on her collar. Not your typical stray.

Several people had tried to approach the gorgeous black and silver shepherd, only to have her dance away. Until Cassie showed up and Sadeé laid claim to her.

"Sadeé, huh?"

She'd been curious about the unusual name, too, and looked it up. "Means 'beautiful girl' in Hebrew. Also means 'dog' in the Shoshone language."

He laughed. "Then I'd say she's well-named."

A half hour passed while they ate the whole plate of homemade oatmeal raisin cookies and got acquainted. Cassie gave him a rundown on her education and her plans for the

future. That's when he changed the subject and asked about the dust storm she'd created while flying down his lane. "I thought for a minute you were doing a time trial for the Stateline Speedway."

Cassie described her run-in with the two men. Spoken aloud, her story sounded lamer than she'd first thought. Her voice trailed off with a shrug. "Probably my overactive imagination."

"Mackay's police presence is small. Maybe you ought to report what happened to the sheriff in Hastings Bluff. Especially since you got pictures."

She shrugged. "I'm beginning to think I overreacted."

Coot frowned but said no more on the subject. "Well, now we've done the polite. Let's talk about why you drove all this way to see me."

She'd had plenty of experience with hardheaded men in her family who thought 'grin and bear it' was the answer for all their injuries. "Mr. Harbins, Doc told me about your accident with the cultivator."

Coot took a sip of his drink. "That man saved my life, and then hooked me up with a fancy specialist down in Idaho Falls who saved my leg. I'm grateful to them both, but it's time I got back to work. A farm don't run itself, you know."

"Did your surgeon prescribe additional physical therapy after you left rehab?"

He nodded. "Yeah, but I can't be gone three days a week

so some little gal can give me a rubdown—no offense. Our son came over from Wyoming to take care of things here while I was laid up. A week in the hospital and another three weeks in rehab is a long time. He's gone back home now. Got his own place to look after."

Belinda, Coot's wife, stepped into the room at that moment with an offer of more lemonade. "Lester, you need to hush up and listen for a change. If this girl can help you, then do what she says." The older woman grabbed the empty cookie plate and winked at Cassie as she left the room. "Stubborn man thinks he knows it all."

"Look, Doc means well, and I appreciate you coming all the way down here, but let's talk truth. I'm gonna limp the rest of my life. I've come to terms with that."

Cassie studied the farmer and decided his wife had the right of it. He was an obstinate old coot. Probably how he got his nickname—through sheer cussedness. "That's not necessarily true. You don't have to limp or hurt doing it. Therapy can help."

He shook his head in disbelief.

Men and common sense—two antithetical concepts when it came to health. She might need a different approach. "Mr. Harbins, you know I'm fresh out of school?"

"Yeah."

"And since I'm not employed yet, this is like a favor to Doc."

His eyebrows drew together in a cautious nod.

"I need this assignment. I need the practical experience for my resume to have any hope of landing a decent paying job." She gave him her best pleading look. "Doc thinks I can help you, and so do I. We could start out easy, three days a week, an hour each time. You pick the days. I can get here as early as you like so you don't lose much daylight. Won't you please reconsider?"

Coot opened his mouth like he wanted to say something, but nothing came out.

Okay. Time to pull out the big guns. "You know my daddy, don't you, Mr. Harbins?"

"Call me Coot. Or Lester. And yeah, I know Cody Cameron. He did me a good turn some years back when I first bought the land. Hauled in a team of horses and brought a gaggle of men down to help me clear rocks and pull stumps. He's a good man."

"Dad used to tell us stories about a crazy guy from back east who thought he could grow potatoes in a rock field."

Coot chuckled, but he squared his shoulders. "Rocks rule the land where I come from. And crazy wasn't the worst thing the folks around here called me, but I proved 'em wrong. Today, I grow the best certified, organic, specialty seed potatoes available in the state. I chose this place deliberate. It's got good soil, but it's a small acreage, surrounded by mountains, and remote enough so it doesn't interest the big boys." He got to his feet, leaned heavily on his cane, and stutter-stepped over to the wall. "Come see this."

Cassie followed him to where six photographs were lined up in a row. Each photo, taken from the same perspective, displayed a little brass plaque at the bottom with a year inscribed.

"Look here." He tapped the first framed photo on the left. "This is what the land looked like when I first bought it back in 1987."

The picture Coot pointed to showed him and his wife with a baby on one hip standing on ground overrun with scrub pine and boulders, some bigger than a car. The next picture, taken five years later, showed the couple with three children like stair steps. Behind them, a quarter of the valley was cleared and furrowed with a bountiful crop of blooming potato plants.

The subsequent pictures, all taken at five-year spans, showed the children through their growing up years and then what could only be grandchildren. The early farmhouse had been replaced by the current two-story structure. A big tractor tire hung from a giant oak tree in one, replaced by the swing set that now sat out front in another. A riot of color filled the flower gardens—yellow sunflowers taller than most men, blue delphinium, flame-colored zinnias, pink peonies, with each garden growing progressively larger. In the last shot, cultivated fields filled the camera's angle from edge to edge.

"This is a wonderful legacy." Cassie brushed a fingertip

over each year's plaque.

"And one I'm proud of." He squared his shoulders.

She turned to face him. "You should be. And yet, it's such a shame."

A scowl replaced his pleasure. "What do you mean?"

"Your dream. It spans thirty years. I can't conceive of the guts and hard work it took to turn a patch of trash land into one of the most successful small farms in the state. You're right, Mr. Harbins … Coot. I can't help you. Only you can do that. But you've already determined your dream has ended. It's okay. I understand. You're ready to slide into retirement."

Silence fell over the room.

Had she pushed too hard?

A moment more and he let out a long wheeze. A second wheeze left him clutching his chest and doubled over.

Good Lord, he was having a heart attack.

Cassie put an arm around his shoulders. Her mind scrambled over every bit of first-aid she'd ever learned. "Let's get you to a chair, Mr. Harbins. Put your feet up. I'll call your wife and get you an aspirin." If they didn't have any, surely there were a few tablets in the first-aid kit she kept in her car. Hopefully, they hadn't expired.

"Aspirin?" Tears streamed down his cheeks as another spasm wracked him. He stumbled toward the chair and dropped his bulk into it with a huff.

Cassie's brows drew together in confusion. "Yes, aspirin.

For a heart—" She stood straight. "You're not having a heart attack, are you?"

Coot pulled a white handkerchief from his pocket and mopped his face, still chuckling.

She backed away from him, hands on hips. "I thought you were dying."

He wiped his eyes once more and stuffed the handkerchief back in his pocket. "You're too smart for me, girl. Too smart for your own good, too. All right, let's do this before I change my mind. And once a week, not three times. I'll expect you on Mondays by eight sharp."

A slow smile stretched her lips. "Two days. Mondays and Wednesdays. Eight is fine. I'll just run out to my car and grab my bag. Might as well get started now."

She dropped her equipment bag on the ground and dug through the glove compartment for something to tie her hair back. No luck. Maybe in the trunk.

A quick search unearthed the small tote she used to carry to calf roping events. Inside it, beneath a pair of old rodeo gloves now stiff with age was a packet of piggin strips. She took two of the long leather strings meant to whip-tie a calf's legs together, and secured her hair into two ponytails, what her mom always called *dog ears*.

For the next hour, they kept up a steady conversation as she led Coot through a series of gentle stretches and exercises before teaching him some simple tricks to strengthen his

muscles on the days she didn't come. They talked about the heat, the stalker who'd followed her friend, Lucy, to Hastings Bluff, her brother Garrett's wedding, the potato crop yield Coot anticipated this year, her dad's love for the wild mustangs, and the preserve he'd set up for them.

Coot settled into his chair and kneaded his sore leg after they finished and then steered the conversation to the story on everyone's lips today—the rash of vandalisms plaguing the county between Hastings Bluff and Mackay.

"So, these scamps paint graffiti on barns, put goats on roofs, torch outhouses, and they're still on the loose? Why hasn't your deputy boyfriend caught them by now? It's been six months."

She stopped packing her equipment and looked at him. "First off, Deputy Naughton is not my boyfriend. He's too bossy, and anyway, we don't even like each other most of the time. I know Derek because he's a friend of the family. I know about the vandalism cases because he enlisted my brothers to be part of the task force looking into the incidents. They meet out at our ranch more often than not and sometimes I hear them talk, that's all. Second, whoever is doing all this damage is careful. They never leave a trail, and the acts are sporadic. It's difficult to anticipate where or when or even how they'll strike next. And third, Derek seems more hung up on catching speeders—mainly me—than a bunch of juvenile delinquents."

Coot scratched his jaw before he spoke. "Any chance it's

the same cowards that shot at your father's mustangs a month or so back?"

Of all the subjects they'd touched on, Coot seemed most interested in the vandals. Could they be responsible for the death of the wild horse? Her brothers attributed the crime to the stalker who'd threatened Lucy, even though the timing seemed suspect. "Could be. Except three-foot tall nasty words spray painted on the side of a barn and setting fire to an outdoor toilet seems juvenile compared to killing a horse."

"Mmm. I'd be curious to see a map showing all the places they've hit."

Did the old man know more than he let on? "What aren't you saying, Coot?"

"Just looking at the facts. These hooligans started up about the same time some of my neighbors started seeing unusual traffic in the mountains through here. I've never been a fan of coincidence." He shrugged.

"Explain 'unusual.'"

"A cargo van. Like the ones the telephone company uses."

"Phone lines go down in the mountains all the time."

"Yeah, but this one don't belong to the telephone company. No logo for one thing. Handwritten license plate for another, the temporary kind you get from a dealer. Only, like I said, it's been going on since January. One run the third week of every month. They never stop and barely even slow down no matter the weather. Pretty brazen, considering how deep the

ruts can get and how low the van's undercarriage hangs. I keep expecting to hear how they lost a muffler or tore off the oil pan."

Everything he said was circumstantial. Suspicious, bothersome, and maybe a little scary, but nothing concrete. Kind of like her run-in with the two guys in the green truck.

"What are they carrying that has everyone so worried?"

"Can't tell. No windows in the rear cargo area."

Nosiness was hardwired into Idaho DNA, especially here in the rural areas where everyone knew everything about everybody. She could see how a mysterious van would pique curiosity. "Have you reported it to the police?"

"Riiiight." His face screwed up into a mass of wrinkles, like he'd gotten a hearty whiff of skunk perfume. "Like I said, Mackay's law enforcement is limited."

She didn't know what to say. On the surface, it seemed a stretch to make a connection, and yet it had a ring of truth. Call it intuition, instinct, a gut feeling, or ESP, the same sixth sense that told her to run from the guys in the truck resonated with Coot's story.

"Why don't we take a look at those pictures you snapped," he said. "See if we can figure out what got those boys riled up."

Cassie showed him the three cell phone pics. In one photo Billy and Tattoo Guy stood facing each other. The second picture caught both men with glares of surprise and the truck tilted up on the jack. The third image showed only part of the men, but revealed the truck's license plate and the contents in the bed with the tarp thrown back.

"Well, lookee here." Coot whistled. "Can you make it bigger?"

She used her fingers to stretch the screen and zoom in.

"Looks like spray paint to me. See the name, Krylon? And all those five-gallon gas cans?" Coot added. "What do you think they need all that gasoline for?"

"What's this?" She pointed to a pair of wooden crates partially hidden by the tarp. "Dyno something or other. I don't recognize this stencil, do you?"

Coot looked both puzzled and concerned. "Nope, but paired with this other stuff it can't be good."

An all-over shiver almost made her drop the cell phone.

"You need to show these to your boyfriend."

She nodded. "I think you're right."

"You ever drove the back way through the mountains?"

She shook her head no.

"It's a mite longer, and you can't go as fast, but it's a real pretty drive. Nice views from the higher elevations. The road winds down to State Road 75 on the other side of the ridge, which runs right by the Triple C. You won't run into any unwanted traffic that way."

"I like the way you think, Coot. You got a map I can look at?"

Chapter Three

Derek waited at a distance while the Challis firefighters contained the small blaze. He'd seen enough thunderstorms back home in Texas to know what had happened here, but he owed the fire officer the courtesy of hearing his verdict.

The massive western red cedar had stood sentinel over the land for at least two centuries. At one-hundred-fifty feet tall, its girth easily measured eight feet in diameter, maybe more. Now, split in two at the midway point, half of the upper trunk and branches dangled from the jagged break and fanned out over the tee box on the ninth hole. The other half of the split tree top sprawled over the smoldering remains of a maintenance shed. He stepped over the burn marks that scarred the ground and radiated outward from the tree in a perfect diagram of the cedar's root system.

Not vandals. Not this time.

Chief Joe Barney barked a few more orders to his men before striding over. "Deputy Naughton, this …" He waved one hand toward the ruined tree. "Is nothing more than Mother Nature expressing herself with a lightning strike. Sorry you had to come all the way out here."

"No problem, Chief. I was in the area. Shame to lose a tree that old." Derek shook the other man's hand before returning to his police cruiser.

The irony of the moment struck him as he settled behind the wheel of the dark blue Blazer. Here he was, a deputy from Hastings Bluff on a potential arson investigation at the Challis Golf Course while the sheriff of Challis attended a meeting in Hastings Bluff to discuss the recent rash of vandalisms.

Derek glanced at his wristwatch before pulling out of the country club parking lot. Late for his own meeting. He could make better time with the siren …

His hand dropped away from the squawk button. No siren. The locals raised enough stink since he'd cracked down on speeders. They wouldn't take kindly to a "do as I say, not as I do" attitude.

One particular offender came to mind. Cassidy Cameron. The woman had a reckless streak and a lead foot that had garnered her several warnings over the past year, from both him and Kyle, his fellow deputy. With her history of traffic citations, one more offense and she'd lose that precious driver's license.

Turning south on Route 93, he settled in at a comfortable fifty-five miles per hour. The fourteen-mile stretch back to Hastings Bluff ran long, straight, and, thankfully, light on traffic. And boring enough for his mind to wander.

Cassidy's face appeared in the dark glass of his mind. The

darned woman had taken up residence in his head … along with the memory of the single kiss they'd shared more than a year ago. A bone-melting brush of lips that promised paradise on Earth.

Flashbacks from the weeks he'd spent with her in Atlanta came unbidden. She'd gone there on a physical therapy internship, but when one of her patients, a federal agent, inadvertently made Cassidy the target of a drug dealing murderer, her brothers decided she needed someone to watch over her. James sent Derek. Matchmaking by the nosy sheriff, but Derek had jumped at the chance like a hormonal teenager.

To her credit, Cassidy had taken his appearance in stride. Didn't even balk when he moved into her apartment. Which still surprised him. They'd talked for hours on end, laughed, joked, watched movies, went for runs. And she'd revealed glimpses of the sweet, vulnerable girl underneath.

He'd never had a woman for a friend before, but Cassidy was smart and funny. He liked her. A lot. Maybe too much.

Derek let out a pent-up breath and recalled the long nights on her sofa while she slept in the bedroom twenty feet away. The woman had no idea of her effect on men. On him. And she'd relegated him to the friend zone.

Yeah, forget that. There was a whole heck of a lot more than friendship between them.

Static interrupted. He thumbed the mic to speak. "Naughton here. That you, Lorraine?"

A few seconds of silence followed before the dispatcher answered. "Where are you, Derek? An army of Camerons just invaded the place. You're late for your own meeting."

He should have called in his status instead of mooning over his lack of a love life. "Sorry. Got a report of a fire over at the golf course. Turned out to be a lightning strike. I'm ten minutes out. Tell James to go ahead and get started."

"I would, but the sheriff's not here either. He said for you to go ahead without him. Wait … I think Sheriff Castle just drove up, too."

Great. "What about Kyle?"

"He's here. I'll tell him to delay until you arrive."

"Roger." Derek stroked the neatly trimmed day-old beard that lined his jaw. Time to get his mind back on business.

At the four-mile sign, he spotted a car approaching from a side road off to the right. He groaned when the vehicle made a running stop and fishtailed onto the road in front of him. Only one person drove a red Honda Civic around here.

"Why?" He pounded the steering wheel. "Why her? Why now?"

He thought about ignoring her transgression, but he'd let her go too many times already. Without thinking further, he hit the siren and stamped on the accelerator. A tiny smile curled one side of his mouth. Time to face the consequences.

Startled by the sound of a siren, Cassie looked up to find

blue flashing lights filling the rearview mirror. A glance at her speedometer—only seventy-eight—elicited a groan. She eased off the gas. What was the speed limit through here anyway?

"This can't be happening." Her teeth ground together. She had to get the pictures to James.

Frustration washed over her like a storm surge. It was bad enough Derek had shown up in Atlanta to—as he claimed— keep her safe. Did he have to harass her at home, too?

She tapped the brakes to show her compliance. Derek could be reasonable. If she remained calm, kept her temper, and explained the importance of what she'd found in the pictures, he might even give her an escort into town.

"Yeah, when elephants move to Idaho," she muttered.

The shoulder widened ahead. A good place to pull over. She flipped on her right blinker.

Derek pulled in behind her on the side of the road, blue strobe still whirling. At least he cut the confounded siren. The dying warble sounded like a lovesick cat.

He didn't get out right away. Two minutes passed. And then another two. Her fingers drummed a staccato beat on the steering wheel.

The SUV's door finally opened and all six-foot-three inches of brawny policeman unfolded. Arrogant and bossy? You know it. But, wow, did he look good in a uniform.

He adjusted his sunglasses and started her way.

It wasn't fair the way his khaki shirt stretched taut across

his chest. Or how the shadow of his beard gave him a dangerous appeal. Or that she'd fallen a little in love with him while he'd only fallen in lust with her.

A sharp rap on the window scattered her unruly thoughts. She looked over, startled to find his face mere inches from her own.

Cassie flashed him the biggest smile she could muster along with a little finger wave. She needed him agreeable and since sugar caught more flies ... if she didn't choke first.

Beside her, Sadeé's tail thumped against the seat.

Cassie had a brief moment to wonder why her dog didn't bristle the way she had with Billy before Derek's deep voice interrupted.

"Lower the window." His voice held not a hint of leniency. "Now."

Her chin lifted as though it had a mind of its own, but she did as he said. "What do you want, Derek?" Semi-sweet was the best she could achieve right now.

"You know the drill. Driver's license, car registration, proof of insurance."

"I'm surprised you don't have my information memorized by now," she retorted. "Look, I don't have time for your games. I have to—"

"Driver's license. Ma'am." His jaw did that twitchy thing, like when she irritated him. Except now he seemed more angry than annoyed.

Cassie reeled in the snippy answer on the tip of her tongue and dug through her purse. She handed the license over. "Here you go, Officer. Can you please hurry this along? I'm on my way to—"

"It's obvious you're in a hurry. I clocked you well above the speed limit. Again. Now hand over the registration and proof of insurance."

She fished the papers out of the glove box and slapped them into his waiting hand. "Don't you have anything better to do, Deputy Naughton? Shouldn't you go cite Polly Prescott for gossiping? Or arrest Doc Burdette for dispensing drugs? I'm sure there's a tourist jaywalking somewhere. I can't believe James pays you to harass me like this."

"Keep up the smart mouth and I'll haul your pretty little butt to jail."

One thing she knew about Derek, he didn't make idle threats. His comment shut her up for all of five seconds, long enough for her outrage to ignite. She yanked on the door handle while he studied her cards and shoved it open hard enough it caught Derek on the hip and forced him back a step.

Cassie got out and closed the distance between them.

"Sadeé, stay. Sit." Derek commanded her dog.

He dared command her dog? Worse, Sadeé obeyed.

"And you ... get back in your vehicle." Derek took hold of Cassie's arm and tried to steer her to the car.

She jerked free and planted both hands on her hips. An

inner voice screamed this wasn't a good idea, but she'd had enough of Derek Naughton and his heavy-handed attitude toward women drivers. They'd reached a truce on the long trip from Atlanta, only because she'd let him drive ninety-five percent of the way. But this fixation he had with the way she drove had crossed the line.

A two-handed shove to his diaphragm surprised him. He shuffled back another step.

"I'm trying to tell you I need to see James. I have important informa—"

"You'll see the sheriff all right." Derek cut her off again. A ruddy flush darkened his cheeks. "You know I was going to give you a ticket, but your behavior just upped the stakes. Cassidy Cameron, you're under arrest. You have the right to remain silent."

Under arrest? He couldn't do that. "You can't do that."

"Yes, I can. Anything you say or do may be used against you in a court of law."

"Arrested for what? I haven't done anything."

"Not done anything? How about failure to stop at a stop sign, failure to use a turn signal, reckless driving, reckless endangerment of an animal, exceeding the speed limit, disobeying a direct order from a police officer, obstructing an officer in the performance of his duty, assaulting an officer of the law, and now resisting arrest. You have the right to consult an attorney before speaking to the police and to have an attorney present during questioning."

Her teeth ground together. He was playing with her. A prank, that's all. He couldn't be serious.

"The speeding ticket alone will cost you your license. Add in all the other points you're racking up and you might never get it back. If you cannot afford an attorney, one will be appointed for you."

"Stop it. This isn't funny." It was her turn to take a step back. Why was he doing this? Losing her license would mean she couldn't take the job with Dr. Wilkes in the fall, couldn't work with Coot, or even go to town. Which would leave her stuck at the ranch. For months.

She circled around to the other side of her car to put some much needed distance between them.

Sadeé stared through the windows, tracking Cassie's every move.

Undeterred, Derek followed her. "No, it's not funny. Why can't you obey a simple law like everyone else? Why don't you see the danger of speeding? One miscue, one wrong—"

"Why do you want to ruin my life, Derek?"

He removed his sunglasses and pinched the bridge of his nose before turning those amazing green eyes on her. A pained expression flitted across his face, a brief regret gone in a flash. He reached out to touch her hair but let his hand fall away. "You look like a teenager with your hair like that. When were you going to tell me about moving to Idaho Falls?" His voice

dropped to a whisper. "Or did you plan to pull another disappearing stunt like when you ran off to Atlanta without telling anyone?"

Guilt and embarrassment flooded through her. She hadn't told anyone about her temporary move to Atlanta until after she'd gotten there. Now, frustration and anxiety over what she'd captured in the pictures plus a healthy dose of regret and disappointment over Derek created a potent overload. The two of them had no future by his decree, but he wouldn't let her go.

Common sense fled. Anger ignited as it always did whenever she found herself in the wrong. "I don't have time for your games." She pulled the leather thong from one of her ponytails.

His signature stony look returned. A mule had nothing on Derek when it came to stubborn. He shoved his shades on again and crossed his arms over his chest.

Her inner voice screeched a warning this time—Bad idea. Really bad idea. She shoved him again. Eight inches taller than her and at least a hundred pounds of solid muscle heavier, no way she could budge him unless he allowed it.

He thought to play with her, huh?

Derek held out a hand in a placating gesture. "Baby, you need to get yourself under control."

In a practiced move too fast to follow, she grabbed his right wrist and had the piggin strip looped around it before he could pull away.

"What do you think you're doing, Cassidy?"

Ignoring him, she grabbed his other hand and bound it to the first one before he could jerk away. Roped and tied in less than five seconds. Just like old times. She hadn't lost her touch.

Derek's grin faded when he tried to break free of the restraints. "Untie me."

"What am I doing, Derek? I just hogtied a pigheaded man who can't hear because he won't listen. Well, you're gonna listen now." With that, she hooked her leg behind his knee and swept his feet out from under him.

He went down hard and wound up on his back. His Stetson flew off. The annoying sunglasses came to rest on the tip of his nose.

Sadeé gave one sharp bark and whined but didn't leave the car.

Cassie wanted to laugh at the stunned look on Derek's face, but right now she had a whole lot of ticked-off cowboy to deal with. Before he could catch his breath, she turned her back on him, straddled his legs, and yanked her remaining ponytail free. Three more seconds and his ankles were trussed, too. She fought the urge to throw her hands up in victory.

"Baby, you are so going to regret this. Untie me. I won't tell you again."

Chapter Four

Cassie leaned back and dusted her hands. Not bad for someone who hadn't touched a rope in years. She twisted around on Derek's legs to smirk at him. "Now, as I was say—"

Derek lunged to a sitting position, sunglasses flying off to one side when he dropped his bound hands over her head and pinned her arms.

"Aaagh!" Too late, she tried to squirm away. Okay, she hadn't seen that move coming. In her defense, animals gave up once they'd been tied.

He growled in her ear. "Undo my hands or I'll … oof."

The elbow she planted in his ribs made his abs contract.

"You'll what? Talk me to death? Lock me up in one of your cells?" She renewed her efforts to wriggle free.

"Little girl, you are in so much trouble." His laugh held more menace than humor.

"Don't call me that," she snarled.

The man had arms like twin pythons. The harder she fought, the tighter he squeezed. "You've lost your edge, Derek," she managed to squeak. "Letting a woman get the best of you. What will the guys say?" With little air to spare, the

taunt sounded more like a breathless lover's whisper than the insult she intended.

"Because I let you, Baby. Only because I let you. Now, untie me before you pass out."

Sheer perversity made her shake her head no.

His arms constricted another fraction. "What's that? I didn't hear you."

Spots danced at the edge of her vision. She couldn't move her arms, didn't have enough leverage to kick, and he was too darned tall to head butt. Where was her ferocious guard dog when she needed her? Sadeé should be ripping Derek to shreds.

As though conjured, Sadeé woofed once, darted forward to lick Cassie's face, and then leaped away again with an excited yip. The crazy dog dropped her head and shoulders to the ground, rump still up in the air, with the bushy shepherd's tail whipping back and forth like a pendulum on steroids. She woofed again and lunged at Derek … and jumped away again.

The vice around Cassie's chest loosened a smidgeon.

"Sadeé, sit," Derek ordered.

The authoritative tone fell a little short, undermined no doubt by a smothered half-laugh, but the dog sank to her haunches anyway. The manic look in her eyes stated clearly how much she wanted in on whatever game these crazy humans were playing.

How did Derek do that? Make Sadeé obey him? Feeling a sense of betrayal, Cassie attempted to slide down and out of

Derek's clutches … without success.

"You are so stubborn, woman." In one fluid motion, he rolled them onto their sides. "Since it looks like we've reached a stalemate we might as well get comfortable."

Okay, he outmatched her in weight, height, and strength. She had a sneaking suspicion he might win in the obstinate department, too.

Her head rested on his bulging bicep. The strong beat of his heart pulsed against her back. His arms relaxed their stranglehold on her diaphragm and sweet air rushed into her oxygen-starved lungs. Other than a rock digging into her hip, it felt nice to lie there.

Derek buried his face in her hair and rooted through the tangled mess to nuzzle her ear. "Mmmm, vanilla."

She tensed. "Derek? What are you doing?"

"You smell like your mom's sugar cookies. I love sugar cookies."

She should tell him to stop. Instead, her head tilted to one side. Her eyelids fluttered.

He nipped the tender skin of her neck.

Her head jerked at the sound of a motor, her movement clipping his chin.

"Ow!" he yelped.

"Someone's coming."

The vehicle slowed and pulled in behind Derek's SUV with a single, short whoop. Great. Another cop. She could see

the tires beneath Derek's Blazer and then the black boots that stepped onto the ground.

Sadeé came to attention with a low growl. The intimidating sound made the hair on Cassie's arms stand on end. Now, the fool dog wanted to protect.

"Derek?" a man's voice called out.

Cassie exhaled softly. James. He might be Derek's boss, but he was also a close friend of her family.

Sadeé settled onto her belly and rested her head on her paws.

"Over here," Derek shouted.

The Hastings Bluff sheriff stepped around the rear of Derek's cruiser, one hand on the half drawn firearm holstered at his hip. He stopped mid-stride, tipped his hat back … and doubled over in laughter.

The guffaw spooked a dozen or more brown thrashers from the telephone line overhead.

CCC

Derek bit off the caustic remark he wanted to make and settled for a, "Glad you think this is funny."

Wicked merriment twinkled in the sheriff's eyes. "So, is this a routine traffic stop gone wrong? Or a three-ring circus?"

Lying on the ground with his hands and feet hogtied did seem kind of ridiculous. Trussed up by a slip of a girl, no less. If this was a circus, he sure as shooting wasn't the ringmaster. More like one of the clowns. "If you're done, Sheriff, I could use a hand with my prisoner."

"Looks like you might be her prisoner."

Okay, definitely one of the clowns. James would milk this goat rodeo for years.

Pressed up against him, he could feel every movement Cassidy made. When her chest expanded, he gave her another quick Heimlich maneuver.

"Ja-eeeemms," Whatever she intended to say whooshed away with her expelled breath.

A concerned Sadeé whined and scooted closer, ears drooping like wilted lettuce.

He was asking a lot for a highly trained dog like Sadeé to follow a command that went against her protective instincts and training. He issued a sharp *ch* sound, and she quieted.

"I stopped Miss Cameron, here, for speeding," Derek explained. "She presented her license, registration, and proof of insurance as requested but then exited her vehicle against my direct order. That's when she attacked me."

"That's not what—oomph." Cassidy's attempted rebuttal earned her another squeeze.

The silly grin never left James's face. "Let me see if I have this right. A woman who can't weigh more than a buck-twenty got the drop on a police officer who just happens to be a former Navy SEAL. She overpowers him, trusses him up like a Thanksgiving turkey, and drops him to the ground even though he's twice her size? That your story?"

"I …" Anything he said would only make him look even more foolish and inept. Derek opted for action instead. He hauled her up with him to a sitting position.

"You're crush—" She produced another strangled squeak.

James whipped out a lethal-looking knife. "Okay, here's how we do this. You," he said pointing at Cassidy. "Will be quiet while I release Deputy Naughton."

He sliced through the thin leather bindings.

"Of course you'd take his side," she spat. "Good old boys—"

James's cocky smile hardened. "You're about one second away from a rag stuffed in your mouth and handcuffs. Your choice. Nod if you understand."

The soft body in Derek's arms went rigid as a two-by-four. Feisty, mule-headed woman. "He'll do it, Baby," he whispered.

"I hope James tells everybody how I kicked your butt, Derek." She pitched her voice low so only he could hear.

Prickly as a cactus, Cassidy ignored James's outstretched hand, got to her feet under her own power, and brushed at her clothes. Dust, bits of grass, and who knew what else covered both of them—like they'd been rolling in the dirt on the side of the road.

Unable to help himself, Derek swatted her backside with a heavy-handed swipe.

Ten thousand volts of fury turned on him. The air between

them buzzed like the stuttering neon sign over Sidewinders Saloon.

Hands out to either side, he shrugged with wide-eyed innocence. "You missed a spot." He reached down to retrieve his sunglasses.

That's when she kicked him in the shin. Hard.

"Sheesh, Cassidy." He hopped on one foot and rubbed his injured leg. "What'd you do that for?"

Sadeé sprang to her feet with another excited yip and wove circles around their legs.

"Now, Cass—" James started to say.

"You saw him. He assaulted me. My dog even thinks so. I'm filing a complaint."

Sadeé's tail slowed and then stopped. She looked from Derek to Cassidy.

"That's it." Derek snatched his Stetson from the ground, whacked it against his leg a couple of times, and slammed the hat on his head. He stalked over to Cassidy and leaned down until they breathed the same air. "I've already read you your rights. Now you're going to jail."

She looked from him to James and stamped her foot. "Are you going to let him do this? It's bad enough he singles me out for all these ridiculous speeding charges. You're the sheriff. Do something."

James raised his hands and backed away. "I told you to behave, Cass. You struck a police officer."

Not waiting for her tantrum to build, Derek clapped a handcuff around one slender wrist and pulled her other arm behind her back to secure it.

Sadeé growled, more of a puzzled I-don't-know-what-to-do warning than any real threat.

Derek looked at the dog, at Cassidy, and then tipped his head back to stare at the heavens. If he tried to separate the two, Sadeé would go nuts. He'd have to take them both in.

Wrapping a hand around Cassidy's arm, he led her to his Blazer and opened the rear door.

Sadeé jumped in, happy again.

Cassidy spluttered nonstop, somewhat less enthusiastic than the dog.

With one hand on top of her head, Derek guided her down and inside. "In you go."

"Wait." She balked, one foot on the floorboard and the other still on the ground. "What's going to happen?"

"Mug shot, fingerprints, strip search, jail time."

Her eyes shimmered like cobalt crystals, filled with a curious blend of anger, shock, and trepidation.

He grinned, aiming for a truly evil smile. "Have to make sure you're not hiding any drugs, contraband, or concealed weapons on your person."

She folded like a Chinese fan.

"I'll get your purse. Anything else you need from your car?"

Her blank look gave him pause. Had he laid it on too thick? "Don't worry, I'll lock it up. Your stuff will be safe until I can get someone out here to collect it."

James stopped him on the way to her Honda. "I sure hope you know what you're doing." He made a tsking sound and shook his head as he strode off to his own vehicle.

"I hope so, too." Derek murmured.

Her front passenger seat, console, floorboard, and backseat were strewn with … stuff. He grabbed what he thought was a purse with a long strap, raised the windows, locked the doors, and pocketed the keys.

The drive to Hastings Bluff, with James following them, lasted all of ten minutes, though it seemed more like an hour.

Cassidy remained silent the entire time, her head turned to stare out the window.

For the life of him, he couldn't see a good end to this day. The speeding ticket alone would ensure she lost her driver's license, which would restrict her freedom for the foreseeable future. Would six months give him enough time to convince her to stay?

He pulled in behind the sheriff's office to avoid undue attention while James parked in front. The gossips in this town would nose out the news of Cassidy's arrest soon enough. Nothing got by those old biddies. The NSA and CIA could learn a few things about gathering intelligence from a small town grapevine.

"Hey." He studied Cassidy's profile in the rearview mirror. "You gonna give me anymore trouble?"

The look on her face gutted him. Silent tears left tracks down her cheeks. He'd never seen her shoulders slump this way.

She turned away without answering.

Now, didn't that make him feel lower than a snake's belly in a wagon rut?

His fellow deputy, Kyle Witherspoon, appeared at the back door. "You coming in anytime soon? We need to get this meeting started."

Unclenching his hands from the steering wheel, Derek indulged in a slow shoulder roll and got out of the car. He'd forgotten all about the task force meeting. And now he'd have to parade Cassidy in front of James, Kyle, and Eli Castle, the sheriff of Challis, not to mention her brothers.

Garrett Cameron had been one of his teammates during their former black ops years. Kyle and James, too. He counted them friends. Wade and Jonas Cameron, as well. That might change in the next few minutes.

Kyle leaned over and peered in at the backseat passenger. "Is that …? Aw man, what've you done?"

Censure from Kyle didn't worry him. From James either. Garrett on the other hand packed a mean left hook. Derek rubbed his jaw in anticipation of the bruises sure to come. Sometimes he wished he'd stayed on with the government. The job had been simple back then. Find the bad guys. Shoot the bad guys. Mission accomplished.

He opened the rear door and motioned Cassidy out. "C'mere. Let me get these cuffs off."

Long legs swung out, the movement awkward without the use of her hands. "Aren't you afraid I'll assault you?" She ducked her head and got her feet under her.

Still spunky. "Look, I'm sorry things got out of hand. You're not really under arrest."

A spark of hope lit her eyes. "Will you waive the ticket?"

Much as he wanted her smile, he wouldn't compromise his sworn oath to uphold the law. "No, Baby, the speeding ticket stands. You've had plenty of warnings."

Sadeé clambered out, stretched one hind leg and then the other.

"This ticket will put me over on points, Derek. I'll lose my license."

Her pleading look made him feel like pond scum. "I know."

"You'd stoop that low? Ruin my life just to claim a victory in this stupid battle of wills?"

What could he say to that?

Her lips compressed into a taut line. "Then you better put me in a cell before you unlock these cuffs, 'cause I swear I want to hurt you right now." She flounced off toward the office before he could free her, Sadeé on her heels.

Kyle opened the door for her.

Inside, the smell of leather, polished wood, and old sweat greeted them. The scarred, hardwood floors creaked. For the first time since he left Texas as a gangly eighteen-year-old, Derek didn't know what to do. This battle of dominance between them could end any chance he had with her.

Garrett, Wade, and Jonas Cameron were the first ones they encountered. Their smiles vanished at the sight of their sister in handcuffs. Three pairs of predatory blue eyes promised consequences Derek didn't want to think about.

"Well, well, look at what we have here. Nice bracelets, Sassy Cassie." Trent Crutchfield, the deputy from Challis, looked entirely too smug. Why would Sheriff Castle bring this greenhorn?

Cassidy locked eyes with him. "Trent? You're trying to be a cop now? What moron hired you?" She dismissed him with an eye roll.

Sheriff Castle turned the shade of a ripe tomato, surpassed only by the explosive hue on the deputy's face.

As if this day couldn't get any worse, Crutchfield pulled out his cell phone. "I've got to have a picture of this."

Derek muscled Cassidy behind him and glared at the irritating man. For a long count of three, he envisioned his hands around Trent's skinny neck. Deputy Crutchfield might be an annoying little Chihuahua with a junkyard dog complex, but he deserved a semblance of respect as a law enforcement brother. For now.

"You might want to rethink that idea, Crutchfield." Jonas Cameron didn't seem to have Derek's same qualms. He might be the youngest of the brothers and not as big as the other two, but that didn't diminish his threat by any stretch of the imagination. He towered over the Challis deputy. "I'd hate for your face to get in the way when that phone of yours finds its way under my boot heel."

"Are you threatening me?" Trent bowed up like a Bantam rooster claiming his territory, one hand drifting to the weapon at his hip.

Sadeé snarled, seeming to grow larger as she confronted Trent.

The deputy took a step back. "Dogs aren't allowed in here," he said with a decided hitch in his voice.

"Stand down, Crutchfield." Sheriff Castle finally asserted his authority. "This isn't your jurisdiction. You're out of line."

Derek whirled Cassidy around and unlocked the shackles. The sooner he got her out of here, the better. He should never have brought her in.

"Here, now, you can't do that." Trent tried to force his way through the mass of Camerons. "The manual states that when a suspect is forcibly restrained—"

Derek ignored the sounds of a scuffle and spoke to Cassidy. "I'll get someone to take you home."

Cassidy marched into the six-by-six jail cell with Sadeé

right behind her, slammed the barred door, and curled up on the narrow cot with her back to the world.

"Derek?" His name on James's lips held a wealth of condemnation. He hadn't seen him come in.

Garrett and Wade stood with massive arms folded over their chests and chuckled.

"What's so funny?" Jonas glared at his brothers. "He arrested Cass and locked her up like a common criminal."

"It's not like that," Derek shouted. He couldn't remember ever losing control of a situation like this.

"Leave it be, Jo. It's a rite of passage," Wade said. "All men go through it when the right woman comes along,"

"Not that you'd know anything about that." Garrett slapped his little brother on the back.

Had they all gone soft in the head? Did they not hear a word he said? "Cassidy is not under arrest. Well, she was … but she's not now."

Fantastic. Now he sounded like a twit.

"You can't un-arrest—"

"Shut up, Trent."

The three words yelled in unison by the other men in the room did the trick. Trent's mouth closed like a trap door.

"I believe we've delayed this meeting long enough." Derek shot the Cameron brothers a look, daring them to argue. "Let's get on with it."

Chapter Five

Consequences sucked. She hadn't even been going all that fast.

With a slow, disbelieving head shake, Cassie entered the tiny jail cell and sank down on the cot. Old Ben Franklin had the right of it when he said, "What begins in anger ends in shame." She was living proof. Why did that weasel, Trent Crutchfield, have to be here?

Derek said she wasn't under arrest. Did he mean it? She could recover from a suspended license, but no reputable medical organization would hire a healthcare worker with a criminal record.

Another tear drizzled its way down her cheek like rain on a window. She turned her face to the cinderblock wall and curled up like a roly-poly. What a horrible day. And it wasn't over. She still had to face Mom and Dad. See them try to hide their disappointment in her. Again.

Sadeé nose-poked her shoulder and settled her chin in the crook of Cassie's neck. Why couldn't people show unconditional love the way pets did?

She pressed a kiss to the dog's muzzle. Despair made a

poor companion, and she'd never been one to sit and brood. Time to face reality and deal with the mess in her life. She sat up … and blinked at the lack of audience.

Raised voices at the other end of the long room drew her attention to where Derek, James, Kyle, her three brothers, and Sheriff Castle sat around the small table. Trent, the gutless wonder, didn't merit a chair. He stood off to one side. All these years since high school and he still hovered on the periphery, never quite belonging, never accepted. Which didn't stop him from invoking the wrath of his father, the mayor of Challis, on anyone who scorned him. What had she done to Trent to make him hate her so much? Other than laugh her head off when he asked her to a dance, that is.

Well, kudos to him for choosing an honorable field such as law enforcement, but a gun? Really?

An irreverent thought left her choking on a giggle. Did Sheriff Castle give him a single bullet to keep in his pocket like in the old Mayberry sitcom?

Cassie lay silent and motionless while the men discussed the rash of vandalism incidents. It soon became apparent they had too great an area to cover, too little manpower, and no viable leads.

A small, spiteful smile curled the corners of her mouth. That would change once she showed them the pictures on her phone.

Her grin faded as quickly as it formed. All the self-righteous justification in the world wouldn't change her predicament. Now, instead of leaving Hastings Bluff at the end of the summer, instead of starting the life she'd been working toward, she was stuck in limbo. She could already hear Mallory's exasperated huff.

Fickle fate? Or had providence provided a last opportunity to make things right with her family? She rubbed a hand over her heart. All the wishing in the world wouldn't make it so, but her mood lightened as a plan began to take shape, a way to fix things with her sister. First, she had to hand over the breakthrough needed in the vandalism cases. The only question was whom to tell?

She might be the one in the wrong, might rue the strain between her and Derek, but all life on earth would cease before she shared her pictures with him. A girl had to keep some pride. Besides, he was just as responsible for this mess as she.

Not her brothers either. They still saw her as a flighty, temperamental teenager without a dab of common sense.

Which left James. Or Kyle. After the others left, she would speak to one of them, explain about her run-in with Billy and Tattoo Guy, and show them the damning pictures. Maybe she'd mention Coot's story about the van and his suspicions that it might have a connection to the vandalism incidents.

CCC

"Uh, could I speak to you for a moment?" Cassie followed James into his office.

Sheriff Castle and Trent were first to leave. Then the others—Garrett back to the ranch, Wade and Jonas to collect her car, and Kyle on some unknown mission. Derek lingered longest, insistent upon taking her home until Lorraine, the dispatcher, sent him off on a call.

"Make it quick. I missed lunch." James settled behind the desk and busied himself flipping through a stack of papers.

Okay, this didn't sound promising. She sat in the uncomfortable wooden chair in front of his desk. "First, this isn't about Derek or what happened earlier. It was my fault. I deserved the ticket."

He looked up at her, eyebrows lifted.

Now that she had James alone, all the qualms over how the Mackay police would respond came back full force. "I let myself get in a hurry. You see, I saw two guys on the side of the road this morning, about halfway between here and Mackay. They had a flat tire."

"Tell me you didn't stop."

"I had Sadeé with me, kept my doors locked. I let the window down only enough to offer to send help."

"Dadgummit Cass, you know better—"

She shrugged. "Let me finish. You can fuss later. I think they might be involved in the vandalism—"

"Hold it right there." James picked up the phone on his desk and dialed a number. "Derek, get back here. Now." He hung up without waiting for an answer.

"I don't want to talk to him." She chewed on her bottom lip to keep from saying more. It shouldn't be this difficult to give the police valuable information.

"Tough." James went back to his papers and ignored her.

Ten minutes later, Derek walked into James's office dragging an extra chair with him. He sat beside her and called Sadeé over.

Sadeé crawled to him, rolled over, and exposed her belly for a rub.

Her dog. Traitor.

"Now that we're all calmed down, Cassie wants to tell her story. I think you'll want to hear what she has to say."

Cassie wanted to slap the smirk off Derek's face but took a deep breath instead.

Both men bristled when she recounted the run-in and subsequent chase. The eye rolls from both James and Derek conveyed clearer than words what they thought about her not notifying the Mackay police.

Her words trailed off after that. She mentioned the pictures in passing, but didn't bother telling them about Coot's suspicions or the mysterious van. This was a mistake.

Derek she could excuse. He was still angry with her after their altercation. Not James, though. He shouldn't let personal irritation get in the way of doing his duty as sheriff of Hastings Bluff. More than that, he was Garrett's best friend, which made him her friend. Or so she'd thought. Her family had adopted

him when Garrett brought him home from a mission to recover from a bullet wound. In all the years since, before and after he became sheriff, he'd never treated her like a dimwit. Until now. She looked away, desperate to hide how much their ridicule hurt.

James leaned back in his chair, his voice filled with exaggerated patience. "Okay, Cass. Show me these pictures."

"I can't. They're on my cell phone. In my car."

Derek leaned forward, elbows on his knees. "You thought the Mackay P.D. would make light of your story. Why'd you think we'd do otherwise?"

Right. Why? She was still the same screwup that no one believed. Pent up frustration gave way to the familiar sense of betrayal. "You think I'm lying?"

Derek looked away. "Not intentionally."

The hits kept coming. She had to get out of here.

"Look, I appreciate that you want to help, but you've given us nothing." James wouldn't look at her either.

"Hey." Derek's voice was soft, cajoling. "It's not that we don't believe you. We're stretched pretty thin and—"

"My information isn't worth checking out." She didn't want his pity.

"Tell you what," James added, his expression pained. "E-mail those pictures to me when you get home, and I'll take a look at them."

"Baby, listen—" Derek reached for her hand.

"Don't." She pulled away. "Just … don't."

"At least one good thing has come of this." James's evil chuckle did little to ease the tension. "You won't be driving through No Man's Land by yourself anymore. Not smart, Cass."

An emotional void settled in the middle of her chest. Nothing ever changed here. She squeezed her eyes shut.

James came around the desk and patted her on the shoulder. A clear dismissal. "Want to join me at the diner? My treat."

"No." She had no idea what to do next, but it wouldn't be with either of them.

After a few seconds of uncomfortable silence, Derek rose and stepped aside. "Grab your stuff. I'll run you out to the ranch."

"No, thank you." She slung her purse over one shoulder and started for the front door.

"How will you get home?" He persisted.

"Not your concern."

Sadeé followed her but stopped at the door. With a pitiful moan, the dog looked from her to Derek and back again. Even the dog chose his side.

Cassie hadn't thought it possible to hurt more than she already did. "Stay, Sadeé," she commanded in a husky whisper right before she closed the door and set off at a brisk pace for the nearest corner.

Out of sight of the sheriff's office, she leaned against the wall and held back the tears that fought for release. The last thing she needed was someone to see her bawling.

A few minutes later, Derek's Blazer nosed around the corner of the sheriff's office. He drove slow, head turning side to side.

Sadeé sat beside him in the front seat.

Cassie ducked inside Fancy's Hair and Nail Salon.

"You need an appointment, Hon?"

Cassie whirled around. "Oh, hi, Doreen. Sorry, I didn't see you. No, no appointment. I needed to get out of the sun for a minute. That's all."

She left before the woman could say anything more and scurried in the opposite direction Derek had gone. Two blocks past the sheriff's office, she crossed the street and darted down a through-alley. After another three blocks, she doubled back and took a left turn that led to Wade's office.

Of course, the doors to Cameron Security Services were locked tight. No sign of Wade, Lucy, Mallory, or Casey, the high schooler who worked part-time. She'd hoped to catch a ride with one of them. Or use the office phone to call her mom. Now she'd have to ask to use the phone in one of the stores where everybody and their brother would listen in.

Not today. She'd had enough disapproval to last a lifetime. Eight miles might seem like a long way, but sore legs and a little sweat were a small price to pay. She set off at a brisk pace for home.

A number of cars and trucks, and a pack of motorcycles passed her as she trudged alongside Route 93. At one point, a dusty pickup sprayed her with gravel as it zoomed by. She moved further off the road after that. Several drivers she knew stopped to offer a lift, but she waved them off. They'd have too many questions.

The shortcut that crossed the Sinclair property and Little Crooked Stream arrived before she realized it. She, Mallory, and her brothers had often taken this path while growing up. It led away from the highway and curious passersby, but more important, it cut a good mile off her journey.

It was also wooded and remote, which made her nervous after everything that had happened today. She wasn't a child anymore. The days of innocence and safety were long gone.

Quick, before she changed her mind, Cassie sprinted across the highway and entered the tree line that hid her from the highway traffic. She gave a last glance over her shoulder ... and hesitated.

A truck, the same one that had spewed gravel over her a few minutes earlier she thought, approached from the opposite direction. It slowed.

She ducked behind a clump of bushes on instinct. What were the chances?

Dark green GMC with a hemi. Not many of those around these parts.

The driver wore a white undershirt. His left arm hung out the window, better to showcase the impressive ink that ran from shoulder to wrist—a coiled snake.

Her heart revved to a painful rate.

A second man remained in shadow, but she had no doubts as to his identity. Billy. He said they'd find her.

The truck slowed to a crawl before pulling onto the shoulder.

Cassie didn't hang around to see what happened next. Staying low, she scurried through the overgrown foliage and moved deeper into the trees until her lungs burned. She needed to slow down, get herself under control before something worse than a skinned knee happened.

Half an hour more, burbling sounds joined assorted bird calls, insect buzzes, and twigs crunching underfoot. Little Crooked, an offshoot of the Salmon River, wasn't overly deep this time of year. All she had to do was make it across the natural stepping stone bridge at the bend where it turned east and she'd be almost home.

To her surprise, the water lapped at the top of the bank, well above normal. A souvenir from the morning storms no doubt. A spill among the rocks could be painful, dangerous even, not to mention the discomfort of wet clothes and feet for the rest of her journey. Not much choice. Cross the stream or retrace her steps back to the highway and risk running into Billy and Snake Man. Her mother would worry when she didn't make it home before dark.

The first rock was easy, above the water and close to the bank. The middle stones required a longer stride, but only the last two steps posed a concern. Farther apart and partially submerged, they would take a bit of a leap to reach.

The crossing went smooth until she reached the next to last stone. Her foot slipped on the landing. Ankle deep in the water, she wobbled, arms twirling like a windmill. On the last, longer leap, she landed solid, but her momentum carried her forward … into the rushing water.

A sharp pain wracked her knee. Her head went under, but she shot up fast with a shriek, slipping and stumbling her way up the rocky bank. Idaho streams and rivers resulted from snow melt in the higher elevations. No matter how hot the weather got in the summertime, you could count on icy water.

Soaked through but still clutching her purse, Cassie dropped onto her back on the grass. One good thing came from not having her cell phone. It would never have survived the dunking.

A familiar bark disturbed the silence. Movement in the woods caught her eye, and then a dark shadow streaked across the open meadow. Sadeé never hesitated, skipping from rock to rock across the Little Crooked with the accuracy of a tightrope walker. And then the big shepherd arrived at her side with a frisky dance and little puppy-like yips.

Cassie forgot all about her wet, bedraggled state. "Sadeé, I thought you stayed with Derek. What are you doing here?"

CCC

Three hours later, after a detour around an electrified fence and an encounter with a bull that sent Cassie running for her life, she and Sadeé reached the long private road that led home. Not far now.

With the last vestiges of twilight hanging on, Sadeé found a low spot and wriggled underneath the rails that lined the drive. Cassie climbed over and dropped to the ground just as a police cruiser with lights flashing barreled down the road toward her.

Not again.

Derek stopped the Blazer in a cloud of dust. "Where have you been? I've got half the county out searching for you. Your mom is a mess."

"Go away, Derek. You're not my keeper." She stormed off as fast as her weary legs would move.

This time, Sadeé pranced at Cassie's side without a second look at Derek.

"Good dog," she said and fondled the dog's ears. "Let's go home."

"Cassidy, wait."

She stopped but refused to turn around. "What, Derek?"

"I ... I'm sorry. Get in the cruiser. Let me take you home."

A ride would be most welcome about now. Just not with

him. She started walking again.

"Please."

Well, crud. He would play the please card. With a loud huff, she raised both arms out to the side and let them drop. "Fine. Just don't talk to me."

She stomped to the rear door and yanked.

It didn't open.

"Up front, Cassidy. You're not my prisoner." He opened the passenger door for her and then clicked the rear door locks to let Sadeé jump in.

Cassie held her tongue for the few minutes it took to reach the ranch house. When they pulled up in front, her entire family converged on the cruiser.

Garrett reached her first, but their mom shouldered him aside and pulled Cassie into a brutal hug. "Cassidy Elizabeth Cameron, I've been so worried." Soft sobs wracked her mother's frame. "Why didn't you call?"

"I'm sorry you worried, Mom. I left my cell phone in the car. And then I ran into a few obstacles I didn't remember."

"Met Sinclair's new bull, huh?" Jonas smirked.

Laughter bubbled up. "Yeah. He's scary."

Mom released her and took both of Derek's hands. "Thank you for finding my daughter."

He had the grace to blush. "I didn't find her, ma'am. She was almost home when I saw her climbing the fence."

Everybody started talking at once—about her trip to see

Coot Harbins, being stopped by Derek and hauled into jail, why she shouldn't have walked home alone, why she was wet and dirty, and more.

"Sorry I worried you. Look, I'm sweaty, humiliated, and really tired. I'm going around back to shuck these grubby clothes in the mud room. After that, I want a long, hot bath, something to eat, and my bed. I promise to give you all the gory details tomorrow. Okay?" She didn't wait for their response.

Sadeé followed her.

Cassie sat on the low patio wall and peeled off her soggy sneakers and socks. No blisters. Small blessings.

Derek rounded the corner of the house. "I'd like to see those pictures you took if you don't mind."

Give him another chance to ridicule her? Fat chance. "I mind."

"Look, I'm sorry about all that happened today."

"Why?"

"Why? What do you mean?"

"Why are you sorry?"

"Well, you're upset … and … I feel bad … and …"

"Got it. Well, you've apologized. Hope you feel better now."

"Baby—"

"You don't get to call me that."

"You're still angry."

She closed her eyes and counted, willing herself to not clobber him. "Yes, Derek. I'm still angry. Your 'sorry' hasn't fixed anything other than to soothe your bruised conscience."

She started toward the house.

Sadeé went with her but started with the whiny sounds again. Clearly, the dog didn't like the discord between her and Derek.

"What do you want, Cassidy? Blood?"

She stopped at the door, back rigid. "No, not blood."

"Then tell me. I'm not a mind reader."

She turned. The last rays of sunshine slanted across the yard and burnished him in a fiery halo. His icy green eyes remained fixed on her. Turbulent. "I want something far more precious than blood. Something you aren't capable of giving. Good-bye, Derek."

The door closed behind her with a quiet snick.

After stripping down to her underwear, Cassie headed for the stairs with Sadeé bounding ahead. Halfway up, she noticed the mud and burs matted in Sadeé's coat. They both needed a shower. And food.

Chapter Six

The kitchen door closed in his face with a finality that left Derek panicking for reasons he didn't fully understand.

"Whatever." He turned away. Cassidy was safe. And she had Sadeé to guard her. That's all that mattered.

By the time he reached his cruiser at the front of the house, all the Camerons had gone back inside. Just as well. He couldn't handle anymore flesh wounds. What he really wanted right now was a big, juicy burger with an ice cold beverage to wash it down. Maybe two. And he knew where to get them.

After a stop at his small apartment to change out of uniform, Derek set off for Sidewinders on the outskirts of town. The local watering hole had a rowdy reputation, but they dished up the greasiest, tastiest burgers in Custer County. His stomach rumbled in anticipation.

A sparse parking lot greeted him. Not unusual for a Monday, which suited him fine. He didn't have the patience to deal with testosterone-driven stupidity. That came with Friday nights when too many guys crowded into a too small room, all of them trying to drink each other under the table. Add in half-priced drinks for the ladies, and it was just a matter of time before things got out of hand.

Derek shook his head and recalled the past weekend when he and James had jailed six drunken cowboys to let them sleep it off. He didn't get it. Why would a woman wear clothes that left nothing to the imagination, dangle herself like a pork chop in front of a pack of starving wolves, and then cry foul when they decided on her as the main course for dinner?

He settled onto a bar stool, dropped his Stetson on the counter, and ordered his meal. The drink arrived first. He downed it in one long guzzle. When the burger arrived, he attacked it like he hadn't eaten in days. "Hit me again, Tate," he waved his empty glass at the bartender. "Another burger, too."

Tate Murtaugh, bartender, bouncer, and owner all rolled into one, called the order into the kitchen before he filled a new glass and brought it over. "Keep eating like this and you'll soon look like me." He patted his thickening waistline. "And you might want to go easy on the pop. That much sugar and caffeine this time of night and you won't sleep a wink. Not to mention what it does to your teeth."

"When did you become my momma?"

Tate snickered. "Last weekend when you hauled those drunken idiots out of here." The portly barkeep mopped his way down the counter with a well-used towel.

Derek polished off the rest of the first burger in two bites, gave a satisfied belch, and glanced around the dimly lit room.

Only a dozen or so other patrons hung out. Two men he didn't know sat at the opposite end of the bar. Three guys and a girl, all locals, were shooting pool in the back corner. The rest, some familiar, some not, were scattered in ones and twos among the tables.

Tate set the second burger in front of him.

"Thanks, man." Derek reached for the ketchup.

"No problem ... aw, crap." Tate stared past Derek. "I wish that girl would find some other place to go fishing."

Derek looked over Tate's shoulder at the mirrored wall behind the bar and spotted the woman who'd just walked in. Colleen Weldon. In a skimpy red dress made of some kind of stretchy material that hugged every one of her abundant curves. The front of the dress dipped dangerously low while the hem rode high enough to make a man hold his breath in hopes she'd bend over.

She stopped inside the door and took a long moment to survey the room. When she spotted Derek, a small smile touched her lips.

He turned around on the stool, hamburger forgotten, and fixed his steady gaze on her. If Cassie didn't want to play, there were plenty of others who did. Colleen could be a much needed distraction after the day he'd weathered.

Blonde and lethal to a man's wits, Colleen sidled up to the bar and wriggled onto the stool next to his. "Hey, Tate."

"Colleen. You want something to drink?"

"Yeah. I'll have whatever he's having." She inclined her head toward Derek.

"This is—" Derek started to say.

"Coming right up," Tate interrupted.

"So, Mr. Deputy, what brings you out on a Monday night?" Colleen ran her long red nails down his bare forearm.

"Here's your drink." Tate plunked a tall glass on a coaster in front of her and added a straw, but didn't stick around for small talk.

She raised the glass for a sip.

Derek followed the sultry movement and zoomed in on her dark cherry red lips.

"Ugh." Her nose wrinkled with a look of distaste. "What is this? It tastes like … Coca-Cola." She set the glass down with a thunk, spilling some of the foam over the sides.

"Good guess." Derek grinned and raised his own glass in salute. From his experience, women like Colleen didn't have much of a sense of humor, especially not if they provided the amusement. He took a huge bite of his second burger and waited. She'd get all huffy and stalk off any second now. Cut her losses and move on. And save him from some serious regret.

Her eyes narrowed, but then she leaned over and nudged his arm with her shoulder. "Why come here if you're not going to drink?"

He finished chewing, swallowed, took another sip, and

wiped his mouth with a napkin. "I'm off duty, but still on call. And these …" He gestured at his plate. "Are the best burgers in six counties."

She called to the bartender, waggling her glass. "Tate, how about a little Jack?" Turning to Derek again, she gave him a long, speculative look. "What do you say, Deputy, you up for some fun tonight?

"Well, darlin', it depends on what you call fun."

Before she could answer, another woman walked in the front door, saw Colleen, and rushed over.

While the two women greeted one another with air kisses, and oohs and ahs over the other's clothes, Tate doctored Colleen's drink as requested. Leaning over the counter, he whispered to Derek, "I wouldn't fish in those waters if I was you."

"Huh?"

"Colleen's trolling for a breadwinner and uses a short skirt and what the good Lord gave her as bait. Mess around with her, and Cassie Cameron will pack up and leave faster than you can spit."

Derek scowled after Tate when the other man walked away. Small towns all had one thing in common—everybody got up in everybody else's business. Besides, he'd already ruined things with Cassidy. The aggravating woman wouldn't give him the time of day after today's events.

Something you aren't capable of giving.

He couldn't get her last words out of his head. Could still see her closing the door in his face. Cassidy wasn't a casual hookup kind of girl. He'd known that from the get go. And he'd tried to seduce her anyway. Women never put up much resistance when he turned on the charm. Until this one. She wanted the dream, the happily ever after.

The very thought should send him running like a scalded dog, but she was the forbidden fruit, the Thou Shalt Not that made him want to snatch the apple and take a bite. He didn't want to run, didn't care she was Garrett's baby sister, and didn't that realization chap his hide.

Derek nodded, more to himself than to Tate. There'd be no forgiveness if he hooked up with Colleen Weldon. If he still wanted a shot with Cassidy and if he had any chance at winning her, he'd best walk out of here right now. Alone.

He slid off the stool and dropped some cash on the bar.

"Too much thinking makes Derek a dull boy." Colleen stopped him with a touchy-feely hand on his chest. "What do you say we dance and then see where the night takes us?"

"No can do, darlin'." He tried to sidestep her.

"C'mon. One dance won't hurt." She pressed up against him, her hands reaching around to roam up and down his back.

Behind him, a group of new arrivals poured in, their voices loud and laughing. A second later, a profound silence filled the joint.

With a sense of foreboding, Derek looked over at the

mirror … and into the fiery blue eyes of Jonas Cameron.

Derek detached Colleen's arms from his body and stepped away from the too-willing woman. Every eye in the place fixed on him, sensing the sudden tension. Even the group at the pool table stopped their play.

A trilling ringtone saved him. He pulled his phone from the pocket of his jeans. "Yeah, James?"

Derek listened with rapt attention, already moving toward the door. "On my way," he said and pocketed his cell.

"Hold on a second, Naughton."

Jonas, the youngest and only unattached Cameron brother, knew full well what went on in a place like this. The rascal could charm the boots off anything with a double-X chromosome. And often did. Tonight, however, he'd gone into over-protective brother mode. Jo would never believe Colleen's flirtations were unwelcome. No doubt, he'd been the recipient of her charms at one time or another. This wretched day was fast becoming a Greek tragedy.

"Can't. Vandals hit Pioneer Dairy. Got a half-mile stretch of barbed wire fence down and three hundred milk cows loose on the highway. Gotta go." He started toward the door again, but paused before leaving. "We could use some help." His gaze swept from Jonas to the three other men with him, all hands from the Triple C. He didn't wait for an answer or bother with a good-bye for Colleen.

His rear tires spun a little as the cruiser left the parking lot.

Sometimes life took you where you least expected, but never in his wildest imagination had he thought he'd ever want to settle down with one woman.

CCC

Midnight arrived before they called it quits. Derek couldn't remember ever being this tired.

With thirty-odd men pitching in, it didn't take long to move most of the herd back into the pastures. Cows, like people, became disgruntled when thrust out of their comfort zone. Once they turned the lead cow in the right direction, the others couldn't follow fast enough.

Derek had to take off his hat to Jonas and the three hands from the Triple C. Without them and their knowhow, the entire crew would still be out searching for stragglers. Even so, it took another three hours for everyone not assigned to milking duty to construct a temporary fence.

He groaned. His hands hurt, his back ached, and he had two painful bruises on his shins, one Cassie had gifted him with earlier in the day and the other from a big heifer that took exception when he swatted her backside. He chuckled at the similarities between the two incidents as he limped toward his car.

James caught up with Derek and walked with him to where they'd parked side by side. "From the way you're hobbling, I'm surprised you can find something funny in all this. Wanna share?"

"Got kicked by one of Jack's cows when I smacked her rump. Same reaction I got from Cassidy this afternoon."

James laughed with him but soon turned serious. "You did the initial investigation here. What do you think? Same perp?"

"Too dark and too crazy to find much, but my gut says it's the same guy. I'll come back at daybreak for a more thorough look, see if I can find his calling card." The vandals had taken to spray-painting a giant "V" somewhere on their last four crime scenes. "Dude's been watching too many movies."

"I'm getting real tired of looking like Barney Fife here."

"Know what you mean, but there's only so much we can do. Not like the old days, is it?" Derek leaned against the side of his car and yawned. It was times like this he missed his job with the Bureau of International Intelligence, when he, James, and Garrett had worked together in an elite squad. They'd been adrenalin junkies back then, part of the criteria for being invited into the covert organization that went into hotspots all around the world. Only the best of the best.

But he'd moved on. They all had. Age did that to a man. Stole your immortality. Made you realize your days were numbered. That's when you became ... careful. And a liability.

It had taken some adjustment, but Derek found contentment in his role as a public servant. Besides, he'd had plenty of excitement over the past year what with TJ and the drug lord from Honduras, and then the maniac who'd stalked Lucy. The Camerons were like true north on a compass, drawing trouble like iron filings.

"As of right now, you're assigned full time to catching this guy," James told him. "I called Jeb Wharton in to take over your regular duties."

Derek blinked. "Jeb's retired."

"And bored out of his gourd. He jumped at the chance to put on a uniform again. Temp work is fine with him. He understands it's just until we catch whoever's doing this."

"Does that mean I can contact some low friends in high places?"

James nodded. "Fowler owes me a few favors. Do whatever it takes to stop this nonsense."

"Roger that."

Derek said good night and poured himself into the Blazer, too tired to do anything but be thankful he was done with cows and fences. By the time he grabbed a shower and fell into bed, he'd be lucky to get four hours sleep before the alarm rang to come back out here.

Someone rapped on his window. Derek groaned, knowing who it was without looking. He lowered the window. "S'up, Jo?"

Jonas Cameron leaned down so they were eye to eye. "I know you and Garrett are thick. And you've been a good friend of the family, but I think it's best if you stay away from the ranch for a while."

"You mean away from Cassidy."

"Exactly."

"Not happening. What you saw at Sidewinders didn't look good. I realize that. Colleen Weldon came in. Pickings were slim. She settled on me. I'll admit the woman's a tempting handful, and yes, I thought about having a little fun … for all of ten seconds. Any man with blood still pumping through his veins who says he wouldn't is a liar. But she's not what I want. You saw her making a move and me trying to extricate myself from her clutches without making her mad. All I wanted was a burger. End of story."

Jonas didn't say anything for a long time. Finally, he straightened up. "You've always been a straight shooter, but if you hurt my sister I will reshape your face."

Derek nodded. "I swear my intentions toward Cassidy are honorable. Know this, if I do somehow hurt her, it won't be intentional. And I will let you do whatever you want to my face."

The faint light of the dash offered enough light to see Jonas nod once before he walked away.

Breathing a sigh of relief, Derek turned toward home. Shower, sleep, and then back out to Pioneer Dairy for another recon. After that …

He scratched his head and searched for an excuse to visit the Triple C.

Chapter Seven

Tired, anxious, and overwhelmed—not the best prescription for a good night's rest. After tossing in her bed for endless hours, Cassie finally got up on the dark side of dawn and made her way to the barn with Sadeé trailing her like a shadow.

Yesterday's stresses might account for the fatigue, and the run-in with the two men offered plenty of reason for her worry. Everything else she blamed on Derek. The aggravating man wouldn't get out of her head. Even now, in the quiet peace of a newborn morning, the tall Texan dominated her thoughts. Common sense told her nothing good could come from tangling with him, but sometimes the heart wanted what the heart wanted, wise or not. Could she settle for what little he could give?

"Well, aren't you the early bird? I thought city girls on vacation slept till noon every day." Rascal Sutcliff had been foreman for the Triple C Ranch since the day her dad bought the land some forty-odd years ago. He walked a little slower these days, moved a little stiffer. How long before rickety old bones and arthritis forced him into retirement like her dad?

"Who are you calling a city girl, Rascal? I have never slept 'til noon in my whole life. Besides, no way anyone could sleep in around here, not with alarm clocks that crow before the sun wakes up."

He chuckled. "If you're looking for something to do, stalls always need mucking. You remember how to use a pitchfork?"

"Of course."

An hour and a half later, Cassie swiped a sleeve across her face and put the pitchfork, muck bucket, and wheelbarrow away. Her body rebelled from the unfamiliar activity. Pitching horse manure mixed with straw onto a waist-high cart worked an entirely different set of muscles than she was used to. Not a bad kind of ache, though.

Sadeé frisked by her side on the way back to the house, glad to be out of the barn. She steered clear of the horses and didn't think much of the chickens. City dog for sure.

Four weeks had flown by since the gorgeous black and silver shepherd came into Cassie's life. Four weeks without a response to the 'found dog' notices Mom had posted in the newspaper and online. Seemed odd since it was obvious someone had invested a significant amount of time and money in the dog's training. Sadeé definitely didn't fit the typical stray profile.

"I think the good Lord sent you here to help me through this summer, girl."

Cassie took the single sharp bark as agreement and

scratched behind the dog's ears. She couldn't help but hope no one came forward to claim her.

Blue sky stretched overhead. Not a cloud in sight. Hot, but not the oppressive heat of the past few weeks. A perfect day for a ride. Did her brothers still keep the reels and fishing gear in the little shed near the bend of the river?

The more Cassie thought about saddling up, the better the idea sounded. Out in the open, with no one around, she could air out her muddied feelings about Derek. Besides, Buffy needed the exercise. The beautiful dun-colored quarter horse had won a barrel racing championship for her once upon a time, but years of inadequate exercise had left the mare fat and indolent.

Cassie scuffed both boot soles on the stiff-bristled mat by the back door before stepping inside to hang her hat on a wall peg.

Sadeé went straight to her water bowl and then stretched out on the cool tile floor of the mud room. Mom tolerated the dog's presence in the house, but not in her kitchen, and no begging at the dinner table.

The clink of pots, pans, and murmured voices clued Cassie that meal preparations were in full swing. The men rose before daybreak to start the daily chores, but everybody returned to the house for breakfast at seven-thirty sharp. Mom skewered anyone who came late to her table. Like dinner in the evenings, she expected the family to be in their seats on time,

washed, hungry, and with no excuses. Of course, not everyone made it for every meal. Garrett and TJ had their own home across the valley now. Even Mom had to cut the newlyweds some slack.

"Morning, Mom."

"Good morning, sweetheart." Her mother looked up with a smile as she bustled from stove to counter to refrigerator and back again. When she leaned over to kiss Cassie's cheek, her nose got all wrinkly. "Been helping Rascal in the barn, huh? Why don't you go wash up and then come help us with breakfast. Garrett and TJ are coming this morning."

"Okay." Mom had a thing about horse poop. She didn't like it. Not in her house anyway.

Cassie glanced at Lucy who hovered over the stove. A frown of concentration creased her forehead as she whisked what looked like sausage gravy in the cast iron skillet. The girl could sure focus, which probably contributed to her incredible skill with computers. Cooking on the other hand—not her forte.

"Hey Luce. I see Mom put you to work."

Lucy looked up for all of a split second before returning her attention to the pan. "Hi, Cassie. Sorry, I have to concentrate. Cooking's not as easy as your Mom makes it out to be. This gravy for example requires an exact rhythm. Stir too fast or without sufficient heat and it won't set up. Too slow or too hot and it lumps or sticks." The circular movements she made with one hand never faltered.

Cassie stifled a grin. She'd played guinea pig for Lucy's cooking and knew all about those dreaded lumps. Drawing up her courage, she turned to her sister. "Good morning Mal."

All three women stopped what they were doing and stared.

Up to her elbows in flour, Mallory swiped at a wisp of hair and left a white smudge on her cheek. "Morning," came her answer after several seconds. Returning her attention to the wooden biscuit bowl, she scooped up the mound of dough, plopped it on the floured counter, and took the rolling pin to it.

Okay, that was awkward. Repairing bridges shouldn't be this uncomfortable. Cassie raced upstairs to wash and change her soiled clothes.

When she skipped down again, TJ and Garrett had just opened the front door. She changed directions, hurried over to them, and wrapped both arms around her brother's waist.

Garrett stiffened before giving her the tiniest squeeze in return.

Humor and despair battled within her. Affectionate displays didn't come easy for her family, but lately, they seemed to handle her like nitro glycerin, like one wrong move and she'd blow up in their faces.

Perhaps with a little less pride, a tighter clamp on her flashpoint temper, and a whole lot of patience they'd let her crawl back into their affections. Cassie turned to TJ who didn't hesitate to pull her into a hug.

After breakfast and once the dishes were washed and put

away, Cassie declined an invitation to go shopping with TJ and Lucy. "I would love to, but I need to call Doc Burdette and update him on my visit with Coot Harbins yesterday. I should have called him last night."

They let her go without a fuss, something she both appreciated and regretted. Living away from Hastings Bluff, she'd had no opportunity to get to know either of the women who'd captured the hearts of her two older brothers. That would change, too.

She grabbed the portable phone and dialed Doc Burdette from her mother's office. Sandy Reeves, his receptionist, answered.

"Hey, Sandy. It's Cassidy Cameron. Can I speak to Doc?"

"Hi, Cassie. Glad you're back for the summer. You calling about Coot Harbins?"

"Yeah, I should've called yesterday, but I was late getting back."

"Can you hold? Doc's with a patient, but I think he's about done."

"No problem."

Johnny Cash's deep voice crooned to her over the line while she waited. Merle Haggard followed with his signature mix of twang and steel guitar. None of this modern pop-country-rock stuff for Doc. Cassie dropped into the desk chair and pressed the speaker button. Another soft ballad filled the small room.

Sadeé's wet nose nudged her. A moment more and the dog curled up by Cassie's feet.

Doc's voice came on the line. "How'd it go with Coot yesterday?"

"Well, he's aptly named. Stubborn as a stick, but we hit it off. His son went home to tend his own farm once Coot was released. Now he doesn't feel he can leave for what he calls a little exercise and massage. He's got a point. Two hours to Idaho Falls and another two hours back cuts a big chunk out of the work day."

"You talked him around though, right?"

"Yeah, you could say that. We reached a compromise after I accused him of succumbing to old age." Remembering the faux heart attack brought a chuckle. "I suggested three days a week, he countered with one day. We settled on two."

Doc laughed with her. "You're too much like your daddy the way you bulldoze over people. Pull some ideas together for a treatment plan and come see me tomorrow."

"Well, there's a slight problem." She hesitated, reluctant to explain why she couldn't work with Coot.

"No," her sister said behind her.

Cassie found TJ and Lucy standing in the doorway, Mallory behind them. "Hold on a sec, Doc." Muting the call, Cassie turned to the girls. "What?"

"We'll drive you," Lucy said.

"No, you can't—"

"Yes, we can," TJ overrode her objection. "We want to help you, Cassie."

"But you don't even know the arrangements."

"Doesn't matter." Mallory tossed her head. "Between the three of us, we can work it out. Or maybe we'll all go and make a day of it. TJ and Lucy have been begging the guys to go sightseeing. They've seen nothing of Idaho beyond Hastings Bluff and the ranch."

"Come on, Cass."

"Let us do this for you."

"You gonna stay cooped up here? Let Derek win?" Mallory went for the kill shot. She'd always known how to hit for greatest impact.

For once, Cassie checked her pride. "Okay. If you're sure?"

Three palms lifted high in the doorway and high-fived each other.

"Uh, Doc. Looks like my problem has worked itself out. I start with Coot next Monday. What time should I come by tomorrow?"

"How about noon? And if you want to bring some of those chicken salad sandwiches your mama makes, it wouldn't hurt my feelings none. We can eat while we talk."

She looked to the three other girls. One by one they nodded.

Cassie said good-bye to Doc, but before she had the

receiver settled in the cradle her new supporters crowded around.

"Time to spill the details," TJ said. "I'm dying to know how you wound up in jail."

No way they'd let her out of this. "I'm not sure where to start. Other than the time I spent with Coot, I can't remember a worse day."

"Worse than when you snuck off with Danny Horton to go swimming and wound up breaking his nose because he thought you meant skinny dipping? And then Jonas found out and gave him two black eyes, which got you both grounded for a month." Mallory's eyes twinkled.

Cassie's heart warmed at her sister's overture.

"Oooh, save that for later. I want to hear about Derek first," TJ said.

"You left before breakfast. Start there," Mallory said.

"Okay. I wanted to get ahead of the storm, or in this case, behind it since my route lay in the opposite direction. It's been years since I traveled Route 93. I'd forgotten how desolate it is. And despite someone …" She nodded toward her feet. "Being scared to death of storms, Sadeé bucked up and came along."

The shepherd's ears twitched upon hearing her name. Soulful, golden-brown eyes rolled up and met her stare.

Cassie retold the story of the two men with the flat tire, how Billy's aggressive come-on had tripped all her alarms, and his comment about finding her later. "I don't know what got

into me. He was scary, but he also made me angry. I hate bullies. Especially guys who think size gives them the right to run roughshod over women. The pictures were a knee-jerk reaction, a way to balance the scales against a threat that really wasn't a threat." A twinge of guilt poked her conscience. "Maybe with a little spite mixed in."

"He threatened you. Never doubt it." TJ crossed her arms over her chest. "What happened next?"

Cassie described the chase, right up to the point where the green truck followed her onto the road to the Harbins' farm only to turn around and speed off.

"You reported all this to the police in Mackay, right?" Mallory had her hands on her hips, a sure sign her sister wanted to kick someone's butt.

"No. Once I explained to Coot what happened, I realized how stupid my story sounded. I mean, I can't say for sure they were chasing me. And I hit their truck. On purpose. Maybe they followed me to Coot's to get my insurance information."

"Then why didn't they call the police and stick around?" Lucy's face puckered in a frown. "What that guy said, what they did … I agree with TJ. Maybe not overt, but definitely a threat. You were smart to take defensive action. What did Mr. Harbins say?"

"He kind of agreed that the Mackay police wouldn't do much. He told me about a van that makes a crazy, mad dash trip through the mountains every month. It runs people off the road sometimes and has everybody in the area buzzing. Several people reported it to the cops, but … they haven't really done anything wrong." She shrugged. "Anyway, Coot suggested I might have better luck telling James. I was on my way to his office to do that when Derek showed up."

TJ rubbed her hands together and grinned. "I want to hear this part. Garrett said Derek stopped you on the Challis Road. If you went south toward Mackay, how'd you wind up north of Hastings Bluff?"

"Coot thought those two guys might wait for me to leave. He suggested I take the back road through the mountains to where it intersects with State Road 75. From there it's just a few miles to Route 93 north of town. Just my luck, I turned in front of Derek." Heat filled Cassie's cheeks. "I might have been going a tad fast."

"Did you explain all this to Derek?" Lucy asked.

"I tried. He wouldn't listen."

They doubled over with laughter when Cassie described how she'd hogtied Derek and then wound up on the ground, neither one giving an inch. Their chuckles faded when she told them how he'd hauled her to jail in handcuffs, about Trent Crutchfield's spiteful comments, the stupid pride that left her with only her feet to get home, and then seeing Billy and his friend pass by.

"I don't mean this in a hurtful way, but I'm kind of glad you're grounded." Mallory seemed to plead for understanding.

"You're safe here."

Cassie nodded at her sister. "Thanks, Mal. Looks like I'm stuck on the ranch for the foreseeable future. The thing that really irks, though, is how Derek and James blew me off like a child caught telling a whopper. James graciously offered to look at the pictures if it would set my mind at ease."

An uncomfortable silence followed until Mallory said, "So they haven't seen the pictures yet. What's in them that you think is so important?"

Cassie couldn't contain her smirk. "Full face pics of Billy and his friend, a shot of their license plate, and a very clear look at the contents in the back of their truck."

"Which was …?" TJ motioned with her fingers to continue.

"A dozen cases of spray paint, a bunch of five-gallon gas cans, and a couple of wooden crates."

"Oh, my gosh," Lucy exclaimed. "You think they're the vandals."

"Why didn't you make James look at the pictures?" TJ asked.

"Derek left my phone in the car. By then, they'd already decided I was exaggerating."

"Where's your phone now? I want to see," Mallory said.

"In my bedroom. Be right back." Cassie dashed upstairs and pulled her cell phone off the charger. Unlocking it revealed a string of missed calls, voice mails, and text messages, all from Derek. She ignored them and opened the phone's camera roll on her way down the stairs.

TJ whistled when she saw the pictures. "That's a lot of paint."

"Worse, it's enough gasoline to set the whole town on fire," Lucy added.

"Mal?" Cassie didn't like the look of her sister's ashen face.

"Those crates—see that funky orange sticker?" Mallory used her fingers to enlarge the image.

TJ pointed at one of the boxes. "You mean this crazed porcupine thing?"

"Looks like a Rorschach image to me," Cassie said

Lucy frowned. "I'm not sure, but it looks like the symbol for explosives."

"It is. The Dyno stenciling you see—that's Dyno Nobel. They manufacture commercial explosives. All the mining operations around here use them." Mallory turned to Cassie. "You have to show these to James right away. It's only pranks so far, but this …" She tapped the picture again. "Goes way beyond pranks and graffiti."

"So, what do I do?" Cassie asked.

"The proper question is what do we do?" TJ corrected. "We're with you in this."

"First, e-mail the photos to James. You can't make him see what you see, but if he doesn't sit up and take a serious

look at these, we need to vote in a new sheriff next election."
Mallory's expression turned wicked. "I'd give a month's pay to
see his expression when he opens your e-mail."

"Should I tell him about Coot's suspicions about the van?"

"No, I don't think so," Lucy said. "There's nothing to
connect it to the vandals, and it's not in their jurisdiction. Tell
you what, though, when we visit Coot on Monday ..." She
gestured to herself, TJ, and Mallory. "We'll go visit his
neighbors and try to find out what's got them buzzing."

TJ lowered her voice. "Can you call Coot and find out if
this mysterious van made a run yesterday?"

"Why?" three voices asked.

"I overheard Garrett on the phone early this morning. The
vandals hit Pioneer Dairy last night. Seems awfully
coincidental."

Chapter Eight

No clues. No hints. Not one lead. Stymied on how to proceed with the investigation, Derek closed the file folder and set it aside.

He'd gone back to Pioneer Dairy at sunrise and walked the length of the makeshift fence they'd thrown up last night. Most of the original posts had been broken or uprooted and strewn amidst snarls of barbed wire. At the far end of the destruction, a John Deere lay on its side in the ditch, ensnarled in more wire. A couple of calls had confirmed the tractor came from the Worsham place two miles over. That's where he found the first calling card—a big, red "V" painted on the green cowling. Jack Behr reported another "V" spray-painted on one of his cows, this one in purple.

Tire tracks had gouged deep ruts in the pasture where the culprits made doughnuts, probably to spook the cows as they lumbered in for the evening milking.

Derek scratched his head. How could they do so much damage in the daytime without anyone noticing? And how did they get a spooked cow to stand still long enough to spray paint its forehead?

What started out as simple acts of malicious mischief—a torched outhouse, frightened goats, and graffiti— had escalated to felony charges of malicious injury to property with this incident. Neither he nor James thought the dead mustang fit the profile, but to replace the fence alone would cost Jack upwards of five thousand dollars. Who knew how much the cleanup would run, or the loss in milk production from his traumatized cows, or the damage to Henry Worsham's tractor.

The longer these supposed random pranks went on, the more irate and suspicious people in the county became. They wanted the culprits caught, the nonsense stopped.

He and the other cops in the county did, too. They were sick of looking like bozos, but no matter how many times he went over the case notes, nothing jumped out at him. He needed a break, a snitch, a lead.

Weariness hit hard as he leaned back in his desk chair. Cassidy's cryptic words still reverberated through his mind. *Something you aren't capable of giving.*

Double talk. He didn't do hearts and flowers. Never needed to. But she wanted it, and until he figured out how to deliver, she wouldn't return his phone calls. Wouldn't even respond to his texts.

"Derek," James sauntered from his office, a sheaf of papers in his hand. "New bulletins from RISS and N-Dex came in. Pass them on to Kyle when you finish." He set the papers on the desk.

Every Tuesday, James pulled reports from the Regional Information Sharing Systems and the National Data Exchange. Law enforcement agencies across the nation used them, and James had everyone who worked for him read through the reports, even Lorraine, the dispatcher.

"Man, you look awful." James frowned at Derek. "Go home when you finish these. Get some rack time. I think we can manage for a half day without you."

"Think I will." Sleep. A novel concept. If only he could get his brain to shut down long enough to reach REM stage. Derek dropped the vandalism folder in the file drawer, locked it away, and then skimmed through the bulletins.

A surveillance investigation of a $1.8 billion dollar white-collar bank fraud scheme in Boise.

Two new narcotics distribution bands in Fullerton, California.

A joint effort of state and federal agencies from San Diego to Vancouver in a crackdown on human trafficking along the Pacific Coast corridor.

Weapons deals in Las Vegas.

A breakthrough in a rash of crash and grab robberies of high-end jewelry stores in Seattle.

A suspected terrorist cell operating out of Portland.

A serial arsonist in Cheyenne.

And at the bottom of the page, a quick mention of their piddly series of vandalisms in the remote area of Custer

County, Idaho.

He laid the reports on Kyle's desk and grabbed his hat.

"Hold up, Derek." James's voice halted him before he reached the door. "Get in here. You need to see this."

All thoughts of rest evaporated like dew in the morning sun.

"Remember those pictures Cassie harped on? She sent them in an e-mail. Take a look." He turned his monitor so Derek could see the three images. In the first picture, two men in profile stood next to a truck. The second image revealed full face views of the same two men, angry this time. The third photo showed the vehicle—a dark green, GMC Sierra 2500HD with a temporary Colorado license plate—and its load.

Derek let his breath out in a whoosh. "That's a lot of spray paint."

James enlarged the snapshot and centered in on the contents of the truck bed revealed by the thrown back tarp. "I think maybe we should've taken Cassie a bit more seriously yesterday. Might have prevented last night's stunt. What worries me now is the amount of gasoline. Let me print a copy of these."

"Wait." Derek pointed at the orange sticker on one of the wooden boxes. "Are those explosives?"

"Looks like it to me," James confirmed.

All this time, they'd blamed over-privileged teenagers with too much time on their hands and too much money at their disposal. Now it seemed there might be more to this mystery than just kids playing pranks.

"Lookee here." James zoomed in again. He pointed at the area under the tarp. "Unless I miss my guess, that's a hard shell rifle case under there, maybe more than one."

"Assault weapons?"

James shrugged. "My badge says don't jump to conclusions, but my gut's telling me a different story. We missed something."

"Run the license plate. Post the photos on the N-Dex. See if we get a hit." Derek grabbed the copies from the printer and turned on his heel.

"Where you headed?"

"To question a certain hardheaded young lady." Cassidy might ignore his calls and texts, but she couldn't very well flout an official visit.

CCC

After TJ, Lucy, and Mallory took off, Cassie looked for her mother. She found her in the rose garden out front, in well-worn jeans, one of Dad's long-sleeved chambray shirts with the sleeves rolled up, and heavy duty gloves. She knelt by a rose bush and wielded a pair of shears like someone on a mission.

"Isn't it a little early in the season to prune? I thought you waited until after first frost." Cassie sat cross-legged on the grass nearby while Sadeé explored.

Her mom looked up with a sunny smile. "I've learned a

good trim throughout the year extends the blooms by several weeks. Also makes it easier to cut back the canes in the fall."

Made sense. Kind of like how she'd let all the bad stuff build up between her and Mallory. She had to prune away all the hard feelings to get to the heart of the matter.

"I haven't had a chance to tell you …" Her mother brushed a strand of hair from her face. "But you here at the ranch, at home this summer, makes me very happy."

"I'm sorry I rushed my visits when I came home before."

"You had your life in the city, and college."

"I did, but the city can be a lonely place. It's hard with only strangers to depend on, not knowing if you can trust them. It's good to have kin who always have your back." At least most of them.

Mom shucked off her garden gloves and dropped down on the grass beside Cassie. "That's not always true. You remember the stories about my parents. How they washed their hands of me when I married your father. They died without ever speaking to me again. Not that I regret marrying your father, quite the opposite. I would choose him over them every time. And don't forget Cody's father. Cold. And meaner than a … Well, I can't think of an animal nasty enough to compare that man to."

"I'm sorry. I didn't mean to dredge up bad memories."

"It's okay, sweetheart. I made peace with the past a long time ago. It's not all about blood relations; it's about family.

Sometimes common experiences, close relationships, and shared commitments bind people tighter than genes. Take James. Or TJ and Lucy. Derek and Kyle. They're family now. I love and trust them like my own."

Cassie ducked her head, plucked a handful of grass, and tossed the blades aside. She'd turned her back on her family for a long time, and now others had taken her place.

"I've missed this." Cassie waved a hand in a wide sweep. "I don't know how to make it right again."

Mom leaned over and bumped shoulders. "You're always welcome here, Cass."

Welcome. As in a visit. "I think I'll saddle Buffy and go for a ride. I've got some stuff I need to sort out in my head."

"And I need to finish these roses before we both get all sappy, as you kids say. If you hurry, you might catch your father in the barn. He wanted to ride out and check on his precious wild horses this afternoon. If you don't mind some company."

Cassie stood and kissed her mother's cheek. "Thanks, Mom. Seems like the older I get the smarter you become."

Her mother's soft laughter tinkled like wind chimes and lifted some of the darkness.

Cassie stared in open-mouthed wonder at the vista before her. Barren and broken or lush and wild, the ever-changing landscape and vibrant colors stole her breath. She'd ridden this

land too many times to count, knew all the twists and turns better than the face she stared at in the mirror each morning, yet the grandeur still rendered her breathless.

"Close your mouth, Sprite." Her dad chuckled. "Not much has changed. You've just forgotten."

She grinned at him, unable to remember the last time he'd called her that. Too many years.

"It's like I've rediscovered part of my soul out here. I didn't realize how much I've missed this."

A man of few words, he nodded and nudged Rowdy with his heels. The big quarter horse quickened his pace.

"How far now?" She urged Buffy to keep up.

Dice Canyon lay twenty-six miles from the house as the crow flies, but six miles longer by land because of the hills and arroyos. Too far for a comfortable day trip on horseback. Instead, her dad drove most of the way with a trailer behind. They'd unloaded and saddled the horses, and ridden out on the last leg a short time ago.

"An hour, hour and a half tops. Smart to leave the dog. She'd tear up her paws out here."

Sadeé didn't take the command to stay very well. She'd pout when they returned.

Cassie had always loved alone time with her father. He liked the quiet, too. Neither ever felt the need to fill the silence with unnecessary words. When they reached the canyon edge, the mustangs weren't there.

"They'll come. Stream's down yonder." He pointed toward the boxed end of the gorge. "Let's unsaddle our horses. Let them rest while we eat."

Cassie spread a blanket on the ground near the lip and stared at the zigzag trail that led down. The descent was close to a thousand feet to the canyon floor. One day she intended to make the trip.

A little more than an hour later, the ground began to rumble. A mere vibration at first, it soon became thunder.

"Here they come." Dad shaded his eyes with one hand and squinted into the sun.

Moments later, the wild mustangs cleared the bottleneck at the mouth of the canyon. The herd—roans, chestnuts, paints, brown, red, black, white—loped at a lazy pace behind the dominant stallion. Wild creatures. Protected and free, only because her dad had set aside this land for them.

"Count them for me, Sprite."

She cupped a hand over her eyes and began the tricky task of counting the horses. "Sixty-three," she said minutes later.

"Good. Same as last week."

"How often do you check on them?"

"I try to get out here twice a week."

One of his beloved mustangs had been killed not long ago, shot like a fish in a barrel by some cowardly cretin James had yet to identify. "You know, I have a good bit of free time on my hands lately. I could help. Maybe come out one day a week in your place."

He chewed on a twig of bunchgrass and watched the horses drink from the sparkling stream. "Figured you'd offer. Sure you haven't gone city-soft? You remember how to hitch the trailer?"

"Old age must've caught up with you if you don't remember all the times I hauled Buffy to rodeos. Some stuff you don't forget. How about I take Fridays?"

He nodded and glanced up at the sun. "Deal. Best we start back. Don't want your mother to worry."

On the return trip, Buffy's labored breathing slowed them down. It would take a while to get her back in shape.

Rascal came out from the barn to help unload the horses from the trailer.

"We got this, Cass," Dad said. "Go on up to the house and wash up. Tell your momma I'll be along."

She brushed most of the dust off her clothes before sticking her head in the door. "Hey, Mom. We're back."

Sadeé greeted her with an aloofness that didn't last. Before long, she was whimpering with joy and dancing around the room.

Cassie knelt on the floor to hug the dog and receive wet kisses. She could always count on Sadeé to bring a smile.

"Thank heavens." Her mom wiped her hands on a dishcloth and hurried over. "Your dog stayed by the door the whole time like you were never coming home. Everything okay at the canyon? It's not like your dad to miss supper."

"Sorry, Mom. My fault. Dad took pity on us. I haven't ridden that far in a long time, and Buffy's not in the best shape. He and Rascal are taking care of the horses."

"I set plates in the oven for you. Go wash up. Derek's been here all afternoon. He's waiting in the family room."

The euphoria from the afternoon disappeared. From her experience, men didn't have a lot of patience. If Derek stayed all those hours, surly wouldn't begin to describe his mood. "Thanks."

Cassie considered a fast trip upstairs to clean up first, but decided against it. He'd think she did it for him, and the man didn't need any encouragement. She started toward the family room.

Four brawny men—her three brothers and one livid deputy—glared at her from the doorway.

Uh-oh.

A detached part of her registered the way Derek's forearms flexed as he clenched and unclenched his fists. A vein pulsed in his forehead. He stood tense as a panther ready to spring. And his eyes—emerald ice chips.

Now she understood why Garrett sometimes slipped and called him Iceman.

"Uh, what's up guys?"

Derek stepped forward. "Where in the name of Hades have you been, woman?"

Chapter Nine

Too late, Derek realized his mistake. Chastising Cassidy in her own home, in front of her brothers, wouldn't endear him to her.

A kaleidoscope of emotions flickered across Cassidy's face, wariness predominant until the pained look of a wounded creature settled in. She seemed to shrink in on herself.

A feeling unlike any he'd ever felt before seized him. He'd worried about her, was concerned she might be hurt. And then he'd hurt her himself with his impatient anger.

Garrett muscled past Derek to loom over his sister like the Grim Reaper. "Why didn't you show me the pictures, Cass?"

Up went her defenses. Back went the shoulders. Loner Cassidy stood here now, ready to prove how much she didn't need anyone.

Derek's lungs seized. How many more ways could he screw up his chances with her?

"Those guys you ran into are behind all the vandalism crap. You knew this and didn't say anything." Wade sided with his brother.

Jonas lined up alongside them as well. "You willfully

withheld vital information. Do you want to get arrested again?"

Women in general didn't understand that males of the species are hardwired from birth with all the subtlety of a grizzly bear in defense of its territory. Cassidy didn't get it. Her brothers didn't handle fear or anxiety well, not when it involved a direct threat to their sister.

So what was his excuse? Because he didn't have a brotherly bone in his body when it came to Cassidy.

She braced for the storm, hard and unyielding, alone against the world.

A low rumble brought them all up short, a serious warning of a boundary crossed. Sadeé positioned herself in front of Cassidy, head lowered, ears back, and muzzle twitching. The dog's eyes focused on the brothers with scary intensity.

Garrett, Wade, and Jonas all took a step back.

Not good. Sadeé recognized the brothers, but that wouldn't deter the dog from defending Cassidy.

Derek uttered the *ch* sound and snapped his fingers.

The growl subsided. Sadeé sat on the floor in front of Cassidy, but the bushy tail swishing over the hardwood floor fooled no one.

Derek held his arms out and tried to herd Garrett, Wade, and Jonas out of the room. "Hey, guys, let's take it down a notch. How about you let me handle this, okay?"

Mallory stormed into the room at that moment. She flung an arm around her twin's shoulders. "You're the one who needs to back off."

TJ took up position on the other side of Cassidy and confronted Garrett. "Why are you yelling at your sister?"

Garrett didn't play nice-nice. Outnumbered, he'd faced down enemy combatants and come away the victor again and again. "Come on, angel. This doesn't concern you …"

Fierce, aggressive, and deadly, the seasoned warrior wilted under his new bride's censure. The man stood a foot taller and a lot wider, but his size didn't intimidate her one iota.

"Cassie's my friend and you guys are bullying her. That makes it my concern." TJ jabbed Garrett's sternum with her index finger.

Derek didn't know whether to laugh, groan, or applaud. Long, pointed nails ought to be outlawed. Whoever dubbed women the weaker sex sure had no clue about the way the world really worked.

Lucy, Wade's computer genius girlfriend, joined the fray. She wiggled her way to the front, and stood with nostrils flaring and high color in her cheeks. "You plan to beat her into submission next?"

Yep, reason had departed the premises. Lucy's words confirmed it.

Wade took another step back, bumped into a table, knocked over a vase of roses, righted it, and mumbled what sounded like "Sorry" under his breath.

Any man with a grain of sense would tuck tail when

confronted by a trio of angry mama bears. Not Jonas, though. Wild, arrogant, and still free from Cupid's mischief, the youngest brother settled into his Superman pose—chin jutting, wide stance, and arms crossed over his chest. "You girls need to trot your little fannies back to the kitchen. This is Task Force business and nothing to do with you."

Derek winced.

Garrett and Wade did, too.

For a man with a reputation as a lover, Jonas showed all the finesse of a donkey.

Derek braced for World War III.

Sure enough, three seriously ticked off women exploded.

Make that four. Sadeé rose to her feet again, her lips drawn back in a snarl to bare some wicked-looking teeth.

Derek elbowed his way between the two factions. "Stop. We can talk—"

A blast of male and female voices drowned him out.

"You've done enough—"

"Stay out of this—"

"It's not—"

"Who are you telling—"

"Enough!" Cody entered the room. The Cameron patriarch forced his way into the battle, shoved Wade and Jonas aside, and confronted Derek and Garrett. "What in blazes is going on?"

Derek's mouth opened and closed. He had no idea what to

say.

Apparently, Garrett didn't either.

Cody turned to the girls. "Well?"

More than a little miffed, an irate TJ pointed her dagger-like finger at her new husband. "These cavemen ganged up on Cassie. They threatened her."

A trio of feminine noses lifted high, while Cassie's chin remained conspicuously low.

Derek's mouth dropped in consternation. Threatened? A look at his cohorts confirmed their appalled surprise, too.

Wade recovered first. "Not true."

"She's not a criminal—"

"Silly, hysterical women—"

"I said enough!" Cody yelled. He looked from the girls to his sons, stared at Derek for a long moment, and settled last on Cassidy. "Ah, Sprite. What'd you do this time?"

With the first sign of aggression toward Cassidy, Sadeé had gone into full alert. The dog didn't care about right or wrong. A menacing rumble issued from her throat.

Derek uttered another soft *ch*.

Sadeé obeyed and backed off. The hostility dialed down to a safer DEFCON 3.

Cate came in then, using the apron to wipe her hands. She did a slow perusal around the room.

No one said a word.

"Derek, sit." Cate pointed to one of the oversized

armchairs. "Do not move. Don't say a word."

He dared a quick look at Cassidy … and almost lost it. Her lower lip quivered. Tears clung to her lashes, tears she fought hard to hold back. So much hurt lay in those sapphire eyes. Somehow he found the chair and collapsed into it.

"Garrett, TJ?" Cate went on. "It's time you two went home."

"But—" Garrett started to say.

Cate held up one hand.

TJ sniffed and walked out, not waiting for her husband. Paradise might be a reach for the newlyweds this evening.

"Wade, I'm sure you and Jonas have chores to do in the barn. Mallory, you and Lucy go with them."

The girls departed first, righteous indignation oozing from every pore.

The guys followed, muttering under their breath.

"Cody, you need to leave, too. We'll speak about this later."

With a nod, Cody turned on his heel and left, not that it surprised Derek. He didn't know a single man who would willingly remain in the middle of a mess like this.

"Cassie, sweetheart, sit down over here, please." Cate led her to the loveseat opposite Derek's chair.

She sat, Sadeé at her feet, but refused to look at her mother or him. Though fragile and beaten down, Cassidy still took a moment to scratch behind Sadeé's ears to comfort the dog.

It took every ounce of Derek's control to not go over there and pull her into his arms.

"You two need to deal with whatever this is between you." Cate left the room.

Derek squirmed, uncomfortable in the heavy silence. The future lay before him, his for the taking, but with each tick of the clock he felt it slip away. A tightrope couldn't be any narrower than the line he walked. One more careless word and Cassidy would bolt. It's how she dealt with emotional overload.

Some deep, primal instinct told him if she ran this time, he'd never get another shot.

He drew in a deep breath, released it in a slow exhale, and offered up a silent prayer for the first time in his life. *God, I know we're not on close terms, but You know this precious woman. Her belief in You makes me want to believe, too. Please don't let me mess this up again.*

"What are you thinking, Baby?"

She took a long time to respond.

"The battery was zapped by the time I got my phone from the car last night. I sent the photos to James after breakfast this morning. I told you all I know in your office."

"Not that. I screwed up there, and I'll apologize, but first, I want to know what's going on in your pretty head because from where I sit, it looks serious." He kept his voice soft, persuasive.

Cassidy continued to study her hands.

His guts twisted.

"I think …" The pause lasted so long he didn't think she would continue. "I should have left after the wedding. If I hadn't stayed on, I wouldn't have run into those guys. Wouldn't have gotten the ticket and ruined my chances for a job with Dr. Wilkes. Or created this rift in my family."

He forced a chuckle. "The speeding ticket was just a matter of time."

She still wouldn't look at him, but her jaw tightened.

"You know, you're wrong on every count." He tried again. "Without those pictures, we wouldn't have a clue how to move on this case. As for finding a job, you graduated with honors. Your resume has at least a dozen golden references and awards, not to mention the fancy internship in Atlanta. You can get any job you want. Anywhere. Even here."

Deep blue eyes collided with his at last.

"Cassidy, I'm not mad at you. Your brothers aren't either. Men go a little bit psycho when people they care about are in danger. It's like we failed in our primary role as protector."

"But—"

He held his hand up. "No buts. If you hadn't stayed, what would happen to Sadeé?"

A snort was her answer.

Movement over Cassie's shoulder drew his eye. Cate and

Cody stood in the doorway.

Derek chose his next words with care. "Baby, there's no rift in your family."

"You heard my dad. Everything's always my fault, even when it's not." Cassidy's voice broke. "And this afternoon Mom told me how you, Kyle, and James are family now. TJ and Lucy, too. And then she said ..." Another hitch. "She said I'm always welcome."

The stricken look on her parents' faces spoke volumes. They had no idea how much their careless words had hurt their youngest daughter. When Cate started forward, Derek shook his head to stop her. Cassidy didn't need to see her parents' pain. She'd assume the blame for that as well.

"Don't read too much into their words. I seriously doubt they meant it like you think. They love you. You're not the one at fault here."

"But I'm always the one blamed." She leaned forward and buried her face in her hands.

Behind her, Cody pulled his wife away.

Unable to stand it any longer, Derek moved to the loveseat. He wanted to comfort her, needed to touch her. "It's okay, Baby. Let it out. I've got you. I'm not going anywhere."

She took the tissue he offered and didn't resist when his arms wrapped around her.

Some little while later, after the sobs quieted, Cassidy pulled away. "Sorry. I got your shirt all wet."

He lifted her chin and thumbed away the tears. "So, does this mean you're not completely disgusted with me?"

The renewed sparkle in her sapphire eyes gave Derek hope. "Well, you're not … repulsive." She reached for another tissue.

Fifty pounds of heartache lifted from his chest. "Hey, I can work with not repulsive."

She choked back a giggle. "Do you want to talk about the pictures?"

"No."

"Oh."

He loved the way her eyebrows drew together in a frown. "You tried to explain. I didn't listen. I'm sorrier than you can imagine. I claim ignorance because my intelligence drops fifty points whenever I'm around you."

She attempted another smile. "So, is that good or bad?"

"Good, or at least not bad. I mean, uh …" Panic overcame him, like a noose tightening around his heart. "I'm not making a commitment or anything. No promises. Just … I think I need some time to figure this out."

Cassidy stirred emotions he'd never wanted. He scrubbed a hand through his short hair.

Her hand captured his chin and, with gentle force, she turned his head until their eyes locked. "No promises." Her soft lips brushed his, a whisper of a kiss. And then Cassidy rose and left the room.

CCC

The weather guy on the TV the next morning said to watch for a cold front to slide in from the north. The thermometer would continue to drop throughout the day and give noticeable relief from the dog days of the past month.

Derek parked in front of the Calico Diner ten minutes ahead of schedule. Goose bumps pebbled his arms as he hurried inside. For a Texas boy like him, it seemed wrong to be shivering in August. Even in the mornings. "Hey, Dee Dee." He waved at the owner as she bustled among the few lingering guests.

Hopefully, the old timers were wrong in their predictions for another fierce winter. Last year's record snowfall about did him in. Back in his hometown of Laredo, people spent their entire lives without seeing snow. Heck, forty degrees down there qualified as storm of the century stuff. Downright arctic.

"Mornin', Derek. Others aren't here yet. Grab a seat. I'll get your coffee in a sec."

He nodded and sauntered to the left side of the eatery. The booth at the far end afforded as much privacy as you could get in the diner.

Every Wednesday, once the breakfast rush thinned, he met James and Kyle here to eat and a quick debrief. Today, they would no doubt discuss Cassidy's photos and the boneheaded confrontation he'd set off with the Camerons yesterday.

Explaining that little skirmish held as much appeal as a trip to the dentist.

James entered a few minutes later only to stop at the first table to chat with old Judd Wheeler.

Wizened and leathery, Judd looked like he might've seen two turns of the century, but he refused to let old age dictate life. A few minutes more and James clapped the old timer on the back and headed toward the rear.

Derek chuckled. He liked this softer side of his battle-hardened friend.

Just as James dropped onto the bench across from Derek, Dee Dee approached their table with three mugs in hand. She poured the coffee, set the pot aside, and whipped out her order pad. "Rodeo Roundup?"

"Works for me," Derek said. Three eggs over easy, hash browns, sausage, bacon and ham, toast, a five-stack of silver dollar pancakes topped with a big glob of huckleberry jam, and a large orange juice. Perfect. Especially since breakfast didn't happen for him most days.

"Same for me, but …" James glanced at his watch. "But bring Kyle one of those bran muffins. Maybe he'll make it on time next week."

Dee Dee laughed and scurried off to start their order.

By tacit agreement, neither spoke while they drank their coffee.

Kyle rushed in at ten minutes past nine and slid in beside

Derek. "Sorry. Stopped a hot little BMW with expired Nevada plates. At this rate, Derek's speed trap should garner us enough fines by Christmas to fund the new video systems for the cruisers."

"Routine traffic check. Not a speed trap." Derek scowled. After moving to Hastings Bluff, he'd parked his cruiser on a side road south of town a couple of times with the express intention of deterring speeders. It appalled him how fast everyone drove here. He'd found the speeders all right, but he also hit a mother lode of expired registrations, no insurance, burned out headlamps, busted exhaust systems, and even one stolen vehicle.

"Got a few items higher up on the wish list," James said. "Like replacements for our expired vests."

"Roger that," Derek said. Most people had no idea armored vests didn't last forever.

Kyle's mouth formed a pout. Hollywood good looks had given him the call sign Romeo during his time in service. Superior skills and sheer cussedness had earned him a spot on the same clandestine government team Derek had served on though.

Their food arrived, and Dee Dee settled two huge plates of food in front of Derek and James. She set a smaller plate in front of Kyle.

He looked at the sad little muffin, at Dee Dee, at Derek, and then at James. "Uh, what's this?"

"Breakfast for people who're late." James buttered his toast.

Kyle shoved the plate away. "I'm not eating it."

Dee Dee laughed and motioned another server forward. "Okay, Shea. You can bring his food now."

Shea Townsend. Beautiful, blonde, and with curves to make a man melt. And eyes the light blue color of a cloudless summer sky. Mm-mmm. What she did for a white double-breasted chef's jacket and funny hat.

If a certain feisty brunette hadn't put kinks in his brain, this one might just pique his interest. Derek took a big gulp of coffee … and spluttered. "Hot, hot." He reached for the glass of ice water.

Shea set another Rodeo Roundup in front of Kyle. "Here you go." Her ready smile enchanted without effort but also showed not a lick of interest in any of them beyond their role as customers.

"Thanks," James called after her.

Derek turned a quizzical eye on his boss. The sheriff had a reputation with women—heck, they all did—but gorgeous Shea didn't trip any switches for him either.

Kyle, on the other hand, about broke his neck as he watched her sashay back to the kitchen. "Mm-mm. That is one fine woman."

James's frown said he didn't much care for the direction of his deputy's thoughts. "Off limits. You stay away." He pointed his knife at Kyle. "Shea's a nice girl."

Interesting. James showed all the classic symptoms of an older, protective brother where Shea was concerned.

Kyle opened his mouth, thought better of whatever he wanted to say, and shoved in an entire sausage patty instead.

For the next several minutes forks scraped over plates, glasses and cups clinked on the table, and a lot of satisfied chewing sounds filled the air. With their hunger knocked back, James directed the conversation to Derek. "What else did Cassie say?"

"Not much. But the brothers got a bit worked up when I showed them the pictures. Especially after she disappeared for most of the afternoon. Turns out Cody took her with him to check on his mustangs. TJ, Lucy, and Mallory jumped to her defense when the boys got a little rowdy. That prompted a regular battle of the sexes until Cate kicked everyone out." Derek refilled his cup and raised the coffeepot toward the other two. "More?"

They both held their cups out.

"What pictures?" Kyle asked around a mouthful of egg he'd liberally doused with hot sauce.

Derek swore the man had a cast iron gullet.

James handed over the folder with the pictures. "Seems our little Cassie had a run-in with some bad guys. She snapped these pictures with her phone."

Kyle studied the photos and gave a low whistle. "You

think …?"

"Yep," James said. "I ran the plates. Truck's registered to some company called Fleet Corp."

"A transportation group?" Derek pushed his empty plate aside and picked up his coffee cup.

"Dunno. Fleet Corp is a subsidiary of Midwest Distributors held by Alexander Services, which is owned by Mag-something-or-other. I got lost after the sixth level. Never did find the parent company."

"Which means we're back at square one with no leads." Derek shook his head. In the old days, they'd snap their fingers and get the full, immediate resources of the Navy and later, the Bureau of International Intelligence. Kevin Fowler, the former director of their covert team with the BII, never skimped. "You think you could persuade a certain government bureaucrat to lend us a hand?"

Kyle waved at one of the pictures. "Hey, I saw this truck."

Excitement bloomed in Derek's belly. "You sure?"

"Fifty-thousand dollar prissy green GMC pickup, shiny as a showroom floor model? Yeah, I'm sure."

"When? Where?" James said.

"Monday. Late afternoon. Two dudes cruised around town before they parked out front of the diner and came in."

Chapter Ten

Derek poured the last of the coffee into his cup and raised the empty pot to get Dee Dee's attention. When she acknowledged him with a nod, he resumed his study of the photos. Something seemed off about the whole situation, had from the first.

The big guy—Billy, Cassidy had called him—might tip the scales at two-fifty, two-sixty. Five years ago he might have been a danger, though not for Derek. Kyle or James either, for that matter. Big bodies like Billy's required a lot of maintenance, but it didn't look like he did much more than lift a fork these days.

Still, the law of physics won out more often than not. A man his size posed a real danger to someone untrained in hand-to-hand combat. Or to someone half his size. Like Cassidy.

A picture of her in a confrontation with these men, alone on the side of the road, heated Derek's blood. He tamped down his anger and turned his attention to the other guy. Smaller than Billy, he wore faded jeans, scuffed boots, and a wife beater undershirt to show off some very impressive ink. A serpent coiled around one arm from wrist to shoulder. Scales, talons,

long flickering tongue—incredible detail. The kind of artistry found only in larger, metropolitan cities. Given his swarthy skin tone, black hair, mud-colored eyes, and other gang-related tats, Derek guessed Los Angeles.

Another elusive difference set him apart from Billy. Intelligence lurked in those murky brown depths. A calculating cleverness that made nasty look nice. Definitely the more dangerous of the two men.

Dee Dee arrived with a fresh pot of coffee and topped off their cups.

"You got a minute to sit and chat with us?" Derek asked.

Kyle pulled a chair over from another table for her.

"Sure. Give me a couple of minutes to finish up with Judd and Caleb."

Once the last two customers paid, Dee Dee returned with her own cup of coffee in hand. "What's up, boys?"

Derek showed her the photos. "Kyle saw this truck parked out front of the diner Monday afternoon. You remember these guys?"

She studied the picture for all of three seconds. "Yep."

"How about you tell us what all went down from the moment they walked in to when they left." He pulled a pen and small notepad from the leg pocket of his cargo pants.

James cradled his coffee cup in both hands, apparently content to let Derek take the lead.

"Not many customers here when they came in," Dee Dee

said. "Just Harve and Gordon Reddy. The big guy there swaggered in and took the first seat at the counter. I thought it might break under his bulk, but it didn't. The other guy followed a step or two behind. He seemed fidgety. Looked around like a thief casing the joint and eyeballed Harve and Gordy until I thought they might snap. You know how prickly Harve gets."

"I'm surprised he didn't call them on it."

She shook her head. "Tonto there left a seat between him and his buddy. He asked for coffee. Black. Tubby ordered a big glass of milk and three slices of apple pie all for himself."

"Tonto and Tubby, huh?" James choked on a laugh.

Kyle smothered a snicker.

"They say or do anything?" Derek asked.

"Didn't talk much, but they did perk up quite a bit when Shea took her break. She came out from the kitchen, tossed her apron on the counter, and gave those boys one of her patented, heart-stopping smiles. Then she poured herself a glass of lemonade and sashayed over to one of the booths by the window. I swear that girl doesn't have a clue how gorgeous she is or an ounce of self-preservation."

In his peripheral vision, Derek caught the way James and Kyle leaned in.

Shea Townsend drove all the men in town a little crazy with her angelic beauty. When she'd arrived in Hastings Bluff a little over a year ago, her sweet personality had seemed too

good to be true. But she was the real deal. It didn't take long for everyone to see she had a heart big as Mount Borah and not a mean thought in her head. Even the women liked her. Maybe because she showed no interest in any of the men hereabout.

Far as he could see, Shea didn't have time for a man in her life. She worked most days at the diner, catered a few events here and there, substituted at the grammar school in Challis now and then, sang in the church choir, and did volunteer work in the community. Now that he thought on it, he couldn't recall ever seeing her out on a date. And yet she always had a ready smile, even for bottom feeders like Tonto and Tubby.

"Those two ..." Dee Dee's laugh held little humor. "About broke their necks watching her."

Derek clamped his teeth together. It irked him how some men leered openly at a pretty girl. There were lots of ways to admire a neat figure without intimidation. He couldn't abide a man who demeaned a woman.

Dee Dee looked from Derek to Kyle, but then she zeroed in on James with a knowing look. "You should've seen how excited those two got when Mallory Cameron waltzed through the front door a few minutes later."

A flush stained James's neck and rose to darken the normal ruddy color of his cheeks.

The air took on a heavy quality, but Dee Dee sipped her coffee unconcerned. "Shea and Mallory meet up here a lot since they agreed to help Miz Tillberry with the summer book program. Those two guys whispered back and forth like teenage boys at a pep rally. Nothing I wanted to hear, I'm sure."

"Please tell me they didn't approach the girls or speak to them." Derek asked the question more to head off James's growing fury than to prompt Dee Dee. She didn't need encouragement.

"No, but I could tell their stares made the girls uncomfortable. So much so, they cut their visit short. Shea even frowned at them when she scurried back to the kitchen. And Mallory ..." Dee Dee shook her head. "Poor girl couldn't get out of here fast enough. When Tubby realized she was about to leave, he stuffed the entire third slice of pie in his mouth. Never seen such a hog of a man. Tonto hurried over to the cash register to pay their bill."

"Don't suppose they used a credit card?" Kyle asked.

"Nope. Cash. Had a wad of crisp, new bills in his wallet, the kind you have to lick your fingers to separate. I made him wait while I spoke to Harve and Gordy and asked them to follow Mallory home, just in case. They'd also noticed how Tubby and Tonto were in a hurry to leave after Mallory got up. Harve told me later those two rode his bumper until Mal turned off toward the Triple C. They whipped around Harve then and lit out like they had a date with the devil."

"You didn't think it important enough to notify me?" James's voice held an edge that would make a lesser person buckle. Not Dee Dee.

"Don't get all snippy with me, James Evers. You know as well as I do men look at pretty girls all the time. It's a fact of life, an involuntary itch. I'm sure you've scratched a few of those yourself through the years. Do you really want me to report every time a cowboy stares a little too long at some sweet girl? Or only when it's Mallory they got their eye on?"

"You said you didn't like the way they hurried after Mallory." Derek sided with James, but right now he needed to refocus everyone's attention before one of them snapped. "Enough so you felt the need to arrange an escort for her but not enough to report it to one of us?"

James continued to glare, while Kyle watched with avid interest.

Dee Dee sniffed. "Those two men made my skin crawl, but last I heard dirty clothes, greasy hair, and roving eyes don't break the law. They didn't do anything wrong. And I made sure they didn't. I'm not Loretta Tuttle, you know."

The left corner of his mouth twitched. Miz Loretta Tuttle was a delightful lady in her mid-fifties whose husband had passed a year ago. She called the Hastings Bluff Police Department two or three times a week about something. Whoever had nightshift would make a trip out to her place, do a cursory inspection around the grounds, and give her a ton of reassurance and comfort. All would be right in her world again … until the next time.

An abrupt realization sobered him. Hadn't they given Cassidy the same lip service? Listened, patted her on the back, and sent her on her way? And now James chastised Dee Dee because she didn't report the same gut instinct.

"Tell you what." Dee Dee's voice held unmistakable indignation. "I'll call you the next time my antennas start to twitch, but you better respond pronto."

"I will." James backed off. A little. At least the vein pulsing in his forehead had slowed.

"Thanks for your help with our questions. I think we have enough for now." Derek extracted a few bills from his wallet and handed them to her. "My turn to buy."

Waiting until she left, Derek shared a thought with James and Kyle. "They mistook Mallory for Cassidy."

"And now they know where both of them live," Kyle added.

"They won't trespass on Triple C land, not if they want to draw another breath. Best let the brothers and Cody know. They'll brief the ranch hands and keep a closer watch over the twins."

"Don't you think you should tell the girls, too?" Kyle asked.

Derek chuckled. "Remind me again how you got your call sign, Romeo? 'Cause it sure wasn't for your knowledge of women."

"Look here, son," James went on in a fatherly tone, which

made Derek laugh again. James might be the oldest, but no more than five years separated all three of them.

Undeterred, James went on. "Think of women like coins, always spinning in the air. On one side, they're all soft and cooperative. On the other, they're thorny, obstinate, and more ornery than a mule. Unfortunately, a man can't know which side they'll land on, much less how long it will last."

Kyle's eyebrows had drawn together until they almost touched in the middle.

"What Father James is trying to say ..." Derek tried to help. "If you give a woman orders, half the time they'll do exactly the opposite out of sheer spite. They always have to prove they're smarter than us. Frankly, it's not worth the risk or the attitude. We tell their daddy and brothers, let them watch over the girls, and everyone stays safe and happy."

Across the room, Dee Dee gave a disgusted snort and disappeared into the kitchen.

Kyle mumbled through a mouthful of pancake. "God gave goats more sense than He did either of you."

"What?" Derek frowned while James gave the other deputy a death glower.

Chewing sounds. A slurp of coffee. A fork clattered on the plate, and Kyle finally wiped the paper napkin across his mouth. "For the record, I think you're wrong. It's like with any mission; good intel leads to good decisions. Mallory and Cassidy should know the truth so they can make informed decisions. They're not foolish or stupid. Both of you should know that. But there's a bigger issue you've both missed."

James crossed his arms over his chest. "What issue?"

"Tell me," Kyle said. "You believe there's a chance those two guys pulled the Pioneer Dairy prank? And the other incidents?"

"It's a strong possibility, and the best lead we've got." James's posture remained stiff.

"Look at the facts." Kyle raised a finger to tick off his points. "Two men—a low life redneck and a Hispanic thug by the looks of him. Strangers who are familiar with the area. A brand new truck with a sticker price higher than most folks in these parts earn in a year. Temporary tags and a registration buried deep, not to mention a truck load of highly suspicious stuff. What do you think they plan to do with the paint and gasoline? And not just anybody can walk in Dyno Nobel and buy a whole crate of explosives. Add in those guns under the tarp and you have to ask why two grown men want to torch an outhouse or paint graffiti on a silo in a place they're not connected to. Why steal a tractor, tear up a fence, and spook a herd of cows? How do they know where to pull these pranks, and more disconcerting, how do they know to do them when they won't get caught? Hey, I'm no math whiz, but this don't add up."

Derek looked at James. "He's right. It doesn't make sense. There's more at play here."

CCC

Two days passed after the epiphany at the diner. Forty-eight hours without a single lead to show for their efforts. Derek set the case file he'd labeled Tonto & Tubby on his desk.

James had renewed his efforts to trace the truck's registration, but it seemed the deeper he delved, the more convoluted the maze became.

Kyle focused his time on running the two men's pictures through various facial recognition programs. He'd also posted their photos on the national databases. They needed a hit, a break of some kind. And soon.

Derek reread everything in the files, and obsessed over the pictures taken at each vandalized location. He'd even gone out and walked the sites again to no avail. He had nothing to go on.

And no Cassidy either.

After their little confrontation the other night when he'd bared his soul and then gotten cold feet, he'd tried to call her every day.

She refused his calls, ignored his voice mails, wouldn't respond to his text messages, and wouldn't get out of his head.

He was so messed up. Just that morning he'd fired off yet another text the moment he woke, before his feet even hit the floor.

WHY WON'T YOU ANSWER? PLEASE DON'T SAY YOU'VE GIVEN UP ON ME.

The answering tone moments later launched his heart into orbit:

NO PROMISES.

Now, as he entered the office, Derek struggled to hold his grin in check. Those two little words, noncommittal and ambiguous, promised nothing and everything, and held the power to turn his world upside down. He'd reread her text at least a dozen times.

He grabbed a cup of coffee and settled in at his desk. On the spur of the moment, he tapped out another text:

YOU'RE ALWAYS OUT RIDING WHEN I COME
BY. WILL YOU TAKE ME WITH YOU ONE DAY?
SHOW ME THIS LAND YOU LOVE SO MUCH?

Her reply came within seconds:

MAYBE.

His spirits soared again. Definitely hope.

Lorraine's raised eyebrow brought him down to earth again. Time to stop mooning and get to work.

Derek opened the case file and spread out the photos on his desk. Colored sticky notes with the dates of each event helped him sort them in chronological order. His desk soon looked like a rainbow.

January 20: Jackson Homestead—graffiti on silo.

February 17: Lawson's Barn—six pigs in gunny sacks suspended from barn ceiling.

March 16: Morrow Farm—outhouse overturned/torched.

April 20: Main's Barn—a dozen goats on tractor shed roof.

May 17: Dice Canyon/Triple C Ranch—one wild horse shot and killed.

June 15: Abandoned property—pornographic graffiti on barn.

July 20: Pioneer Dairy Farm—tractor stolen/wrecked; fence destroyed; cows stampeded.

Except for the dead horse out at the canyon and this last incident of destroyed property, the pranks all seemed juvenile, stuff teenagers would dream up. "Lorraine, we got a map of the county somewhere?" He yelled across the room to the dispatcher.

A few moments later, she handed him a folded travel map.

The acts were as random as the dates, victims, and locations. He smoothed the creases from the map with restless fingers. "Willard Jackson's place, Lawson's …" He got up and went into James's office, opened the shallow middle drawer of the sheriff's desk, and confiscated a half-eaten bag of jelly beans.

Back at his desk, he placed a single candy at each of the vandalism sites. All but one—Dice Canyon—was located within an eighteen mile stretch on the eastern side of Route 93.

He went over to the twelve-month calendar on the wall where they managed their shift schedules and tagged the dates with the post-it notes. All but one event fell on a Wednesday.

The Dice Canyon incident occurred in the wee hours of a Tuesday. But they all happened in the third week of the month.

"Lorraine," Derek called again, his radar pinging.

She left her desk and walked over. "Now what?"

He started taking down the post-its from the wall calendar. "Can you get this map blown up? I need it poster size, say three-by-five feet. Soon as possible. And some colored pins."

Chapter Eleven

The crunch of gravel drew Cassie to the bedroom window. She flicked the curtain aside and looked down at the Blazer pulling up in front of the house.

Derek. And James.

It wasn't enough for Derek to call and text her at all hours of the day and night. Now he had to show up at the ranch unannounced? Didn't he understand? She wasn't ready to face him again, not after he'd halfway expressed his feelings … and then panicked.

With scuffed boots in hand, Cassie raced down the stairs, pausing in the kitchen only long enough to cram her feet in.

Sadeé padded behind, quiet as a wraith.

Masculine voices carried from the front of the house. With the lunch hour just gone, it was unusual to find all the Cameron men at home. Garrett and Jonas spent most of their days at the big barn while Wade had mentioned last night how his security business ran him ragged with all the new work he'd picked up. Did they expect Derek and James this morning?

The thought rankled that Derek might not be here to see her.

"Stay, girl." She kissed the top of the dog's head. "Sorry, but you'll give me away." With a final rub, Cassie blocked Sadeé from following, closed the door with a soft scrape, and sprinted for the barn.

Inside, her path led to the loft ladder, up eight steps, and then over onto the top of the adjacent stall.

Lancelot, Wade's dun stallion, startled and shied away as Cassie swayed above his stall.

"Shhh, boy. It's just me." Wade would kill her if his mount got spooked and injured himself. Not to mention what two thousand pounds of panicky horse flesh could do to a human body in an enclosed space. If she survived the eight-foot fall onto the hard concrete floor.

Cassie hesitated with one foot still on the rung and both hands glued to the ladder. How many years since she'd done this?

Too many. The stall had been empty the last time she'd attempted it, and fear hadn't yet found its way into her personal dictionary. Cassie looked up to where daylight spilled through the loft entrance. Dust motes floated on hazy, lazy sunbeams. She could reach the hiding place in mere seconds by ladder—

The deep timbre of male voices intruded.

No time. She'd expected the guys to shoot the bull for a while like men always do, not head to the barn. Unless they had come to look for her. Or did they want privacy?

Each second brought the voices closer.

Panic hovered a little too close for comfort. Time had run out. Cassie transferred her weight onto the two-inch wooden wall and let go of the ladder. She teetered on the precarious perch for a moment, torso undulating, arms stretched wide. Inch by fearful inch, she made her way across the tightrope width of the stall to the rear wall. Almost there. Another shuffle step forward and outstretched fingers clutched at the two-by-six support beam. Relief left her legs shaky even as euphoria surged. She'd done it.

The voices grew louder. No time to celebrate.

Cassie reached high to find the nail spikes on the back side of the post. Hammered in years ago by her twelve-year-old hands, they were invisible unless you knew to look for them. A fist closed around a high spike. Toes found purchase on another.

The climb to the underside of the loft took no more than five seconds. All the planks looked the same until she shoved against the fourth one.

The board lifted with a soft creak.

One more step up allowed a shoulder shove that moved the twelve-inch wide plank aside. The narrow gap looked smaller than she remembered. Snug. Not a … skinny teenager … anymore. Horrified by a terrible vision of being wedged there and found by Jonas, Cassie pushed through with a new burst of energy.

Her hips popped through. "Ow." Scraped, pinched, and

bruised, she eased the loose board back into place.

"You hear something?" Her dad asked and then louder, "Cassie, you in here?"

She went still as the dawn. No one knew about her hidey hole or how she used to come here when life got hard.

Muted daylight filtered through the forty-year clutter of old equipment and stacked boxes in the loft, remnants of her parents' early life together. The year she turned twelve she spent the entire summer creating the space by dragging one or two pieces into place each week so no one would notice.

The men stood below her now, but the inch thick loft floor and the clutter of junk muffled their voices and made it impossible to hear what they said.

Boots thudded up the ladder. Footsteps clomped around the loft a few feet away from where she crouched. "Mallory? Cassie? Are you up here?"

James.

Her lungs burned with the effort to remain quiet.

Only after he retreated down the ladder again did she allow a sweet breath of air. Below, the voices faded as they moved away.

In a careful half slide/half crawl, she squirmed her way to the pile of old feed sacks stacked in the corner and sank down amid years of undisturbed dust.

CCC

Cassie pressed an ear to the loose board. Ten long minutes

had passed since she last heard voices. The silence seemed loud in the confined space, but her hideaway remained undiscovered. Time to get out of here.

A slow belly-crawl through a tunnel in the clutter—her secret passageway—opened onto the open area of the loft. Taking slow, cautious steps she avoided squeaky boards. From the big hayloft window, she could see the front of the house and the long, gravel drive ... and a dust trail behind Derek's Blazer as he drove away.

An odd sense of regret trumped the relief of successfully avoiding him. At some point, they had to either move forward with this crazy attraction or walk away from it. Ignoring it sure didn't work.

She found no sign of the others, not that they weren't nearby. Jonas in particular had a sneaky side.

The horses offered a few soft whinnies, but no other sounds came from below. After five more minutes, she deemed it safe to leave and started down the ladder.

Movement stopped her in her tracks. Mallory crept through the shadows close to the wall, peeked out the door, and sauntered forth.

Had her sister been hiding, too? Maybe she heard what the men talked about.

Cassie hurtled down the ladder, dusted her hands together at the bottom, and rushed outside. "Mal, wait up."

Mallory, already halfway to the house, ignored her.

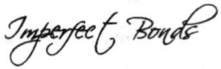

A quick jog and Cassie caught up. "I saw you in the barn just now."

Too late she recognized the closed off expression and flared nostrils. Mallory was livid.

"You hid." An accusation.

"Yeah. But I couldn't make out a word they said." Cassie leaned in, voice lowered to a conspiratorial whisper. "Did you?"

"Yes, I heard, but it's none of your business." Caustic Mallory stood here, her glare a poison dart.

Cassie reeled from the venom in her sister's words. What happened to their truce? To them wanting to mend the breach? What did she do this time?

Déjà vu swamped her. Memories from the past invaded, all the times Mallory had rejected her.

A desperate urge to lash out consumed Cassie, but with maturity came wisdom. Some things you had to fight for. She squared her shoulders. "Okay, what did I do?"

Mallory whirled to face her. "Not everything is about you."

"What then? Why are you so angry? Is it the family? The ranch? Are those guys I ran into causing a problem?"

Mallory looked away, a confirmation of Cassie's fears.

"That's it, isn't it? I brought my troubles here. I screwed up again." Bitterness had a vile taste, especially when doused with truth.

Mallory sneered. "What's it matter? You'll just run again."

"I never ran away."

"Yeah, you did. You took off after graduation without a word. You left a note, Cass. A lousy piece of paper. Mom cried for days. And when you didn't call—"

"I did call."

"Not for two weeks. Mom made Dad drive to Boise to make sure you weren't living in a dump. And then she sent one of us back every month to see if you still lived."

Cassie recoiled. "You came … I didn't know … I never saw—"

"You weren't supposed to. Mom told us to stay out of sight and not crowd you." Strong emotion stained Mallory's cheeks. Tears swam in her furious blue eyes. She might be the calmer twin, the reasonable one, but not today. Restraint had stretched too thin.

A sick feeling formed in the pit of Cassie's stomach. Mal was right. This wasn't about her. Whatever she'd overheard in the barn had upset her badly. And she'd turned her fury on the first available target.

A confrontation between them was inevitable if they had any chance of healing all the hurts between them. But not now, not in the middle of the yard like this. She couldn't even face Derek. How would she deal with Mallory and the ghosts of the past?

But if not now—when?

With a resigned sigh, Cassie stood her ground. Sometimes you don't get to pick when or where your battles happened.

"You knocked us all for a loop when you decided to stay after the wedding," Mallory said with a sneer. "I mean, how many times in all the years since you left did you come home?"

Their mother raced from the house toward them, wiping her hands on her apron. Flour streaked one cheek. "Mallory, don't. Let it go. Girls, please. It's okay."

Sadeé slipped out behind Mom and raced to Cassie's side.

"No," Cassie said, glaring at her sister. "It's not okay. It's never been okay. Go on, Mallory. Finish."

"Six times, Cass. Six measly times in seven long years. Four trips for Christmas, last summer for Mom and Dad's party, and this year for Garrett and TJ's wedding. Why did you stay now? I mean, three days is your max before you cut and run."

"I wanted … It doesn't matter. I don't have a driver's license now, so leaving isn't an option. Would you please explain what you heard in the barn? I have a right to know if my family is in danger, especially if it's because of me."

"You forfeited your rights when you abandoned us."

Hurt boiled to the surface, betrayal left to fester for too long. Mallory's words had the same effect as flint striking stone. One … two … three … Cassie never made it to ten. "I didn't abandon anyone. Don't you get it? You abandoned me long before I left. You made it impossible for me to stay," she yelled. "You, dear sister, are the reason I had to get out of here."

Mallory's complexion turned ashen.

A knife twisted in Cassie's gut. She felt Mallory's pain. The twin bond they'd shared their whole life remained as strong as ever, undiminished by time and animosity.

"You left because of me?" Mallory's voice broke.

Cassie didn't trust herself to speak. The hurt was too great.

Mom sniffled off to one side, her apron a mangled mess.

Sadeé sat in silence, ears low. Those beautiful golden brown eyes seemed full of sadness.

The truth would open old wounds, pour salt in them. Then again, maybe that's what they needed, a cleansing. She had nothing to lose.

Cassie lifted her hands out to either side, let them drop, and fought to hide the defeat that coursed through her. "I gave us until graduation to fix things. I'd tried so hard for years, did all I could think of to make it right between us. By then, though, we'd already forced the rest of the family to choose sides. It wasn't fair to Mom and Dad, or our brothers. Since I screwed everything up, it made the most sense for me to leave. I still don't understand what I did to make you hate me."

Mallory turned in a slow circle, hands clenched in her hair. She looked … lost. Tormented. "You think I pushed you away? That I hate you?"

"Don't you?"

"No. You've got it all wrong."

"Of course, I do. I'm always wrong. Tell me something new."

"That's not—"

Cassie held up a hand. They were done here. "Listen for once, Mallory. Hear this if you hear nothing else. Doc's offered me a job. He says there's a need for physical therapy services in the rural parts of the county, not much right now, but he thinks it will grow. I'll move into the apartment in town."

"But—"

"No." Cassie turned and started for the house, Sadeé in step. "I'm done with punishment for unknown sins," she tossed over one shoulder. "I'll try to stay out of your way, but this is my home, my family, and my town, too. Deal with it."

Mallory caught up at the door and grabbed her arm. A suspicious wetness shimmered in the eyes so much like Cassie's own, but this time they held a light that defied the dark emotions from earlier. "Wait ... I ..."

"Come with me." Mom had gotten herself under control and now led them to the family room. "Sit. Finish this. Get it all out. Do I need to stay and referee?"

Mallory dropped onto the couch.

Cassie took the overstuffed armchair to her right. "No. You should go."

Twin sisters, once as close as any two people could be,

now distant and subdued. The hurt ran deep, but Cassie wanted more than anything to mend this breach. "I don't know how to do this, Mal. I'm a stranger here. Everyone treats me like I might break."

"You want to know why? Because every argument with you, the slightest disagreement turns into a no-holds-barred, win-at-all-cost battle. It's like you have to win. Here's a clue. I'm not your enemy. None of us are. We're your family."

The harsh tone as much as the words cut a little deeper. Cassie had always thought of Mallory as passive, non-confrontational, maybe even a little timorous. Not so, at least not today.

Mal leaned forward. "I'm done with the 'Fragile, Handle with Care' stuff. Did you know after you said you wanted to stay on after the wedding, Mom begged us not to upset poor little Cassie. 'Your sister is sensitive and high strung,' she mimicked their mother's voice. "'Give her time to realize what she left behind.' Well, you've had time. Seven years' worth. And now you waltz in, announce your intention to return to the fold, and claim that I'm to blame?" Bitterness poured out in an ugly laugh.

"All those years ago, why did you push me away?"

Mallory flung herself back in the chair and took a long time to answer. "Remember our first rodeo? The barrel race where Rhubarb got hurt? You wanted to win more than anything, but you sat in fourth place when my turn came. I can

still see you bawling behind the chute. It seemed like you needed to beat me at … anything. Well, guess what? I threw that race. And I've looked out for your thankless ego ever since."

The memory returned, fresh as the day she'd sat in the saddle, wracked with disappointment and yet filled with excitement because her ten-year-old twin needed only a clean run to take first place. But Mallory yanked on the reins too soon, too hard. Rhubarb, her quarter horse, clipped the third barrel and knocked it over.

Her disqualification moved Cassie into third place. The framed green ribbon still hung in the bedroom.

Mallory wasn't done. "All those years in school I avoided competition of any kind between us because of your jealousy."

Jealous? The past continued its parade. Ninth grade Mallory who'd walked away from a spot on the high school varsity basketball team. Declined a nomination to the Homecoming Court. Refused to date Clive Richey, captain of the football team and the most popular boy in school … because Cassie had a crush on him.

Mal had it right in so many ways … and yet so wrong.

For the first time ever, Cassie had no pithy comeback. "Everything came easy for you. Barrel racing, roping, grades, boys, sports, friends. Mallory, the smart student, the beautiful twin, the perfect girl. No matter how hard I tried, I never measured up. Do you have any idea how many times I heard,

'Why aren't you more like your sister?' I was okay with it, though. Really. I mean, who needed friends when we had each other? But then one day you didn't want us anymore. You pulled away. And I had no idea what I'd done or how to fix it. I tried so hard to live up to your standard. Not jealous, Mal. Unworthy."

"I thought you hated me." Mallory's anger had fled and left her own pain exposed. "I thought if I stayed out of your way …"

The fabric of Cassie's world ripped. She'd spent years behind a mask so no one would see how much the rejection hurt her. Today, with one stroke, Mallory destroyed those defenses. Emotions churned with the need for expression, but accusations at this point would ruin any chance to reconnect with her twin.

"Do you remember how we used to fight? How we'd roll around on the ground the way Garrett and Wade did when they wrestled? Only we always ended up in a fit of giggles. When everything went bad between us, I tried to start arguments just to get you to fight back. But you never did."

Mallory wiped her eyes with a sleeve.

"Graduation day seemed appropriate," Cassie went on. "I'd all but given up by then, not to mention offending everyone of importance. It's not pleasant as the bratty twin. Everybody dislikes you."

"Not much fun as the perfect twin either, especially when

you're far from perfect."

The admission didn't surprise Cassie. She might be a poor imitation of her twin, but not once had envy ever entered the equation. "At least our bond hasn't broken. I still feel when you're happy or sad, angry or hurt. Do you feel it, too?"

Mallory nodded.

"For the record, I know I'm less than you, Mal. But I'm okay with that. I've always been proud of you."

"That's baloney. You're not less than anybody, especially me. You're one of the strongest, most determined people I know. Why do you still push me away?"

"I don't know. Self-defense, maybe, or habit. Rejection has a mean kick, doesn't it?"

"Oh, man, does it ever. For the record, you're so much more than you think you are. Can we fix this, Cass?"

"I don't know, but I'm willing to try."

"You're right about another thing." Mallory gripped Cassie's hand and squeezed. "You deserve to know what the guys said in the barn."

Chapter Twelve

Cassie leaned forward in the armchair with a silent prayer. *Please, Jesus, don't let me mess up again.* For the first time in forever, a glimmer of hope beckoned. Painful as it was, she had a real chance to reconnect with her twin and her family.

The frown on Mallory's face didn't bode well. Whatever she'd overheard in the barn could not be good. "Tell me what the guys said, Mal."

"James and Derek came to the ranch to speak with Dad, Garrett, Wade, and Jonas. About us. They checked the barn to make sure we weren't there first." A tiny smirk softened the indignation. "I have a secret place to hide. Apparently, you do, too."

Cassie nodded. "I'll show you sometime if you want."

The severe line of Mallory's mouth relaxed a little more. "I want." She closed her eyes and took a deep breath. "He makes me so mad."

"Who? Derek or James?"

"James. Derek and Jonas, too. Garrett and Wade actually seem more human since TJ and Lucy took them in hand."

"I've noticed." A remarkable change had occurred with

Garrett since her visit last summer, back when Derek first kissed ... Nope, not going there. Wade seemed in the midst of the same metamorphosis this summer. Not exactly soft—no one would call any of the Cameron men pliable—but calmer, more human. She quite liked them this way.

"Well, rest assured, Jonas, James, and Derek still drag their knuckles. I'm surprised their egos fit in the same vehicle with them."

Cassie felt a momentary relief. Mallory's rant was no longer directed at her. "I agree. Science might have proved the existence of protons, neutrons, and electrons, but they forgot about the morons."

That garnered a laugh.

"Tell me what they said."

Mallory seemed to fold in on herself. "Dad called out your name. I couldn't see them, but I could hear pretty well. One of them went up the ladder to the loft but came down a few minutes later."

"James. I recognized his voice."

"Thought so."

Cassie tried to picture where her sister might have hidden. Under the hay? In the tack room? Maybe one of the storage areas? Her eyes narrowed on Mallory's hair. She reached across to pick ...oats? "You hid in the feed room? Where?"

A sly smile emerged. "Pull an empty fifty-pound sack over your head and wedge yourself on the bottom shelf among the other bags … people see what they expect."

"You're lucky you didn't get locked in."

It was Mallory's turn to reach across and brush Cassie's shoulder. "From the look of these cobwebs, I'd say you hid somewhere in the loft."

Cassie nodded with her own secret smile, and the conversation turned serious again.

"To make a long story short, the two guys you had the run-in with? Yeah, well, Kyle saw them at the diner Monday afternoon. I did, too."

"What?"

"I meet Shea there every Monday. You remember Shea? She catered Mom's party last summer. Anyway, we got rooked into helping Miz Tilberry with her summer book program. Now we meet at the diner every week to divvy up assignments. Those two guys were at the counter. I didn't make the connection to your pictures until I heard James talk about it in the barn. You're right. Those two lowlifes are a nasty piece of work. I feel dirty just remembering the way they leered. Bottom line, James and Derek believe they mistook me for you. Even Dee Dee called them bad news. She got Harve Reddy to follow me home when I left. Just in case. Good thing, too. Your new friends tailed him until I turned off for home. Apparently, they're still hanging around, which explains why Derek and James came out today. To warn the men."

Cassie groaned. Garrett, Wade, and Jonas had always

taken their role of big brother way too seriously. Their protective attitude, for the most part, had taken the form of insult to any males who wandered into their sisters' orbit. When rude failed, which didn't happen often, they stepped up the intimidation factor. The three of them in full He-Man mode scared her. Add in their military reputations and an awe-inspiring array of weapons they used as a not so subtle threat … yeah. Can't blame a guy for choosing safer pastures.

"That doesn't explain why you're so upset."

"Then let me tell you. They *instructed* Dad and our brothers to keep a close eye on us. I believe Derek's words were—" Mallory's voice deepened in imitation. "Make sure the girls don't do anything foolish because we all know they can be ornery as mules. Cassidy in particular takes spiteful delight in doing the exact opposite of what I tell her, even when she knows it's for her own good."

A rush of heat streaked from the top of Cassie's head to her toes. "Derek said that?"

"Wait 'til you hear what James said." Her voice dropped in mimicry again, but with a nuance of hurt this time. "Cass and Mal are like my little sisters, cute as ladybugs but reckless. If I had my way, they wouldn't leave the ranch without an armed escort."

Cassie sucked in a breath with a hiss. James saw Mallory as a girl, not a woman. Was the man blind? A flash of clarity interrupted Cassie's dismay. Not blind. He had a chronic case of denial, most likely because of his relationship with their brothers. Regardless, his words had hurt her sister.

"You care about him, don't you?"

Mallory's eyes went all swimmy, but a few rapid blinks cleared them. "Stupid, huh?"

"Have you kissed him?"

"No." She sounded forlorn. "But he's hugged me a couple of times. Not a brotherly squeeze either. Tight, like he doesn't want to let go. Then he gets scared and pushes me away."

She ached for her twin, knew how it felt to care for someone who didn't feel the same way. "Have you thought about dating someone else? It might shake him up."

Mallory gave a rueful chuckle. "You've been gone too long. Hastings Bluff has a limited menu of acceptable males, although I did invite Kyle to lunch several months ago. To celebrate his birthday. He wanted to know if James had okayed it."

Cassie cocked one eyebrow high. "Well, that stinks. But it kind of makes sense, too. I've seen how James looks at you, like you're the pie and he's starved. I suspect he considers you off limits for himself because of Garrett. I mean, lusting after the sister of your best friend probably violates some kind of man code. And yet, it seems he's posted a no trespassing sign around you."

"Enough about me. What about you and Derek? Because I have to tell you, those ice cold green eyes start to smolder whenever you walk in a room. That boy's got it bad."

Yeah, she knew all about the way they smoldered. For now, she had other responsibilities, and Derek created an unwanted distraction. Not to mention overbearing and irritating. "We're both mature women capable of logical decisions based on facts. Shame on them for withholding important information from us. I, for one, can't go anywhere anyway unless somebody drives me … which leads me to Monday and my session with Coot. Are we still on? I sure can't see Garrett, Wade, or Jonas as my chauffeur."

Mallory grinned at last but with the dogged look Cassie remembered from childhood. Her twin had faced down a stubborn old goat, a vicious rooster, and any number of wayward calves. When Mal decided on something, the woman became a force of nature. "Have one of them drive? Ugh." She shuddered. "Do you still keep your Smith & Wesson under the car seat? Good. I've got a Diamondback DB9, and I know both TJ and Lucy carry. I do believe we fulfill the requirement for an armed escort."

Cassie laughed and held her hand up for her sister to slap.

"Okay, now that we've solved the world's problems, I have a long ride ahead of me. I told Dad I'd help him check on the mustangs, and Fridays are my day."

"And I've got a magazine article to finish and a deadline to meet. See you at dinner."

They reached for each other. "I missed you so much,"

Cassie whispered."

"Not as much as I missed you. I don't know if we can recapture what we had before, but I intend to try. As for Derek and James ..." Mallory stepped back and snapped her fingers. "Keeping us in the dark will bite them in the butt."

CCC

Cassie led Buffy out of the horse trailer and into the barn, sweaty and dust-caked from the long ride out to Dice Canyon and back. Sixty-three mustangs. She'd counted twice to be sure.

Twenty minutes later, with Buffy settled in her stall, Cassie grabbed a pitchfork to scoop up the fresh muck. A quick glance at the big clock on the barn wall showed fifteen minutes until dinner. Enough time for her to get cleaned up. She patted the tired horse good night, hefted the steamy forkful, and closed the stall door.

Footfalls sounded behind her. A spigot turned on, followed by the sound of water spilling into a metal bucket. Seemed late for Rascal to top off the water troughs. The old foreman usually had the animals fed and tucked in for the night by now.

"Hey," Mallory called out from behind her.

Cassie turned. "Yeah—aaagh!"

Cold water hit her square in the chest, soaked her shirt and jeans, and splashed her face. "What'd you do that for?" she spluttered, blinking away the water.

Mallory doubled over and chortled.

So, big sister wanted to play? Cassie flung the muck on the pitchfork at her sister.

The raucous laughter became an outraged shriek. "Eeew! Nasty! Not fair." Straw and horse manure stuck to Mallory's shirt and jeans.

Cassie threw the rake aside as they started to circle each other. After a long count of ten Cass let out a banshee screech and launched herself at her twin, going for a headlock.

Mallory knew her too well. Shoulders lifted high in imitation of a turtle she pulled the same sneaky leg sweep Cassie had used on Derek.

"Oooof!" Air rushed from her lungs as Cassie landed flat on her back.

Somehow Mal had fallen with her.

The two wrestled, rolled over and over in the dirt, and grappled for the upper hand. They collided with the mostly empty manure cart and tipped it over. Dung-matted straw spilled onto the floor.

With a great heave, Cassie maneuvered Mallory onto her back and sat atop her, only to find herself flipped and pinned in a similar position a second later.

And then Mallory started to laugh. Not the snarky "I put one over you" chuckle, but deep, hysterical, out of control guffaws. Just like old times. "I give. My arms … legs … feel like noodles."

"Why'd you quit? I was about to tap out," Cassie wheezed and rolled to face her sister, chest heaving, and promptly fell victim to another spate of laughter. How long had it been since they'd tumbled about like their brothers, only without the fists? Fifteen years? Eyes closed, she wanted nothing more than to prolong this moment.

Their laughter subsided into chuckles and then into sporadic giggles until, slowly, awareness of another presence intruded. Cassie cracked an eyelid—and peered up at four bigger than life men who stared down in stupefied wonder.

Garrett scowled, his bushy eyebrows drawn so tight they almost met in the middle.

Wade's mouth hung open.

Jonas's signature devil-may-care smirk begged to be slapped, not because he'd done anything to deserve it but because sooner or later he would.

But it was Dad's smile that made her heart hiccup. His deep blue eyes, a color he'd passed on to all of his children, danced with delight.

Cassie poked her sister. "We got company."

"Ow." Mallory turned to look at their audience. "Oh, uh … hi?"

"Heard a lot of squawks. Thought a couple of weasels got into the barn." Impossible as it seemed, Dad's grin stretched wider.

Mallory rolled her eyes.

"Cody?" Mom's voice called from somewhere outside the barn. "What's going on? Did the boys get into another fight?"

Cassie struggled to sit upright. Bad enough to get caught by their father and brothers. The guys would shrug it off, but their mom frowned on horsing around.

Sure enough, Mom, who stood shorter than Cassie and Mallory by a good four inches, pushed Garrett and Wade aside and came to an abrupt halt in front of them. "Oh," was all she said.

Cassie scrambled to her feet and reached a hand down to haul Mallory up. "We were ... uh ... horsing around."

Mal winced but then nodded in vigorous agreement. "Yeah, all in fun. No broken bones or anything."

Mom didn't look convinced from the way she took in the overturned manure cart, the pitchfork on the ground, and scattered hay. Her nose wrinkled before she turned to Cassie and Mallory again. "Is that smell ..."

Seeing Mom's face pucker up as her words trailed off almost loosed the giggles again.

"Yep," Jonas said. "It's horse—"

Dad thumped him on the back of the head. "Your insight isn't needed, son. Let's get cleaned up for dinner."

The brothers trailed after Dad, with reluctance from the way they kept looking back and snickering.

Mom seemed at a loss for words, but then she propped one hand on her hip and pointed toward the back of the barn. "Get this mess cleaned up. When you're done, hit the outdoor shower. You can use some of the empty feed sacks for towels. And girls? If you can't get your clothes clean enough for my washer, burn them. Boots, too. You're not tracking this filth into my house. Understand?"

"Yes, ma'am," Cassie and Mallory said together. They held off another fit of laughter until their mom disappeared through the barn door.

"You have horse poop in your hair." Cassie pointed at her sister's head. "And there's a big smear on your cheek."

"Well you've got a brown glob of it in your ear."

"Yuk!"

The better part of an hour later, they left the outdoor wooden enclosure with wet hair dripping down their backs. Wrapped in burlap, each held their sodden and somewhat cleaner clothes and well-scrubbed boots.

"I don't care what Mom says, it's not a shower." Mallory shivered as they trudged toward the house. "A shower infers two temperatures—cold and hot. Not cold and icy."

"I agree. Dad just rigged the water faucet higher up on the wall."

"So, you never did tell me about you and Derek?"

A "none of your business" retort remained on the tip of Cassie's tongue. Their truce was too new, too delicate. She opted for a shrug and silence instead.

"You know, if we're gonna give this twin-bond thing

another go, trust is essential. I have never betrayed your confidence. I never will. Look, I'll go first."

"First?"

"Yeah. About James." Mallory went quiet for several seconds, a thoughtful expression on her face. "It's not like we're a couple, and yet we are. Everyone in town treats us like we're together. We receive invitations as a couple, talk, and go for long horseback rides. He takes me fishing, and sometimes we meet for lunch or have dinner. It's unspoken, but we don't date other people. We're comfortable, and yet there's this edgy tension, too."

"You're in love with him."

"Yes." Sadness enveloped her sister. "Remember, Ronald Higbee?"

Cassie thought for a moment. "Yeah. As I recall he took a whip to one of his horses, and when Dad found out, he beat the tar out of him. It took both Garrett and Wade to pull him off."

"A mean, wicked man. Mom tossed him a five dollar bill and brought the horse home. Took Dad a long time to win that horse's trust. James reminds me of that mare sometimes, the way he acts all leery and cautious."

"Have you spoken to Garrett about James?"

"What? No!" Mal recoiled with an expression akin to horror.

"Sorry. Stupid question, but who knows James better than his best friend?"

"Friend or not, he'd ambush James and beat the snot out of him if he thought he might … would … you know."

Cassie laughed. "Which makes James's reticence understandable. Looks like you're going to have to talk with the man himself."

"To James?" Her look of horror returned. "He's a guy, Cass. Guys don't discuss feelings. Might as well talk about cramps, periods, and feminine products. He doesn't even talk about his past. All I know is he joined the Army at eighteen right after his father died, met Garrett in Ranger School, and the two have remained BFFs ever since. He grew up on a ranch somewhere in south Texas and has a younger brother who still lives there with their mother. Whenever I dig for more he shuts down."

What a fine pair they made. Mallory loved a man who wanted her but refused to act on his desires, while she loved a man who would act on his desires in a heartbeat but didn't want any more than that. They faced the same choices—take what their men would give or walk away and maybe keep their souls intact.

"Okay, your turn to dish," Mallory prompted.

The walk from the barn to the house had never taken so long, but if Cassie wanted to repair this rift with her twin, she had to put her heart out there. "You're right. There's some serious sizzle between me and Derek, but he's a one-night stand kind of guy. Love 'em and leave 'em. Told me so

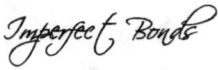

himself. My head tells me getting involved with Derek is a bad idea, but my traitorous body doesn't care. If I accept his terms and then he walks away later … I don't want to be that woman, Mal. I could never stay here and watch him move on to someone new."

"Aren't we a pitiful pair?" Mallory bumped her shoulder. "C'mon, I'm starving. Let's face Mom so we can get a real shower with hot water and shampoo meant for humans."

Chapter Thirteen

Derek set off for the Triple C the next morning, but slowed at the split in the road. He had to fight his inclination to follow the right fork to the house. That way led to Cassidy. Not that she'd be there. It didn't matter if he called ahead or dropped in unannounced, somehow the stubborn, sassy girl always managed to disappear. Pretty tricky for someone without a driver's license.

She wouldn't answer his calls, and except for two short responses on Friday, she didn't respond to his texts either. He hadn't seen or heard from the annoying girl since, but he'd spent all of Saturday and Sunday thinking about her. Even now, a visual of her dark hair and blue eyes left him in a stupor. He'd never chased after a girl. Never needed to or wanted to until now.

"I'll catch up with you, Baby," he'd murmur. "Not now, but soon."

Bearing left, the road rose in elevation through a stand of Ponderosa pines until it opened onto a scenic panorama of the valley. He slowed, came to a stop, and stared out the window for a long time. The Triple C ranch house stood across the

valley, a full mile as the crow flies, longer by road. Where Cate and Cody Cameron had raised their five kids.

The two-story structure, built of native timber that Cody had cleared from the land, boasted a wide, wraparound verandah. A broad chimney dominated the front, constructed from rock he'd hauled from the river himself. A red barn rose behind the house where the family housed six horses, one ornery goat, and their personal vehicles.

At a break in the tree line a mile or so beyond, he could see Wade's new home under construction. No doubt another wedding invitation would be forthcoming.

Derek got out of the car and looked over the roof in the opposite direction. The business end of the Triple C Ranch operations sprawled along the valley floor. Some distance beyond what the family called the Big Barn, he could just make out where a gabled roof poked through the trees. The home Garrett built for TJ.

A grin stretched Derek's mouth. The Cameron bachelors were dropping like tin cans on a shooting range. Would Jonas follow the trend and stake out his own plot of ground? What about the girls?

The thought of Cassidy's home built on property ceded by her father bothered him for some inexplicable reason. A husband should provide for his wife. No man worth his salt would allow his woman's father to pay for her needs. And Cassidy deserved to be cherished. Not that it made any difference to him.

A frown chased the grin away. He didn't like the vision in his head of Cassidy in a long, white dress, a lacy veil over her lustrous dark curls, and blue eyes gazing in adoration at the faceless man who waited at the altar.

He climbed back in the Blazer but didn't restart the engine right away. The image faded slowly, but not the mood it had conjured. His gaze traveled to the far side of the valley, across the river to a plateau low in the hills—miles from the other homes. Would Cody Cameron consider selling a piece of his property?

Frugal by nature, Derek knew he could afford it. His Navy paychecks had added up over the years, especially given all his deployment time in the skeevy locations where he'd been assigned. He'd sent a hefty sum home to his mom every paycheck for years, but no longer. Not since his little brother had turned the ranch around. And then his pay had tripled with the move to the Bureau … as had his investments.

The Cassidy-invoked feeling made his chest feel like a war zone.

Pushing her out of his head took more effort than it should, but he had a job to do. With a quick flick of his wrist, the engine roared to life. The Blazer started down the slope.

Impressive best described this portion of the Triple C. The sprawling barn shared the same deep red color as the smaller family barn and sported the same white crossbeams for trim, but the similarities ended there. This barn had twenty-four horse stalls, three adjacent corrals, a free-standing bunkhouse, feed sheds, equipment sheds, a small medical facility, and vast acreage of fenced pastureland—all dedicated to the breeding, raising, training, and sale of quarter horses.

Derek spotted Jonas working with a pregnant mare in one of the corrals. He parked his Blazer alongside the row of trucks in front of the barn.

"Hey, man. Meet Duchess, and yep, before you ask, she should deliver any day now." Jonas stroked the mare's muzzle. "She's been awful fidgety this last week. Can't rest, won't eat. I'm the only one she tolerates near her."

"Guess your manly charms work on two-legged and four-legged females."

Jo chuckled. "Hey, if you got it …"

Derek tipped his hat back and looked around. "Garrett and Wade about?"

"They're riding check on the line fences. Why? What's up?"

"Got some intel on those two guys sniffing after Cassidy and Mallory. Thought I'd update all of you at the same time."

Jonas glanced at his wristwatch. "I'll send a text and let them know you're here. C'mon. You can help me get Duchess settled while we wait."

Inside her stall, Duchess, a smallish roan at only fourteen and a half hands, bumped against the walls as she turned in a complete circle. Even with a distended belly, she was beautiful. Her coat, all glossy and sleek, gleamed in the shaft of sunlight spilling through the open doors. When Jonas tried to slip a feedbag of oats over her head, she snorted and sidled away. An offered apple slice earned him a head shake. The little mama definitely seemed out of sorts.

Jo gave up and hung the nosebag on a hook outside the door. "Duchess is usually sweet and docile, but she hasn't eaten since yesterday morning and then only a few bites. Can't rest either. I might have to call the vet out to induce her before she's too tired and weak to deliver."

Derek knew more about cows than horses, but calving couldn't differ all that much from foaling. Same principles applied. He grabbed a soft bristle brush and stepped into the stall with Duchess, humming a lullaby his mom used to sing. Quick movements could startle a skittish mare, so he kept his movements slow with a murmured, "Easy girl." Before long, Duchess allowed him to stroke her velvety nose.

He ran his hands along her neck and flank and then followed the same path again with the soft-bristled brush with the lightest of touches. "Sweet little mama."

Duchess's skin rippled under his touch. She turned her head to look at him and rolled her eyes but allowed him to continue.

At her soft whinny, he added a little pressure. "That's my good girl."

He kept the brush strokes long and slow, firm but not hard, all the while he hummed the melody and crooned. "Everything's gonna be fine, beautiful lady."

After a full circuit around the horse, Derek ran his hands down her legs until she let him lift a foot. He used a pick on her already clean hooves, more for the familiar physical touch than a need for maintenance. The Camerons took exquisite care of their animals.

Duchess snorted again but then calmed even more under his ministrations. Her head drooped. Long lashes flickered as she settled into a semi-doze.

Derek backed out of the stall, closed the gate behind him, and turned to find all three brothers studying him. "This her first foal?"

Jo nodded. "Yeah, how'd you do that?"

He shrugged and led them away from the dozing mare. "First-time mamas are always a little anxious. Duchess just needed some reassurance."

"You work with horses before?" Wade asked.

"Nope." Derek shook his head, feeling more than a little foolish. "Grew up on a cattle ranch. I figured if it worked for cows …"

"You have a way with animals," Garrett said, stopping near the barn door. "I've seen how Cassie's dog responds to you, too. Not something you can teach. You ever get tired of chasing bad guys and giving out tickets, come see me."

Heat climbed Derek's neck, but he nodded. Garrett didn't offer praise lightly. None of the Camerons did. "Thanks. I'll keep it in mind."

"Jo mentioned you had something to tell us." Wade brought them back to the point of the visit. Horse talk was done.

Derek stepped closer to make the conversation less of a them versus him stance and more of a collaborative circle. "Had a couple reports on those two overgrown juvenile delinquents we think are behind the vandalisms. Thought you'd want to know they're still around."

Garrett's expression turned hard. "Details."

"James shared their pictures with the police departments in Custer and adjacent counties. A report from Saturday put them north of Challis. Another report on Sunday, this one from a gas station manager in Mackay, included a clip from a security camera. Seems our two persons of interest ditched the green GMC and got themselves a late model blue Silverado."

"They're trolling along Route 93," Wade said. "Looking for a new site to wreak their brand of havoc ... or looking for Cass or Mal?"

Furrows etched Garrett's forehead. "Pricey wheels. Hard to reconcile those two with that kind of money."

"Stolen?" Jonas asked.

"Nope. James checked," Derek shook his head. "He widened the query since we got squat on the first attempt."

"Could be one owns the GMC and the other the Chevy," Wade offered, always the voice of logic.

"Nah, don't think so," Derek said, knowing they'd eventually reach the same conclusion he, James, and Kyle had. "We ran the license. Both vehicle registrations show they're owned by a corporation, but the owner name is buried deep."

"There's a deep bankroll behind them then." Jonas's concern turned to confusion. "Doesn't make sense. I mean, why go to all the effort and expense to pull a bunch of juvenile pranks way out here?"

Several seconds of thoughtful silence ensued. Derek kept his smile under wraps while the three brothers worked their way through the puzzle.

"Diversion," Garrett concluded.

Wade said, "Camouflage."

Jonas chimed in a split second behind his brothers. "They want to distract the local law enforcement, but from what?"

Derek nodded. "That's the big question. Whoever's behind all this knows we have limited resources. They want to draw our attention to a particular area and away from somewhere else."

"We need to map out the occurrences."

"Pinpoint locations and dates."

"Find the trend."

Being out of active service for a few years had done nothing to dampen the brothers' instincts and quick wits. Derek allowed a grim smile. "Got one started. Wanted to see when you guys could stop by the office and have a look. The more eyes the better."

Jonas frowned and glanced over at Duchess's stall.

"Or I could bring it out to you," Derek added.

All three brothers nodded at that.

"How about tonight?" Garrett suggested. "Come for dinner. I'll let Mom know. Afterward, we can have a look-see at what you put together."

"You really think Cass and Mal are in danger?" Jonas asked.

Derek thought about it for a second before he answered. "All my instincts are screaming to lock 'em up somewhere safe." He couldn't restrain himself from asking about her any longer. "How's Cassidy doing?"

"Docile as a lamb," Jonas said with smug assurance. "Hasn't left the property since you clipped her wings. Now I think about it, neither has Mal. Nary a complaint from either of them."

Derek's eyebrows drew into a razor-straight line. "Now, why does that scare me? Those two don't have a biddable bone in their bodies. Are you sure?"

"Dad put the word out to Rascal and all the hands." Garrett scratched his chin like maybe he wasn't all that sure. "They'd holler if either of the girls tried to leave."

The other two brothers looked at each other.

Jonas pulled out his cell phone again and punched in a number. After a second, he tapped in a second number. And then a third. "Hey, Mom. Is Cassie around? No? How about Mal? Well, where'd they go? You sure they took the horses? Okay, okay. Sorry. Yes, ma'am. Bye."

"Somebody you can call to see if the horses are gone?" Derek wanted more assurance than a supposition offered.

"Mom said she heard Mal, Cass, and Lucy talking last night about an early morning ride. We left Rascal to finish inspecting the fences.

"Lucy's not cleared to ride. Her shoulder's still healing from the surgery." Wade ran a hand through his hair.

"TJ said she needed my truck today." Garrett whipped out his phone and dialed. "She's not answering."

Wade waved his cell phone. "Lucy either."

Derek started toward his Blazer. "Think I'll head over to the house and see if the horses are there or not."

"Let us know what you find," Wade said.

Cassie couldn't remember the last time she'd laughed so much.

TJ had arrived in Garrett's monstrous red truck just as the sun breached the horizon. How tiny she'd looked behind the wheel with the driver's seat pulled forward as far as it would go. What really set the tone for the day though was when she hauled out a step-stool to climb back in when they set off for the appointment with Coot.

"Hey, without it I'd need a rope to get up there. Just remind me to reset the seat before I get home. Garrett gets a little crazy when I leave it all the way forward. Kind of like I do when he leaves the toilet seat up."

They'd had to leave a brokenhearted Sadeé behind. Big as Garrett's truck was, the ride would be long and uncomfortable for four adults plus a seventy-pound dog. Even so, the day had gone better than any of them expected.

They'd pumped Coot for information about the mysterious van and got him to provide introductions to neighbors who shared his concerns. Then, while Cassie put him through his physical therapy paces, TJ, Lucy, and Mallory had canvassed the area in search of more details. And find them, they did.

"What did you make of Harold Detwiler's claim about someone locked in the back of the van?" Lucy asked. The owner of the Quick Stop Coot frequented had told them about the time the mystery van stopped at his store to clean mud from the windshield after a bad rain. Harold offered them the use of his water hose and claimed to hear what sounded like sobs inside the cargo area. "He said the noise stopped after one of the men slammed his fist a couple of times against the side of the van."

Lucy shook her head. "Not enough information for a logical conclusion. I mean, it could have been an animal or maybe his kids waking from a nap. That doesn't make him or

his cohort animal abusers or kidnappers. For all we know, old Harold's hearing aid fritzed out."

"Who would stuff their kids in the cargo hold of van with no windows?" TJ asked.

"Or bang on the side with their fists to hush them?" Cassie added.

Lucy held her one good hand up in surrender. "I know. I know. It sounds suspicious, but it's still hearsay and speculation. I have to point out the law's perspective. Look at the facts we have. First, the locals are bothered by a mysterious van that travels way too fast over the mountain roads . Second, the one time the van stops, a man in his seventies, who wears a hearing aid and stood at least twenty yards away by his own estimation, claimed to hear something in the cargo space. Said noise elicited an angry response from the driver of the van who then banged on the side of the vehicle. Third, those actions don't fit what the locals consider normal behavior, so the shop owner assumed a worst case scenario. He shared his opinion, which was adopted by the other locals. That's mob mentality, ladies. Accusations and speculation based on fear, hearsay, and opinion."

"You're discounting what we learned today?" Mallory asked.

"Not exactly. The human brain is an amazing machine. It operates in problem solving mode all the time. Insufficient data? No big deal. The mind filters through possible scenarios and fills in the blanks. Erroneously most of the time, which is why eye witness accounts are often suspect. The television industry, shows like NCIS, Criminal Minds, and all the CSI spin offs have exacerbated the issue. They condition us to expect and even desire drama."

"Hmm. Never thought of that," Cassie said.

Lucy offered a shrug. "Bottom line, people fill in the blanks when insufficient data doesn't allow a proper conclusion. In other words, we enhance the mundane."

TJ glanced away from the road to stare wide-eyed at the former government Wunderkind. "So, what, we just wait?"

Mallory's brow wrinkled into a thoughtful frown. "Lucy's right. Innocent until proven guilty and all that legal jazz."

"Well, we do have one viable lead." TJ turned onto the long drive that led to the ranch. "That lady reporter Grandma Rosier mentioned. We need to find out why she's investigating our mystery van. And since we're almost home, I propose we table the matter for now."

"I have some publishing contacts in Seattle," Mallory told them. "If there's an investigative reporter with one of the television stations here on assignment, I'll find her."

The house came into view and silence descended. There, at the bottom of the front steps, stood a group of very large, very unhappy men.

"Uh-oh," TJ said.

"Uh-oh is right." Lucy twisted in the front passenger seat

to pin Cassie and Mallory with a stare. "Let's see—five men standing side by side, arms crossed, jaws clenched, muscles flexed—looks like the robust version of the welcome wagon. Did we do something wrong?"

Mallory looked guilty as sin.

Cassie bumped her sister's shoulder and gave her a stern frown. "Not a thing."

"Okay, let me put it another way. What did you two forget to tell us?" TJ demanded.

"Well, we might've overhead the guys in the barn on Friday," Cassie admitted. "They decided Mal and I couldn't leave the ranch without an armed escort. Of course, they didn't bother to tell either of us because women don't obey when a man makes a demand."

"Imagine that. Let me guess. James's words. No, Derek's." Lucy's thoughtful expression morphed into irritation.

"That would be a yes on both counts," Mallory confirmed.

TJ's focus bounced between the road ahead and the other girls. "What a crock. And Garrett went along with it? I want the full story, but later. Right now, we need to figure out how to handle the gaggle of bruised egos up ahead."

"I got this," Cassie said.

"They want to start something, I say bring it on," Mallory added.

"Girls, I suggest we keep what we learned today hush-hush until we can present concrete evidence. I wouldn't put it past these guys to try and ground all of us." TJ eased the big truck to a stop. "Not that they could."

Garrett had TJ's door open before the engine died. He lifted her out and let her slide down the length of his body. "Angel, why didn't you answer your phone? You know how I worry."

Cassie gaped at her macho, alpha male, warrior brother.

"No signal in the mountains." TJ seemed to melt against her newly wedded husband. The two of them became lost in their own world as he led her toward the house.

"Get a room." Mallory muttered under her breath as she clambered out behind Cassie.

Wade didn't lag far behind his brother. He wrenched open the front passenger door and lifted Lucy out. "Hey, Tiger."

"Hey," Lucy replied, her voice dropped to a breathless whisper. She and Wade followed after Garrett and TJ.

Mallory arched one eyebrow at the three remaining men.

Cassie raised a matching eyebrow. She could almost feel the tension simmer among Derek, James, and Jonas. "Wait for the explosion," she whispered to Mallory. "Wait for it …"

Chapter Fourteen

Cassie glanced at Mallory, saw her twin's belligerent expression, and matched it. More than one person had complained about how the single arched eyebrows they had perfected annoyed the heck out of people. She shuffled sideways until their shoulders touched, almost like old times with the two of them in a face-off against the world. Or in this instance, with three scary, really big men who looked like they wanted to rip something apart.

Derek, James, and Jonas maintained a polite, non-threatening, social distance after Garrett and Wade moved away, not that it tempered the aggression radiating from the trio. Long seconds of friction-encrusted silence stretched between the two factions.

She'd expected a battle of wills, but this confrontation had explosive potential, the kind none of them might recover from.

"Mind explaining where you've been?" Derek spoke first. "And why none of you would answer your phones?"

His voice held an edge of … worry? Anger? Relief?

Yes to all three. He hid his frustration well, but Cassie recognized the rigid set of his spine. These men dealt in action, not diplomacy, and yet he attempted civility.

"Excuse me?"

Mom and Dad chose that moment to join the others. Sadeé darted through the door behind them and hightailed it straight to Cassie, yipping and frisking like a puppy. It was impossible to maintain her resentment in the glow of Sadeé's excitement.

Cassie squatted to greet the dog with soft words, laughter, and a few quick rubs. When she straightened again, Derek stood nose to nose with her, or rather her nose to his chest.

"You're not supposed to leave the ranch without one of us along. Mallory either." His voice dipped into the gruff zone but still chased courtesy.

Keeping eye contact with those icy green orbs proved difficult given the severe angle of her tilted head. Why did he have to be so blasted tall? The sheer size of the man blocked out everything around her.

Mallory trembled beside her. Only a slight quake but noticeable nonetheless.

Not Cassie. Derek's posturing might intimidate most people, but all that overpowering male dominance didn't daunt her. Unable to lift her chin any higher, she crossed her arms instead. Her elbows dug into the slab of muscles he called a chest.

He didn't blink or even budge.

"And I'm supposed to know this—how? Did you put me on house arrest and not tell me? For your information, I don't need your approval to leave the ranch, Derek. As for Mallory … yeah, I'm calling hogwash. You can't put her on restriction. She hasn't done anything wrong."

James joined the fray, but when he opened his mouth to speak, Derek stopped him.

Good thing, because Mallory had puffed up like a blowfish. Shoulders squared, chin jutting out, she all but dared the sheriff to say something.

The tension radiating from Derek eased. He took a step back, one hand rubbing his chin. "We were worried."

The switch from frontal attack to conciliation threw Cassie. She wasn't sure how to react, so she kept her mouth shut.

"All I'm saying is those lowlifes who threatened you are still hanging around," Derek went on. "Until we catch them, you girls are in danger. You need to stop haring off like—"

He apparently valued his life since he didn't finish that sentence.

Cassie uncrossed her arms and slammed fists on her hips. "You mean the same guys who set fire to Ben Morrow's outhouse and tore down Jack Behr's fence? You've had half a year to catch them. Forgive me, but I refuse to hide like a frightened bunny for another six months while you play cops and robbers." She moved to go around him.

He sidestepped and blocked her. "You need to listen to me, Baby."

The tight control she'd held on her emotions snapped. "I did listen, Derek. You told my brothers and my dad how Billy and his pal mistook Mallory for me. Told them to not tell us because we'd do the opposite of what we were ordered. Oh, and let's not forget how I can't be trusted to know commonsense if it slapped me in the face. Message received. I'm a screw-up. I always have been, but you ..." She shoved Derek. "And you ..." She glared at James. "Don't you ever disrespect my sister."

Derek and James wore identical shocked expressions.

Mallory linked her arm with Cassie's.

Cassie's bottom lip trembled, but a painful bite with her top teeth halted the quiver. A furious exhale ruffled her bangs. Earlier, in the truck, she'd determined to hold onto her anger, but renegade tears welled up anyway. Why did she always cry when she got mad?

She dug in her purse and presented the Smith & Wesson with a flourish. "News flash, Captain America. I can protect myself."

Both men flinched, but Derek pressed her arm down. "Put the weapon away, Cassidy."

Behind them, TJ pulled a Sig Sauer from her jacket pocket and waved it in the air. "I'm packing, too."

Garrett grabbed her hand.

"Me, three," Lucy piped up, revealing the small holstered Beretta tucked into her arm sling.

"Hey, don't leave me out. I can hit center mass at twenty-five yards with every shot." Mallory fumbled in her purse until James stopped her.

"I think that more than meets your criteria of 'armed escort,'" Cassie said.

Derek closed his eyes, lifted his face to the sky, and pinched the bridge of his nose. "You heard."

"Every word."

Mallory shook off James's hand. "We both did."

"I checked. No one was around." James sputtered and crowded in on Mallory's other side. "I even went up to the loft."

"Arrogance, thy name is man." The smug in Mallory's smirk would rile the Dalai Lama himself.

James's normal ruddy complexion turned the color of an eggplant. "Princess, you need to stop while you're ahead." His clenched teeth made it difficult to understand what he said.

Arrogant indeed. Unrequited love sucked. Maybe the time had come for her and her sister to cut their losses with these two. Better to just rip off the Band-Aid, make it quick. It would hurt for a while, a very long while. "You made a bad assumption, boys. Never underestimate your enemy. Isn't that part of a SEAL's creed, Derek?"

Quiet descended. Even the mundane, everyday sounds vanished as if all of nature held its collective breath. The others leaned in and watched but kept a discreet distance.

A wave of sickness washed over Cassie. She didn't want to do this in front of everyone, didn't want to do it at all.

Derek donned his Master of the Universe persona and seemed to grow larger without effort. But then he deflated and became just a man again. "You're right. We should have informed you of the danger. You're both smart and more than capable of making intelligent, informed decisions. My head knows that, but my gut still screams to make sure you stay safe. I was wrong. I'm sorry."

Cassie's mouth dropped.

"Hear me out. You're wrong, too. You are not a screw-up. Far from it. And we are not your enemies."

"Frenemies then," Mallory taunted.

James yanked Mal's arm and moved her a few steps away.

A small smile tweaked the corners of Derek's mouth. "Not frenemies either. Far from it."

"Then stop treating us like we're your helpless little sisters. We're grown women." Cassie glared at James, pleased when the sheriff dropped his eyes.

A tap to her cheek drew her gaze back to Derek. "Trust me, Baby. I'm well aware of your womanly assets. There is nothing brotherly in the way I feel about you."

A blush warmed its way into her cheeks. It was her turn to duck her head. Smooth-talking Derek with his horn dog ways just wouldn't quit. And deep down, she didn't want him to. Hope, like a weed, was a difficult thing to kill.

"Now, you have to admit …" He went on. "James and I do have a slight advantage given our unique backgrounds. We've dealt with the likes of Tubby and Tonto before. We know what to expect and how to deal with them. I need you to trust us on this. Trust me."

"Tubby and Tonto?" She couldn't hold back a smile.

Derek chuckled. "That's what Dee Dee calls them. It fits. What do you say to a do-over? I promise to keep both you and Mallory in the loop from here on out, but you have to listen with an open mind, even if you don't like what you hear. Your safety is my—our—top priority. Deal?"

Cassie exchanged a look with her sister. "Agreed. We can do reasonable. I trust you, Derek. I always have, even when you go Neanderthal."

It was his turn to cock an eyebrow at her. "Okay, now we have the sticky stuff out of the way, would you please explain where the four of you got off to today? Because, Baby, the caveman clubs came out when none of us could reach you."

TJ, Lucy, and Mallory joined her in regaling the guys with an edited version of their morning journey. Derek didn't like her commitment to Coot's physical therapy, but he seemed to grudgingly accept it. With stipulations.

She'd won this battle of wills and could afford a little graciousness, and so agreed to his terms. Besides, a satellite phone that actually worked in the mountains and all the way through No Man's Land wasn't a hardship. And since Derek said he wanted to hear her ideas, she decided daily conversations with him might further their relationship— regarding the case, of course.

CCC

"I don't care, Trent. Tell your boss, but you're not getting our files."

Derek slammed down the phone receiver and headed for the tiny break room. He needed coffee, a distraction, something to take his mind off the day's futility.

He'd wasted the whole morning worrying about a hardheaded woman, only to have her hand him his butt once she returned. Iceman stayed lethal under pressure. Icy. It's how he first got his nickname, back when he served with the SEAL teams. The more dangerous the situation, the calmer he became, able to focus, to see in every direction, and process everything around him in a microsecond. He didn't know how or why. It was just part of him.

Until one little woman upset his careful equilibrium and put him on his knees. He hated feeling out of control.

It didn't get any better after he and James returned to the office—both with their tails tucked between their legs. They'd devoted the whole afternoon to catching up on reports. He stretched his neck and got a satisfying crack. Paperwork had to be the worst form of punishment ever.

He punched the doorjamb. Wanted to punch it again but knew it wouldn't help his mood. Instead, he lifted the carafe of what looked like oil sludge and eyed the contents. This bilge, loosely disguised as coffee, on top of everything else, would probably eat a hole in his stomach. His gut still churned from the call with that nitwit, Trent.

"Hey, man. Somebody put sand in your shorts?" James stood in the doorway, hands braced on either side of the entry.

Derek set the coffeepot back on the burner and switched it off. "To paraphrase something Cassidy said recently, 'What moron hired Trent Crutchfield?' Sometimes, I want to rip—"

"Don't finish that thought." James held up a hand. "At least not out loud. Plausible deniability. That way you can claim self-defense or temporary insanity, and I won't have to arrest you for premeditated assault. I thought Trent called this morning for an update?"

"The worthless little punk calls every day. Doesn't have a lick of experience, can't fight his way out of a jar of jelly, has mush for brains, and yet he thinks he knows more than all the rest of us put together. He's a danger to himself and anyone in a fifty-mile radius."

"So, what'd he want this time?"

"You mean what'd he demand? Seems Sheriff Castle requires a copy of everything we have on the vandalism cases, including the pictures Cassidy took and all the background info we've gathered so far. Tried to tell me he was taking over the investigation into Tubby and Tonto. Not in this lifetime."

"Cut the boy some slack. He's trying to prove himself to

Eli. You remember those days."

"No, I don't. I never acted like him, and as long as I'm in charge of this case, he's not getting a thing. Sheriff Castle wants something, he can ask for it himself. I don't trust Trent as far as I can throw the fool, and I'm pretty sure I can shotput him off the side of a mountain."

"So, all that shouting before you slammed the phone down means you graciously declined his request?"

Derek flashed his mission-ready grin—lots of teeth and little mirth. "Polite enough to satisfy your grandmother."

"My grandma lives in a log cabin in the Rockies and hunts grizzlies."

"I know."

Chapter Fifteen

The sultry summer days of the past three weeks faded one into another, too fast for Cassie's liking. July became August, only to pass in a blur without any sign of Billy or the tattooed guy, thank goodness.

With the map spread open on the hood of the truck, she ran her index finger along the line Dad had marked. Time had gotten away from her this morning, resulting in a later than normal start for her weekly trip to check on the wild horses.

The canyon's eastern perspective offered the best view of the valley and the mustangs preferred to graze there, but she could take the truck closer up by the north rim, close enough to cut the time on horseback by half. It was a shorter driver, too. She'd need binoculars, but at least she could take Sadeé with her this time.

The black and silver shepherd perched on the front passenger seat, her whole body wriggling. She gave an excited yip when Cassie looked her way. It didn't take much to make her happy, but the funny dog would pout for hours when left behind.

With a sigh, she decided on the northern route. The shorter

ride today would give her city-bred dog an easier run and, hopefully, not tear up the pads of her feet. And they'd still get home before dark to keep her mother's anxiety at bay.

No one liked it when Mom worried. She made sure of it.

Cassie closed the door of the horse trailer behind Buffy and went through her checklist one more time, something Dad had drilled into her. Rifle, binoculars, riding gloves, kerchief, hat, knife, rope, first-aid kit, rucksack with apples, energy bars, water, and the latest addition—the satellite phone Derek insisted she carry whenever she left the ranch. Everything a good girl scout might need and a few more besides. She threw the truck into first gear, waved to Rascal, and pulled away.

Two hours later, she parked the truck and unloaded and saddled Buffy, strung the rucksack over the saddle horn, added the canteen, saddle bags, and rifle in its sling, and mounted. Four or so miles to go. With her face tipped to the sun, she nudged Buffy into a steady, ground-eating trot. What more could a girl ask for? She had her horse, her dog, and the whole outdoors all to herself.

Wellbeing filled her, a sense that all was right with the world. What would Derek think about the land out here?

Sadeé ranged wide, but never out of sight. So many new sights, sounds, and smells. The poor girl would wear herself out at this rate.

As Cassie relaxed into the ride, thoughts of her tall Texan filled her head. Not an unusual occurrence but awkward when the ladies at church caught her woolgathering. Worse when one of her brothers had to poke her back to attention at the dinner table.

Men were supposed to be simple creatures at heart, or so she'd been led to believe. Feed them copious amounts of red meat, let them think they were large and in charge, and give them leeway to periodically slake their more aggressive tendencies with other Neanderthals.

Except Derek confused her.

He called or texted every day, something she hadn't expected. And he came out to the ranch several times a week. Lately, though, the heat was missing. He'd gone from boiling with lust to more like sap from a tapped sugar maple in the winter. The subtle—and sometimes not so subtle—innuendos fell by the wayside, traded for small talk and laughter. He even teased her the way her brothers did.

She didn't want another brother.

Which raised the question, what did she want? How much of herself was she willing to give to the man who turned her inside out?

The temperature climbed as the miles disappeared beneath Buffy's hooves. Glad for the kerchief around her neck, Cassie mopped sweat from her face. The canyon wasn't far now.

A distant rumble made her smile. Sound carried a long way out here, especially the thunder of running horses. Dad often spoke of when he first saw the herd roaming wild and

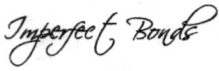

free over the open land. But vulnerable to predators of both the four-legged and two-legged variety. He'd used some of the first profits from the Triple C to purchase five thousand acres of unwanted range bordered on three sides by the Lost River Range foothills. Well within the boundaries of his new property, he'd set aside five hundred of those acres as a preserve for the wild horses.

Dice Canyon made up part of the preserve. The classical box-shaped gulch stood significantly wider than the other gorges, with lush grass, shade trees, and two icy streams that flowed from the mountains. The walls were mostly non-scalable except for a rough trail on the eastern edge and another on the north face, but at close to a thousand feet, they made for a long descent and an even tougher ascent.

Thirty minutes later, she caught sight of a dazzling glare ahead. A little farther and the glare became a late model pickup with an abundance of chrome. Too fancy for a work truck. What was it doing out here? So close to the canyon?

Cassie pulled on Buffy's reins and stood in the stirrups to search the area. No sign of anyone.

She urged her horse past the truck and closer to the canyon's edge where she dismounted and pulled the little Remington 7mm-08 rifle from its sling.

Sadeé came racing over. Her ears stood straight up, fur bristling. The beginnings of a snarl showed lots of teeth. Not a good sign.

Cassie look around again before peering over the north face and spotted three men. One stood on a flat rock near the bottom while the other two picked their way down the narrow trail.

The one in the rear stopped, threw his head back, and tilted a bottle to his mouth, before handing it off to his companion.

The man nearest the canyon floor yelled something she couldn't make out. A second later, he raised a gun to his shoulder.

"No!" Cassie's shout blended with the gunshot and a screech from one of the horses. The echoes ricocheted off the rocks walls.

Down on the valley floor, one of the horses dropped to its knees. And then fell over on its side.

The rest of the herd, alerted to the danger, tossed their heads and snorted. Many of them stirred in agitated circles.

Mocking laughter filled the canyon followed by a second gunshot.

Another animal screamed and fell.

The herd bolted. The two downed animals never had a chance, trampled by the stampeding horses.

Dust rose high into the air. The sound of the horses racing through the canyon rattled the rocks with earthshaking vibrations. A cacophony of horror flew on the wind—screams of pain, frightened cries, an explosion of thunder like freight trains colliding, and behind it all, the demonic laughter of the murderers.

Cassie stood frozen, horrified, sickened. The rifle slipped from her fingers right before she spewed the contents of her stomach.

More shots rang out.

The nightmare had to stop. With a ruthless swipe of a sleeve across her mouth, she snatched up the Remington and dropped to her belly at the side of the cliff. Stock braced against her shoulder, she tracked the shooter through the sights until the crosshairs centered on his chest. One second passed. Three. Five.

She couldn't do it, she couldn't shoot the man.

Furious, she jerked the barrel up and fired, aimed toward the second man and fired again. Added a third shot above the last man. The three shots struck nearby outcroppings. The resultant hailstorm of rock slivers and fragments sent the men in a mad scramble for whatever cover they could find.

The man at the bottom who'd shot the horses raised his rifle and fired again. At her! The shot didn't come close, but Cassie hit the ground amid a barrage of gunfire from the other two.

Not the outcome she'd expected. At least they'd stopped shooting at the herd, but now what?

They would come after her.

Her mind went to work. Forty minutes. That's how long it

would take them to climb back up. Less if they threw caution to the wind. She glanced over at their fancy truck. Buffy couldn't outrun that thing, but she could slow them down.

A gurgling, thrashing sound pulled her attention from the truck. She whipped around, her heart breaking. "No, no, noooo." She wailed.

Buffy lay on the ground, sides heaving.

Cassie raced over to the horse. "Buffy."

Flecks of bloody froth coated the animal's mouth. A steady stream of blood flowed from a tiny hole in her chest and pooled on the ground. Buffy struggled, unable to gain her feet.

"Oh, Buffy, what have I done?" Tears blurred Cassie's vision. Her voice broke. She dropped to her knees near the horse's head. Buffy had helped her win the calf roping and barrel racing crowns, had listened without judgment for so many years to all her dreams and heartaches. The sweet horse didn't have a mean bone in her body. Not Buffy.

The horse's groans came nonstop now, deeper, and more labored, with an occasional gut wrenching cry of pain laced with fear. Her legs still thrashed, but weaker now. The horse lifted her head and looked at Cassie, her eyes wild with pain and fear, but then it dropped back to the ground with a thud.

Sadeé settled on the ground beside the horse with a whimper. The dog knew the truth as well as she did. It would take hours for help to arrive. Buffy didn't have hours.

"I'm so sorry. I'm so sorry." Cassie wrapped her arms

around the horse's neck, both giving and taking comfort. Part of her dissolved into grief-stricken sobs while a separate, harder part searched for and embraced numbness. She knew what had to be done. No animal should suffer like this.

ccc

Dry-eyed and grim, Cassie submersed herself in the emotional void she'd sought and found. Staying low, she slung her knapsack over her shoulder and crawled to the canyon wall to peer over.

The three men had made substantial headway climbing up the narrow trail. Another fifteen minutes and they'd reach the top.

She fired another shot, close enough this time to give them a nasty scare.

Cursing rose from below, followed by the sound of scurrying and the clatter of loose rocks.

Good. That should slow them up a bit. She crawled away to a safe distance before sprinting to their truck.

She looked in the ignition for the key, checked behind the visor, in the console and cup holder. No such luck.

Not daring to waste any more time searching, she popped the hood release and pulled her knife from the scabbard at her hip. The sharp blade made quick work of every belt, wire, hose, tube, and cable she could reach.

At the rear of the vehicle, she slit the tarp covering the truck bed and sucked in a deep breath. Paint, gas cans, and boxes of who knew what lined the cargo area. She skimmed through the items. "My, my, would you look at that."

They had a hand-held stun gun stowed in with the other stuff. She grabbed it along with a few other necessities, stuffed everything into her knapsack, and raced back to check on the men.

More guarded now, they'd made some progress, but not much.

She backed away and called Sadeé to her side. They didn't have much time.

"Find Derek." She pointed back the way they'd come. "Go. Find Derek." It was the one command that might get the dog to leave her. No way help could get here in time, but at least Sadeé would be safe.

The dog lowered her head to her paws with a long, keening whine. She didn't budge.

"Go," Cassie said with more command. "Find Derek."

With obvious reluctance, the shepherd rose to her feet and ran a few steps before she stopped to look back.

"Go. Find Derek."

Sadeé turned and raced off.

With a hand over her eyes, Cassie watched until the dog disappeared. Solitude no longer felt like an old friend.

Grief was for survivors, and since she had yet to earn that status, Cassie set off in a lope south along the canyon's rim. She had one shot at getting out of this.

After thirty yards, she stopped and backtracked, careful to fit her feet exactly into the footprints she'd left in the loose sand. When she reached the cluster of boulders near where the men would emerge, she climbed up to hide and take stock: rifle reloaded, cable ties in her back pocket, rope coiled and laid out on a nearby rock, a pocket full of golf ball-sized rocks, and the stun gun. Only one more thing to do. She pulled the sat phone out and dialed.

Derek answered before the second ring. "Cassidy."

She choked off a sob.

"Baby, what's wrong? You're scaring me."

His concern unleashed a flood of emotion. "They killed B-B-Buffy."

"What? Who did? Are you okay? Cassidy, talk to me. Where are you?"

"D-dice Canyon," she choked out. "Three men. They were shooting at the mustangs. I-I-I fired over their heads to make them stop. They shot back and … hit Buffy." Another sob. "I had to … had to …" She couldn't say the words.

"Shhh, Baby. It's okay. You're okay. Where are the men now?"

She took a shuddering breath. "Climbing up from the canyon. They'll reach the top soon."

"Listen to me, Cassidy. You need to get out of there. Take their horses and go."

"They have a truck. I couldn't find the keys, so I cut all

the wires."

"Is Sadeé with you?"

"Y-yes." He'd freak if he knew she'd sent the dog away.

"Okay, here's what you do. Find a place for both of you to hide. Even with Sadeé to protect you, the odds are bad. Use the "quiet" command and she won't attack them unless you tell her or if they get too close. I will come for you, Cassidy, but you have to stay safe until I get there. Promise me you'll do this."

"I have to hang up now, Derek. Tell my family—"

"No. You will not say good-bye. Promise me you won't do anything foolish. Cassidy? Baby?"

She couldn't tell him what he wanted to hear so she disconnected the call and powered down the phone.

Chapter Sixteen

Derek grabbed a handhold in the rear compartment of the emergency Life Flight helicopter and pulled himself inside next to James.

The paramedic who rode with them closed the cabin door and raised his thumb to the pilot.

Frank Yarbrough, a veteran of the first Iraqi war and the lead pilot of Life Flight operations for Custer County, opened the throttle. Seconds later, they were airborne and rising fast in a northwest direction. The G-forces were subtle, but enough to press Derek back into the small jumper seat.

Iceman. He was Iceman.

Uncle Sam had invested half a million dollars to make him an elite warrior. SEALs were trained to action. Deadly. They learned early how to shut out anything unessential to the mission. And he'd spent the better part of the last eleven years, ever since his eighteenth birthday, perfecting those skills in one cesspool or another around the world. Never in all that time had his focus faltered. Not while serving in the Navy, later with the Bureau of International Intelligence, and not as a civilian law enforcement officer.

Until now.

A hard jab to the ribs and a steely glare snapped him back to attention. He could read James's thoughts—*Get your head in the game.*

Derek acknowledged the rebuke with a sharp nod. He needed to compartmentalize more than he ever had before. Had to shut down the rage, a fury unlike anything he'd experienced since witnessing the atrocities in Afghanistan. He'd be no good to Cassidy without focus, but the next twenty minutes of waiting might very well unhinge him.

Time was the enemy of the moment.

He leaned forward and yelled at the pilot. "Can't you make this thing go any faster?"

Frank ignored him. The aviation helmets the pilot, co-pilot, and crewmen wore had built-in noise attenuation features and communication channels. Talking with them would be impossible without a compatible headset.

Derek poked the pilot's shoulder to get his attention. When Frank turned his head, Derek raised one fist to shoulder level and pumped it fast up and down several times—the military signal for "hurry the heck up."

Frank blew him off by jabbing an index finger at the dials and making a slicing motion across his throat.

Message received.

Ice. Where was his Iceman alter ego?

Willing the toe-tapping to stop, he ran his hands over the

AR-15, examining the rifle from stock to sights. Next, he patted the Sig Sauer P-229 on his hip. And the second Sig tucked in a sheath holster at the small of his back. Extra ammo—stuffed in vest pockets. Ka-Bar knife—strapped to his thigh. Flash bangs, flares, binoculars, zip ties …

With his third weapons check completed, he moved to operational protocol. Define the objective. Analyze the data. Plan the op. Execute. Even when a mission went belly up, which happened more often than it should, he and his teammates had pre-considered, well-honed, and practiced responses. The mission was everything, but none of those prior ops held anywhere near the degree of importance as this one.

"Hey," James leaned over and shouted over the roar of the blades. "Cass is smart. She won't do anything stupid."

"They shot her horse," Derek yelled back. "What would you do?"

James looked away, mouthing a few off-color remarks before his lips sealed tight in a hard line.

A vibration in Derek's pocket alerted him to an incoming call. He looked at the display. Garrett. With one finger in his ear, he pressed the cell tight against the other ear. "Yell. We're in the air."

"Ten men en route. ETA in fifty-five."

Derek looked at his watch and gave a silent whistle before repeating the information to James. No way trucks could make that kind of time towing fully loaded horse trailers. Garrett

intended to come all the way by vehicle. They'd need a load of luck to not blow an axle or tear out a transmission moving that fast. "Roger. Our ETA in five."

Garrett's voice hitched. "Hey, that's my little sister."

"I know." Derek disconnected and slipped the phone back in his pocket, pushing thoughts of Cassidy to a hidden stronghold in his heart. Worrying wouldn't help her.

James gave him a shoulder bump and held out an open ammo box of … grenades?

Amazed, but not surprised by his friend's resourcefulness, Derek helped himself to four of the explosives and tucked them into pouches on his utility vest.

The co-pilot twisted sideways from the left seat and yelled, "LZ. Eleven o'clock. ETA in two." He made a circling motion with one finger to indicate they'd circle the area first for a quick aerial recon. Derek made a mental note to thank Frank for busting it to get here.

With the landing zone in sight, Derek felt some of the pressure ease for the first time since Cassidy called. Waiting was over. Time for action.

James pulled paper and pen from somewhere, wrote a note, and showed it to the co-pilot and then Derek: 3 FEET WE JUMP. HELO DUSTOFF.

The co-pilot nodded. They would come in hot, hover three feet off the ground long enough for Derek and James to bail, and then speed off to a safe distance. A standard maneuver used by military medevac Dustoff units when working hostile territory. The less time a bird spent on the ground, the better their chances of getting away unscathed.

The aircraft banked and came around for a broadside view of the target area.

"Would you look at that?" James pointed toward the dark blue truck.

Derek raised his binoculars.

A male sat on the ground, his back against a spindly scrub pine and a white bandage wrapped around one thigh. He appeared to be secured to the tree with his arms behind him.

A second, much larger man lay on his belly near the canyon's edge. Both hands were stretched behind his back and tied to his feet.

Derek winced. Bent like a bow and strung tight had to hurt. But then he allowed himself an ugly chuckle. His sweet little Cassidy had a mean streak.

Sadeé stood sentry halfway between the two men, head swiveling back and forth as she kept watch over them.

Derek widened his search, his heart knocking harder than ever. Where was she?

He spotted Buffy lying on her side, not moving. Cassidy had curled up next to her and had one arm draped over the horse's neck.

"Oh, Baby. I'm so sorry," he murmured.

He hated this for her but couldn't suppress a hodgepodge

of emotions—fear, relief, sorrow, anger, pride, and even laughter for the way she'd dealt with two of her enemies.

The helicopter began its descent. Feelings could wait. Right now, she needed him strong. And lethal.

"Don't see the third target," James yelled. "Split up." He tapped his chest and pointed north, and then pointed at Derek and motioned south. Toward Cassidy.

When the helicopter settled into a hover near the ground, he and James jumped out and surveyed the immediate area with weapons ready. A second later, the helicopter swooped away, and he and James headed in opposite directions.

Sadeé rose to her feet with a bark when she recognized Derek.

"Stay. Watch," Derek commanded the dog.

Ever obedient, the shepherd resumed her vigil.

Derek hurried forward in a crouch, his weapon sweeping back and forth in a continuous arc while his ears and eyes took in everything. At the canyon's edge, he peered over the side and scanned the cliff face before searching the nearby cluster of boulders. Not many other places to hide. He hurried along the rim.

His recon led him past Cassie. He ignored her for now and continued on another hundred yards until satisfied no threat remained in his search area. Ever watchful, he loped back to kneel at her side.

She combed her fingers through the dead horse's mane in

a continuous motion—the only part of the animal not covered in blood and gore.

"Baby, where's the third guy?" Please, please don't say you killed him.

Tear tracks left dirty trails down her face, evidence of the heartbreak. One eye had a faint, purple cast around it. She'd have a shiner by tomorrow.

Derek ached to hold her, but he didn't. Not yet. Not until they'd neutralized the danger, because once he had her in his arms, he'd be hard pressed to let her go again.

Spasms rippled through her, a succession of quick, tiny inhalations that shook her body. Between sniffles, she made a vague gesture toward where James still searched. "H-h-he ran off."

He studied the mottled bruising on her face. Unable to resist touching her a moment longer, he traced a knuckle along her jaw in a whisper-soft caress. Her skin reminded him of rose petals. "Are you hurt?"

A single millibar of pressure eased inside him when she shook her head no.

"Did you recognize any of them?"

A deep, shuddering breath preceded her response. "Not the one who ran off, but the guy with his face in the dirt is Billy. I clobbered him with the rifle and then gave him a hit with the stun gun."

Derek whirled to stare at the guy on his belly. It could be.

He looked big enough.

"Sadeé nailed Trent," she added. "Took a chunk out of his leg."

He whipped around to stare at her this time. "What did you say?"

"I applied a compression dressing to stop the bleeding, but he needs medical attention."

Derek looked at the smaller man tied to the tree. "Trent? Deputy Crutchfield?"

"Yes." Cassie wiped her face with a sleeve and winced. "I told you he's bad news."

Derek cupped her chin and angled her face up to his.

Turbulent eyes met his, a cauldron of emotions swirling in the depths, dark blue like a storm-ravaged ocean. No, not blue. That was too tame. Might as well describe lightning as white or call the sun yellow.

"Hey." James trotted over. "You find anything?"

Derek stood. "She says the third man took off." He nodded in the opposite direction.

"I found his tracks and followed a ways, but he got too much of a head start to catch on foot." James nodded at Cassie. "She okay?"

"Yeah. A little banged up."

"Them?" James nodded at the two bound prisoners.

"She didn't recognize the one who ran, but the big guy is Billy, the one we call Tubby. The other is …" He hesitated.

The gravity of the situation started to dawn on him. What a mess. "We have to do this by the book, man. Clean. No screw-ups."

James's stare sharpened. "Talk to me."

Cassie staggered upright, most of her weight supported by Derek. "She's says the one tied to the tree is the one who shot the horses. It's Trent Crutchfield."

CCC

Derek scooped Cassie into his arms and carried her to a rock near where the helicopter had landed. With the danger gone, the adrenaline crash hit him harder than he'd ever experienced before. He sat and held her on his lap, rocking while she cried, unable to let her go for even a moment.

Her tears weren't pretty. She cried for real, like her heart had shattered into a million bits. The great sobs should have torn someone her size in half.

When she burrowed into his chest, clinging to him as if for dear life, he thought his own heart would burst.

Sometime later, once her tears had subsided, she mumbled against his chest. "I'm okay now, Derek. Just don't let go. Not yet."

His arms tightened.

James left the paramedic to assess their captives' injuries and came over to check on Cassie. "Remind me to never get on your bad side, Cass," he said with a chuckle. "I always thought women were cute when they got angry, and love how you girls

get all fiery eyed and fierce." He gave Cassie a smart salute. "But you, honey, are gorgeous."

"I had help. I sent Sadeé away, to keep her safe, but she came back."

"Tell me about it." James pointed at the dog. "Sadeé took a chunk out of our boy, Trent. He's gonna limp for a long time."

Cassie's head jerked up, some of that fire sparking in her eyes. "Our boy? You're claiming him?"

"Nah, not me. Derek or Kyle either. I told Eli he was making a mistake. Talk to me, Cass. What happened here?"

Her mouth settled into a hard line. She'd set her grief aside, though involuntary shivers still made her body shudder. She filled them in on everything that happened up to when she called Derek. "I didn't have much choice but to deal with them. I tried to even the odds. I cut the wires under the hood of their truck."

Derek tensed and then forced himself to relax. She'd done the best she could given the circumstances. He ran one hand up and down her back, the soothing motion as much for him as for her.

"When I checked on them again, they'd gotten close. I'm not ashamed to admit that I thought seriously about shooting all three of them. It would be so easy to pick them off from the top. I couldn't do it, though, so I threw rocks instead."

"What?" Derek took her by both arms and set her apart.

"Do you have a death wish, woman? Or are you just plain crazy?"

"Shhh."

His jaw dropped. Many hardened soldiers had trembled before his anger and she ... shushed him?

"I made All State as a pitcher my last two years of high school. Twenty feet is nothing, especially from a height advantage. And I was careful. I pegged Billy with the first throw. Hard enough I think his fingers are broken."

"Three fingers to be exact." James's bark of laughter drew a glare from Derek, but it also brought forth a tenuous smile from Cassie. "I threatened him with a gag if he didn't shut up his complaining."

"Anyway, he dropped his rifle and the thing slid halfway to the bottom. That's when he charged, mad and stupid." She squirmed then.

Derek realized he'd drawn her into his arms again and was squeezing. He loosened his hold, but only a fraction.

"I was ready for him when he climbed over the edge. Bent the Remington's stock when I cracked his head. Almost hit a homerun."

James burst out laughing at that.

"I lost the satellite phone in the scuffle, though. It sailed over the edge of the canyon. Who knows where it ended up?"

Derek had to admit the visual she'd conjured was funny. He tamped his own chuckles down. The last thing Cassidy

needed was encouragement. She deserved to be kissed and spanked, maybe even locked up in a cell for the rest of her life. She was so darn ferocious and fearless. No, not fearless, not from the way her hands still trembled. Why did she always downplay her vulnerability?

"What about Trent and the other guy?" James prodded.

Trent didn't follow Billy right away, thank goodness. Once he got up his nerve, he fired two quick shots and charged over the top. I think he meant to shoot me, but he's always been stupid as a stick. I mean, even an idiot knows rifles aren't effective in close. While he was trying to draw a bead, I cracked him on the shoulder and made him drop the gun. He got in a lucky hit with his fist, though." She touched her injured cheek. "That's when Sadeé appeared like a rabbit out of a top hat. I'd sent her off before all this went down to find you, to keep her safe." Cassie paused to glare at the dog. "So much for obedience."

Sadeé wagged her tail, not the least bit repentant.

Cassie's disapproval became a reluctant smile. "She's pretty awesome. Made Trent squeal like a little girl and kept him pinned down while I tied up Billy. The other guy changed his route and popped over the rim about twenty yards to the north. He took off and never looked back."

Yet another validation of why he always listened to his gut feelings. Sadeé had more than proven her value. Even so, his fists still yearned for a go at Trent's face. Derek offered a silent prayer of thanks instead.

Have mercy on my soul, Lord, because this woman is gonna be the death of me.

Imperfect Bonds

Chapter Seventeen

Derek sucked a breath deep into his lungs, held it as long as he could, and then released it in a long, slow count. A semblance of calm returned.

A day had passed since Cassidy's call. Twenty-four hours mostly spent dealing with lawyers, judges, doctors, the state police, reporters, photographers, and more bureaucrats than any small town should have. This latest turn of events left a foul taste in his mouth and had him questioning everything he believed in, even the oath he'd sworn. Sometimes the law just plain got it wrong.

He turned down the long drive to the Triple C Ranch, not quite sure how he'd wound up on the wrong side of right.

Garrett came out to greet him. "Pretty sad hound dog expression you got there. Guess we won't like whatever it is you got to say. C'mon in. Everyone's in the family room."

Derek removed his hat and followed Garrett inside, ignoring the vibration of the cell phone in his pocket.

He spotted Cassie right away. She sat on the love seat next to her sister, with the rest of her family gathered around. Sadeé lay on the floor at her feet.

"Cate, Cody." He nodded at her parents.

"No need to make polite, Derek." Cody Cameron stepped forward. Gruff and no nonsense, his anger from the previous day hadn't abated one iota. "Tell us straight out what's gonna happen to that good for nothing—"

"Cody." Cate's touch gentled her husband's wrath. "Let him speak, dear."

No way to sugarcoat what he had to say. Derek met Cassidy's eyes across the room. "Trent's been released."

Nothing. No explosion, no surprise, not even a blink. The only indication she'd heard him was the way her body seemed to wilt.

His cell phone hummed in his pocket again as he looked around the room. He ignored it. Whoever was calling could wait.

Wade answered his unspoken question. "Lucy did some research. She says the wild horses don't qualify under the Bureau of Land Management's Wild and Free-Roaming whatever law because they're not on public land. Dad can't press charges because his preserve's not a sanctioned herd management area, and he doesn't own the horses. And we can't press charges for trespassing because the property's not posted. Is that about right?"

Derek nodded. "Trent claims to have received an anonymous tip about shooters at the canyon. Says he went to investigate, caught those two red-handed, and was taking them in when Cassidy opened fire."

"That's not true. Trent shot the horses. I saw him." Spots of heat tinted Cassie's cheeks.

He almost smiled then, preferring her outrage over the zombie-like defeat she'd shown. Hands up in surrender, he said, "Hey, I'm on your side. The judge made the call with a little encouragement from Melvin Crutchfield, the esteemed mayor of Challis. At least James had the good sense to call in the State Police. Once their forensics team finds the spent shell casings, the fingerprints and ballistics will tell the story. For now though, it's Trent's word against yours."

"But—" She stopped mid-sentence. A lot of her fire faded.

She'd called him for help. Not her dad, not her brothers, not James. Him. She'd clung to his hand throughout the questioning and again when Doc treated her. And now, he'd added to her burden. Would she feel he'd let her down?

"There's more." He looked down at his mangled hat, steeled himself for her look of betrayal, and addressed the room. "Trent intends to file charges against Cassidy for assault with a deadly weapon, battery, and interfering with a criminal investigation. James and Sheriff Castle were trying to talk him out of it when I left, but you might want to get in touch with your lawyer."

Mallory gripped Cassie's hand while the others drew in tight around her until Derek was sure a mouse couldn't sneak through. He'd seen what Garrett was capable of in a hostile

situation and heard stories of Wade's stint in Afghanistan. He'd also witnessed firsthand how the entire Cameron clan had closed ranks when danger threatened first TJ and then Lucy. In a faceoff with them, whether on the open range or in a courtroom—yeah, he wanted to be on their side.

The sound of crunching gravel had heads turning toward the window. A few seconds later, James barged in. "You." He pointed at Derek. "Need to answer your blasted phone."

To most, the sheriff of Hastings Bluff came across as detached and dispassionate, cold and uncaring, a façade he'd cultivated for years, but Derek had worked with James on too many missions to not recognize the fever in his former teammate's eyes. He stepped aside and gave James the floor, even as a sprig of hope unfurled.

James took a long look around the room and made eye contact with each person before he moved to the next one. When he reached Garrett, the two locked stares as something unspoken passed between them. And then the two of them glanced at Derek.

He recognized that look, knew these two men almost as well as he knew himself. James wanted the team back together. For a mission. One that called for special resources and unique skills. Excitement flared inside him. He'd missed this feeling.

"A call came in a little while ago. We have new information on the case."

Jonas, ever the wiseacre, spoke up. "Let me guess. Kevin

Fowler."

From the way James glared at him, Jonas must've hit the mark.

Tension built in the room faster than an air hose could fill a tire. Garrett draped an arm around his new bride's shoulders, while Wade pulled Lucy in close to his side. A safe bet they weren't Fowler's biggest fans.

James's death stare turned to one of speculation. "Yeah, the bureau man himself. Care to share how you know this?"

"I thought Fowler only chased international drug dealers and terrorists," Cody said. "Why's he interested in my mustangs?"

"Why indeed?" Jonas leaned against the wall, hands in his pockets, legs crossed at the ankle, and one eyebrow lifted.

Something about the blasé attitude didn't ring true, the humor forced. Dark secrets lurked behind the twinkle in Jonas's eyes, almost mocking. Something seemed off. All five of the blue-eyed, dark-haired siblings took after their father, with very little of Cate in their physical appearance. Except Jonas. He'd inherited her dimples, deep indentations brought out by a genuine smile.

Jonas's smile was there, but not the dimples.

With the spotlight off him for the moment, Derek took a really close look at the other man. He'd worked with Garrett long enough in the Bureau to know his story, and he'd heard plenty about Wade's time in Afghanistan. But what he knew of

Jonas would fit in a thimble. After graduating early from college, Jo enlisted in the Marines, served a year stateside, and then spent another two years bumming around Europe and North Africa as a civilian. Nothing about where he served, what he did, or the places he visited. No stories either. Not even his rank.

Derek tapped his hat against his leg, annoyed at not picking up on the inconsistencies before. The military branches might be vastly different in culture, but not in their commitment requirements. And a single year of service didn't cut it, not for enlisted ranks or officers. At minimum, the Marine Corps demanded a four-year stint.

"James? What's going on?" Cassidy asked.

The stare down between James and Jonas continued a few seconds longer before James answered.

"A few weeks back, I had Kyle post your pictures on some shared law enforcement websites. Last night, he added Tubby's fingerprints. We got a hit this morning. One of Fowler's information analysts made the connection. Tubby is implicated in one of Fowler's cases."

"How does this involve Trent?" Cassie asked.

"Drugs. He's been using since high school. Too much time on his hands and too much money to throw around. Using led to dealing, and now he's in so deep he can't get out. His position as a deputy for the Challis PD brought him to the attention of the Herrera Organization. According to Billy, they strong-armed Trent into working for them.

"What does this Herrera have to do with the mustangs?" Cassidy asked.

"According to Billy, he and the guy with the snake tat had one job, to create distractions on specific dates along Route 93. Trent provided eyes and ears inside the police department, and told them where to pull their stunts. He suggested Dice Canyon.

"Trent shot the horses to get back at me because I wouldn't go with him to the prom?" She wore a look of incredulity.

James nodded. "Seems that way."

"I don't like where this is leading." Garrett scrubbed a hand through his short hair until it stood on end. "Fowler resigned as director of the North, Central, and South American region with the Bureau when they tried to promote him into a leadership role. He went back to work for them in his former role, but in a contractor capacity. He now gets to pick and choose his cases—and prefers the nastier ones that cross multiple borders."

Cassie's eyes widened with each bit of information.

"When's he coming?" Jonas asked like it was a foregone conclusion.

"Tonight," James said. "He wants to meet with all of us at nine."

CCC

Cassie checked her phone again—five minutes to eight. Another hour before Agent Fowler arrived.

How had a simple act of goodwill gone so wrong? She'd stopped for Billy and his friend because guilt wouldn't let her pass a stranded motorist and not offer help. Maybe Derek was right. Trouble did seem to follow her around.

Was it bad luck? Had she ticked off some cosmic being and brought evil to her family's doorstep?

No. There was … is only one God. Most of her regrets and consequences came from poor choices she'd made over the years. But she could change, couldn't she? Her lips quoted a favorite scripture from Jeremiah, one that had sustained her since childhood. "For I know the plans I have for you …" she whispered aloud. "Plans to prosper you and not to harm you, plans to give you hope and a future."

She'd retreated to her bedroom after dinner, sick of everyone treating her like a Fabergé egg, but the walls closed in. Maybe fresh air would help.

Sadeé followed her downstairs, through the kitchen, and out the back door.

At the barn, Cassie turned aside. The horses would have settled for the night. They didn't need her restlessness. And she couldn't face the empty stall.

At the corral, she climbed up to sit on the top and hooked her feet behind the second rail. Quiet reigned, broken only by familiar night noises, some heard, others called up from memory. Funny, she'd forgotten how sound carried out here. The wind rustled through the leaves in a papery murmur. Tree frogs serenaded the night. The last few birds still awake sang a sleepy lullaby. A twig snapped somewhere in the woods where a nocturnal creature crept unseen. The contented snuffles from the horses in the pasture brought a smile. For a moment, she imagined she could hear the steady rushing of the river.

This land fed her soul, and she'd put herself on a starvation diet. No more.

Overhead a million tiny pinpricks of light danced on the inky canvas. The full moon hung low on the eastern horizon, just beginning its ascent. Shadowy ribbon-like clouds drifted across its face.

Awareness prickled the hair on her arms. She smiled as a feeling like warm honey spread through her. Only one person elicited such a response.

Derek stopped behind her, not quite touching but near enough she felt the heat of his body. His large, calloused hands settled onto the rail on either side of her.

Sadeé greeted him with a tail wag and a look of adoration, but not even Derek held the same allure as the woods at night. The dog slipped away to explore.

"Why does she like you?"

"Who?" Derek's voice was a warm breath against Cassie's ear.

The subtle hint of his cologne teased her nose and launched a swarm of butterflies inside her belly. "Sadeé. She accepts Mom and Dad, Lucy and TJ, but barely tolerates my brothers or James. But you … that day in your office … why did she obey you and not me?"

He leaned closer until the rough beard outlining his jaw rasped against her shirt sleeve. "I don't know. My manly charm maybe. Does it work on you?"

Derek had charisma in spades, but she'd been surrounded by gorgeous, Hercules-sized men her whole life. Except Derek made her feel small and feminine. And special. "You trained Sadeé, didn't you? For me. Why?"

The cat-like rubbing stopped. The warmth from his body disappeared, leaving her to mourn the loss, but only for a moment. He climbed up and sat next to her on the fence.

She leaned into him. "Tell me, Derek."

"When you went to Atlanta …" He stared off into the distance. "I didn't know anyone there. There was no one I could ask to check on you. I hated it."

The implication of his words took a moment to sink in. "You kept tabs on me."

"Yeah."

"While I was in school, too?"

"Yeah."

"Why?"

He still wouldn't look at her. "I've asked myself that same

question a hundred times. I mean, we kissed. Once. If you can even call it a kiss. More like a couple of twelve-year-old kids fumbling in the dark. It wasn't even hot, and then you shut me down. Fast."

Not hot? She'd almost combusted.

He went on, "But it was enough to light this crazy need inside me to make sure you stayed safe when I wasn't around."

The moon peeked out between the clouds and bathed his profile in silver and shadows. He exuded sensuality, but not in a soft way. A trait most women would find hard to resist. His gorgeous face might have been cut from granite, his jaw designed to take a punch. And yet, Derek Naughton—hardened Navy SEAL, self-professed player, and relationship phobic— had a tender side. He cared about her.

Wonder and warmth infused Cassie. "And?"

"And then I followed you to Atlanta and discovered I liked you. A lot. You're fun and smart. Easy to talk to. I don't think I've ever in my whole life just hung out with a woman before." He shifted on the fence rail and looked at her then. "That's when I realized you're one of those forever kinds of girl."

"Thank you."

"You're welcome." He looked away. "Sheesh, this is hard. Feels like high school all over again. I've never had a girl for a friend. I'd still like to ... to .... You know. But I don't want to ruin whatever this is we have."

Uncharted territory for both of them, but while she wanted to see where their feelings might lead, Derek shied away, skittish as one of Dad's wild horses.

Cassie sighed. Here they were, alone with a full moon on the rise. All he had to do was bend a little. Touch his lips to hers.

"Hey." His voice pulled her out of the fantasy. "What are you thinking?"

Not a chance she'd confess where her wayward thoughts had gone. "Nothing much."

"Tell me."

Her mind scrambled for an answer. "Buffy. The Vampire Slayer."

"What?" He chuckled, but his amusement held an undertone of confusion. "That's the last thing I expected to hear. Well, maybe not the last thing. If you'd said the Texas Rangers had a chance of getting into the World Series this year I might have keeled over."

She shrugged. It was the last thing she'd expected to come out of her mouth, too.

"Vampires? Seriously?"

"No, not vampires. In the house it felt like the walls were closing in. I came out for some fresh air, only when I got to the barn I couldn't go inside. The horses were settled in for the night. I used to give Buffy an apple every evening. Sometimes, after I'd groomed her, she would lie down in her stall and roll in the fresh hay."

"I get it. Word association. Buffy the Vampire Slayer. A distraction."

"I guess." So lame, but he seemed to buy it. Could she talk to him about what was really bothering her? Or would it scare him off?

"I'm so sorry about Buffy, Baby."

Those ever-present tears pricked at her eyes again. And then she blurted out, "Derek, do you think people can change? I mean, really change?"

He took a long time to respond. "Seems like a simple enough question, but the answer is complex."

"I don't understand."

"Well, there are certain things no one can change. DNA is one example. The past is another. They shape you into who you are today. Other things can be altered in a superficial way with contact lens, hair dye, and cosmetics."

"That's not—"

"I know. What you're most concerned about are the intangibles—personality, attitude, behavior, beliefs, and the bonds we form—they're the foundation of who we are. I think changes in these areas occur naturally. The real question is do you think people can change the way they look at and respond to things in the present. And yes, I believe it's possible. Not easy, but doable."

"Explain."

"Self-awareness is the first step. Conviction. You have to recognize and accept a need to change. Next you define a plan and set it in play. Commitment is the key. How bad do you want to change?"

"Sounds like a military exercise."

He chuckled. "It is. Define the objective. Establish a plan. Accomplish the goal. A bit simplified, but, hey, it's worked for me. So what is it you want to change about yourself? Because from where I sit, this Cassidy is just about perfect."

A bitter laugh left her teetering on the fence. "Ha. Perfect is the last adjective I would use to describe me. What you said before, about intangibles, bonds in particular, isn't that a two-way street?"

Derek slung an arm around her waist to steady her, but that only sent those soaring butterflies into a nose dive. "Bonds are strong ties you feel toward another individual. You might influence or encourage a reciprocal feeling, but it's not something you can command."

"You mean … like love? How one person can have strong feelings for someone, but not be loved in return?"

Was she talking about them?

"Don't know much about love. I was thinking more about ties that form between soldiers who face life and death situations. Unbreakable bonds. They might fade with time and distance, but they can't be severed."

Her head dipped.

"Hey, every decision we make is imperfect, Baby. They're riddled with consequences and what-ifs. You can't know if a different decision would be better or worse. All we can do is make the best choice we can, given what we know at that moment, and then own that decision. Bonds you make are yours. If they're not returned, that's on the other person. Don't second-guess yourself. That only steals from the future and doesn't change a thing."

Cassie's lips parted in wonder. Dark and light, hard and soft, insensitive and considerate, the man was a walking, talking dichotomy. It would take years to tap all the layers Derek hid, and she wanted those years.

Headlights pierced the night and saved her from answering.

"We'd better get back to the house." Derek swung his legs over the fence, dropped to the ground, and reached for her. His hands almost spanned her waist as he swung her down. "That's probably Fowler."

Chapter Eighteen

Cassie stepped inside the kitchen, blinded for a moment by the transition from dark sky to incandescent lights, and almost mowed down her diminutive sister-in-law.

"Hey, I was about to sound a missing person alert." TJ dodged to one side, her eyes shifting from Cassie to Derek and back again. A glimmer of a smile touched her lips.

TJ's knowing look combined with the heat of Derek's hand on Cassie's back spread warmth to her face. "I, uh, needed some fresh air."

"Fresh air, right." TJ hooked her arm through Cassie's. "Come on upstairs. I think Uncle Sam's bogeyman has finally arrived. Let's get your hair brushed before we meet with Agent Fowler."

Derek frowned. "There's nothing wrong with her hair."

That warm honey feeling spread through Cassie again.

TJ leaned in and said in a loud whisper, "Girl stuff. You don't want to know."

"Okay, that's my cue to leave." Derek skirted around them and hurried toward the family room. "See you in a few."

Sadeé padded after Derek.

TJ chuckled. "Works every time. I love the panicked look men get when they think you're going to talk about ..." She made air quotation marks with her fingers. "Feminine stuff."

Cassie chuckled and followed her up the stairs. "So, are you going to tell me what this is all about?"

"Shh. Not here. We'll talk upstairs."

Mallory waited in the doorway of her bedroom. "About time." She motioned them inside with a quick look both ways to see if anyone followed and shut the door.

Lucy sat on the bed inside the room.

TJ flopped onto the bed next to her. "Mal's about to burst, but refuses to say a word until she has us all together."

"I didn't want to repeat myself." Mallory dropped to the floor in a cross-legged position. Lucy's yoga influence, no doubt. "I heard back from that reporter."

The words didn't make sense at first. Cassie searched her memory for ... ah, the woman who claimed to be from a Seattle television station. Mallory, TJ, and Lucy had heard from one of Coot's neighbors how she'd nosed around asking questions about the mystery van, even describing it right down to the Colorado temporary plates. "You found her?"

"Yes. She's an investigative reporter. I called her on Wednesday at the Seattle station where she's supposed to work, but no one knew her. Their personnel office gave me an extension number, but I had to leave a voice mail."

Cassie crossed her arms and leaned against the door. She

had a feeling she might need the support. "Go on."

"When I didn't hear back by Thursday night, I called again with a vague explanation. I left another message yesterday, and again this morning." Mallory shrugged. "She finally called back tonight during dinner and left a voice mail."

They all understood why Mal had missed the call. Cell phones at Mom's table? Uh, no.

"What did she say?" Cassie asked.

"Listen for yourself." Mallory tapped the speaker button and played the recording.

"Miss Cameron." A terse, feminine voice said, her voice tinged by a faint accent. "Listen carefully because I don't have a lot of time. Stop asking questions about the van and about me. The men behind this operation—if they learn of your snooping—believe me when I say death would be a kindness for both of us."

The hang-up click had a finality about it that made Cassie shiver. "Wow."

Lucy's face had paled. "What is this reporter's name?"

"Ysolde Hermón."

Lucy stood and began to pace. "We have to tell James and Derek."

Mallory glanced at TJ and then Cassie. "Why? What do you know, Lucy?"

Lucy shifted her weight from one foot to the other. "Ysolde Hermón is not a reporter. She's an undercover agent

with the Bureau."

Dread filled Lucy's eyes. And something else—fear.

"I met Ysolde Hermón briefly when she passed through Atlanta," Lucy explained. "She's been working a South American drug and human slavery ring for years. Word was this cartel intended to expand into the western United States and Canada, and eventually form an alliance with the Middle Eastern and African traffickers."

Not much scared Lucy. Cassie first met her during her time in Atlanta when the former BII agent got hurt in a cyber drug bust gone wrong.

"Ysolde's parents emigrated here from Honduras—right after the younger daughter was kidnapped by this cartel." Lucy started to pace. "She was fourteen. It's been ten years. Ysolde's been looking for her ever since."

"I figured drugs, alcohol, maybe even weapons dealing." Cassie slid down the door until she sat on the floor. "What do you mean by human trafficking?"

"I don't know, Cassie, anything, everything. It's all so depraved. Adoptions, slave labor, organ harvesting, kidnapping, prostitution, sex exploitation, you name it. They target babies, children, teenagers, young women, and even young men. Anything goes in that industry—and it is an industry, a juggernaut."

CCC

Cassie followed the others downstairs and watched in bemusement as each girl succumbed to an invisible gravitational pull—TJ to Garrett, Lucy to Wade, and Mallory to James. Before she realized it, she'd worked her way to Derek's side.

Sadeé nudged her leg, drawing a quick scratch behind the black ears.

Their visitor shook hands and spoke with her parents. Whatever he said to Mom brought a blush to her cheeks and a scowl to Dad's face.

Beside them, Jonas chuckled.

Agent Kevin Fowler. She'd heard tales from TJ and Lucy about how Fowler was dedicated to his work, maybe even ruthless. He always got the job done, no matter the cost. Perhaps in another setting he might seem average or even nondescript, but not here standing among giants like her brothers, Dad, James, and Derek. The very oddity of his smaller size brought attention.

She placed him at maybe five-eight, give or take an inch, with sandy hair cropped close in an almost but not quite military cut. A tint of white at his temples suggested he could claim more years than Garrett but less than Dad.

He turned then and faced the rest of the group. Gray, almost colorless eyes, assessed each person there. "Ah, the Camerons en masse, such an imposing lot. I believe I've met all of you except for Mallory's lovely lookalike hiding behind the deputy. Derek, please introduce me."

Like the Red Sea, the others parted for him when he approached and took Cassie's hand.

Derek cleared his throat, though it sounded more like a growl. "Cassidy Cameron. Agent Kevin Fowler."

"A pleasure, my dear." He held her hand for a moment longer than the handshake required.

A soft rumble issued from Sadeé's throat. Not a threatening sound, but neither was it welcoming.

Had she really considered the agent unremarkable? Cassie shivered under the hypnotic intensity of his gaze. Authority emanated from the man, along with something else, something dangerous. "Hello."

"Well, now that we all know each other, let's have a seat in the family room." Mom, ever the hostess, pointed the way. "Would you care for something to drink, Mr. Fowler?"

Cassie waited until Fowler turned away before she wiped her palms on her pants.

"Thank you, but no. It's enough you agreed to see me this late."

Garrett and Wade brought extra chairs in from the dining room so everyone could sit. Everyone except Derek who planted himself directly behind Cassie.

Fowler positioned his chair so he faced the group. "As I said, it's late, so let me get to the point. I asked to speak with all of you together because I've learned from experience. To you, family supersedes confidential, top secret, or need to know. This way, I can ensure a uniform message is delivered … including the consequences should what I reveal be shared outside this group."

That garnered a few raised eyebrows.

Fowler turned to James. "Sheriff Evers, as a duly elected law enforcement officer and a former operative of the Bureau of International Intelligence, you are hereby sworn to confidentiality regarding everything you are told tonight. By extension, your oath will encompass all those present."

James looked around the room and received nods—some hesitant—from everyone. "So be it."

"Very well." Fowler turned his attention to the group again. "I'm here in response to a picture and an inquiry Sheriff Evers posted on the Regional Information Sharing Systems, a national database used by law enforcement agencies, including my organization."

He pulled a photo from his inside jacket pocket and held it up. "One of my analysts saw the post and flagged it. From the brief phone conversation I had with the sheriff earlier today, I understand Cassidy took this picture. The big man is William Kershisnik, a.k.a. Billy, Big K, or B.K. He's a small time thug for hire. The other man is Arturo Zavala. Both Kershisnik and Zavala are implicated in one of my cases. Cassidy, would you please tell me about your encounter with Billy?"

She explained about the encounter with the two men on

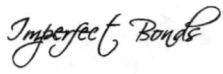

the highway, the subsequent car chase, of seeing Billy and his tattooed friend later that same day in Hastings Bluff, and the incident out at Dice Canyon. She did not mention Coot's story of the mystery van roaming the mountain roads, her suspicions the two issues might be related, or the results of Mallory's call to the reporter. She couldn't bear another eye roll.

Derek and James added details regarding the rash of vandalism in the area and their suspicions about Billy and his pal.

"Your turn, Fowler," Garrett said. "Tell us about the case Billy and Zavala are implicated in and how does it involve us?"

The agent's right leg bounced up and down for several beats. "Zavala does odd jobs for a Denver company called Midwest Distributors."

"That's a shell," James interrupted. "I ran the truck's license. It's registered to Fleet Corp, which is held by Midwest, which is owned by Alexander Services, and then Magna Carta Enterprises. I never did find the parent company."

"You are correct. Midwest is one of many subsidiaries under numerous blanket corporations the Diego Herrera Organization utilizes."

Cassie turned wide eyes on Mallory, and then Lucy and TJ.

A flurry of questions and comments erupted, coming so fast Cassie couldn't tell who said what.

"What is this Herrera's primary business?"

"Why would a Colombian company hire a couple of thugs to prank a remote county in Idaho?"

"Only thing comes out of Columbia are drugs, oil, and bananas. I doubt we're talking oil or bananas."

"Why does the bureau have an interest in Herrera?"

Fowler let them go on for another few seconds before he held up his hand. "Sheriff, you and your deputies likely know about the recent joint effort of state and federal agencies in the trafficking crackdown along the Pacific coast."

Derek's hand touched Cassie's shoulder.

"This is about human trafficking?" Garrett asked. "Does this Herrera group have anything to do with Rafael Castillo?"

"In part," Fowler answered. "Diego Herrera funded Castillo. Now that Castillo is gone, they've absorbed his operations in Honduras and are now focused on owning the Americas' transportation corridors. They run any and everything from Bogotá up through Central America, Mexico, the United States, and into Canada with distribution points all along the way. The crackdown in California, Oregon, and Washington succeeded only in shifting the western corridor further inland and splitting it up among multiple temporary routes. Once the heat dies down, they'll likely go back to the coast since it offers the shortest, fastest route north. For now, Route 93 is one of the new routes, from Las Vegas to Calgary."

"So, the pranks are what, a distraction?" Wade asked.

Fowler nodded. "Local police don't pay much attention to

the traffic on their roads. Derek's little speed trap with its random stops for license checks has caused them a bit of aggravation, which is why they dispatched Arturo here."

"To make sure the police presence in the area stays busy elsewhere when they make their monthly runs." Derek pressed a hand to his forehead.

"Yes."

The sour taste of fear rose in Cassie's throat. She took no delight in having her suspicions proven.

"Las Vegas to Calgary, that's more than a thousand miles. Are you saying they do this all along the route?" James asked.

"No. Only here and one other place near the Canadian border. For the most part, local law enforcement chooses to look the other way at traffic violations. You made them nervous enough to take action."

"Uh ..." Cassie raised her hand like a fourth grader, realized what she'd done, and snatched her arm down. She already knew the answer to her question, but had to ask it anyway. "What type of vehicles does this Herrera group use?"

"Our intel suggests they use panel vans, one or two per run. All arranged through third and fourth party sources, of course. The transporters can't finger the higher ups if they don't know who they are. Smaller cargoes also invite less scrutiny and incur less financial risk if caught."

Fowler's eyes narrowed on her. "For an insignificant dot on the map, Hastings Bluff seems to draw a lot of illegal attention. I attributed TJ's difficulties to chance. Even with Lucy, I could make a case for coincidence. But three times? Do you have something more to add Cassidy?"

Her lungs labored, her breath came in short gasps that raced against her heartbeat. Hastings Bluff wasn't the nexus Fowler spoke of. She was the trouble magnet.

All eyes turned to Cassie.

"Tell them," Lucy urged.

TJ and Mallory nodded their agreement.

"Tell us what?" Derek asked.

Sadeé sat up and laid her head in Cassie's lap.

A deep breath helped, but didn't eliminate the quaver in her voice. "I know about the van. It leaves Route 93 north of Mackay and runs through the mountains. Coot told me about it. He and his neighbors reported it to the Mackay police, but they never followed up."

"The van never stops," Mallory added. "Only one time it did. And the owner of the gas station claims he heard crying sounds from inside."

"What?" Garrett exploded out of his chair.

TJ nodded. "When the driver banged his fist on the side of the van, the crying stopped."

"More importantly," Lucy said. "The van makes this run once a month about the same time the vandalisms have occurred."

"A reporter has been asking questions, too," Mallory

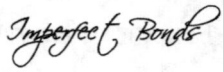

added. "She left a message tonight telling us to butt out."

James stood. He looked annoyed. "Why didn't you tell us any of this?"

"Why?" Mallory laughed at him. "You didn't believe Cassie when she tried to tell you about those guys. Why on earth would she tell you about the van and open herself to more of your and Derek's snarky attitude?"

James's face turned dark red.

Derek hung his head.

Fowler's laser stare came to rest on Cassidy. "I wonder what else you might know," he murmured. "Perhaps we should have a little chat. For now, tell me—what reporter and who the heck is Coot?"

Chapter Nineteen

"Get a move on, slow poke. Mom's waiting at the front door." Cassie banged on her sister's bedroom door again. "She's tapping her toe and you know what that means."

Some things never changed. Mom hated being late to anything, but especially for church. Sundays for the Cameron family meant preaching and singing, followed by dinner, often with an invitation extended to friends they met there. At least that's how it used to be, until Garrett left home followed by Wade and Jonas. And then her.

Except her brothers had come home.

Echoes of the past stirred. An unexpected longing filled her. She hadn't been back to the little white church on the outskirts of town since her high school commencement ceremony. Not once in seven years. Would the parishioners remember her?

Cassie studied her reflection in the hall mirror and smoothed back a lock of hair. Of course they would. She'd known most of the church members her whole life. Besides, having her mirror image beside her would provide a hint.

She rubbed at an imaginary mascara smudge and then

tugged at the scooped neckline of her dress. The real question was would they welcome her home?

The bedroom door opened. Mallory stuck her head out, spotted Cassie at the mirror, and took off down the stairs, heels clattering on the oak floor. "Who's the slow poke now?" She yelled over her shoulder.

Cassie darted after her with a grin. Just like old times.

"I swear, a herd of turtles moves faster than you girls," Mom scolded as she hurried down the front steps after them. "Wade, Lucy, and Jonas left ten minutes ago, and your father is out front with the engine running. You know how impatient he is." The laugh lines had deepened around her eyes belying her displeasure. She had her family together again. All of them.

An unexpected surprise awaited them at the church. Derek stood outside the front door, decked out in his khaki uniform. He waved with a hurry-up gesture. "We're about two minutes away from doing the walk of shame down the aisle." He took her hand, tucked it inside his elbow, and hustled her inside. "You trying to make an entrance?"

"Oh, they'll stare anyway. And whisper. Just wait."

He opened the door and held it for her parents and Mallory and then all but dragged Cassie down the aisle behind them to the pew near the front where Garrett, TJ, Wade, Lucy, and Jonas waited.

Sure enough, heads turned, fingers pointed, and whispers filled the air.

Cassie scooted in next to Mallory, leaving Derek to squeeze in beside her at the end of the row. "Is James coming?" she asked for her sister's benefit.

"No. We drew straws. He lost. Somebody has to man the office."

When the music started, one lady left the choir loft and walked to the front of the dais. The music director gave her a handheld microphone.

"Who's that?" Cassie leaned in and asked her sister.

"You remember Wilbur Townsend?" Mallory whispered. "Starlight Catering? He used to provide the food for the Hasting Bluff annual picnic and all the big events at the Challis Country Club."

Cassie nodded.

"That's Shea, his niece. She's the one I told you that I meet with at the dinner every week. Mr. Townsend retired last year, and moved to Florida leaving Shea the business."

"Should I know her? She looks familiar."

"You might remember her from Mom's party last summer. She catered the event. Dee Dee has her cooking part-time at the diner, too, and she does some substitute teaching at the elementary school in Challis."

"Shh." Mom admonished them with a frown.

Mallory's mouth stretched wide in an oops grimace. "Later," she mouthed.

The young woman sang the lead in the remix of Amazing

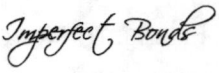

Grace/My Chains Are Gone. Blonde, beautiful, and blessed with a voice angels would envy—why did some women get looks and talent?

Cassie wanted to be jealous, especially given the rapt attention Derek paid to the singer, but the powerful, emotional rendition captivated her, too.

Shea held the closing notes until the music faded away, but where applause and a hearty amen or two would typically follow, a hush held the congregation in thrall. After several seconds of awed silence, the people rose in a standing ovation as Shea returned to her seat in the choir loft.

After the sermon and the closing benediction, Cassie and Derek accompanied the rest of her family outside for the obligatory meet and greet in the churchyard.

Jonas provoked a few raised eyebrows when he singled out Shea Townsend. Odd. He always made a point of steering clear of anything that might be construed as a relationship. And yet, he had to know their laughter and smiles would feed the gossips for a week or more.

Derek pulled Cassie aside. "I can't stay."

"Why? I thought you'd come back to the ranch for lunch."

"I'd love to, but I have to get back. Fowler called a meeting this afternoon. Sheriff Castle's coming over for it."

The knot in her belly tightened. She'd been on edge ever since Trent tried to have her arrested for assault. "About Trent?"

"I don't think you have to worry about Crutchfield. He's got his own problems since he hit Fowler's radar." Derek nodded toward the parking lot. "C'mon, your daddy's getting impatient."

Sure enough, Dad paced back and forth, every now and then slapping his Sunday-best black Stetson against his leg. The doors stood open to the midnight blue King Ranch F-150, still as shiny as the day he drove it off the lot in Idaho Falls last year.

Derek's palm landed on the small of her back as he steered her toward the truck, but then he shoved both hands in his pockets and concentrated on his boots. "I, uh, want to ask you something, but I don't want you to take it the wrong way. It's just …"

She stopped and faced him. "You want me to forego Coot's therapy sessions."

"Yeah." He looked back toward the church, at her dad's truck behind her, off in the distance. "It bothers me—a lot— you on the road or out on the range where I can't get to you. And it's not like forever, just until we finish this case."

Not forever. No commitment. The eternal spark of hope that lived in her heart ebbed and flowed like the tide. "Well then, you're in luck. Dad's already laid down the law. He doesn't want me going out to the canyon without him anymore. But, Derek, I can't stop seeing Coot. We've just gotten started with his program."

Derek leveled those icy green eyes on her, except icy didn't seem to fit the moment. Molten seemed more apt.

She shivered anyway.

"I didn't think so." He took her hand. "I'll bring you a new satellite phone. Will you at least promise to keep it with you? And take Sadeé wherever you go, and no more sleuthing."

She crossed her heart. "I promise. No more snooping. No more questions. The sat phone and Sadeé go where I go. My gun, too. And since someone saw fit to pull my license, I'll always have backup."

"You're going to Coot's tomorrow then?"

"Yes. We've agreed on Mondays and Wednesdays for six more weeks. Would it put your mind at ease if I call when we set out and when we arrive?"

The intensity of his stare didn't change, but he nodded. "Yeah, it would."

"Okay then."

The engine revved behind her. Dad had his own way of getting your attention.

Cassie smiled and turned to go. When Derek didn't release her hand, she laughed and tugged.

His grip loosened slowly until she pulled free and danced away. With a finger wave and a saucy grin, she scrambled into the back seat of her dad's truck.

CCC

"What do you mean you don't know where he is?" Derek clenched his fists and then unclenched them. He had an insatiable urge to hit something.

"I spoke to his father, the mayor, on the way over," Sheriff Eli Castle said. "Trent didn't come home last night, and no one's seen him since we met here yesterday morning. The mayor and his wife are worried."

"I'd be worried, too, with Fowler in the mix," James offered. "My bet is Trent's hiding under a rock somewhere."

What a mess. Without Trent's report and signature, they couldn't hold onto Tubby much longer. And Cassidy's testimony wouldn't help. According to her, Trent did the shooting. Tubs here did nothing more than brandish a weapon, call her a nasty name, and threaten to "get her."

The front door squeaked open. Fowler entered, made a quick survey of the room and joined them.

Derek breathed a sigh of relief that Lorraine had Saturdays and Sundays off. Thirty-plus years of working for the various sheriffs of Hastings Bluff had given the dispatcher/office manager/administrative assistant a wealth of institutional knowledge but, as with all good things, Lorraine came with a downside. Confidentiality was a suggestion to her.

"Good afternoon, gentlemen."

The agent's raspy voice never failed to raise Derek's hackles.

Fowler pulled up a chair. "I hear you've misplaced a deputy."

Derek locked on to Fowler's words like an onboard radar system acquiring a target. No way the man had overheard their conversation, not unless he had cochlear implants or superhero hearing. Now that Derek thought about it, he wouldn't discount either possibility. Fowler and his ilk had a way of pulling impossible rabbits out of stranger places than hats.

"Where is he?" Derek asked.

"Let's just say Deputy Trent Crutchfield has a new home for the foreseeable future. He won't bother you or the Cameron sisters anymore." Fowler pulled a sheaf of papers from his inside jacket pocket and handed it to James. "Sheriff Evers, this is a federal court order. Your prisoner, William Kershisnik, has been remanded to the BII. My agents should arrive shortly to remove him."

They all turned to look at Billy who snored in one of the cells at the far end of the room.

Derek knew better than to demand specifics. James did, too. Eli Castle on the other hand had yet to experience the immovable wall otherwise known as Agent Kevin Fowler.

The portly sheriff stood and confronted the seated agent. "What have you done with my deputy? Is he under arrest? On what charge and by whose authority? I demand—"

"Sit down, Sheriff," the agent cut him off, his voice hard.

Derek winced. Fowler didn't do demands.

"Both you and the mayor of your town are in enough trouble with Homeland Security because of your connection to Trent Crutchfield," Fowler continued. "You don't want to wind up on my bad side as well."

Like a fish pulled from the water and gasping for breath, Sheriff Castle's mouth opened and closed while he grappled with Fowler's words. The disgruntled sheriff finally conceded and lowered his bulk into the chair.

Derek's admiration for the man went up a notch. You don't get reelected seven times in a row and not learn to pick your battles.

"Thank you," Fowler said. "William Kershisnik and Trent Crutchfield are implicated in an investigation which involves national security. This puts both men under the jurisdiction of the Department of Homeland Security and, by extension, the Bureau of International Intelligence. A third person of interest, Arturo Zavala—the man with the serpent tattoo—remains at large and is considered armed and dangerous. I am requesting assistance from the law enforcement agencies of Custer and surrounding counties in locating this man. Any information should be reported to this number." Fowler held out a business card.

Sheriff Castle took the proffered card and tucked it in his breast pocket.

Fowler glanced at his wristwatch. "By now the mayor and his wife have been apprised of their son's incarceration. I have

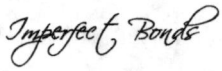

no doubt they're screaming for a lawyer, to the media, and to anyone who might listen. I'm asking you to exercise your influence with them and get them to desist. The last thing we need is a nosy reporter showing up. Neither do you want a spotlight on the criminal you hired to protect the citizens of your town. In return for your help, I'll ensure both you and the mayor come out of this clean as a fresh coat of paint."

Sheriff Castle turned to James with eyebrows lifted.

James nodded. "He can do it."

"Do we have a deal?" Fowler asked.

"I'll do my part." Sheriff Castle leveled a finger at the agent. "You do yours."

"C'mon, Eli, I'll walk out with you." James herded the Challis sheriff toward the door.

A multitude of questions swirled through Derek's head, but he wouldn't raise them before James returned. Instead, he grabbed some water from the fridge in the break room, handed a bottle to Fowler, and set a second one aside for James. Unscrewing the cap, Derek guzzled half of his bottle.

"Eli means well," James returned and picked up his water.

Fowler nodded. "Civilians always do. Is everything set?"

"Yeah," Derek answered. "I sent Garrett a text message and told him to be here in fifteen minutes with his brothers. Kyle's due any minute."

He tipped up his bottle and drained it. Something about this case bothered him. He just didn't know what.

CCC

Half an hour later, the group assembled around a desk in the front of the office. Derek tapped Kyle Abbott's shoulder with the rolled up Custer County map. "Clear that stuff off for me, will ya?"

His former teammate in the BII and current fellow deputy for Hastings Bluff cleared the papers and other paraphernalia from the littered desk and helped spread out the map. A coffee cup, stapler, tape dispenser, and a book weighted the corners to hold it open.

Chairs squeaked and rollers scraped across the floor as Fowler, James, Garrett, Wade, and Jonas scooted closer. Altogether their numbers made seven. Perfect for a team, especially since five of them had once worked together.

"What are these?" Fowler waved at the various colored markings on the map.

"This is Custer County. The red circles represent the vandalism sites over the past six months. Dates are noted to the side." Derek ran his finger from point to point. "These blue slash marks north of Mackay represent the point where we believe the transport van leaves Route 93 to travel through the mountain roads. The second pair of blue slashes here on State Road 75 near Hastings Bluff is where it comes out of the mountains at Idaho 75 and rejoins Route 93 north of town."

Kyle shoulder-bumped Derek. "I think word of your speed

trap got around."

Derek returned the bump, only with more force. "It's not a speed trap, jerk. Look how many expired licenses, missing registrations, and lack of insurance we've identified. Get serious."

"Kyle is correct. I believe that is precisely what happened. Word of your, uh, license checks has indeed spread. " Fowler said.

The others focused hard stares on the agent.

"Dominos, gentlemen, with a little bit of kismet thrown in for good measure. The location of Derek's, er, checkpoint just south of Hastings Bluff is a bottleneck for all Route 93 traffic north and southbound. You perform these stops often enough and at random enough times to make it a concern to anyone who wishes to avoid scrutiny from the authorities. Someone who can't afford to be stopped, questioned, or searched."

No one looked away. No one blinked.

"We believe the Herrera organization is behind these activities," Fowler continued. "Opinion is they learned of Derek's checkpoint and hired Zavala and Kershisnik to provide distractions to draw the local law enforcement's attention while they follow an alternate route around the roadblock. Their plan worked fine until a chance encounter with Cassidy led to her taking their pictures. When James posted the photos on several national data bases, one of my analysts found them."

"Route 93?" Garrett asked. "Most people think the known

world ends at the state line."

Fowler leaned back in his chair, threaded his fingers together, and rested his hands on his stomach.

Derek tensed. He knew Fowler's mannerisms. He'd settled in for story time. Their little get together had turned from a brainstorming session into a mission briefing in a heartbeat. He looked around the room. From the expressions of the other men, they had drawn the same conclusion. Things were about to get real.

"The entity we're dealing with started in Colombia, an assortment of small drug cartels who bloodied themselves as each one tried to establish dominance. In a brilliant and totally unexpected move, they joined forces, banded together under a single, fictitious name—Diego Herrera—and established a board of directors, not unlike American corporate structures. The Herrera organization discovered power and safety in numbers, as well as anonymity and protection for the leaders. This allowed them to prosper. Now they intend to monopolize the transport of illicit goods through the western United States and Canada."

"What you're not saying is that Herrera has political connections now," Garrett, the unofficial leader of their unofficial team said.

Fowler nodded. "Their precipitate growth took us by surprise. We didn't react fast enough. Now, there are political nuances to consider."

"You mean they bought their way into our government," Garrett continued. "So, instead of taking them down from the top, you have to slice off a few tentacles to establish, or in this case, re-establish a semblance of control. Is that the reason behind the Pacific Coast crackdown? To slow their expansion? A Mexican standoff?"

"Yes."

"And you're making Route 93 an example," Garrett persisted.

Fowler took a moment to answer. "That is one way to look at it."

An answer, and yet not an answer. Derek pushed away from the desk and leaned back with hands clasped behind his head. Unease continued to build in his gut. The agent had tics and tells just like everyone else, and Derek knew them. Knew the evasive words and relaxed pose hid a deeper truth. When had Fowler become a political creature?

"So, what are they hiding and what do you want from us?" Garrett, as usual, got to the heart of the matter.

Chapter Twenty

Like the rest of the men in James's office, Derek's years of military training, discipline, and experience had conditioned him to not question orders or a superior officer, and especially not one who had never hesitated to dirty his hands alongside them. Fowler had once saved Derek's life, and he'd returned the favor—more than once. The question was could he still trust the man?

Yes, up to a point.

"I need your help setting a trap," Fowler answered Garrett's question. "According to the trend you've identified …" He pointed at the linear calendar on the wall Derek had used to layout the vandalism incidents. "Their next run should be eight to ten days from now."

Fowler the man, the soldier, the agent would do everything in his power to see the job done right and would look after his men in the process, no matter the cost. It was the innocent bystanders Derek worried about now, the ones Fowler viewed as expendable, a justifiable loss, collateral damage.

War on home turf changed priorities. Those innocents Fowler discounted were people Derek cared about. "Doesn't add up," he said.

All eyes focused toward him.

"Excuse me?" Fowler's raspy voice deepened, full of disapproval.

"Allow me to think out loud for a minute, okay?" Derek leaned forward and rested his forearms on the desk.

Fowler nodded.

"The vandalism incidents are meant to distract local law enforcement from potentially stopping one of their transport vans, correct?"

Another nod.

"Then the vandalism incidents and the cargo runs have to be synchronized." Derek went to the calendar tacked to the wall and pointed at a date. "Which means, as you pointed out, the next stunt and whatever event they want to hide should occur here." He pointed to the dates on the calendar. "Next week. Monday, maybe Tuesday. Not this past Friday."

Fowler's heavy eyebrows flattened into a straight line.

"Tubby's involvement at the canyon day before yesterday raises several questions. Was the shooting of the horses an intended distraction? In which case, did Herrera move up the schedule? If so, why? Or, if the shooting is unrelated to Herrera, why was Tubby involved? And if it is unrelated, will Tubby's arrest force Herrera to change plans?"

"Go on," Garrett said.

Fowler neither nodded nor spoke, but his clenched jaw

revealed displeasure.

"If they've been watching, they'd know Dad rides out to Dice Canyon on Mondays. They wouldn't know about Cassie's rides on Fridays since she's only done it twice." Jonas raised one eyebrow. "They probably expected Dad to find the dead horses on Monday. Which suggests Friday's shooting is a prelude to a run this week."

"Give me five minutes alone with Billy, and I'll find out." Garrett's clenched fists had turned his knuckles white.

Derek had no doubt he could make Billy squeal.

"I'm with Derek," Kyle said. "Something doesn't add up. You mentioned this Herrera group had both direct and indirect ties to drug trafficking. Sales and distribution, right?"

Fowler stared at the deputy for a long time before answering. "Yes."

"Weapons trafficking, too?"

"Yes." Fowler showed signs of impatience now.

"And human trafficking?"

"What is your point, deputy?" Fowler snarled.

"All of this stuff has been crossing our borders for decades," Kyle responded. "It's always been handled by the Drug Enforcement Administration, the Bureau of Alcohol, Tobacco, Firearms, and Explosives, or the Department of Health and Human Services. On the other hand, the Bureau of International Intelligence only concerns itself when international jurisdictions overlap, and specifically in cases

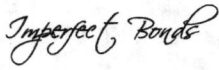

where verifiable threats exist against the national security of our country or its leaders. My point is, where's the national security risk? What's the BII doing in the middle of this?"

Fowler didn't blink, didn't twitch, or even seem to breathe, but the pressure in the room escalated to manifold proportions.

Derek forced his lungs to contract, to release the breath he'd unconsciously held in response to the rising tension. Need to know was a military term that pigeon-holed data, thereby restricting it to the fewest number of people in the smallest amount necessary to affect an end result. No more. No less. No questions. Every mission he'd ever participated in operated in this fashion. All of them knew this.

Kyle knew it. And he'd touched the nerve anyway.

Fowler's glare at the youngest member of their team softened to a degree only slightly harder than tempered steel. "This is TS/SCI, Kyle. Do you understand? Do the rest of you get it?"

Derek's breath hitched again. Not need to know—Top Secret, Sensitive Compartmented Information. Many of the military's top echelon and most of the government's elected officials didn't have access at this level.

No one spoke. A heavy silence enveloped the room broken only by the hum of the refrigerator and the sound of a vehicle passing outside. Sweat beaded on Derek's forehead. Had his hearing been keener, he'd for sure hear seven different hearts thumping hard.

"I'll tell you what I can," Fowler went on. "You'll have to trust me on the rest, and if you can't, leave now."

No one budged. One by one they all answered, "I'm in."

"Very well. Over the past six months a rash of abductions has occurred across the nation. Girls of all ages are being targeted with one thing in common—privilege. They're daughters, wives, sisters, cousins, mothers, friends, and girlfriends of wealthy, affluent people. We're not sure if this is a temporary trend, some third world country thumbing their noses at the Great Satan, or if it's a concerted effort to undermine our country's governing structure by blackmailing and compromising our leaders. Whatever the game, I intend to stop it. Hastings Bluff appears to be the first viable battleground."

"You don't think they'll change the route after Kershisnik's and Trent's arrest?" Wade spoke up this time. He looked like he wanted to rip somebody's head off.

"It's a possibility," Fowler replied.

"But you don't believe it," Wade persisted.

Didn't believe or didn't want to believe? A piece of the puzzle glimmered in Derek's mind. His own words came back to him. Fowler would do everything in his power to see the job done. He would use any means necessary … and anybody.

"Our intelligence suggests the organization is too big to react that fast," Fowler went on. "And in the grand scheme of things, this run is a drop in the bucket of their business."

"You're saying Herrera isn't behind the abductions, only the delivery?" Wade asked.

"You intend to draw them out, don't you? How?" Jonas the jokester had remained quiet throughout the meeting. He didn't look amused now.

"No," Derek said.

Once again, six pairs of questioning eyes turned his way.

"No," he repeated with more force. "You will not use Cassidy or Mallory to bait a trap."

The tension in the room went arctic.

"Not your call, deputy," Fowler snapped at Derek before he turned to face the wrath of the other men. "You're all proven entities. I know you and trust your skills, experience, and decision-making abilities. I prefer to use you in this op, but I can easily bring in another team. As for Cassidy and Mallory, they've already agreed to help."

CCC

Escape smelled like fresh-brewed coffee. Cassie inhaled and let the rich aroma fill her lungs, the perfect rescue from a night spent tossing and turning. She yawned, stretched, and then leaned on the kitchen island to stare out the window while the coffee dripped.

Outside, the darkness paled and gave way to a monochrome gloom. No pink streaks to herald the Monday dawn. No sun to brighten the day. Not even the rooster crowed.

The rain had started sometime in the night. It continued now, soft and slow in what Mom called a quiet soaking.

Beside her, Sadeé's ears perked up. The faithful shadow lifted her head and looked toward the dining room, tail thumping against the hardwood floor.

A moment later, Mallory appeared. "Hey," she murmured. "Make enough to share?"

Cassie waved her twin over. "You're up early." She filled two cups, set them on the island, and grabbed the sugar bowl from the cupboard while Mallory fetched the creamer from the fridge. Twins. They even took their coffee the same way. Light and sweet.

"You look the way I feel. Guess neither of us got much sleep last night after James's and Derek's little visit. The nerve of those two. James might be the sheriff, but his authority does not extend to telling me what I can and can't do, who I can and can't see. So, are you going this morning, or not?"

A raised eyebrow was the only response Cassie offered at first. She let the silence play out a little longer before answering. "I told Derek I would think about it, and I did."

Mallory lifted her cup and blew across the surface of the steaming brew before she raised it to her lips. "For what, all of two seconds?"

"More like five. It was hard enough getting Coot to agree to physical therapy. I'm not about to drop him now that we've gotten started. Derek knows how important this is to me." She

took another sip and looked at her sister. "So, yes, I'm going. That is, if you are. TJ's got a job interview at the elementary school over in Challis, and Lucy's too fresh off her shoulder surgery to hold the wheel for that distance, so I kind of need you to drive."

"Count me in. I still can't believe James and Derek drove out here last night just to rant and rail about Fowler. I mean, it's not like the man would put us in danger. Would he?"

Cassie met her sister's worried eyes across the counter. The agent's inquiry—Would you be willing to help us if we needed you?—seemed innocuous enough but didn't explain Derek's and James's outraged reaction. "Well, they did bring the new sat phone."

Garrett, Wade, James, and Derek all sang Fowler's praises from their time working for him in the BII, and yet they had reservations. TJ never said much about her experience with the agent, but her few carefully chosen words made it plain she had trust issues with him. Jonas seemed ambivalent, neither condemning nor supportive. Only Lucy stood up for Fowler. She claimed he was trustworthy and just doing his job.

"My truck is in for a brake job," Mallory said. "You think your car can handle the mountain roads with all this rain?"

The roads might pose a problem for a vehicle as low slung as her Accord. And if Lucy came, too, it would be too cramped to include Sadeé. "I think we're safe taking Route 93 with Billy in jail and the other guy nowhere around. We'll have to leave

Sadeé, though. With you, me, Lucy, and all my equipment, there won't be room for her, which will tick Derek off even more since I promised to keep her with me."

"Good morning," As though the mention of her name had summoned her, Lucy appeared in the kitchen doorway. "If we're still going to Coot's, you need to get a move on. It's already a quarter past six."

Cassie jumped up from her chair, rinsed her cup in the sink, and took off toward the stairs behind Mallory. They usually left by six-thirty. "Coffee's ready. We'll be down in ten."

Fifteen minutes later, they left an unhappy Sadeé behind and climbed in the red Honda, Mallory behind the wheel, Lucy belted into the front passenger seat, and Cassie stuffed in the back with the ice chest and equipment.

She had the new satellite phone, which left only one more thing to check. "Run your hand under the driver's seat, Mal. Make sure my gun's there," Cassie said.

When Mallory nodded, Cassie made herself comfortable for the long ride.

The rain continued to fall in a slow, monotonous drizzle. Oddly enough, they didn't talk much on the drive until halfway through the journey Mallory called their attention to the vehicle behind them. "I'm not one to jump at rabbits, but that vehicle's been following us since we left Hastings Bluff."

Cassie turned to look through the rear window and spotted

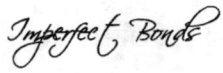

the dark blur. "Slow down, Mal. Let's see if they'll pass us."

She let off the gas and dropped their speed from sixty-five to forty-five. "They slowed, too."

An uneasy feeling settled in Cassie's gut when the other vehicle kept pace with them. The truck—she was sure it was a truck even though she couldn't make out details—maintained the same distance.

Shoving her equipment bag on top of the cooler on the floor, Cassie pulled the seat back forward to reveal access to the trunk. Using her iPhone as a flashlight, she squirmed and wriggled the upper half of her body into the opening and groped around. The leather case was here somewhere. She didn't remember taking it out.

Arms extended, fingers searching, she scrabbled through the jumble in the trunk and identified an assortment of stuff— her rodeo bag, some miscellaneous clothes, one boot, a small cardboard box, more clothing, the hard plastic tool kit with its molded handle, and … there … the squarish, leather case. Cassie backed out of the small opening.

"What in the world are you doing?" Lucy asked.

Cassie unsnapped the case and brandished her find. "Binoculars." She turned to the rear window, fitted the glasses to her eyes, and found the vehicle. Several twists of the zoom let her focus in close.

"What do you see?" Mallory shouted from the front.

"A green F-150. Two men."

"Zavala?" Mal's voice held an edge of tension.

"Can't tell." Cassie dropped the glasses and turned to look at Mallory and Lucy. "Speed up, Mal. Let's see if they hang with us."

Their speed rose to fifty, sixty, seventy, before Mallory settled in at eighty miles per hour, the max her little Honda could handle without shaking apart.

"Uh-oh," Mallory looked at the rearview mirror and the road ahead, back and forth like a metronome. "They're closing on us."

Cassie almost gave herself a black eye when she whipped around and raised the binoculars again. The truck was closer now. The driver's sleeveless white undershirt made a startling contrast against his darker skin. The passenger wore … a suit? Colors and shapes, but no features. Or tattoos.

"How far are we from the turnoff?" Lucy asked.

Cassie looked around at the familiar stretch of road. "About two miles. I think." She raised the glasses again and zoomed in on the pursuing truck. Closer now, she could make out the two men, one black, the other white, but not enough to determine if the driver was Zavala. A sense of déjà vu overwhelmed her, bringing back the fear from her previous run-in. Leaning forward between the seats, she pointed ahead. "There. Half a mile."

"I see it." Mallory glanced at the rearview mirror again. "Wait. They're slowing down. They've backed off."

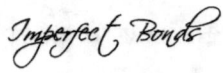

A quick glance back confirmed it. The truck had let the distance between them grow again. What game were they playing?

"It's like they're trying to scare us. But for what purpose?" Lucy wore a puzzled frown, a sure sign she'd gone into analytical mode.

Mallory slowed enough to make the turn.

A few moments later, the truck turned behind them but instead of following, they pulled onto the shoulder. Another curve and they were lost to sight.

Mallory pulled into Coot's front yard a few minutes later and cut the engine. Her hands shook when she took them off the steering wheel. "I don't understand what just happened, but I think we should call James."

"Let's think about this for a minute," Lucy said. "It felt like a threat, but what did they do? They never even got close, unlike Cassie's encounter with Billy and Zavala. For all we know, the truck behind us could've been a couple of good old boys who get their jollies scaring a bunch of girls."

"I see your point, but if I couldn't see them with binoculars, doesn't it stand to reason they couldn't see us. How would they know we were girls?"

"Then perhaps they were using us as a speedometer or a pace car. You know, setting their speed to ours. We don't know for sure if it was Zavala. Or one of his cronies."

Chapter Twenty-One

The rain stopped not long after they arrived at Coot's. Cassie took her time setting things up and getting him ready for his physical therapy routine.

While she put him through several slow stretches, Mallory and Lucy regaled him with an account of their imagined highway encounter.

Except imagined didn't seem right.

"I think you should call that boyfriend of yours, the one who works for the sheriff, and tell him what happened to you girls on the way down this morning."

"I don't know …"

"Coot's right." Mallory's crossed arms said she'd be difficult to convince otherwise.

Lucy, who stood at Mal's side, nodded her agreement.

"Would you excuse for a moment, Coot?" Cassie gave him her sweetest smile as she herded Mal and Lucy to the other side of the room.

"If Derek finds out what happened, he'll tell James who'll tell the Three Musketeers," Cassie tried to whisper, but knew her agitation let it carry across the room. "They'll want me to

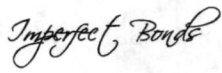

discontinue Coot's treatments. I can't do that."

"Yeah, well if we don't tell them and they find out, we won't have to worry about going anywhere for a long, long time," Mallory huffed.

"Hey, Belinda," Coot yelled out.

A few moments later his wife, Belinda, appeared in the doorway. "What are you going on about, Lester?"

"Need you to call around and find out if anybody's seen a green Ford truck hanging around these parts today. A real shiny one, with lots of fancy chrome trim."

She frowned at him for a few seconds before looking at Cassie. Then she nodded, motioned to Mallory and Lucy to follower her, and left without a word.

"Okay, let's get started." Coot rubbed his hands together. "If those guys are still lurking about, Belinda will find out. And if they are, you aren't leaving till you call your man."

Relieved with the simple solution, Cassie nodded and got to work. An hour and thirty minutes later, she motioned Coot over to the big comfy armchair.

Coot sank into depths of the chair and stretched his leg out on the ottoman with a sigh. Every week the old grump fussed nonstop about how much the workout hurt and then complained about the soreness afterward. But even he couldn't deny the improvement. He'd given up the cane a week ago, and today, his limp seemed barely there.

"Straighten your leg. That's it. Flatten the knee and point

your toes. Now flex. Again."

He complied with a moan, but sounded more like a kid lapping at an ice cream.

His wife and the two girls returned. "I got everybody in a twenty-mile radius on the lookout for your green truck, but so far no one's seen a thing," Belinda said.

I'm not sure if that's good or bad, but it's sure a relief." Lucy settled onto a nearby chair.

"So, now what?" Mallory asked.

Thoughts of today's encounter with the truck disturbed Cassie more than she wanted to admit, but she refused to let it interfere with her job. "Head home, I guess. I don't see a need to call Derek or James right now, but we should probably tell them when we get back."

"I understand your dilemma, girls," Coot said. "But I'm also a great believer in listening to your gut. And my gut says you're not happy about all this."

Cassie squirted a drop of massage oil on her hands and kneaded his calf, easy at first, and then deeper.

He flinched when Cassie dug her thumbs in around the scar, but then he always did.

"Easy there, kiddo."

"Sorry." She kept right on increasing the pressure, just like she always did.

"All I'm saying in better safe than sorry. If you don't want to call your boyfriends or your brothers to come get you,

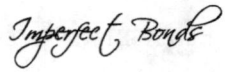

maybe you should rethink the route you choose to go home."

"Are the mountain roads passable after all this rain?" Mallory asked. "My Honda doesn't have four-wheel drive, and it sits pretty low to the ground.

"County does a good job keeping the roads graded. They drain well and the rain stopped some time ago. Tell you what, stick around and have lunch with me and the wife. See what they look like after a couple more hours to dry out. And if those guys haven't shown their face by then, I doubt they will."

Cassie patted his leg and wiped her hands on a towel. He made sense.

CCC

Cassie sat in the back of the Honda, hands braced against the seat in front of her. When the car's rear tires slewed sideways, she grimaced at the vibration from the floorboard as the undercarriage scraped over mud and gravel.

The short drive from Coot's place off Trail Creek north to Walker Road hadn't posed a problem, but then they had to wind their way north and west, climbing in altitude. Their route paralleled first Bradshaw Creek and then Road Creek as it narrowed into one of those faint gray lines found on a map, roads sometimes dubbed scenic but often unnamed.

"Sorry." Mallory apologized. If she gripped the steering wheel any harder her fingers would leave indents.

Lucy sat in the front passenger seat with a wild-eyed, worried look and a death grip on her door handle. Her gaze shifted like a pendulum between Mallory and the road.

Some of the elevations through here rose higher than the timberline, as much as twelve thousand feet. Thank goodness the route they took topped out at little over seven thousand and had plenty of room for two vehicles to pass, at least on a good day.

Today wasn't the best of days.

"You're doing fine, Mal. No worries." Cassie cringed at the hollowness of her voice.

Several roads crisscrossed the Lost River Range, following the trails cut by early settlers. On the west-facing side of the mountains, dense forests of spruce, cedar, maple, birch, oak, and other hardwoods proliferated, the kind that would ignite the autumn landscape in a blaze of color in another two months.

The eastern slopes, the side they now traveled, seemed alien in comparison, all rock and sparse vegetation. Not an issue during the winter since snow closed most of the mountain roads, but the barrenness created an erosion problem during the summer months. The county, in their pinch-penny wisdom, decided to forego maintenance for the more problematic areas, which resulted in a curious mix of asphalt and graded hardpan that turned into ruts when it rained.

Mallory fought the slide until the car's wheels settled into the twin furrows again, but the dragging, sludgy sound didn't let up. She pointed ahead. "We're almost to the crest."

"Great." Cassie responded with enthusiasm she didn't feel. Although paved for most of the way down, the opposite side descended at a much steeper angle. Their slip and slide would simply go faster now. Her little car might never be the same.

"You're doing fine," Lucy encouraged from the passenger seat.

"Next time it rains, I don't care if they like it or not, we're bringing one of the guys along. And a couple of shotguns, too," Mal quipped, never taking her eyes from the road.

Cassie looked at her watch. At this rate, it would take them forever to get home. "I called Derek when we left Coot's. Had to leave a message, but I promised to tell him when we started home. Maybe I should call him back and let him know it's taking longer than expected. Maybe we should call Mom, too. Let her know we'll be late."

Brrrrrng. Brrrrrng.

The strident ring coming from her equipment bag startled all three of them.

Lucy jerked around. "What's that?"

Cassie shrugged. Not her cell phone. Had to be the new satellite phone Derek provided to replace the one she lost at Dice Canyon. Few people had this new number. No one had actually called on it yet.

To her credit, Mallory's focus didn't waver from the road.

Brrrrrng. Brrrrrng.

"It's the satellite phone." Cassie fumbled in the bag and found the phone. "Hello."

"Cassie, thank goodness you picked up." TJ spoke fast, her voice agitated. "I'm at your house. Coot called here trying to find someone who could get in touch with you."

"Hold on, TJ. Let me put you on speaker." Cassie repeated TJ's words while she studied the phone's face. Finally locating the speaker button, she pressed it. "Okay. Go ahead."

"Coot knew about the satellite phone, but didn't have the number. He said one of his neighbors spotted the truck you were worried about. The green one. It's about fifteen minutes behind you."

Lucy's eyes, already wide from watching the treacherous terrain, widened even more. "Can you go any faster, Mal?"

Mallory sat up straighter in her seat. "Uh, have you looked at this mess they call a road? Speed is not an option here."

"I take it the green truck is a bad thing?" TJ asked over the phone.

"Yeah. We think so," Cassie replied.

"What do you mean think so?"

"It's complicated." Cassie rubbed her forehead. "Two guys in a green truck kind of crowded us on Route 93 on the way down to Coot's. But they never got close enough to see their faces, and didn't do anything other than follow us for a while. Not that they could do much else with no other roads along that stretch. Like I said, it's complicated."

"Yeah, but now he's following you for real. You need to get out of there."

"Mallory's right, TJ. We're deep in the mountains. With all the rain, the roads are a disaster. Our top speed is eight miles an hour."

"Don't you have a map? Can't you find another route?" TJ's voice rose with each word, a sure sign of her escalating worry.

Mallory tapped on the brake as they approached the first curve on the descent. "Uh-uh. I'm not turning down any of these side roads. They're no more than ruts. We wouldn't make it ten feet before getting stuck."

"That truck has to weigh twice as much as this car," Lucy said. "It will have more traction and a greater clearance, which will allow them to make better time than us."

The Honda hit a puddle of standing water and fishtailed toward the sheer drop off on the other side.

Lucy sucked in air through clenched teeth with a hissing sound.

"I got it. I'm good," Mallory said in a breathy explosion of words.

"You're good," Cassie agreed, willing her pulse to slow as the car righted itself. "You're good."

"Everything okay?" TJ's worried voice came over the line.

"We're okay," Cassie repeated, feeling more hopeful than

confident. Her insides fluttered from the surge of adrenalin.

"Okay, we can't get off this road, and we can't outrun the truck. What do we do?" Lucy stared straight ahead, her body taut and unmoving.

What indeed. Cassie said the first thing that came to mind. "I'll call Derek. He'll know."

"Yeah. That's good," TJ said. "You call Derek. I'm calling Garrett. One of them will know what to do. Keep me posted, okay?"

"We will. Thanks for the head's up."

An oppressive silence filled the car after TJ rang off. The rhythmic sound of tires on the wet road and the purr of the Honda's engine brought home how alone they were out here.

Cassie dialed Derek's cell phone and counted the rings. After the fourth buzz, she stabbed the off button. A voice mail wouldn't do. Who knew when he'd check for messages?

She tried again. Same result. Why didn't he pick up? "He's not answering."

"Try calling the office number," Lucy suggested. "Someone's always there."

After finding the number in her cell phone contacts, Cassie dialed.

"Sheriff's office."

Lorraine's familiar voice brought a moment of relief. "Lorraine, hi, this is Cassidy Cameron. Is Derek there? Or James?"

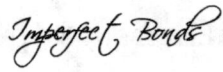

"No, honey, they left word they'd be out of the office the rest of the afternoon. Can I help you?"

The last thing she wanted to do was share any of this with Lorraine. She'd turn it into a scandal and spread it all over the county before sundown. "Uh, can you get a message to one of them? Tell them I need to speak with them as soon as possible?"

"Jeb Wharton's out on a call, but I'm sure I can get him for you."

"No, no. Just Derek. Or James. Thanks, Lorraine."

"Okay, no Derek and no James," Mallory said when Cassie disconnected the call. "We can't rely on help getting here in time anyway, and it's a given that truck will catch up to us, right? What then? Put your analytical mind to work, Lucy."

"They'll try to get us to stop. Barring that, they might shoot the tires out. It's what I would do." Lucy's frown of concentration didn't engender confidence. "They could also shoot at us, ram the car from behind, run us off the road. Or they might even ignore us."

"You don't believe that any more than I do," Mallory grumbled.

Cassie had to side with Mallory this time. "Hope is not a strategy, guessing their moves won't help us, and wishing won't make our dreams come true."

Lucy nodded. "You're right. I doubt their intentions are good."

"Fowler talked about drug runners, arms trafficking, and abductions, but he never mentioned murder." Cassie prayed she was right. "My bet is they'll try to run us off the road and kidnap us."

Mallory stared at the mirror again. "Uh, Cass, Luce?"

"What?" Lucy asked.

"I hate to tell you, but the truck? Yeah, I just caught a glimpse of it."

Cassie whirled around. "Where? I don't see it."

"Still a ways back, but they're moving a lot faster than us. And we have another problem. I spotted a white van four turns ahead of us."

"We're boxed in?" Cassie's heart thundered.

"We need a plan. Now." Lucy looked at Mal and then Cassie, her frown deepened, cutting furrows in her forehead. "Any ideas? Because I'm coming up short here."

"Okay, here's what we do." Cassie leaned forward between the two front seats. "The road makes a sharp turn to the north leading into the next set of hairpins. Line of sight will be lost for a few moments. We won't see them and they won't see us." She dropped the satellite phone into Lucy's lap. "Take the sat phone, Lucy. Mal will stop the car as soon as we round the next bend. You get out and hide while we continue on."

"What? No. I'm not bailing on you." Lucy shook her head.

"It's not bailing. Your injured arm makes you a liability if

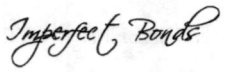

we have to fight or run. This way you can stay in touch with TJ and the guys," Cassie argued.

"And what if you don't get away, what if they abduct you, how do we find you then?" Lucy made no bones about disliking the idea.

Cassie reached forward and brushed a strand of hair behind Lucy's ear. "You'll swap earrings with us."

"Of course!" Mallory slapped the steering wheel with an open palm. "The earrings Wade gave you with the GPS transponders."

Lucy touched her ear. "Yeah, when that Cypher creep was trying to kidnap me."

"They're the same chip implants in the herds he monitors, and yet you never take them off," Mallory cracked. "Genius, Cass."

"I'll take one and Mal the other. Wade can track us using his security system," Cassie insisted. "He can find us."

Lucy looked intrigued, but not convinced. Thorough and methodical to a fault, she preferred to examine solutions from all angles. She liked details.

"Our turn is coming up," Mallory warned.

"Discussion time has run out, Lucy. Will you do this?"

She nodded. "Okay, but I don't like it."

"You don't have to like it. I don't like it either, but it's all we have. Mal, take out your right earring while I help Lucy."

Luckily, Mallory wore simple hoops she could flick open

and remove with one hand.

Cassie took out one of Lucy's studs and put it on Mallory's ear. "Lucy, turn your head so I can get to the other one. If nothing happens, if they just pass us by, we'll come back for you quick as we can."

With the second GPS-chipped earring affixed to her own ear, Cassie pointed ahead. "That's it. That's our curve. We can't stop but a second, Lucy. You'll have to hurry."

The car jerked to a halt at the apex of the curve. Scrub brush, trees, and boulders provided plenty of hiding places for Lucy.

Cassie leaned over and opened the passenger door. "Go, Lucy. Take the phone. Run. Hide."

Mallory waited just long enough for Lucy to clear the door before peeling off again. The wheels spun for a second before they grabbed the slick pavement. The car shot forward.

Cassie scrambled into the vacated front passenger seat and yanked the door shut. A moment more and Lucy melted from sight.

"Go. It will take Derek or James at least an hour to get to us, maybe longer. We need to delay this confrontation as long as possible."

Mallory stared at the rearview mirror. "I don't think we have an hour, Cass."

Chapter Twenty-Two

Cassie turned all the way around in her seat to stare out the rear window. "I don't see the truck. How far?"

"They just entered the first hairpin in this set."

The ascent side had long, sweeping zigzag turns. Not so the descent side. A caution sign at the top of the pass established the danger right off. STEEP GRADES NEXT 7 MILES. USE LOWER GEAR.

A second sign a short distance farther announced the first of four sets of tight, curlicue S-turns. CAUTION 4% GRADE NEXT 1.5 MILES.

They'd dropped Lucy back at the first of the third series when the truck topped the rise behind them.

"The brakes are hot, Cass. That's not good." Sweat beaded on Mallory's forehead despite the air conditioning. "Or it could be the engine. Do you smell it?"

It didn't matter if the car overheated. They had to get out of these turns before the truck caught up.

They entered the longest straightaway. One more set of S-turns to go. "The car is fine, Mal. Go faster. We can gain some distance here. Any sign of the van ahead?"

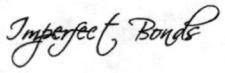

Her sister pressed the accelerator. "Just a glimpse now and again."

Not fast enough, though. Not that it mattered. All they could do was delay the inevitable as long as possible to allow their brothers, Derek, and James time to reach them.

The last series of turns, six this time, one on top of the other, came much too soon. Runoff from the mountain streams made the roads more treacherous, and the eight percent grade here didn't help. They slowed to a crawl to navigate the tight curves.

"Do your best." Cassie gave up staring at the road ahead and twisted in her seat to watch for the truck.

The first four turns passed without sighting either vehicle, but that didn't ease Cassie's worry. Instead of a vertical stack, these curves had been hewn from the side of the mountain and followed its profile in a roundabout fashion that eliminated line of sight from one turn to the next. As they entered the next to last curve, Cassie caught a flash of green and chrome. "I see them. They're three turns back."

"That's not possible. No one can go that fast on these curves." Mal's voice held a touch of panic.

"Don't freak on me now. We knew this would happen." Cassie faced her sister. "Get us through the last two turns. Get us to the plateau. We can't go over the side there."

"Not funny."

"Hey, funny ha-ha, or funny weird? Don't worry. Lucy's

in touch with Wade by now, and TJ will have called Garrett. Hopefully, Lorraine reached Derek or James, too. The cavalry will come for us. You'll see." Inane drivel, but she needed the reassurance as much as her sister did. The waiting would surely kill her if the bad guys didn't.

"Uh … Cass?" Mallory stammered as they came out of the fifth turn.

Cassie jerked around in the seat and felt the blood drain from her face. The white van was ahead, just disappearing around the next curve. Not unexpected, but with the vehicle behind closing them in, a spike of terror surged through her veins.

"Not good."

"Get my gun from my purse. It's on the floor behind my seat."

Cassie leaned between the two seats and reached for the her sister's little handbag. Her fingers closed around it … but then released it. She wormed her way back to a sitting position in the front seat. "No guns."

"What? It's all we have. You know they're carrying."

"Exactly. But murder hasn't been part of their modus operandi so far. Let's not give them cause to change their minds."

"Getting shot might be better than the alternative."

"No. Alive we have a chance. There is no chance with dead."

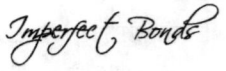

"The truck is trying to squeeze by me," Mallory shrieked.

A sheer rock wall bordered the right side of the road. The opposite side had a two-foot wide shoulder separating them from a steep drop-off.

"Move to the middle. Cut him off. If he comes alongside, he can push us into the mountain. Move, Mal. Now! You can do it."

"I don't like this." The Honda inched over to the middle of the narrow two-lane road.

The driver of the truck backed off, but laid on the horn with several long, angry blasts.

"He's motioning us over."

"Tough." Cassie held her breath as the truck's two left wheels drifted onto the narrow shoulder. The driver stuck his head out the window and shook his fist.

"He's yelling. What should I do?"

"Let your window down. See if you can hear what he's saying."

Mallory pressed the button and let the driver's side window down half way.

"Pull over you crazy—" The driver added a vulgar slur and continued to wave toward the side of the road.

Mallory's face flamed at the insult he'd hurled. "Stupid idiot. Like I'd pull over even if I had a place to stop."

Good. Angry Mallory was infinitely better than the terrified mouse who'd gotten them this far.

"He backed off."

Sure enough, the truck had fallen back several car lengths. Why? She could think of only one reason—to build up speed and ram them. Maybe they should reconsider the guns.

"Oh, crap." Cassie's stomach lurched. "Here he comes again."

Her sister's face had turned a pasty white.

They didn't have a chance in a brawl with the tank-like truck. If they could get through this last turn, the road widened at the bottom and opened up into a wide valley. No sheer walls to crash into. And no ravines to plummet over. If the van didn't block them.

A jarring thump sent the Honda lurching to the right and Cassie flying in a tangle of arms and legs against the dash. Vaguely she registered the screeching metallic sounds of metal on metal. The truck had rammed them.

Mallory stomped on the brakes, which sent the car into a spin. The steering wheel jerked one way while she slammed against the driver's window.

Tires squealed. One side of the car lifted off the ground, teetered for a heart stopping moment, and then did a three-sixty roll. They hit the rock wall on Cassie's side, ricocheted off, and went into another spin.

Cassie bounced off the windshield, landed on top of Mallory, crashed upside down against the ceiling, banged her knee on the gear shift, and then tangled with a huge, white

pillow that slammed her sideways against the front passenger
window. Her head cracked against the glass.

Pinned in place by the airbag, the world continued to spin.
She couldn't move, couldn't breathe. Her ears rang, and her
brain didn't want to function. Lightning sizzled inside her
skull. Only one thought registered. Mallory hadn't made a
sound.

CCC

Derek set the stack of forms aside and rubbed his eyes. He
hated when his turn to man the office rolled around with
nothing but reports and more reports to pass the day. Now, with
Fowler's involvement, the sheer volume of paper had doubled.

He stood and stretched, deciding a fresh pot of caffeine
might help pass the time.

The smell of burned coffee assaulted him the moment he
stepped through the door of the break room.

"Lorraine," he yelled.

"What?" she yelled back from her desk at the other end of
the office.

"Am I the only one that ever washes the coffeepot? Can't
you at least turn the burner off?"

"You turn it off. I don't drink the stuff." The clattering
sound of her fingers on the keyboard resumed.

"Great." He poured the syrupy dregs down the drain,
added a squirt of dishwashing liquid, and set the pot under the
faucet.

The office phone rang. A moment later, Lorraine yelled again. "Derek, James wants to talk to you."

He turned the tap off, dried his hands with a paper towel, and walked back to his desk. Too late for coffee today anyway, but at least they'd have a clean pot for tomorrow morning. "Naughton."

"You heard from the girls?" James's voice sounded tinny over the landline.

"Yeah. Cassidy called when they left the Harbins' place. That was about fifteen minutes ago."

"Good. They should be home in another hour."

"As long as they don't find trouble to poke their nose in."

James didn't speak for a long moment. "That's not as funny as you think."

"I know."

"Call me when they get home."

"Will do."

Not ten minutes passed before another call came in, this one on his cell phone. He frowned at the UNKNOWN NUMBER showing on the screen. He hated telemarketers, almost as much as the bureaucratic reports he had to write. The call stopped after four rings.

Almost immediately, it trilled again. Same number. Persistent buggers.

Annoyed by the interruptions, he grabbed one of the reports from the top of the stack. Might as well get on with it.

They wouldn't fill themselves out.

His desk phone rang.

"Sheesh." He slammed his pen down and snatched up the handset. "Naughton," he snapped.

"I'm on my way to the Triple C." James's no nonsense tone put Derek on alert. "Meet me there fast as you can. Fowler's got something going down."

"He get a bead on the traffickers?"

"Something like that."

"He wants to spring a trap, doesn't he?"

"That would be my guess. You got your gear?"

"I keep my duffel in the Blazer. What about the office?"

"Go ahead and head out now. I called Kyle and Jeb Wharton in to cover."

"Roger."

"Oh, and bring the map with you."

Derek shoved the stack of reports in the drawer, saw his cell phone lying there, and stuffed it in his pocket. With the rolled map under his arm, he stopped at the door and looked over at Lorraine. "James called me to the Cameron ranch. I doubt either of us will be back today. Kyle's out on patrol and Jeb Wharton's coming in for the night shift. Call one of them if you need something."

Lorraine waved a hand and went right back to her computer.

Fifteen minutes to the Triple C. Ten if he busted it.

Excitement put his senses on high alert, the same anticipation he always felt before a mission. He had a feeling they'd see some action this afternoon.

CCC

Derek spotted James's black and white Yukon parked next to two Suburbans in front of the Camerons' ranch house, and pulled in behind the vehicles. Jamming his hat on his head, he grabbed the map and started toward the house.

The door opened before he reached the steps. "You made good time," Garrett stuck his hand out.

A whining Sadeé slipped around him, prancing and whining when she recognized Derek.

"Not like there's any traffic to speak of." He nodded toward the SUVs. "Fowler's?"

"Yup."

"Hey, girl." Derek leaned down to pet the dog. "Why aren't you with Cassidy?"

"That is one miserable pooch. She's been crying all morning." Garrett shook his head. "I swear, I can't remember a dog becoming so attached to a person the way this one has to Cassie."

Derek straightened up. "You got any idea why Fowler called this meeting?"

"Nope, but I'm sure we'll find out soon enough."

Inside, the agent and five more men stood around one side of the long dining room table while James, Wade, and Jonas

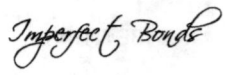

stood on the other side, all of them sizing each other up. They all wore similar clothes, himself and Garrett included—cargo pants, t-shirt, utility vest, and black tactical boots. No doubt the two government vehicles outside held a cache of weapons, too.

Looked like his intuition was right. Fowler wouldn't bring a horde of agents with him unless he had something up his sleeve.

Somehow Derek managed to not rub his hands together. He'd missed this, missed the thrill of living on the edge, working with a finely honed team, and doing things most people couldn't. Or wouldn't. A true brotherhood of adrenalin junkies.

"Hey, Derek," Wade said coming over. He pulled his cell phone out, checked the display, and pocketed it again.

Jonas followed, gripped Derek's shoulder, and took his hand. "Hey, man."

Derek looked around. "Hey, Jo. Where's your mom and dad?"

"Mom's in Boise, I think, doing one of her book signing things."

"Dad's over at the big barn," Garrett added. "He volunteered to mind the ranch while we're off doing whatever it is Fowler's cooked up."

"Deputy Naughton." Fowler said from across the dining table. "Glad you're here. Let me introduce my men. This is Ambrosio, Wang, Rosetti, Moffat, and Kuykendall."

All the handshaking got a little confusing, but Derek committed the new men's names to memory. He thought it unusual that Fowler would pair up strangers for an op without benefit of prior training together. His former SEAL team had prepared, ate, slept, showered, bled, celebrated, and even cried at times together. They'd become so close each member knew what the other would say before the words formed. Same for the Bureau team he'd served on with Garrett, James, and Kyle. Must be something important for Fowler to breach such an unspoken protocol.

"Gentlemen," the agent said. "We have a very small window of opportunity here. Gather around please. Is that the map?"

Derek unrolled the plat on the table and held it open with the help of two of the agents.

Sadeé never left his side.

Jonas fetched several cans from the kitchen pantry to weight the corners of the map. Just as he set the last can in place, his phone vibrated. He pulled it out and checked the display, and dropped it back in his pocket.

Fowler stabbed his index finger at the Utah/Idaho border. "Aerial surveillance identified a white Ford Econoline with temporary dealer tags. The van's rear cargo area has no windows. It's carrying a driver and one passenger. The sighting occurred approximately three hours ago."

"Aerial surveillance?" Garrett asked.

Fowler stared at the eldest Cameron brother for a few seconds, as though trying to decide how much to reveal. "Texas finally got serious about protecting their border. They recently allocated a ton of money to purchase listening devices, surveillance cameras, gunboats, drones, and some pretty nasty weaponry for the Border Patrol. They also approved a small fortune to grease palms, which netted them a lead on the Los Lobos cartel out of Juarez. I simply called in a favor."

"Los Lobos? Never heard of them."

"They're a small time drug cartel operating a fleet of big rigs with false bottoms out of the Juarez/El Paso area," Derek said. "Local scuttlebutt says they're responsible for the network of tunnels that riddle the twelve-hundred mile Mexico/Texas border."

Expendable vermin. By the time the authorities acquired enough proof to make an arrest, the conduit moved to another location with new trucks and new drivers. Catch one and ten more sprang up.

"You are correct," Fowler said. "Recent chatter indicates Los Lobos launched a new pipeline from Texas to Canada."

"Don't tell me—Route 93." Wade's expression showed his disgust.

"And I'll bet Herrera got wind of it and stepped in." This from James.

"Yes on both counts."

"So you borrowed a drone? Must have been some favor.

Those things cost about $3,000 an hour to operate." Garrett pursed his lips, deep in thought.

"The van wasn't due until next week," Wade crossed his arms over his chest. "How'd you know it was coming today?"

"Good to see you're still sharp." Fowler's glare could put lesser men on their knees.

Not Wade, though. He and Lucy had the recent pleasure of working with Fowler when an Afghan cyber terrorist tried to hack into Wade's security system. He'd gone toe to toe with the steely eyed agent and come out with his carcass intact.

Fowler's eyes remained focused on Wade. "We had a … tip. Now, if you're through picking everything apart, I'd like your attention here." He gestured at the map.

Wade seemed to accept his words, as did the others. Military conditioning. As one, the men all bent over the table.

Something seemed … not off, but odd. Fowler owned all the arrogance, confidence, and brazenness in the world. The man held the power of life and death over his men with the missions he assigned and supported, and never missed a chance to let his subordinates know who was in charge. But not this time. He'd kept his focus on Wade and then ducked out on making eye contact with any of the others.

Which was why, when the others all bowed over the map, Derek didn't miss the quick glance that passed between Fowler and Jonas. Or the barest tilt of the chin from the youngest Cameron brother.

Jonas met Derek's stare across the table, lifted one quirky eyebrow, and then bent with the others to study the map.

"As I was saying, a van matching our criteria crossed from Jackpot, Nevada into Idaho on Route 93 approximately three hours ago. Their current rate of speed would put them somewhere near here." He pointed to a spot near Arco.

James and Garrett both frowned. Derek had worked with them in the past enough to know they didn't do approximately. None of them did.

Fowler became aware of their reactions. "What is the problem now?"

"You got a time stamp for that drone footage?" Derek asked.

A fleeting glimpse of annoyance crossed Fowler's face, but he snapped his fingers.

One of the agents, Derek thought it was Kuykendall, flipped through a folder until he found the needed report. "Thirteen-oh-six, sir."

Military time. Six minutes past one in the afternoon civilian time. Every man in the room looked at his watch. Some things didn't change. All branches of the military used the Coordinated Universal Time standard based on the International Atomic Time standard.

"Three and one-half hours, not three." Garrett checked the mileage legend on the map and traced Route 93 north of Arco. "Those extra thirty minutes puts the target here, near Mackay."

They had even less time to devise and implement a plan. Worse, the Harbins farm lay a scant ten minutes north of the Mackay Reservoir. Too close to the girls.

A chill ran down Derek's spine.

Chapter Twenty-Three

Derek tried to convince himself the odds of Cassidy and Mallory running afoul of the van were slim to none, but that didn't prevent the hair on his arms from standing on end. He knew their penchant for drawing trouble.

Across the dining room, James frowned at his cell phone.

"Lose the telephones, gentlemen," Fowler groused. "The clock is ticking. We have fifteen minutes max to plan this operation." Fowler looked around the room, his scowl a challenge.

That was more like the Fowler Derek knew.

A buzzing sound broke the silence.

Garrett ignored Fowler's glare and fumbled his cell phone out of his pocket. "Sorry," he apologized. "I have to take this."

He left the group and headed for the kitchen. "Hey, Angel. This isn't a good time."

Derek itched to look at his own phone again. Too many calls. His earlier sense of uneasiness blossomed into full-blown anxiety.

Fowler rolled his eyes and turned back to the rest of the group. "Now—"

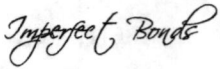

The sound of TJ's agitated voice cut him off, carrying over the line to every ear in the room. All eyes turned to watch.

"Slow down." Garrett froze in the doorway. "Say again." A few seconds of silence followed, but then he turned and looked at them with something akin to alarm.

Not good. Garrett didn't panic. Ever.

With a muttered curse, he hurried back to the table, phone clasped to the side of his face. "Hold on, TJ. I'm putting you on speaker. Start over." He thumbed the volume as high as it would go and set the device on the table.

TJ was already in mid rant, her words rushing out. "… is bad. You have to do something, Garrett. You have to go get them."

Sadeé stirred at Derek's feet. Even she felt the unexpected strain.

Eleven men—Garrett, Derek, James, Jonas, Wade, Fowler, and the five agents—stared at the device like it was a Diamondback about to strike.

"Take a breath, Angel. Breathe and slow down."

A shaky inhale and exhale followed. "Okay. Coot Harbins called the ranch looking for someone to pass an urgent message on to Cassie, Mal, or Lucy. He knew Cassie had a satellite phone, but didn't have the number. The girls had an … encounter with a green truck on the way down. Nothing happened. They didn't even see who was driving, but it followed them for a while and made them all nervous. Coot says his neighbors saw it turn onto East Lake Road not fifteen minutes behind the girls when they left to head home. He thinks it's following them."

Derek planted both hands on the surface of the table and glared at Garrett's cell phone. "They took Route 93 this morning, TJ. Cassidy called me when they left Harbins' place. She didn't mention anything about taking the mountain road home."

"Well, they did. There's more. I talked to Cassie on the sat phone and relayed Coot's message. Mallory was driving. She said the road they're on is a mess and the side roads impassable. There's no way they can go any faster. That truck is bound to catch up with them."

Derek looked at the other men. The same fear he felt was reflected on James's face. The brothers, too.

A hush fell over the room.

"Are you still there?"

"We're here, TJ. Go on." Jonas took charge.

"Cassie said she'd call you for help, Derek."

Derek covered his eyes with one hand and let his head drop. "I had several calls not long ago, all from an unknown number, I thought they were cold calls. I didn't pick up."

"Me either." Jonas's voice had gone hoarse. "I got the same call."

"So did I." All the color had drained from Wade's face. A second later he patted his pants pocket and dug his phone out.

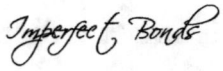

"Wait … It's her. Cassie, are you okay? What's—"

Derek and James forced their way past the others to Wade's side.

"TJ." Garrett picked up his phone and turned aside. "Cassie's on the other phone now. I'll call you back as soon as we know something."

Wade shook his head and whispered, "Not Cassie. Lucy. I'll put her on speaker."

Lucy's voice quivered over the speaker. "Cass said they wouldn't hurt us, Wade, but I'm not so sure. She thought they might want to abduct us instead. That's when she and Mallory took my earrings. They each have one." Her voice broke on a sob.

Sadeé gave a mournful cry.

"What? Why?" Derek asked.

"The earrings have GPS chips in them," Jonas explained. "Wade gave them to Lucy last year when we thought Cypher might try to kidnap her. She wears them all the time now. He can track the transponders. He can find the girls."

"What else, Tiger." Wade's gruff voice took on a softer note whenever he spoke to Lucy.

"She said—" Her voice hitched. "If it came down to fight or flight, my injured arm would hinder them. They put me out on a blind curve, shoved the satellite phone in my hand, and told me to hide. And to call Derek. I tried and tried, but he wouldn't answer. None of you did." Weeping filled the line.

"I'm so sorry, Tiger. Take a deep breath. We need to hear the rest."

Sniffles, hiccups, and several broken huffs later, Lucy continued, "I saw the green truck go by a few minutes ago. It's the same one that followed us on the way down. I'm so afraid for them."

Derek grabbed Wade's arm. "You have your laptop handy? We need a closer look at this mountain."

Wade nodded and walked away still clutching his cell phone. Mere moments later he returned, laptop in hand. He set the phone down on the dining room table and powered up the computer. Before long, a topography map of the area filled the screen, one that showed roads, logging trails, and hiking paths.

"Print it." James instructed.

A click set the printer in Mrs. Cameron's office whirring.

James hurried to retrieve it and laid it down on the table where the men could crowd around.

"Four series of hairpins run down the western side." Derek pointed to some squiggles on the map. "From what Lucy said, this must be where they let her out, at the top of the third series."

"Which puts Cassie and Mallory somewhere between here and … here." James tracked the rest of the descent with his finger.

Wade pulled up a Google Earth map and zoomed in. "I don't see anywhere to pull off until they get past the turns.

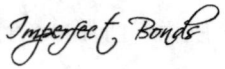

From there, it's four more miles to the highway."

Garrett moved his finger through the turns and onto the straightaway to where the faint gray line intersected with the thicker line marked ID 75. "Too risky to try and take the girls on the curves. Any attempt would happen here."

They'd all latched onto Cassie's abduction theory, more out of hope than reality. Because the alternative, that the men might force them off the road on the hairpin turns, was unacceptable.

"I swear, one of these days I'm gonna lock those girls in a cell and throw away the key." James left the group huddled around the desk and started pacing.

"This doesn't change a thing."

The words brought James to a stop. Every man there turned to stare in disbelief.

"What?" Derek turned his anger on Agent Kevin Fowler.

"Are you crazy?" Wade growled. "It changes everything. Cassie and Mallory are our top priority—"

"Let me finish." Fowler pulled up a chair and sat, seemingly unaffected by the rising tempers. "The mission still exists, just with an added component."

"He's right," Garrett said. "Take a seat and listen up."

Chairs scraped. Clothing rustled. Quiet descended.

"We plant a team here and here to prevent both the target van and the truck from escaping." Garrett pointed at a point north and south of where the mountain road intersected with

Idaho 75. "A third team will take the lead, enter the road here, locate the van and/or the truck, and assess the situation."

"Recon," James said.

Garrett nodded. "A fourth team will follow once we have a SITREP."

Some of the fear paralyzing Derek's brain flowed away. Strategy had always been Garrett's specialty. He had the utmost confidence in his former team leader.

Fowler took over. "Excellent. Naughton, you and Rosetti take the north roadblock. Evers and Moffett, take the south."

Fowler nodded at two more agents on his right. "Yang, Ambrosio, and Garrett will take point. Follow the road until you encounter one of the vehicles, but do not engage. I repeat. You will not engage. Assess and report back, and then continue past to find the second target. Kuykendall, Jonas, and I, will brace for a frontal assault."

"Hammer and anvil," Jonas said.

"Exactly. First two teams, you will stand by to provide support. Are we clear?" Fowler took a moment to look at each man, the way he hadn't done before.

Sidelined. Derek wanted to cuss, spit, or maybe blow something up.

A long, heavy sigh preceded James's nod. From the way his shoulders drooped, he didn't like being left out of the action any more than Derek did, but they would both comply.

Derek ground his teeth together and added his nod.

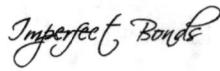

Beside him, a deep growl rumbled from Sadeé's chest.

"And what about me?" Wade's glower would scare a grizzly bear away.

"We need you to man your computer. Find those GPS signals and walk us in."

Calm returned, but the fear in Derek's gut continued to churn. "I'm bringing Sadeé."

Garrett nodded. "Good idea. Okay, men. You know the drill. Let's roll."

CCC

Cassie's body felt like someone had used it for a punching bag. A fireworks display was going off inside her head, and to top it off, she couldn't move. Not an iota. Was this how death would come for her? Pinned under an airbag with her face smushed against the window?

Her eyes didn't want to open. She forced them anyway. No more than a slit, though. The burn was too great.

A haze filled what little she could see. Cornstarch, chalk, and talcum powder. The airbag had deployed, propelled by the nitrogen gas cartridge. She pushed the slowly deflating fabric away from her eyes, only to have it cover her nose and mouth instead. Short on breath, she clawed at the covering until she created a small air pocket.

Chemical dust filled her nostrils and left her coughing. Convinced she wouldn't expire in the new few minutes, her mind began to sort itself out. Reason returned, along with the events of the last few minutes—the van, the crash. "Mal?" she croaked.

No answer. Not even a groan.

A terrible foreboding settled in. Her voice rose in pitch. "Mallory?"

A hissing sound answered. Twitches and pings from the dying car engine. And someone shouting nearby. But no Mallory.

Cassie swallowed hard. She couldn't lose it now, not when her sister needed her.

The passenger door she was compressed against jerked open without warning. She tumbled out of the car and hit her head on the asphalt. Fresh agony exploded. She withdrew her legs from the car and curled into a fetal position. Pain possessed her soul, but queasiness held claim on her body.

"Get up, chica," a disembodied voice said.

Nausea struck in waves until Cassie could no longer deny the revolt. Her stomach tried to expel every bite of food she'd ever eaten.

When the sickness passed, she wiped her mouth with a sleeve, moaned, and lay as still as possible. If she didn't move, maybe her brain wouldn't implode. Maybe she wouldn't puke again.

The respite didn't last. Fire scorched her scalp when someone grabbed her ponytail and used it to drag her away. The rough pavement, rocks, and gravel ripped through her clothes and shredded her skin.

She cried out and clawed at the hands in her hair. Her legs pumped hard, heels scrabbled for purchase, anything to alleviate the searing pain.

Another pair of hands slid under her armpits and lifted until she stood upright. Her knees locked, more to keep from toppling over than an act of defiance.

"This must be our lucky day, amigos. Looks like we found ourselves a matched pair." The mocking voice intimated terrible things that set her stomach roiling again.

Cassie squinted at the man in front of her. Dark hair, pockmarked face, swarthy complexion, wiry build, and a tattoo that ran the length of one arm. Zavala. Just as she suspected.

She backed away but was brought up short when the Neanderthal who'd dragged her from the car tightened his fist in her hair.

"Let's clean her up. See what we have." Zavala snapped his fingers.

The caveman forced Cassie to her knees and tugged her head back until her neck arched.

Zavala emptied a bottle of water over her face.

Cassie gasped and spluttered under the stream until the caveman let go. She fell forward onto her hands and knees.

A third man entered the periphery of her vision. Cassie stopped breathing when she saw her sister's limp body in his arms. He brought her to Zavala and dumped her on the ground.

"Noooo." She tried to crawl to Mallory's side, but Zavala barred her way.

"Your twin lives." Smugness saturated his voice. "For how long depends upon your cooperation."

Tears streamed down her face, but Cassie held the rage and fear in check and pleaded with Zavala. "Please, let me help my sister."

"Save your tears, chica. You'll need them where you're going." Ugly laughter erupted from the others.

Helpless. She hated the feeling. All she could do was hope that Lucy had reached Derek. That he would come. But she had to delay, give him time. Had to keep Mallory safe from these monsters.

Cassie forced herself to look at each one of her captors. To etch their faces in her memory. The man who'd manhandled her was Caucasian, late twenties, with beady eyes, thinning brown hair, and a paunch—another Billy in the making. The one who'd dumped Mallory on the ground like a sack of garbage had lifeless black eyes and a puckered scar along his jaw line.

Zavala gave her a cold, appraising once-over.

She understood what that look meant. An involuntary shudder ripped through her. Please, God, let Derek get here soon. Or Garrett, or anybody. She took a deep breath and ignored her still pounding head. She had one job—to keep herself and her sister alive until help arrived. "What are you going to do to us?"

Zavala's grin exuded menace. He looked at the other men. "What do you think, boys?"

Caveman grunted, his piggy eyes alight with lust.

Scarface rubbed his hands together and grinned, exposing neglected teeth. "Make them pay for all our trouble."

Cassie couldn't hold back a moan.

The fourth man who'd ridden with Zavala in the truck walked up. Tall and slender, with skin dark as ebony, he wore a three-piece suit and shiny leather dress shoes. "No. Do not touch them. I want them undamaged."

The imperious command wiped the leers from the faces of the other three. "A matched pair with eyes the color of the sky will fetch a great price from my clients. They will ride with the others for now. I will take possession of them once we cross the border." A refined accent pegged him as the product of an affluent British education, which somehow made him seem even more dangerous.

A bone-deep fear filled Cassie.

Chapter Twenty-Four

Outsized and outnumbered, it did no good to struggle when the caveman bound her hands behind her back with rope. He added a strip of silver duct tape over her mouth to ensure her silence.

Like escape was an option. She wouldn't leave without Mallory, and her sister had yet to regain consciousness.

Zavala jerked his head toward the van.

Caveman shoved Cassie toward the open door at the rear.

She recoiled, not wanting to enter the dark, cave-like interior.

"Climb in, chica." With one hand gripping her upper arm, Zavala helped Caveman force her inside. "Get comfortable. You have a long ride ahead."

Her sister was already there, sprawled on the floor of the van … next to another bound woman.

Caveman climbed inside, rolled Mallory onto her side, and tied her hands at her back. He applied the nasty duct tape next, and then disappeared.

The door slammed with a clang. Darkness descended. The grating sounds of a key turned in the lock.

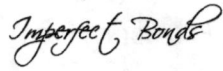

Her heart racing, Cassie wriggled against the rope to test the knots but gave up when they tightened more. If she continued to struggle, her hands might go numb. She'd be useless then.

Voices penetrated from outside the van. Rising in tenor, it sounded like an argument ensued among her captors.

Scooting on her butt to the side of the van, she pressed an ear against the wall.

"Do it. Now." The accented precise enunciation could only belong to the tall black man in the dapper suit. His sharp, authoritative command put an end to the quarrel.

A long silence followed, and then the unmistakable vroom of a truck engine. Gravel crunched, followed by a scraping noise, and then the shrill screech of metal on metal.

She determined her car must be blocking the road. That would explain the awful sounds. They were using Zavala's truck to push the Honda aside.

A new sound insinuated itself, a quiet sob that seemed filled with hopelessness.

Cassie scanned the dark interior.

Distorted shadows took on shape as her eyes adjusted. The mishmash became twelve young girls, some maybe as old as sixteen, others no more than ten, all of them bound and huddled in the far corner.

Despair rocked Cassie as the gravity of the situation became clear. These girls had fallen into the clutches of wicked men with no scruples and no morals, monsters that traded in human capital. She shied away from imagining what the future might hold for them. For her and her sister, too.

A fresh wave of nausea left her stomach in a clench. Not good with her mouth taped shut. She didn't want to die today, certainly not by drowning in her own vomit. Several deep breaths helped clear her wits.

Her eyes adjusted. Insubstantial figures became individuals. Details emerged. The girl she'd heard weeping continued to cry. Two others whimpered even as some of the bigger girls shushed them. Eight Caucasians—a blonde, two redheads, and five with varying shades of brown hair—and four, the smallest of the bunch, with dark skin and skullcaps of tight black curls. All were bound hand and foot. All wore bruises and other signs of mistreatment.

Another moan drew Cassie's attention, this one from behind. She whirled around, muscles going limp with relief.

Mallory's head rocked side to side. Her eyes fluttered. A good sign, right? Not that she'd be much help in figuring out a way to escape.

A kernel of anger unfurled deep inside Cassie's gut. These men had stolen so much. How could she stop them? Glancing at the pitiful huddle of girls again, she locked gazes with one of the older captives. Hope shone there along with something else—expectation.

Cassie jerked her head in a beckoning motion at her

unlikely ally, and tried to look over her shoulder. "Mmmmm."

She repeated the gestures several more times as she scooted across the floor in a series of bumps and lurches until she reached the girl. "Mmmmm mmmm," she repeated.

The van would move soon. How could she make the girl understand?

The girl stretched her feet out and used them to inch her way forward until she sat side by side with Cassie.

Cassie wanted to laugh and cry. She moved her legs into a cross-legged position and leaned forward instead until her forehead rested against the girl's cheek.

Wavy blonde curls tickled Cassie's face as the girl returned the touch. They didn't have time for this, but both needed the few moments of comfort. Not too long, though. "Mm-mmm-mm-mm."

The muffled sounds meant to be words captured Blondie's attention. She drew back with a puzzled frown.

Cassie made the jerky motions with her head and shoulders again. When that didn't work, she twisted around and showed the girl her wriggling hands.

Nodding, the teen mimicked her movements. She spun on her bottom until she could show her own writhing hands.

Leaning over to study the bindings, Cassie wanted to shout a hallelujah. Maybe they had a chance after all. She knew knots, thanks to all her years in the rodeo, long hours spent roping calves, and working with livestock on her dad's ranch.

The simple handcuff knot used to bind the girls posed no problem for her.

She shifted some more until she could reach Blondie's hands. A little more … almost … there.

Another metallic complaint echoed outside. Cassie froze for a second but then resumed her exploration of the knots.

Deft fingers found the ends and worked them with meticulous precision through the first loop. The rope loosened and Blondie broke free.

The first thing the teen did was rip the duct tape from her mouth and launch herself at Cassie. "Thank you, thank you, thank you," she blubbered.

Sweet Sassy Molassy, but the girl was strong. "Mmmmf."

"Oh. Sorry." Blondie attacked the knot binding Cassie's hands.

With her hands free and the tape off, Cassie rubbed her chafed wrists. "Thanks. What's your name?"

"Rebecca."

"My name is Cassie. That's my sister, Mallory over there." She gestured to where Mal lay on the floor. "C'mon. Let's untie the others."

Rebecca nodded and scurried to one of the redheads.

Cassie went to her sister first. "Mal, are you okay?"

Mal's eyes opened. She pushed up to a sitting position, groaned, and lay back down with a hand raised to her head. "Feels like someone bashed me in the head with a Louisville

slugger. What happened? Where are we?"

"I'll catch you up in a minute. First, I need to help Rebecca free the others."

"Who's Rebecca? What others?"

Ignoring her, Cassie moved to the woman lying next to Mal and peeled away the tape on her mouth.

"Let me guess. You're the Cameron twins." The woman spoke with a faint Hispanic accent.

"Yeah. Who are you?" She started on the woman's hands.

"Ysolde Hermón." She sat up and rubbed the red marks around her wrists.

"The reporter from Seattle?"

She nodded. "I thought I made it clear you needed to stay away from these men."

"You did. And we tried. But serendipity can be a real shrew. Looks like you didn't take your own advice."

"I've been tracking these *monstruos* for three years." Ysolde's accent thickened with passion.

"You knew what they were up to, how dangerous they are, and followed them anyway?" Cassie's voice quivered with incredulity.

"The police think their Pacific Coast Highway crackdown did the job. They pat themselves on the back when the truth is, the operation simply moved."

"So, why don't you tell me what's going on here while we free the others."

Ysolde knelt beside one of the young, black girls. "Do you know of the Herrera organization?"

"Tell me." She leaned in closer to concentrate on another knot.

"They're a new world phenomenon. A group of small drug cartels joined forces and swept through South and Central America two years ago. I believe they're sourcing the recent wave of tainted Norco pills sweeping San Diego, LA, and San Francisco."

"You mean the stuff that makes those who ingest it super-crazy strong? And fries their brains?"

The reporter nodded. "There's more. Last year, Hererra started a systematic elimination of smaller cartels that have made inroads into the western United States. They intend to monopolize the transportation corridors."

"What transportation corridors?"

"The routes used to move drugs, weapons, alcohol, stolen goods, and recently, people."

"Human trafficking?" Cassie looked at the girls. She already knew the answer.

"Yes. They've now joined forces with a major organization in North Africa and have ties to several terrorist groups."

"You're talking about slavery and … sex trafficking?"

Ysolde shrugged. "A child costs little to maintain, is easy to replace, and cheap labor is always in demand. As for the

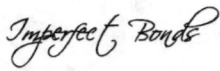

others, fair hair, colored eyes, and light complexions are a novelty among dark skinned cultures. Those with a political axe to grind in particular." She moved to another girl, this one with chestnut colored hair and big blue eyes.

Cassie swallowed hard, trying to dispel the image Ysolde's words wrought. "Can't those countries stop this?"

"It's a matter of economics and politics. Emerging third-world nations require cheap labor to pull them out of poverty. This perversion offers many perks for government officials, either direct from cheap labor, or indirect through bribery. Morality is a convenience only the rich can afford."

They reached Rebecca's side. Only two more girls left to free.

"The Middle East is a different story," Ysolde continued. "There are economic forces at play there, too, but also sociological implications. To them, fornication and adultery are major sins. For the leadership to acknowledge that a depravity such as sex slavery exists within their borders is tantamount to an admission of corruption. These are religious states. The governments are responsible for preserving traditions and upholding the religious laws. This 'hidden population,' as the abducted women are called, would severely challenge their religious and civil authority."

Cassie let out a soft whistle. "So they stick their heads in the sand and pretend the issue doesn't exist."

"Yes. It's easy to blame Nigeria, Cameroon, and other

African countries where terrorism has become commonplace. They kill their own, or worse, sell them like merchandise, but what about those who make the purchases?"

"Nigeria ... Boko Haram?"

"That is one. Understand, these men have no respect for human life, especially female lives. There are many markets in the Middle East, Europe, and parts of Asia. If they succeed in moving us out of the United States, no one will ever find us."

Cassie looked around the interior. What had she gotten herself and her sister into? They had to get out of here, but how? She touched Lucy's earring and took comfort in knowing Wade would track her and Mallory. Derek and the others would come for them.

She just hoped it was in time.

Forcing back disgust, fear, and a rising panic, Cassie focused on the first order of business—find a way out of the van. Preferably without Zavala or the others knowing. "So, how'd they catch you?"

"That serendipity thing you mentioned. I received a tip of a schedule change. They told me it would be the last run on this route, which meant my last chance to get my story. My cameraman and I planned to wait for them near the turnoff they take from 93 into the mountains, but they arrived early, before we could hide our car. We tried to get away, but the front tire blew. I hit a tree."

"Where's the cameraman? Please tell me they ..."

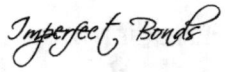

"Killed him? No. Gomez, the coward, ran off and left me."

Cassie's lungs burned. She released the breath she held with a renewed sense of hope. They didn't kill the cameraman, didn't kill Ysolde. "I know you're not really a reporter, but do you know you're lucky to be alive?"

Ysolde didn't respond. Neither could she hide the way her body trembled.

All the girls were free now. Time to check on Mallory.

Her sister sat slumped in a corner with her eyes closed. Her head rested against the wall. She didn't look good.

Cassie's own head still throbbed, but she pushed through the pain and pressed her ear against the door. Angry voices still argued in the distance. The scraping metal sounds continued as well.

She did a quick mental calculation. At least twenty minutes to make it down the mountain, another ten to the turnoff that led back to Route 93. She still had time to figure something out.

Moving to the rear door, she tugged on the lever. Her head fell forward. Of course it was locked.

"Don't tell me you'd jump from a moving vehicle." Ysolde followed close behind.

"That would require a way out." Cassie punched the door, and then flapped her hand to ease the sting.

No windows. No access to the cab. Solid floor. The rear

doors appeared to offer the only way in or out. No locks on the inside to pick. No tools to pry the door open. She frowned when an obscure memory of Jonas flitted through her mind. What did he have to do with doors?

The thought persisted until she worried it free from the deep recesses of the past. Jonas's first truck. A ratty old smoke-burning Ford he'd bought himself. It had a broken tailgate, a too loud muffler, and a door with a broken lock that wouldn't open. Only eight or nine at the time, she'd been too young to do much more than hand him the tools he needed.

Her eyes went wide as she looked with frantic haste around the van. "Help me search for something, anything we might use as a tool."

One girl dug in her pockets and pulled out a set of car keys. Another held out a couple of bobby pins. Yet another found a safety pin.

"I have a hair clip." Ysolde ran a hand through her hair and removed a plastic tortoiseshell claw-like clasp.

Yeah, all that stuff was about as useful as a milk bucket under a bull.

"Will my belt help?" One of the teenagers offered a thin, hot pink, leather belt.

"Maybe. Keep looking," she told them.

Running her hands over the rear door, Cassie found the ridged outline of the panel cover that hid the mechanical workings and pried at it with her fingertips. "Keys," she said to no one in particular. "I need the keys."

A moment later, the bunch of keys fell into her hand.

Using one, she worked it under the seam and ran the key higher up the side, all the way to the corner.

Ping.

A plastic clip popped free and dropped into the well behind the panel cover. Now she could worm her fingers underneath. She tugged. Yanked harder. Lost her handhold, and landed on her bottom.

Behind her, one of the girls giggled.

Fine. Scooting closer, she planted both feet on either side of the panel cover, got another handhold, and tugged again.

Ping, ping.

Two more clips gone.

Ysolde stepped in and grabbed the top side. "You pull the bottom. One, two, three."

The panel cover came free. Ysolde set it aside. "Now what?"

Lock rod. That's what Jonas had called it. A long metal stick that connected to the locking mechanism. When engaged, the door locked. Disengaged, the door opened. All she had to do was find it.

She groped the door again, this time searching for a niche, a recessed area, a well.

Outside, the truck's engine revved and then began to fade. Zavala was leaving?

Both front doors of the van creaked opened.

Cassie stopped, her breathing arrested.

None of the girls moved. No one breathed.

The van rocked with the weight of two men climbing in. A moment later the doors slammed and the engine turned over.

A sudden lurching movement threw Ysolde to her knees. They were moving.

Cassie braced herself and set to work again. Several long minutes passed before her fingers located two locking rods. A quick tug disengaged the first one, but the second played stubborn.

"Give me the belt." This was taking too much time. She wound the inch-wide hot pink strip of leather around the remaining rod, threaded it through the buckle, and yanked. Her knuckles banged against the metal rim and scraped off precious skin. Two nails broke. She lost her grip on the belt and tumbled backward. A bruised tailbone for sure this time.

Dadgummit. She sucked on her injured fingers to keep from howling in frustration. She got to her feet instead, grabbed the ugly pink belt, and yanked again.

The rod let go.

She stumbled and would have fallen again but for the crowd of arms that caught her.

A collective cheer made Cassie look up.

The left rear door stood open, wagging in a gentle back and forth motion.

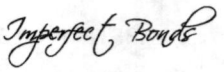

"You did it!" Ysolde's grip on her shoulder would leave more bruises.

"Are we really going to jump?" one of the older girls asked.

Cassie's plan, such as it was, had leaped ahead of her like a wildfire jumping a break. She had no idea what to do when—if—they made it out undiscovered. "Yeah, unless you have a better idea."

"How do we explain to the little girls?" Rebecca asked. "Some of them don't speak English."

"Those who understand can translate." Cassie scurried to her sister's side. "Mal? I need you to wake up." No way would she leave without her sister.

"Yeah, okay. The van's moving."

"Yep. Time for us to blow this place. Can you walk?"

"Not if I don't have to."

"You have to. Up you go." She hoisted her sister up. "Listen, the van is going slow. You have to jump out the back."

Mallory stared at Cassie like she'd found an exotic new species. "You hit your head, too?"

"Not joking. You're first up. Let's go. We got a dozen little girls to rescue, and you're leading the way."

"What?" Mallory looked around, saw the wide-eyed little girls, and clapped a hand to her mouth. "Oh my precious Lord, you aren't joking. What kind of heathens would kidnap children?"

"The worst kind, Miss Cameron. I am Ysolde Hermón. May I call you Mallory?"

"Is she for real?" Mallory whispered to Cassie.

"Yeah, she is. Ready?"

"No."

"Good. Let's go." Cassie guided her to the rear. "Ysolde, hold the door. Don't let it bang whatever you do. Rebecca, line the girls up and lead them over here. This is gonna go fast."

Rebecca nodded and hurried to the girls.

"Roll when you hit the ground. Ysolde will be right behind you." Cassie turned to the reporter. "I need you to look after my sister and gather up the girls as they jump. Get everyone off the road quick as you can and hide. Understand?"

The older woman nodded. "What about you?"

"I'll follow once the others are safe." Two of the older girls were first in line. The whole group of young ones stood behind them, some still weeping. The remainder of the teenagers would bring up the rear. And then her.

She squatted by her sister. "Ready Mal?"

Mallory looked anything but ready. "I guess so."

Ysolde held the door steady. "Sit on the edge, lean forward, and let yourself fall out. The impact will be less than if you force the jump."

Mallory did exactly as told. The van's momentum did the rest.

Cassie didn't wait to see if Mal got up. She took Ysolde's

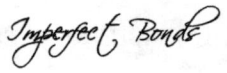

place at the door, and gave the woman a little shove. "Go."

"I just hope I live to write about this." Ysolde toppled out.

Rebecca's line followed like clockwork. Cassie gave each girl a quick squeeze and pressed them forward. Until the last one.

"She's fighting me," Rebecca said.

Huge frightened eyes filled the tiny girl's tear stained face. The van didn't slow on the next turn.

Cassie caught herself and the wailing little girl before they hit the floor. "Sh, sh, sh," she crooned and pulled the child into a hug. "It's okay."

The child wrapped herself around Cassie like a beach towel.

Rebecca fell on her hip with a grunt.

"The van is going faster, Cassie. We have to do this now." Rebecca crawled to the door.

"Wait." She tugged the earring from her ear and skittered across the moving van floor to the lock well. Plink. In went the earring. Wade could trace them now. They wouldn't get away with their crimes. She hurried back to Rebecca and the girl. "Okay. Go. We're right behind you."

Rebecca disappeared through the door.

Cassie whispered soothing inanities as she scooted toward the opening. The girl had no idea what she said, but seemed to take comfort from the tone. Clutching the child tight, Cassie scooted to the rear door, shoved it aside, and fell forward.

Chapter Twenty-Five

Never in a million years had Cassie imagined jumping out of a moving vehicle. One moment she sat perched inside, feet on the bumper, and the next she hit the ground with the girl's elbow in her ribs.

Hands lifted the child from her. More hands pulled Cassie to her feet. "Hurry," Rebecca said, urgency in her voice. "We have to get off the road."

Easier said than done. Breathing didn't come easy after having the wind knocked out of you.

Cassie staggered after Rebecca, unable to think. Not that it mattered. The human mind was wasted at a time like this, oxygen overrated. Her body took over with an overload of adrenalin, enough to ignore the pain, enough to move. Only one imperative existed—escape.

A terrified look back showed the van's taillights disappear around a turn. Then and only then did Cassie's lungs re-inflate.

Rebecca took the lead, gathering up the other girls as they retraced their path uphill.

Cassie kept one ear cocked for the sound of approaching vehicles from either direction, grateful her survival instincts

had finally kicked in. She never let the girls stray far from cover, sending small clusters of girls at a time to cross the open areas.

When they met up with Mallory, Ysolde, and the others, Cassie did a quick headcount. Relief lifted a heavy weight from her heart when she counted all twelve girls.

She studied each one with a frown. Not a single girl wore clothing fit for an overnight stay in the mountains. Heat baked the area during the summer days, but nighttime brought a different tale, especially in the mountain elevations. Temperatures dropped when the sun set. They had no water either. No food or shelter.

They'd been warm inside the van. Had she forced them from the frying pan into the fire? Maybe they should have stayed and waited for rescue.

Have a little faith, Cass. You've come this far.

Faith. A tough call when you couldn't see the next step. Not that they had much choice at the moment.

She took a deep, cleansing breath. They had no room for doubts, would deal with the hardships one at a time. The most pressing need at this moment was to get as far off the road as possible in the event Zavala and his cronies doubled back.

What would Derek do?

The thought brought comfort and renewed hope. He would come. She looked up at the densely forested mountain. Thick undergrowth, a steep incline, and rugged terrain made for a difficult climb. A glance over the side rail showed the easier path, but with less cover.

High road or low road? Hard or easy? Cassie assessed the group and made her decision. "We go up. As far as possible while it's still light."

A few sighs followed but not a single complaint. Her little band of refugees looked to her for leadership, with trust and expectation.

Praying she didn't fail them, Cassie put the younger ones in the middle and led her ragtag band up the mountain and into the forest.

Ysolde took Cassie's command to watch out for Mallory to heart. Draping one of Mal's arms over her shoulder, she supported, shoved, pulled, pushed, cajoled, and worked twice as hard as everyone else to get her charge up the hill.

Mallory's continued wooziness, headache, and occasional bouts of nausea—all classic signs of concussion—presented a growing concern. She needed medical attention, not an uphill hike. Cassie bit her bottom lip and continued to climb.

Rebecca appointed herself rearguard, which gave Cassie a huge boost of confidence. Becca wouldn't allow any of the girls to fall behind.

Zavala might not find them, but Wade could track the signal from Mallory's earring. And Derek would come. All she had to do was keep everyone safe until the cavalry arrived.

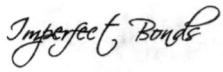

Derek pulled the Blazer to the side of the road and angled it so he could block the road if the targets got by and tried to turn north.

A glimmer of sunlight on chrome some five hundred yards away told him James had maneuvered his Yukon into a similar position on the south side.

"Keep your radios live. Be ready to move."

Fowler's raspy voice grated on Derek's nerves. No, not his voice, the reiterated commands. Missions were planned down to the second and covered every aspect of what could and probably would go wrong. They didn't have that luxury on this op.

Derek had always prided himself for his ability to stay frosty, impartial, and aloof. His teammates expected it. Counted on it. They got in, met the objective, and got out. Emotion had no place in a mission.

Except when family and loved ones challenged your objectivity.

"Copy," James responded.

"Ten-four," Derek said right after.

"Ten-four," Garrett repeated. "Synchronize watches. Time is … seventeen-oh-five. Team Three turning onto target road." Garrett's big red Dodge pickup moved into sight.

Now came the not-so-fun part. The hurry up and wait, and then wait some more. Derek stretched his neck, the popping sounds loud in the vehicle. He hated waiting.

"You okay, man?" Tony Rossetti, the olive-skinned agent from the Bureau asked from the passenger seat.

Sadeé whimpered from the backseat, mimicking Rossetti's concern. She'd taken a liking to the Italian.

"One of those girls …"

"Yeah, I got that much, but you need your head on straight."

Derek nodded. The man was right. "I'm good."

The minutes crawled by until Garrett's voice broke radio silence again. "Two vehicles approaching at slow speed. I repeat. Two vehicles. Green F-150 in the lead. White Econoline van close on his tail."

"Team Four moving in." Fowler's Suburban turned onto the mountain road. "Any sign of the girls?"

"Two men in each vehicle. The driver of the truck is Zavala. We are past both vehicles now. Wait … the back doors of the van are open. Negative on the girls. Say again, no one in the rear of the van. No sign of Cassidy or Mallory."

Four confirmed enemy, but where were the girls? Derek gnawed on his bottom lip.

"Roger," Fowler acknowledged. "Proceed according to plan."

This was it. As much as it galled him to sit on the sideline with Cassidy possibly in danger, he had to trust Garrett and Jonas to do their jobs. Fowler, too.

"Team Four is in position to intercept from the front."

The silence that followed was the longest of Derek's life. To keep his anxiety in check, he focused on his role should Fowler call them in. He and Rosetti would flank right, while James and his partner took the left, both teams waiting for a cue to engage the enemy. Under no circumstance would the targets be allowed to escape.

"Team Three now in position in the rear."

"Roger, Three. Teams One and Two, take up flanking positions. Let's nab our targets and go find those girls."

Derek kicked the Blazer into gear and made the turn onto the smaller road a second before James. Time to get dirty.

CCC

East Lake Road wound down from the mountains and flattened out into a long, straight valley. Dense stands of hardwoods filled most of the open space, leaving a wide shoulder that narrowed where the road intersected with Idaho 75.

Derek pulled onto the right shoulder, while James did the same on the left. With Fowler in the middle, they'd created a lethal, three-prong front. No way the truck or the van could get by them. With Garrett blocking them from behind, the targets were hemmed in.

Angry, anxious, and itching for a fight, Derek let his shark smile emerge.

"Hold position." Fowler's raspy voice barked over the radio. "Wade, I need a report on the GPS signals. Do you copy?"

The line crackled through Wade's response. "First signal is point-two miles from your present position, tracking straight at you, rate of speed twenty-three miles per hour and holding steady. Second signal is three-point-five miles behind the first, but tracking due east. Rate of speed is negligible for measurement. I think that one's on foot.

One in the van, the other one somewhere on the mountain. But Garrett said the van's cargo hold was empty. Did they have one of the girls stashed in the front? On the floor? Or maybe in the truck? The steering wheel creaked under Derek's fingers.

"Steady, man. We don't know anything yet," Rosetti said. When had he become the voice of reason?

Sadeé leaned forward from her perch in the backseat and licked Derek's elbow. Even the dog sensed his mood.

With ruthless determination, he shoved the raw emotions into a box inside the dark place of his mind, slammed the lid, and locked it. No feelings. No fear. No panic. Only ice. He needed the void, a place he could operate from without judgment or guilt. Cassie needed him detached and numb.

"We have them in sight. What is your position, Jonas?"

Fowler's voice pulled Derek back into the mission. Jonas was supposed to be with Fowler.

"Two minutes to position." Jonas's usually ebullient tone had disappeared, replaced by hard determination.

Fowler set a blue strobe on the roof of his vehicle. "Two

minutes. Confirmed. Report when you have line of sight, wind, and angle."

Derek frowned. Surprises were unwelcome in his line of work, those were sniper terms Fowler spouted. A quick search of the tree line on the side opposite him revealed nothing. No Jonas.

A green truck appeared around the curve ahead. A white van followed close behind. The two vehicles slowed immediately. Blue flashing lights had that effect.

Agent Fowler stepped out of the Suburban, careful to remain behind the passenger door, and raised a bullhorn to his mouth. Armored panels gave a man a lot of chutzpah.

"Step out of your vehicles and raise your hands above your heads."

Derek patted the AR-15 rifle, his weapon of choice for distance. If they closed with the tangos, he'd switch to the full frame Sig Sauer P-229. A 230-grain hydra-shock round almost guaranteed a kill shot if you hit the target's chest area.

Two minutes passed with no reaction from either vehicle.

"I have line of sight," Jonas' voice whispered." Two men in the truck. Two men in the cab of the van. No one else."

"Roger." Fowler raised a bullhorn to his mouth. "You are outnumbered. Throw your weapons out the window and step out with both hands in the air."

"Movement from the van," Garrett reported. "Passenger is sprinting to the rear."

"Intercept."

Gunfire erupted from behind the van. Derek had one hand on the door handle, ready to join the battle.

"Hold on, sport. Wait for the word. If we go, we go in hot. You put the gas pedal on the floor and I'll lay down covering fire."

Derek nodded. Normally, this conversation wouldn't be necessary, but he and Rosetti didn't know each other. They couldn't risk miscommunication.

"Two targets from the van neutralized," Garrett growled over the radio.

A block of ice settled in the region of Derek's chest. Not the time to consider the ramifications of what they hadn't found. Neutralize the threat first, interrogate, and then go looking for the girls.

Jonas spoke soft and low over the radio. "The driver of the truck—looks like Zavala—is fidgety. The passenger—he's wearing a suit—is on a cell phone."

Derek searched for Jonas again, in the trees this time. He had to be high up to see into the vehicles.

Again nothing.

"Wade," Fowler growled. "Talk to me. You said one of the signals is here. Verify."

"Coordinates confirmed. First signal is right in front of you. Lagging signal is still moving east at a snail's pace." Wade's voice hitched. He cleared his throat. "Looks like one of the girls got away."

The expected sucker punch didn't come. The hurt and guilt would hit later. Derek remained aloof, refusing to process the implications.

The standoff continued, but Derek and the others never blinked. But neither did the two occupants of the truck.

"Last chance, fellows," Fowler blared through the bullhorn. A moment later he spoke through the radio. "Jonas, on my mark, incapacitate the passenger and then the driver."

Derek blinked at the command. By his reckoning, the tree line stood a good five hundred yards from the truck. He could make a kill shot at three hundred yards. Farther on a good day. Heck, all SEALs could. Maybe even through the window. But aim to not kill the man?

Rossetti echoed his thoughts. "Whoa. The kid's got some mad skills if he can do that."

"Hold," James interrupted. "I see movement. Looks like they got the hint."

"Move in."

The Suburban with Fowler and Kuykendall inched forward. James and Moffett in the Yukon and Derek and Rossetti in the Blazer kept pace. Garrett crept around one side of the van toward the truck, while the two agents with him took the other.

Zavala got out on the driver's side, the snake visible on his upraised arms, a handgun still clutched in his hand but pointed at the sky.

Garrett dropped him with a chop to the neck.

The suit emerged from the passenger side. He held his hands in the air, too, without a weapon.

Six firearms were pointed at the two targets, seven if you included Jonas in his hidden perch.

James and Fowler approached Zavala and the second man, while the remaining team spread out to maintain a clear line of sight.

"Both hands on the hood. Spread your legs." James gave Zavala a helpful shove, patted him down, and cuffed him.

"My name is Sebastian Toure," the man in the suit said. "I am in the United States in an official capacity on behalf of the Nigerian government. I claim diplomatic immunity."

James shoved him toward the truck and proceeded to pat him down and cuff him.

Tall, well dressed, and obviously unused to such treatment, the man struggled and cursed in another language. After a second, he seemed to think better of his actions and calmed. "I called my embassy and notified them of your interference. They have my location, along with photographs of you, your men, and your vehicles. I insist you release me at once."

CCC

Over the past half hour, the incline had grown more difficult. Gnarled roots, deceptive vines, and decades of

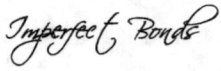

decayed foliage covered the ground and made the uphill trek even more treacherous. Now, with twilight upon them, they slipped, fell, and grappled their way up the slope.

Cassie grabbed a long, exposed root and pulled herself up. Maybe they should have set up camp at the last plateau.

"We have to stop, Cass. Please."

Mallory sounded exhausted. Cassie looked over her shoulder at her sister and the others. Tired and thirsty, they all would benefit from medical attention. A quick glance at the sky told her full dark would soon fall. They needed to make a camp while they could still see. "You're right. Let's backtrack to that flat area we passed five minutes back. I think that's the best we can do for tonight."

They turned like zombies and retraced their steps.

"Is this it?" Rebecca asked a few minutes later.

Cassie nodded. A dense pine thicket provided a windbreak for the small, bowl-shaped clearing. They'd need to huddle together for warmth through the night. The temperature would drop once the sun went down. "Yeah, this will do."

"We're thirsty," one of the older girls said.

"Hush, Nikki," Rebecca scolded. "We're all thirsty, but I don't see any water. Do you?"

Nikki hung her head.

"There are streams all through these mountains. Becca, you get everyone settled in for the night, and I'll go look for one."

"It's getting dark, Cassie. Probably not a good idea."

"I won't go far."

Half an hour later, the tinkling melody of splashing water brought a smile to Cassie's face. On the bank of a fair-sized stream she dropped to her knees and bowed down. Water never tasted so sweet.

Guilt tried to crawl in. With no way to carry water back and the others too weary to walk any farther, they would go thirsty tonight. And the dark made it dangerous. No matter. They'd come this far. She'd bring them at first light. And find food. Mallory had attended a survival course one summer. She'd know what they could eat and what to avoid.

On her return, Cassie scouted an area—not too far from camp, but not too close—that would suffice for bathroom needs. The last of the daylight had fizzled out by the time she reached the others. Satisfied with her efforts, she was startled and delighted to see a small flame flicker through the trees. Whoever had started a fire had earned their Twin Eagles Wilderness Badge tonight.

A ring of stones in the middle of the clearing contained a crackling fire.

Cassie grinned at her sister. "Your work, Mal?"

Mallory sat on the ground, her back against a tree. She looked better. "They did all the work." She waved at the others. "I just told them what to do. The temperature is already dropping."

"Did you find water?" Nikki asked with a hopeful tone.

"I did. It's a hike, and too dark to go tonight, but I promise we'll head out at first light. I found a bathroom area for us, though. It's close by. Who needs to go?"

Every hand shot up.

"I'll take four at a time … you, you, you, and you." She motioned to two of the teenagers and two of the young girls. "We go in a daisy chain. That means you hold the hand in front and the one behind. Got it?"

Less than an hour later, exhaustion took over. The girls curled up like a litter of puppies, arms and legs entwined in their search for warmth.

"I thought they'd come for us by now," Mallory whispered next to Cassie.

"Me, too."

Chapter Twenty-Six

Derek turned to the two Cameron brothers who'd stayed behind with him. "I swear, one of these days someone's going to put a few more holes in that man's head, and I might just volunteer for the job."

Jonas wore his typical amused-at-the-world grin. "I'd say James has dibs. Did you see the look on his face when Fowler ordered him back to town?"

Anger didn't begin to describe the fury that had poured off the sheriff. The man looked like he was wrestling a two-ton steer the way he tried to hold his temper in check. He'd gone along with Fowler, though, mostly because the press had gotten wind of a major drug bust going down and flooded the area. The last thing they needed was a passel of reporters mucking up the works. As the sheriff of Hastings Bluff, damage control fell to James. At least until the government jet arrived to haul the prisoners out of his jail and away from his town.

Fowler always got what he wanted … which apparently didn't include the twins.

Garrett didn't say a word throughout Fowler's and James's argument, but he did a good imitation of a ticking time

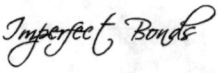

bomb. Clenched jaw, flaring nostrils—all the signs were there, including arctic blue eyes full of lethal intent. Trust was a hard thing to recapture, and Garrett trusted Fowler about as much as he did a snake. It hadn't always been that way between the two. Just since Fowler used TJ as bait in a bid to take down the notorious Honduran drug lord, Castillo. And almost got TJ and Garrett killed.

"I still can't believe he left us to search for the girls alone. He could have left one or two of his men. That's low, even for Fowler," Garrett finally grumbled.

"Kevin Fowler wouldn't leave if he thought we needed help," Jonas said with an air of quiet confidence. "He knows we'll find the girls."

Derek bent down to check the conceal carry holster in his boot, more to hide his surprise than any concern about the weapon. Jonas never took sides, especially not against his brothers.

"Maybe." Garrett sounded unconvinced. He removed his hat, swiped a forearm over his sweaty brow, and slapped the Stetson on again. "I'd bet good money the suit knows more than the other three together. I heard him speaking gibberish on the phone before he surrendered. Too bad about the diplomatic immunity."

"Hausa," Jonas said.

One of Garrett's eyebrows arched high. "What?"

"What's going on, Jo?" Derek didn't try to hide his

surprise any longer. "You're never like this."

"Like what?"

Like a predator without mercy, Derek thought. "Serious, thoughtful," he said instead. "Dangerous. That's not you. Or is it?"

For a moment he wondered if he'd overstepped. Everyone kept secrets they preferred to hold close to the chest. Men respected this line and never crossed it.

Did his brothers realize he had a dark side? From the speculative look on Garrett's face, he guessed not.

"Hausa is the language of Borno, a state in northeastern Nigeria." Jonas's mouth lifted in another jesting smile, almost like the world was his own private slapstick theater. Except this time, the lighthearted humor didn't reach his eyes. Had it ever?

"That's a pretty rough neighborhood, little brother. Nigeria, Chad, Niger, Cameroon … Bad stuff there." Garrett studied Jonas for a few seconds, as though he could dissect his brother's memories. "Not sure I want to hear how you know it."

"You don't."

So, Jonas had his own demons. It might be worthwhile digging into his service records once they found the girls. James would know how.

The thought of the girls brought a return of Derek's scowl. Although he'd never say it—and James wouldn't want to hear it—he was grateful his friend and boss didn't make him go

with Fowler instead. Derek wasn't sure he could've gone, not with Cassidy still missing.

Just the thought of her name set his hands trembling again. It hurt to breathe, that's how much he needed to find her.

Garrett answered his buzzing phone. "Yeah? Got it. Don't worry, man. We'll get her." He turned to Derek and Jonas, and yanked open the front passenger door of the Blazer. "Wade says the second signal is still on the move. Let's go find my sisters."

Putting two fingers between his lips, Derek whistled for Sadeé.

The German shepherd came running and jumped through the opened door into the backseat without a complaint—until Jonas climbed in beside her. She moved to the far side of the seat with a low grumble.

Good. Derek had chosen a German shepherd because of the breed's natural protective instincts. He'd picked Sadeé because of her calm temperament, for her direct and fearless—but not hostile—personality, and an innate aloofness that assured she wouldn't fall into any indiscriminate attachments. After six weeks of working with the dog twenty-four-seven, they built an unbreakable bond. He'd introduced Cassidy by using articles of clothing that carried her scent and then trained the dog to protect her. Now, Sadeé looked first to him as the alpha of their little pack of three, and to Cassidy when he wasn't around. Everybody else fell into one of two categories:

those who posed a threat, and those who didn't.

He took a moment to scratch behind her ears and marveled anew at how attuned she seemed to his emotional state. "We got this girl. We'll find her scent trail, and you can do your magic. Okay?"

Sadeé licked his wrist.

They left Garrett's truck parked on the side of the road and started up the mountain, Derek driving while the two brothers watched for signs that might lead them to the girls. When Jonas spotted what looked like footprints on the shoulder, Derek pulled over and let him out.

Jonas bent low and followed the trail up the mountain. A little more than a mile later, he climbed back in the truck. "Take us to the point where Wade said the signal diverged from the road."

They followed Wade's directions another half mile through a series of hairpin turns before Jonas got out again and motioned them to follow behind him.

Very little shoulder existed on the right side, the uphill lane. No more than three feet with an aluminum guardrail before it dropped away. The mountain allowed even less leeway on the opposite side where it formed a wall along the inside lane.

Jonas peered over the side every few feet but, otherwise, studied the ground with every step. At one point, he crossed to the other side, looked around for a few seconds, only to return

to climb into the back seat again. "Looks like a herd of cattle ran through here. I believe they crossed the road headed up the mountain over there, but I've seen no sign of Cassie's car. Let's continue a little farther."

They found a break in the guardrail after another ten minutes, sheared off and hanging by a flimsy strip of metal.

Jonas and Garrett were out of the vehicle before Derek brought it to a stop in the middle of the lane. They hurried to the side and peered over the edge.

"I see it," Jonas yelled. "About twenty-five feet down. We need rope."

With an order to Sadeé to stay, Derek sprinted to the rear of the Blazer, opened the hatch, and grabbed several lengths of nylon rope and a bag of D-rings. "Did you see …?" He didn't know how to finish his sentence.

"No movement." Garrett's hands moved like lightning as he fashioned a rope seat for himself and added a D-ring. He tossed the other end of the rope to Jonas. "Tie that off, I'm going down."

Jonas wove the rope around one of the guardrail posts with a secure knot. "Go."

Garrett dropped over the side, one hand holding the rappelling rope to his side to assist in his descent down the mountain.

On his knees, Derek peered over the side and got his first glimpse of Cassidy's red Honda wedged sideways between two large pines. Smashed. Crumpled. Shattered windows. The driver's door had been torn off and was nowhere to be seen. His vision blurred.

"See anything?" Jonas yelled.

"They're not here," Garrett yelled back.

Derek's vision cleared. Hope, that undying human trait, refused to give up.

"Looks like the airbag deployed. Passenger door's open. I'm going down a little further." Garrett lowered himself farther.

No explanation needed. Derek held his breath again. They had to know if either of the girls had fallen out.

Long minutes passed before Garrett's head appeared through the foliage. "Nothing. They're not down here. I'm coming up."

"Thank God," Jonas whispered.

Thank God indeed. Derek's hope grew a little stronger.

With the ropes stowed away, Jonas said, "Let's head back to where they started up the mountain."

"Grab that pink shirt from the back," Derek instructed Jonas. "Let Sadeé have a good sniff."

The weight of Garrett's gaze on him felt like a boulder. Derek looked over at him. "What?"

"Why do you have my baby sister's shirt?" The soft spoken question held more than mere curiosity.

Derek felt his face heat, not because he was guilty of

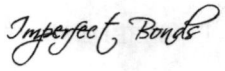

Garrett's suspicions, but because he wanted to be. The man would gut him if he knew of the dreams Cassidy all too often starred in.

"Sadeé knows Cassidy's scent. She can track your sister." Heck, how many times had he sniffed the darn shirt himself?

Garrett's expression didn't change, but he nodded. The silence still felt loaded but no longer dangerous.

Sadeé buried her nose in Cassidy's blouse and whined.

"I know, girl. Let's go find her." When the door opened, the dog bounded out and went to work. She raced one way, spun in a circle, ran off in another direction, returned—total confusion.

Garrett headed downhill from where they parked, obviously intent on doing his own survey.

Derek walked to where Jonas squatted and studied the dirt. "What do you think?"

"Two or three prints where you let me out. More joined them the higher they went. Tracks stop over there." He pointed uphill. "There's a dozen or more prints here."

"Who …?"

Jonas nodded and stood. "Good question. Come look at the other side."

Sadeé continued to twist and turn, visibly agitated. She'd start in one direction, stop and run off in another only to do it all over again.

"Look here." Jonas pointed at the disturbed ground and

trampled brush at the side of the road. "This is where they started their climb."

A sharp whistle brought Sadeé on the run.

Derek gave her another sniff of the shirt, pointed at the ground, and issued a one word command. "Find."

The shepherd dropped her nose to the ground and did that crazy zigzag search again. It didn't take long for her to find what she wanted. The dog's excited yips made his heart hammer. A few seconds later, her tail started wagging with furious intensity and she started to climb.

Cassidy was alive. "We got the scent," he called over his shoulder.

The going was rough in spots, enough so he had to use saplings and exposed roots to pull himself along. How had the girls managed? From the size of some of the footprints, a couple of them had to be quite small.

Jonas appeared behind him. "Garrett took off. He's going after Lucy. Looks like your dog ran off, too."

As if on cue, Sadeé appeared twenty yards ahead. She barked, made eye contact with Derek, barked once more, and disappeared again.

"Well, maybe not. You train Sadeé yourself?" Jonas fell in behind Derek.

"Yeah."

"Thought so."

They followed Sadeé as fast as their human limits

allowed. She returned again and again for them, leading ever upward.

Their speed slowed to a literal crawl once full dark fell. More than once he stumbled over the uneven ground until he was reduced to feeling for handholds.

"I'm amazed they made it this far." Jonas paused to wipe his face. His lungs billowed as hard as Derek's did. "You think maybe we should lay up until morning?"

"No. As long as Sadeé can track her, I'm following."

"Fine with me."

Excited barking erupted up ahead. And then voices.

Derek doubled his pace.

"You smell that?" Jonas asked.

Nose lifted high, Derek sniffed the air. Wood smoke. Somebody up ahead had survival skills.

A hundred yards farther, the incline leveled out into a small clearing where a dozen or more figures huddled around a tiny campfire.

"Derek?"

No sweeter sound existed. His heart swelled with relief, even as his eyes searched for her.

One shape rose and detached itself from the group and started toward him.

The world stood still when his arms closed around the most precious thing in his life. Tears stung his eyes, and he vowed to never let her go, but then Jonas stole her away.

"Cass, you okay?"

"Jonas?"

Shadows obscured her features, but Derek could hear the tears in Cassidy's voice. He needed the physical connection with her. His hand seemed to move of its own volition to touch her arm.

Jonas squeezed his sister like she might vanish if he let her go. He showed the world his irreverent, joking, quirky, and carefree side, but Derek had uncovered another side of the man today. A dangerous and sinister side, but also a soft and vulnerable one. The man was like a dadgum onion with all his layers.

"Is Mal …" Jonas's voice broke. "Is Mallory with you?"

She nodded and pointed toward the fire.

With a quick peck on her forehead, Jonas released Cassidy and hurried to find his other sister.

Cassidy tugged Derek's hand and followed after Jonas.

"Jo?" Mallory cried and staggered to her feet. "You came."

Jonas embraced her and then reached for Cassidy. "Of course, we came. You're my baby sisters." He kissed the tops of their heads.

Derek tried to hang back. The three of them needed this family reunion. But Cassidy wouldn't release his hand. She tugged him closer instead.

Sadeé forced her way into the middle of the laughing,

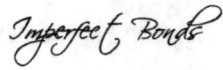

crying siblings. She wound through their legs, her bottlebrush of a tail slapping everyone. Excited little yelps articulated the dog's joy better than any words.

The magic subsided bit by bit until Derek became aware of a dozen or more pairs of eyes trained on them. The girls, some teens, others just kids, and a woman, huddled close together by the fire.

"Cassidy, you want to introduce us to your friends?" Derek whispered in her ear.

A huge smile stretched her mouth wide. "Oh, yes. I don't know all their names—some of them don't speak English very well or at all—but this lady is Ysolde Hermón, the reporter from Seattle who's tracked our van for months."

The older woman stepped forward and shook his and Jonas's hands. "Cassie saved us. We can never repay her."

"No I didn't. We all pitched in. We saved each other." She resumed the introductions. "This is Rebecca and Nikki and ..."

The names ran together. Even if he tried to remember them, there were too many to stick.

After a quick conference by radio with Wade, James, and Garrett to inform them of both Cassidy's and Mallory's safety, and the girls they'd rescued, Derek deemed it too risky to retrace their steps in the dark. The girls needed rest. They would wait for daybreak, visit the stream Cassidy had located, and make their way down. Wade, Garrett, and James would meet them at the bottom with enough vehicles to transport the girls to Hastings Bluff. Lucy, who was now safely back at the Triple C, and TJ would organize food, notify Doc Burdette to stand by, and rustle up fresh clothing for the girls and Ysolde. Kyle was already making the necessary calls to the authorities and the girls' families.

Logistics out of the way, Derek scrounged up additional wood to stoke the fire during the night while Cassidy told the story of how she'd learned about door locks from Jonas.

"Got a question for you, sis," Jonas said to Cassidy. "Why'd you go up the mountain? It's a darn sight harder climbing up, especially for the little ones."

"That very reason. It's more difficult. I thought if we got away from the road and climbed as far as we could, Zavala and his pals might find it too much trouble to come after us. I knew Wade could find us using the signal from Lucy's earring."

Her voice, with the fire crackling softly in the background, created a soundtrack he stored in his memory. The low timber, a bit raspy this late at night, ignited his senses.

"Speaking of which, where's the second earring?" Derek asked. "Wade says the signal's still live and pointing to the van, but James said he couldn't find it."

Cassidy's face lit up in a mischievous grin. "I dropped it in the lock well with the broken rods. Just in case. I didn't want them to get away."

Derek chuckled. Leave it to Cassidy to have the last laugh. "James said he all but tore the vehicle apart looking for it."

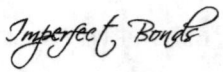

None of them missed when Mallory sniffed and turned away.

James had hurt her by not coming along on the search. She didn't understand the kind of pressure Fowler could apply. Probably wouldn't care if she did. The bottom line in Mal's eyes was he didn't see her as important. He'd chosen duty while Derek had moved heaven and earth to find her sister.

Rough seas lay ahead if James had any hope of worming his way back into Mallory's good graces. If he could. If he even wanted to.

A long time later, slow regular breathing filled the night. Weary to the point of exhaustion the women and girls all slept while Derek and Jonas kept watch. The little flock was their responsibility now. And some habits a soldier couldn't—or wouldn't—break.

Derek sat against a tree with a gently snoring Cassidy draped across his chest. A man could get used to having a beautiful woman in his arms. Smart, sassy, feisty, and humble. Brave, too. She'd put her own life at risk for the others. Who knew warriors came in all shapes and sizes?

Chapter Twenty-Seven

The nocturnal sounds faded away, having succumbed once again to morning. The daytime world stirred.

A small brown fox crept through the underbrush not twenty feet away from where Derek sat. It paused, appearing unafraid at the sight of so many humans in its habitat. Derek followed the animal's progress without turning his head. Throughout the night he'd caught glimpses of a marmot, a few mule deer, and a lone coyote, none of them a threat. The bigger animals that roamed these mountains concerned him more, predators like cougars and bear. Most wildlife kept their distance, leery of so many humans bunched together. They feared people almost as much as they did fire. Still, he'd kept watch. The treasure he and Jonas protected was too precious to risk.

A thin tendril of smoke spiraled up from the almost dead fire. He'd stopped adding wood a few hours ago, since they planned to leave at first light. With no water to soak the ashes, he'd make sure to bury whatever remained with dirt.

Cassidy shivered in his arms and snuggled tighter against him.

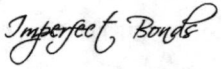

He'd have to wake her soon. For now, though, he wanted to savor the feel of her. A lifetime of waking with her in his arms wouldn't be enough.

One by one, their small group came awake. Some yawned, a few stretched after sleeping on the hard ground, but most just sat up and looked around in confusion.

They'd need Cassidy's 'bathroom' again, and then a trip to the stream she'd found. He squeezed the warm bundle in his arms. "Time to wake up, Baby."

A smile tugged at her rose petal lips. Her eyes open to reveal dark blue pools of groggy contentment. "Good morning."

She mesmerized him. Her smile enchanted while her husky, sleep-raspy voice inflamed. Like one of the sirens of mythology, she'd lured him in and stolen his wits. And he liked it. He looked her up and down. Rumpled, dirty clothes, frightful hair, and a streak of mud on her forehead—she'd never looked more beautiful.

Using his shoulders as a brace, Cassidy pushed to her feet and assessed the others.

"Uh, Cass?" Mallory called from the other side of the clearing where she sat next to Jonas. "Water?"

Cassidy nodded and waved one hand in a follow me gesture. "We can stop by the, er, facilities on the way."

That garnered some chuckles and a couple of "hurry" comments.

Twenty minutes later, they heard the welcome sound of running water.

"Be careful, everyone," Cassidy called out. "I didn't have enough light to scout the area last night. Watch your footing."

Derek looked at Jonas and nodded to the left. The stream meandered the mountainside from above in a series of sweeping turns to where they stood. From that point on as far as he could see, the riverbed ran almost straight down. Not dangerous if you were careful. Only six feet at its widest, and no more than two to three feet deep, but the current moved fast enough to sweep a smaller person off their feet. "Keep the girls with you. Drink upstream, wash downstream, but don't let them wade into the water. And no one goes off by herself. Got it?"

Cassidy bristled. Her lips compressed into a tight line, but she acquiesced with one sharp nod. "Where are you going?"

"Perimeter check. I'm heading up, Jonas will look downstream. A safety precaution. If there's any wildlife in the area, we'll scare them off."

She frowned.

"Hey," he leaned in to whisper against her skin. "We want to give you girls some privacy while you wash up."

The lines in her forehead smoothed out. Cassidy might have the heart of a warrior, but that didn't mean he could treat her like one. He'd have to remember to temper his tone with her. Succinct, no nonsense, maybe even abrupt and harsh, that

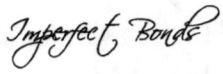

was the language of fighting men the world over. Civilians preferred nice. Soft-hearted women deserved more.

He looked back again before stepping out of sight.

A dozen girls squirmed like hungry puppies as they vied for access to the water. Four of them knelt shoulder to shoulder at the edge of the stream, cupping water into their mouths as fast as they could.

Derek chuckled. Cute.

Jonas found a place where he could jump across. With a final wave, he disappeared into the brush and trees.

CCC

Cassie waited to drink until the others had a turn. She'd had her fill the night before when she discovered the stream. It was only right she wait now.

When the first four girls finished, she herded them a few yards downstream and pantomimed washing her face. "Wash."

During the uphill trek yesterday, Cassie learned the younger girls came from Nigeria and, while English was the primary language, several of the girls came from remote villages and spoke only a local dialect.

Ekemma and Orise, the two girls with the best command of the English language, giggled and translated for the others now. They'd tried to teach Cassie their names and a few words from their dialect but had difficulty with the pronunciation.

"Yarinyar," Ekemma pointed to the others one at a time. "Little girl."

"Yarinyar." Cassie nodded and repeated it several times.

One of the girls rolled up her pants legs and waded into the water.

Cassie motioned her back. "No, no. It's too dangerous. Ekemma, tell her to come back. Not safe."

A string of incomprehensible mumbo-jumbo followed. The girl in the water shook her head and pointed to a nasty scrape on her shin and took another step. The water reached her calves now, swirling around her with enough force to make her stagger and readjust her footing. She bent down to clean the abrasion.

Cassie understood the need to clean the wound, but watching the girl try to maintain her balance on the slick rocks launched a fleet of bumblebees in her stomach. Her breath hitched with every awkward move until, finally, the girl started for shore.

The other four Nigerians had joined them and were gleefully taking off their shoes and socks. Some stripped off their pants.

"No, no. Ekemma, tell them no," Cassie yelled as the newcomers splashed into the stream. "Orise, get them out."

The girls in the water ignored the commands or perhaps couldn't hear them above their squeals and shouts.

In full panic mode, Cassie shucked her tennis shoes and socks, but didn't bother rolling up her jeans. She plunged in after them and grabbed the arm of the first girl she came to.

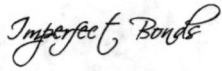

Shaking her head, she shouted "No," over and over while pointing toward the bank. The girl cowered from her and scurried from the water. A second one soon followed and then a third.

Sadeé waited on the bank and herded the drenched girls away from the stream using her fiercest bark.

The last girl had a brave streak, though. She wanted to play. With a grin that showed every one of her white teeth, she danced away, challenging Cassie to catch her.

"No," Cassie pleaded, frantic as the water rose higher on the girl's legs. "It's too dangerous. Come out."

"What are you doing?" Mallory screamed from the bank.

Cassie spared a glance and saw Mal, Ysolde, and Rebecca had moved the other girls well back from the water. Sadeé didn't seem too happy, but she stood guard, looking from the girls to the water and back again.

Enough playtime. She lunged for the remaining girl in the water and caught her wrist.

The girl shrieked with laughter, went limp for a moment, and then jerked away. Her wrist slipped free … but then she lost her balance and went under.

"No," Cassie yelled and made a desperate scramble to reach her.

The current was too strong. The girl couldn't regain her footing. With nothing to anchor her, the rushing water swept her downstream.

A cacophony of screams erupted from the bank.

"No!" Cassie stared after the girl. Derek told her to keep them out of the water. This was her fault. The child wasn't strong enough to save herself.

Without another thought, Cassie waded deeper into the water and followed after the child.

"Cassidy Cameron, no!" Mallory yelled, terror in her voice. "You come back here this minute."

The stream was narrower through here. And deeper. Water rose to her hips in the middle of the channel. Chest deep for the girl. Cassie shuffled her feet as hard and fast as they would move against the current, but not all the rocks on the bottom were smooth.

Something sharp punctured the tough skin of her heel. The reflexive flinch left her trying to stand on one leg. Why hadn't she left her shoes on?

A couple of hops almost got her balance back, but the water had other ideas. She went under, came up spluttering, but couldn't get her feet under her. Worry over losing the girl disappeared as the current swept her away. How could she save another when she couldn't save herself?

Rocks pummeled her feet, legs, arms, hips, and shoulders. Somehow she kept her head above water and avoided cracking it again.

The girl appeared ahead. By some miracle, she'd managed to snag a low hanging branch.

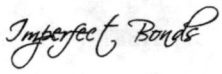

Cassie instinctively reached for the same limb, knowing it might not hold her additional weight. She reached, caught the limb and the girl at the same time, and held on. For a moment she thought it might hold.

Snaaaap.

CCC

Derek stopped to splash his face and gulp down some water. He'd climbed far enough to give the girls privacy, but could still hear them laughing and chattering. Ten more minutes and he'd head back down. The sooner he got them out of these mountains the better. They all needed a bit of medical attention, not to mention food.

A scream brought him to his feet. Several more screams sent him sprinting through the trees back the way he'd come. He lost count of the times he tripped and fell. The third tumble jarred some sense into his head. If he got hurt, who would help them?

He slowed his pace, chose his way with care, but still hurried faster than the terrain allowed. The screams and yelling continued. Something was bloody well wrong, and he'd left them alone.

The girls had moved farther down from where he left them and stood crowded together near the stream. Mallory had her hands cupped around her mouth, yelling, "Jonas. Derek."

Sadeé waded into the water.

Derek whistled her back, but for the second time ever, she

hesitated. "Sadeé. Heel." His tone allowed no room for argument.

The dog left the water, shaking her coat and flinging water everywhere.

No sign of Cassidy.

"Mal," he called. "Where's your sister?"

Mallory sprinted to meet him and almost knocked him over. "One of the girls ..." She pointed at the water. "Cass went in ... They're gone." Sobs shattered through Mallory.

When she collapsed, Derek let her slip to the ground. He hurried to the stream's edge, strode into the stream, and peered downstream. No sign of them. And no wonder. The pull of the current against his legs was strong. A child wouldn't stand a chance. Cassidy might, but not with a struggling child in tow.

He waded back to the bank. Turning to Ysolde, he said, "Stay here. Don't leave. And stay out of the water. I'm going after Cassidy."

She nodded, eyes wide with fear.

He started off downhill with Sadeé dashing ahead, following and searching the stream as they ran. Fifty yards down, he spotted movement on the other side.

Jonas and Derek saw each other at the same time.

"Thought I heard a scream. What's going on?" Jonas yelled.

"One of the girls fell in. Cassidy went after her. Both got swept downstream. I told the reporter to keep the girls there.

You search from that side. I'll continue on this one."

The going proved difficult in places, slowing Derek almost to a standstill at one point.

Sadeé wasn't deterred. She scrambled down and waited for Derek.

Their route sometimes wound away from the stream, but always veered back. When he could get close enough, he searched upstream and down for any sign of the girls.

"Cassidy." He'd yelled her name so many times his voice was hoarse.

The current churned into whitewater at one point, the descent much too steep. Cassidy's pretty little stream had morphed into Class III rapids.

Jonas stood across the stream from him. He looked upstream and then downstream. And went still.

Derek looked where he pointed … saw the drop off.

Cassie kept her arm locked around the girl's waist as they plunged into the current again. The rocks in the riverbed bounced and bruised them both while sweeping them downstream. The channel deepened through a natural gorge. Her toes touched bottom only now and then. The incline steepened here, the current faster.

The child had a stranglehold around her neck, but it took all of Cassie's strength to keep them pointed feet first and holding their heads up.

A loud roar emanated from up ahead and fear surged anew.

Cassie held tight to the little girl. She wanted to laugh at the absurdity of it all. They couldn't have escaped from a fate too horrible to contemplate only to fall over a waterfall to their deaths. She didn't even know the kid's name.

"Shhh, Yarinyar," she whispered, remembering Ekemma's teachings.

She hugged the child tighter … and watched the end approach. Thank you, Lord, for saving Mallory and the others.

The girl heard the roar, turned, and saw the drop off at the last moment. She let out a watery scream and tried to climb up Cassie's body.

Cassie lost her grip on the girl, and then they swept over … weightless … and plummeted toward a pool of water below.

The girl screamed, her arms and legs flailing. Terrified. And Cassie couldn't reach her. Couldn't help her. Couldn't even help herself.

Instinct took over. She righted herself and entered the water feet first. Icy. Bone-cracking cold. And deep.

Thank You, Jesus.

Desperate for air, she kicked for the surface and broke through with a gasp. A fish bowl. They landed in a pool surrounded by huge boulders. At least the water was calm here.

A frantic, gurgling sound pulled her around.

The child struggled in the middle of the pool, arms and

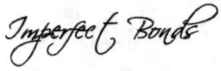

legs thrashing the water. Her head was arched backward. She went under, fought back up choking, only to go under again. She couldn't swim.

Cassie closed the distance between them with quick strokes and realized the danger hadn't gone away. Placid on the surface maybe, but the current remained strong underneath, a relentless pull. She looked around. Another drop. Twenty-five feet away.

In full, mindless panic, the girl fought like a wild animal. She clawed at Cassie and almost got another stranglehold around her neck.

Cassie let them sink under the water.

As anticipated, the child released her and struggled to reach the surface.

This time Cassie managed to turn her around and wedge a forearm around the girl's neck, not tight enough she couldn't breathe, but enough to keep her face up and out of the water. And neutralize her struggles.

Cassie took a couple of much needed breaths and began to sidestroke toward the side of the bowl. They had to get out of this freezing water. Already tired from yesterday's events, no food, and too little sleep, Cassie's muscles quivered. She couldn't tread water for long, not while fighting the current's pull and the hysterical child.

She expended precious energy while making her way around the bowl, searching every inch of the rock enclosure.

Not a crack or crevice to be found. It was as though Mother Nature had polished the stone smooth over millions of years for the sole purpose of trapping unwary trespassers.

Furious barking erupted above.

"Sadeé! Stay!" Bless the dog's heart, she'd found them. But Cassie wouldn't put it past the crazy dog to jump in to try and save them. Instead, she yelled. "Derek. Find Derek."

The shepherd whined, darted away, and returned.

"Go," she cried. Her tears ran too close to the surface now. Sadeé had come but couldn't rescue them. "Find Derek. Please."

He would come, she knew in her heart he would come. He wouldn't give up until he found her. But would it be in time? Cassie gave herself five minutes before her muscles succumbed.

Chapter Twenty-Eight

The stream zigzagged down the mountainside in gentle loops side to side. Until now. For the past twenty yards or so, the water rushed in an almost straight line, the angle of descent increasing. Not good.

Derek stepped onto an outcropping to peer upstream Nothing.

"See anything?" Jonas called from across the way.

"No." Derek looked the other way, but the stream—almost a river now—took a sharp left. The hope he'd held onto was slowly turning to despair.

No. He jumped from the flat rock and started downhill again, following the water's path. He refused to give up. They would find her. They would find her.

A small voice whispered inside his head, a warning of what they might find once they located her.

"No." The unspoken word shouted inside his head. "She's okay. She's okay." *Lord, please let her be okay.*

Sadeé's excited yipping cut through the quiet of the still waking morn.

Derek increased his speed, never breaking stride. He

dodged low hanging limbs but couldn't avoid the twigs, vines, and underbrush that slashed at his face. He swatted them away as best he could and stumbled on toward where the dog continued to bark.

A separate part of him registered Jonas on the other side keeping the same breakneck pace.

The ground dropped straight down, slowing him more than he wanted. Too steep, too steep, ran through his head as he jumped down in some spots, climbed in others, and slid on his butt in one.

The dog's barking drew him on until he found Sadeé doing a frantic back-and-forth dance atop a boulder that towered above him at twice his height.

Derek ran his hands over the rock, searched for handholds, footholds. Nothing. A stand of young pines stood adjacent to the boulder. They might hold his weight. If he could get high enough without them breaking, he might be able to jump to where the dog paced.

How in the world had the four-legged mutt gotten up there?

He searched further, following the granite base downhill to where it met a steep embankment … and found the disturbed area where Sadeé had clawed her way up. Following her trail, he never faltered at the four-foot jump to the flat-topped boulder.

"Find Derek, girl. Find Derek."

Cassidy's voice. Fierce joy filled him but was devoured by a white hot despair an instant later. She sounded so breathless, weary, so … defeated.

He dropped to his knees and peered over the side.

The rocks had formed a natural basin at the bottom of the falls, a perfectly round bowl filled with water. "Cassidy!"

"Derek?"

He spotted her then, close to the bank, almost directly below him. She had the girl, had an arm around her neck to keep her afloat.

"We need help." Strained. Tiring.

He looked around, assessed the situation. Inside of the basin appeared polished. Smooth. With nothing to cling to. And too far away for him to reach her. "You need to find a crack, something you can get your fingers into."

"Already looked," she spluttered. "All the way around. Smooth as a robin's egg."

"Can the kid swim?"

She shook her head.

"Can you get her to float?"

Another head shake. "She'll panic. Take us under."

"Okay. Hold on, Baby. I'll figure something out."

"Current's strong, Derek. I don't know …"

"Hold on, you hear me? Keep fighting."

He could see her strength waning. She was fighting against odds she couldn't hope to beat. Heck, it was a miracle

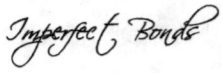

she and the girl still lived after being swept downstream, banged against who knew how many rocks, and dumped over a precipice. But Cassidy couldn't last much longer, not in icy cold water, not against a terrorized kid.

She pointed toward a break in the rocks where the water spilled over in a smooth curtain.

Derek froze at the sight of another waterfall. The blasted current was pulling them toward another drop. "Don't you give up on me now, Cassidy. Hold on. I'll get you out."

"Incoming," Jonas yelled. He'd found some kind of vine and swung across the river in a fair imitation of Tarzan. Crazy, risk-taking fool. But like the well trained operative Derek was coming to believe him to be, Jonas tucked, rolled, and sprang to his feet, graceful as a ballerina.

"She can't last much longer. We need a rope."

"Cassie!"

"Cass!"

Jonas jerked around at the new voices.

Derek looked over his shoulder.

"Over here," Jonas yelled. He turned to Derek with a grin. "It's Garrett and Wade. Looks like the Rangers finally arrived."

Garrett and Wade burst through the trees. "Where's Cassie?" They both asked at the same time.

"She and one of the girls went over the falls," Jonas pointed above and then below. "They're in the pool down there. We need your rope."

"Length?"

Derek looked down for an estimate and his heart almost stopped. Cassie's head dipped below the water. She'd almost run out of gas. "Fifteen feet. She's in trouble. Hurry."

The kid went wild. She fought, kicked, and finally succeeded in climbing on top of Cassidy, pushing her head below the water.

"Oh, heck, no." He shrugged off his pack and dumped his guns—no time to shed the boots—and jumped into space.

Plunging feet first into the water, the icy cold impact sent shock waves through his body. No surprise. He'd trained in worse than this. In two seconds, he reached the struggling pair, yanked the little rug rat away, and pulled a gasping Cassidy up.

"Stop," he growled at the little girl and gave her a rough shake.

The kid went still as a rabbit cornered by a wolf.

"Toss the rope, Jonas!" Derek bellowed.

This could be tricky. He could swim forever, tread water even longer. Could even manage to do so while supporting another person … but two? "You okay, Baby?"

"Yarinyar?"

"What?"

"The girl. Yarinyar," she gasped out.

"I've got her. She's fine. You I'm not so sure about. Can you hang onto my shoulder? The current's pulling us away from the wall."

She nodded.

This untrained slip of a woman had more heart than a lot of the men he knew. But she was fading fast. Her movements had turned jerky, all grace gone.

"Jonas?"

"I'm here." His smiling face peered over the rock. "You having fun yet?"

"Don't make me kick your butt. Get me that rope. Now."

"One rope with a seat harness on its way."

"You hear that, Baby? Your brothers are here."

"Take her f-f-first." Cassidy's teeth chattered.

How had she stood the cold so long? His own muscles had started to twitch. "Can you keep yourself afloat for a few seconds while I get the kid set?"

Another nod. Talking required too much energy.

The kid wanted nothing to do with the rope harness.

Derek finally resorted to brute force and stuffed the kid in the rope seat Jonas had fashioned. "Give me some more slack," he yelled.

More rope dropped. Derek used the excess to wrap the kid's arms and legs, immobilizing her. "Pull her up, but go easy. I had to tie her."

The traumatized child squeezed her eyes closed and whimpered with each bump and scrape.

As soon as the kid cleared the water, Derek locked an arm around Cassidy's waist and pulled her close. "I got you, Baby.

We'll have you out of here in a minute. Let me do the work now."

Her arms flopped around him, her face nestled into the crook of his neck and shoulder, and then she went limp.

Using his free arm, he kept them close to the rock. How could such a wrong situation feel so right? He rubbed his chin over the top of her head and offered up a silent prayer of thanks. Maybe there was something to this God of hers.

After what seemed like forever, but in all likelihood took no more than a minute, Jonas yelled again. "Incoming."

The rope floated down again like a gift from heaven. "Your turn, Baby. Lift your leg up. Good, now the other one." He secured her in the seat harness.

"Your brothers will do all the work now. All you have to do is hold on and use your feet to walk up the rock. Okay?"

"Garrett and Wade are here, too?"

"Yeah. Up you go now."

"My arms feel like Jello," she croaked.

Even papery thin, he still loved her voice. "I believe you can do anything. Hold on now."

She tightened her grip.

All the anxiety flowed out of him when she disappeared over the top. Safe.

"Rope," Jonas yelled. "You need me to haul your carcass up the wall?"

Derek didn't grace the ridiculous question with an answer.

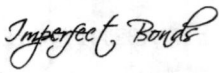

Instead, he caught the rope and pulled himself hand over hand out of the water until he could wind his feet in the rope. Using the break and squat method, he brought his knees to his chest, reacquired the rope with his feet, and reached up. Less than a minute later, he crawled over the boulder and slid down to the ground to Cassidy's side.

"She's beat, man." Jonas had doffed his long-sleeved camo jacket and wrapped it around his sister. Wearing only a short-sleeved t-shirt, he'd get scratched up aplenty on the trek down to the cars.

Cassidy had a hand on Sadeé's head and an arm around the girl. Garrett had handed over his jacket for the kid. The 2X size looked like a tent around her small frame.

"Wade and I are heading back to where Mallory's keeping the girls. We left James there to look after them. I figure it'll take us thirty minutes or so. We'll herd them down to the vehicles from there. You and Jonas stay here with Cassie and the kid. Give them an hour or so to rest and then wind your way down. We'll meet up at the bottom." Garrett clutched Derek's shoulder. "Thanks for saving my baby sister, man. I don't know that I can ever repay you."

"Ditto," Wade added with a slap on Derek's back.

Derek stumbled forward a step. Sheesh. The man was a behemoth, and strong as one of those buffaloes he tagged and monitored. Didn't recognize his own strength. Or he liked jerking with men smaller than him. No matter. They didn't owe him anything. He hadn't rescued Cassidy. He'd rescued himself. Sweat beaded on his forehead despite dripping wet and still frozen from the submersion in the icy mountain water. The thought of what might have happened had he arrived five minutes later …

He didn't finish the thought. Couldn't go there. Instead, he stripped off his sopping jacket, squeezed what excess water he could from it, and spread it on a branch. The boots and socks came next. An hour to let the girls rest. Not nearly enough time to dry their clothes and his boots, but they'd manage.

The two brothers clapped Jonas on the shoulder and then stopped to hand Cassidy and the little girl something. Their shoes. They'd brought their shoes. Thank goodness. They'd need those to get down the mountain. Otherwise, he and Jonas would be carrying them on their backs the whole way.

Derek smiled at the thought, kinda liking the idea.

CCC

"What time is it?" Cassie murmured in Derek's ear.

"Coming up on noon. Hang on, Baby. We're almost there." Derek squeezed her legs.

Twenty minutes ago, after having stumbled and fallen four times in as many minutes, she'd accepted his offer of a piggyback ride. He'd slipped his pack onto her shoulders, squatted down for her to climb on his back, locked his arms under her knees, and stood again without any effort. Not even a grunt.

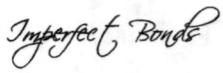

Once it became apparent the little girl couldn't keep up, Jonas had hoisted Yarinyar onto his back right after they set off.

Sadeé led the way, never ranging far ahead.

Hunger gnawed at Cassie. She ached in more places than she thought possible, but it was the weariness that passed all comprehension. Cassie couldn't remember ever being so tired, not even after the week-long roundup her father had once allowed her to go on. She'd never asked to go again.

Concern over her appearance had fled a long time ago. Heck, in the past twenty-four hours she'd been run off the road, crashed into the side of a mountain, pummeled by an airbag, drug by her hair, bound, kidnapped, jumped from the back of a moving vehicle, herded a small army of children up the mountain, got swept downstream in a river, beaten and bruised by the rocks, fallen over a waterfall, and half drowned by a panicky kid. She'd earned the right to look a little bedraggled.

"I hear voices." Jonas had taken the lead, and increased his pace. "Not far now.

Flashing blue and red lights appeared through the thinning underbrush. The welcome party had arrived.

Strong arms lifted her from Derek's back. "Hey, Sprite."

"Daddy." She wrapped her arms around him and gave in to the tears. Through all the terror and desperation, she hadn't cried once. Why now?

He carried her over to the one of the two Emergency

Response Team trucks and set her down.

"Sit here, Cass. Let's check you out." John Bertrand, a boy who'd graduated in her high school class, gave her a reassuring smile. He wore a paramedic uniform and a pair of blue medical gloves.

"Hey, John. You're an EMT, huh?"

"Yeah. And you're a mess."

She pressed for a smile, not sure she succeeded, and plopped onto the floor facing the open rear doors. Déjà Vu. The last time she'd been in this position, the road had risen up to kiss her. Some of her bruises and scrapes were evidence of the meeting.

He handed her a bottle of Gatorade. "Drink. You need to replenish your electrolytes."

"I'd rather have a plate of Mom's French toast and half a cow in bacon."

He laughed. "I know you hurt all over, but show me the worst places."

Once he finished, Mallory, Ysolde, and the other girls from the van crowded around, all talking at once.

Cassie heard only snippets.

"Dehydrated."

"Hungry."

"Bath."

"Sleep."

"Mom and Dad."

"Home."

"Cell phone."

The subdued group from the van stood chattering with each other, even the ones who spoke no English rattled on in their own language.

Cassie looked around. Derek's truck stood off to one side with Dad's truck behind it. And James's Yukon with the flasher going. Garrett's big Ford. The two Emergency Response Team vehicles. "Where's my car?"

Wade came over and gave her bear hug. "Don't worry. We'll get you another one."

What? She loved that car. After returning the squeeze, Cassie pushed away and stood up. Looked right. Left. "Did you already haul it off?"

"Uh, Cass," Garrett appeared at Wade's side. The two of them blocked her in. "It's done for. Let it go."

She sidestepped them and walked toward the small group peering over the embankment.

Dad stood there shaking his head.

James had an arm around Mallory's shoulders.

Mallory had a hand clapped over her mouth.

The other EMT whistled.

"Baby, you don't need to see this." Derek hooked an arm around her waist.

"Is that my car?" She stepped away but took his hand and tugged him along. She still needed an anchor.

The sight sent a wash of shivers through her. The little red Honda purchased the day after high school graduation. She'd saved for four years to buy the used car, and now it lay some fifteen or twenty feet below, sprawled in a snarl of trees. Bent, misshapen, battered, and shattered, it looked nothing like the Civic she'd driven for the past seven years.

"My stuff. My equipment. Can't you get a winch and pull it up?" She turned to Derek. "You know how to use power tools, don't you?"

He snorted. "Cassidy, I'm a Navy SEAL. I am a power tool."

Baaashhhw.

Four fake sneezes broke in sequence behind her, one each from Garrett, Wade, Jonas, and James.

"Glad you finally admit it, dude. I don't know about that power part, though." Jonas grinned.

Chapter Twenty-Nine

"Ladies, I'm sorry you got dragged into this. Please know that the United States recognizes and appreciates your contribution in the capture of these criminals."

Cassie wanted to gag. She had a firsthand understanding now why the others wrinkled their noses whenever Agent Fowler's name came up in conversation. The man really did have a one-track mind—get the job done, no matter the cost.

"Are we done here?" James asked the agent over the Skype connection.

"For now. I'll be in touch when I require your services again."

When, not *if*. The distinction didn't escape Cassie's attention.

"Good." James tapped the power button and ended the connection without further ado. "I'm beginning to hate that man," he growled under his breath.

Mallory nodded and let out an audible sigh of relief. "Are we really done? I mean done, done?"

"Once Fowler gets his hooks in you, you're never truly done with him. But for now, yeah. We're done."

The day seemed like it had lasted a year. They'd risen at the crack of dawn to visit with Ysolde and the kidnapped girls before the Department of Health and Welfare spirited them away, some of the girls to family here in the States and some back to Nigeria. Those who'd lost their families to terrorists would be fostered with Nigerian national emigrants and, hopefully, assimilated into our culture. Much better prospects than what waited for them in Africa. As for Ysolde Hermón, she had more leads to chase in her vendetta against the Herrera organization, reports to file, statements to make, and she'd even hinted about an expose for the media in the not too distant future.

She and Mallory had received a command summons to James's office for a noon Skype debriefing—more like interrogation—with Agent Fowler and members of his staff. Six long, grueling hours later, they were finally done.

"I let your mom know we were running late and that I'd feed you. What do you say? Want to grab a bite to eat?" James closed all his files, dropped them in a desk drawer, and locked it.

"I could eat," Cassie responded, wondering yet again why Sheriff Eli Castle from Challis had been called in to participate for a short part of the Skype call. Kyle, James's other deputy, too. Garrett, Wade, and Jonas all made appearances at some point during the day, but not Derek.

"Me, too." Mallory said.

"I know just the place—Sidewinders. I haven't had one of Tate's greasy cheeseburgers in ages. What do you say?"

"I bet you haven't had one since high school, Cass. Remember those fake licenses we used to sneak in that one time?" Mallory leaned over to bump shoulders.

Cassie winced from the slight impact. Her whole body was sore today. A long sleeved button-up tucked into faded jeans and a kerchief tied around her neck hid most of the scrapes, abrasions, and bruises. "Like I could forget. Tate drove us home himself. And Dad made us shovel manure for a month. Yeah, Sidewinders is good."

She'd proved yesterday she could survive hell, so asking about Derek should be nothing. Right? Screwing up her courage, she asked, "James, where's Derek been all day? Everyone else involved in this business showed up."

"He gave his report first thing this morning. I put him on patrol and told him to stay gone while you were here. Didn't want the two of you distracting each other while we closed this case, especially since he has a tendency to go all caveman where you're concerned."

She ducked her head and tried to hide her smile. Maybe he'd call later tonight.

They left Mallory's truck and piled into James's Yukon for the ride to the honky-tonk on the outskirts of town. Less than five minutes later they pulled into a half-full parking lot. Wednesday nights must be slow at the local watering hole.

Cassie spotted Derek's Blazer in the fourth row and frowned at the flurry of thoughts that ran through her head. Was he off duty? Odd. She didn't know he frequented this place. Or maybe Tate called him in to settle a brawl? But if he had, why would Derek park so far away?

James came around and opened the front passenger door for Mallory and the rear door for Cassie. Neither appeared to have seen Derek's car and strode unseeing toward the bar's entrance.

Cassie lagged behind and tried to ignore an unexpected feeling of disquiet.

The door opened ahead of them and two cowboys came out, serenaded by the loud, strident twang of a rocking country song. They tipped their hats and held the door.

James motioned Cassie in first.

She took several steps inside the darkened, smoke-filled room, her boots scuffing along the aged wooden floor. The smell of spilled beer, cigarettes, stale sweat, and an underlying odor of strong pine cleanser assailed her nostrils. A quick look around showed half the tables occupied and a crowd gathered around the two pool tables in the back, but it was the tall, dark haired Texan who drew her eye. He stood at the bar surrounded by a bevy of women, all of them flirting, squirming, and pawing him. One of the women ran her blood red nails up and down his chest. Miranda Weldon. She and her sister Colleen were the town's sirens.

Cassie's upper lip curled in disgust. Utterly beautiful and sinfully wicked, Miranda drew men like road kill drew buzzards.

Every molecule of oxygen hung up in Cassie's chest when Miranda snaked her hand around Derek's neck and tugged his head down.

His grin revealed white, even teeth and deep dimples, not to mention a naughty side Cassie had often seen. He turned his face away at the last moment so Miranda's lips brushed across his ear.

She laughed, a breathy, sexy hum but refused to release her hold. Instead, she whispered something that brought a flush to Derek's cheeks.

He flashed his grin again and shook his head. "No, I don't think so, sweetheart."

Sweetheart? The man was such a heartbreaker. He would flirt with a scarecrow if it wore lipstick and a skirt. Not that you could call the scrap Miranda wore clothing since it barely covered the essentials.

He looked up then, looked around as though searching … and froze when his green eyes found her.

Hurt coursed through her. She'd known all along Derek Naughton was a player. And yet, he'd been so solicitous, so caring yesterday. He'd hinted for weeks now of wanting more with her, not Miranda, not any of the other women. She had a split second to make up her mind—flight or fight.

The other women must have sensed his distraction. Their smiles faded. Hands faltered. Laughter faded away to an uneasy silence.

Derek pulled Miranda's hand from his neck and took a step away from her. "Cassie."

Miranda turned. A hard glint entered her eyes.

In that moment, Cassie made up her mind. She was tired of running away when things got tough. If she could fight for the relationship with Mallory, she could darn well fight for one with Derek. By his own admission, the man had never had a long term relationship. She just had to teach him a few rules.

"Told ya," Tate Murtaugh chortled from behind the bar. "Mess around with a Cameron, they'll take your head and hand you your butt."

Six long strides brought Cassie to the circle of women. "Excuse me, ladies. I believe you've found something that belongs to me."

Like magic, they stepped away, making room for Cassie … all but one.

"This one's taken, sister. Go find your own man." Miranda sneered at Cassie and reached for Derek again.

Oh, heck no, that floozy did not stake a claim on Derek. Fury boiled up from the fire that had smoldered inside Cassie for the past year. Was she really going to do this? Get into a bar brawl? With Miranda Weldon? Oh criminy, they'd arrest her for real this time.

She reached for Miranda's bony arm at the same time Derek pushed the woman away. Out of reach. "That's what I've been trying to tell you, darlin'. This boy's been taken off the market, and this is the sweet thing you can thank."

"What?" Miranda said. Her mouth hung open.

"What?" Cassie said at the same time. Confusion put her brain into a spin.

"Yep. What say we get out of here, Baby." Derek took Cassie's arm and tugged her toward the door.

James and Mallory stood slack jawed at the entrance. They didn't utter a word when Derek yanked Cassie outside. "I'll see she gets home. Don't wait up."

Tate's cackle followed them out the door.

Cassie regained her senses halfway to Derek's Blazer and dug her feet in. "Let me go. I know what I saw in there. And what do you mean I took you off the market?"

Derek stopped and stood toe to toe with her. "What you saw was me besieged by six of the most aggressive women I've ever encountered and me trying to be polite like my mama taught me. I swear those girls could chew up and spit out a whole unit of Navy SEALs. 'No' doesn't exist in their vocabulary, Miranda in particular. I can't believe you thought I was into that. And yes, you have taken me off the market. You ruined me for anyone else, so deal with it."

She stared, unable to think of a single thing to say.

"Fine. We do this the hard way." He bent low, put a

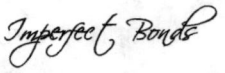

shoulder into her middle, and an arm behind her knees. Straightening, he headed for his truck again.

Upright one moment, thrown over his shoulder the next, Cassie couldn't decide whether to pound on his back or bite him, like either would do any damage to the slab of muscle under her chin. She settled for a squeal, kicked her legs a couple of times, and grinned all the way to the Blazer.

He tossed her in the front passenger seat, hooked the seat belt around her, and stuck a long index finger in her face. "Stay put."

Gravel sprayed everywhere as they sped out of the parking lot. A few minutes later, Derek turned down the road to the Triple C, but instead of taking the right fork that led home, he turned left.

"Where are we going?" she asked in a subdued voice.

His expression, not angry but not smiling either, never wavered. "You'll see."

"Okay, be mysterious. Why are we going this way?"

"Because for once I'm going to talk, and you're going to listen. And I want to show you something."

He stopped on the ridge overlooking the big barn and the pastureland. Even with the fading light the Salmon River still sparkled in the distance. Further to the right, the lights of the ranch house stood out. Home.

Cassie released her seat belt and turned sideways to face him. "I'm listening."

He remained staring straight ahead, his profile strong in the dim light, hands gripping the wheel. "I know it hurt you to see the girls pawing over me. They approached me, and I didn't encourage them. I swear. I was about to leave when you arrived."

She nodded. "I was hurt. At first. And more than a little jealous. But it didn't take me long to figure out they'd ganged up on you. Miranda has a bit of a reputation around these parts. You're not the first man she or her sister have targeted with their little army. I wanted to rip her hair out."

He looked at her then and those drop-dead sexy dimples made an appearance. "I didn't want to have to arrest you again."

"Would have been worth it to see that scrawny witch with a bald spot."

He snorted. And then broke into a fit of laughter. "Thanks for the visual."

"So, tell me. What's so special about this?" She waved at the valley.

He didn't answer. Derek got out of the car instead, jogged around to her side, opened the door, and took her hand. "Come with me."

Cassie found herself looking out across the pastureland.

Derek came up behind her and pulled her back against his chest. His chin rested on top of her head. He pointed. "There, across the valley, on the other side of the river, and up about a

hundred yards. See where the land levels out?"

She nodded.

"I spoke to Cody about buying a couple of acres."

She turned around in his arms. "Dad would never sell a piece of his land, not outside the family anyway."

Derek stared at her for a long time and then returned his gaze to the land he'd pointed out. "What if it was family? How would you feel about that?"

Her eyes closed, squeezed tight until geometric patterns tattooed the back of her lids. She chewed on her bottom lip, stumbling inside her mind to make sense of what he said. "What are you saying, Derek?"

"Nothing. Yet. I'm trying to get the elephant in the corner out in the open."

She giggled. "By shooting it with a grenade launcher?"

"Give me something, Cassidy. My bared soul is bleeding here. I need a read on your feelings."

Her head dipped down as shyness took over. "I ... uh wouldn't be averse to the idea. I rather like the thought of you living near my family. But for how long? By your own admission you've never had or wanted a long term relationship with a woman, so I have to tell you, buying land is a terrible way to get a date."

He tightened his hold. The sound of his strong, steady heartbeat resonated through her. "This is uncharted territory for me, Baby." His voice dropped to a guttural growl. "I want forever. With you."

Cassie's mind went blank, stuck on that single word. "Forever?"

"You drive me insane, Cassidy Elizabeth Cameron. I can't stop thinking about you. You bewitched me last summer, you and that pitiful excuse for a kiss."

"Wait." She looked up at him. "I liked that kiss. It blew my mind."

He chuckled. "We have a lot to talk about, and you have a lot to learn," he said low and slow. "First, I swear I'm gonna die if I don't kiss you. A real kiss." He pulled her flush against his body and claimed her lips.

They remained locked in an embrace long enough for the night sounds to resume. Insects hummed. An owl screeched. Somewhere off in the woods, a small animal scurried through the underbrush.

A long, breathless while later, she pulled away. Not far though. Her legs wouldn't hold her. "I see what you mean. I think I've been deprived my whole life."

Her heartbeat slowed to the rate of a hummingbird's and some of the feeling came back to her toes.

"This is what I want—you and me. Exclusive. Nobody else. And you can't run off to Idaho Falls to work for that fancy doctor either. You have to stay and give us a chance."

And he continued to rock her world. "Wow, you don't want much, do you?" She soothed him by rubbing circles on

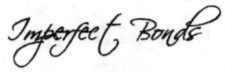

his chest with her fingertips. "I don't know what my folks will say about us … about any of this."

"Your mom and dad like me. Your brothers, too. They know I'm mean enough to fend off your demons and keep you in line at the same time."

A subtle shift allowed her elbow to explain to his ribs what she thought of his comment.

"Oomph." Derek lowered his head and whispered directly in her ear. "I'm kidding. In fact, it's probably me you'll have to keep in line. I mean, I'll make mistakes along the way, do some stupid … er … stuff and—"

She stopped his words with a finger to his lips. "Shut up, Derek. You're a man. Stupid stuff goes with the package. Now come here and kiss this deprived woman again."

He groaned. "I'll grovel forever if it will keep you in my arms. Because that's what I want with you. Forever."

Chapter Thirty

Derek's hands slipped on the steering wheel when he turned onto the lane to the Triple C Ranch. He hadn't had sweaty palms since high school. He wiped his hands on his pants one at a time and took the fork that led to the ranch house.

Dinner with the Camerons. Mrs. Cameron—Cate—had called and extended an invitation. Surely, they wouldn't ask him to share a meal if they were against the idea of their daughter and a … a what? A deputy working for a meager salary? A hardened military man who'd seen and done too much? A Texas boy with no college education or anything else to offer their daughter?

He pulled up in front of the house and had to wipe his hands again.

The front door banged open as he lifted one leg out of the Blazer. Uh-oh. The brothers had decided to greet him outside. En masse. Lord help him. He might not survive the confrontation.

"Naughton," Garrett spoke first and nodded.

Not a good start. His former team leader had never called

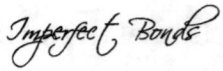

him by his last name. It was always first name, Ice, or Iceman.
Derek nodded but didn't respond. He closed the truck door
behind him with quiet authority.

Wade joined Garrett on the right side, Jonas on the left.
No greetings. No jokes. No handshake or smile. Only arms
crossed over three very broad chests.

Derek swallowed hard. He stood his ground but didn't
advance, ready to leave if things turned ugly. He couldn't fight
with Cassidy's brothers. Not about her.

"You look like a mangy cur with his tail tucked between
his legs." Wade spat on the ground. His expression never
altered.

Derek bristled.

"Looks to me like the mighty Iceman has melted." Jonas's
mouth twitched, but he pressed his lips tighter and held onto
the same grim expression as his two brothers.

"Go ahead. Get it out of your system," Derek growled and
crossed his arms, too. "Just know this. It won't change a thing."

Derek did a wary assessment of the three. He felt
confident he could take Wade, despite the man's size. Jonas, he
didn't know. Little brother was a complete unknown. Garrett
was an even match, a crapshoot. Unless they joined forces …

He squared his shoulders. Any sign of weakness and
they'd pound him into dog meat.

A long, slow breath escaped. He wouldn't fight with
Cassidy's brothers and risk her anger. Only one solution.

"Give my regrets to your mother." He opened the truck door and—

"Hold on, there. You're not running away, are you?" Jonas asked.

"There's a first time for everything, and from where I sit I'd say the Iceman is teetering on the very brink of falling in love. I just wish it wasn't our baby sister he wants to maul." Garrett walked toward the truck.

Derek paused, one leg already in the truck. "Huh?"

"I'm saying I hate the idea of Cassidy falling for any guy, but if it had to happen …" He broke into a grin and stuck his hand out. "I'm glad it's you."

Wade and Jonas joined him, chuckling and slapping Derek on the back.

"Boys, why are you keeping Derek outside? Dinner's almost ready." Cate Cameron stood at the door wiping her hands on the ever present apron.

"Come on in, Derek. Mom made her special pot roast just for you." Garrett tugged on his arm.

The four men walked inside, joking and shoving each other.

CCC

"So, you talk to Cass about the land across the river?"

Derek choked on the sip of water he'd taken, and quickly raised his napkin to his mouth. "Uh, yes, sir. I mentioned it."

"Daddy," Cassidy chastised her father. She sat beside

Derek and patted his back while he coughed.

"What? I don't like loose ends."

Cody Cameron might be in his sixties, but the man was still a force to be reckoned with. The last thing Derek wanted to do was get on his bad side. "Uh—"

"Cody, stop it. You're moving way faster than Cassidy and Derek. It didn't work with me either, remember?" Cate Cameron scolded her husband. "Besides, I kind of like the idea of watching romances bud."

She looked from Derek to Cassidy … to Mallory. Interesting. Had she caught the undercurrents running between Mal and James?

"Thanks, Mom," Cassidy murmured.

Cody propped his elbows on the table and folded his hands together. "All right, but only because I know his intentions."

"Daddy!" Cassie exclaimed again.

Mallory clapped a hand over her mouth to smother a giggle.

TJ and Lucy joined in.

"Cody!" Cate huffed.

The brothers exploded in laughter.

"Uh, sir, no disrespect, but I'd like to move this forward with Cassidy at my own rate." Derek tried hard not to grin at the blush suffusing his woman's face. His woman. Dadgum, but that sounded good.

Cody Cameron's scowl would have frightened a lesser man, but Derek had already withstood Cassidy's three overgrown big brothers. One wiry old man wouldn't get in his way. He hoped.

Her father nodded. Once. But the hard line of his mouth never changed. "I've got my eye on you. Now, what about those kidnappers?"

Cassidy and the rest of her family released a collective sigh.

Derek sent up a silent prayer, something he seemed to do a lot of lately, for the reprieve. "What would you like to know?"

"We done with this business? For good?"

"Yes, sir. According to Agent Fowler, those girls with family have been returned safely. Those whose families were killed by terrorists in Nigeria are being introduced into Nigerian homes here in the States. The two men driving the van and Zavala, the tattooed dude who threatened Cassidy, are in the custody of the BII. I doubt they'll ever see the light of day again."

"Thugs like them tend to disappear when Fowler gets his hands on them. They never see the legal system." Jonas popped a whole dinner roll into his mouth.

Cody lifted one eyebrow at his son and then turned his fierce blue eyes back to Derek. "That so?"

"Yes, sir. We don't ask questions."

"And the other one? The higher ups?"

"The fancy man in the suit pulled diplomatic strings and was airlifted out last night. Knowing Fowler, Mr. Sebastian Toure's name and face have been splattered across every security database in the known world. He won't be of much value to his bosses after this." Derek reached over, took Cassidy's hand in his, and squeezed. One thing for sure, the man would never get within spitting distance of her again.

"Ha," Garrett snorted. "My bet is old Sebastian will disappear one day soon. The man's like a spotlight pointing to the organization behind these kidnappings. I'd say his value has hit a negative number."

"As for the Herrera organization, I doubt our efforts made a dent in their operations. No more than a temporary inconvenience. They'll regroup and set up a new route. That's Fowler's worry now."

"Will you boys go with Fowler? Return to the B-whatever?"

"No." The word echoed round the room as Derek, Garrett, Wade, and Jonas all replied in unison.

Cody gave another single nod. Man was terse in all ways of communications. "Good. Trent?"

"Gone the way of Zavala. Out of Cassidy's life for good." Derek couldn't hold back the tone of satisfaction.

"You know you're the only one who calls her Cassidy. Why is that?" Lucy asked.

"Cassie's the daughter and little sister. Cass is everyone's friend. But Cassidy …" He turned to stare deep into her eyes. "She's the woman who stole my heart."

Shocked silence ensued. For all of five seconds.

"Awwww," TJ, Lucy, Mallory, and Cate crooned from around the table.

Garrett and Wade erupted in belly laughs. "Another one bites the dust. Welcome to the dark side." They did a fist bump even as TJ and Lucy punched them.

"Ewwwww." Jonas made retching noises. "Excuse me. I think I'm gonna be sick."

"Got any brothers, or maybe clones?" Mallory asked with a grin.

"One brother, but he's five years younger than you and never been out of the state of Texas. Doubt he ever will. You think you might like Texas?"

"Maybe," Mal replied. "Then again …"

Growls and chuckles followed her response.

Cody waited in quiet silence until Derek looked at him again. Cassidy's father nodded again. Twice this time.

CCC

"Take a walk with me?" Derek asked when they left the table.

"I need to help—"

Cassidy's mother cut her off. "Go on, sweetie. We got this." Her mother gestured toward Mallory, TJ, and Lucy.

"Okay." Cassidy's entire face lit up when she smiled.

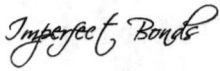

He led her toward the front door, down the steps, and past her mother's rose garden. The petals had closed up hours ago, but their fragrance lingered in the warm night air.

They walked away from the house, away from the road and barn, toward a swale on the western side of the property. Lush grass and a wealth of wild flowers dotted this side of the valley. "Let's sit here. We need to talk."

She settled to the ground in a graceful movement and tucked her legs to one side under her.

Derek folded his long legs and sank down facing her. He needed the space if he wanted to get the words out. Touching her would blow his control to smithereens. Still, he couldn't resist running his index finger along the line of her jaw. So beautiful. So precious. And all his. He'd make sure of it.

"Cassidy, my life so far has been hard and rough. I don't know soft and sweet, but I want it for you. All of it. The house on your dad's land—only if he'll let me buy, though. The white picket fence. A dog. A cat. Some horses and a barn. Church on Sunday followed by dinner with your family. Long, slow rides along the river. Picnics. And one day, a couple of kids with a tire swing in the front yard."

She stared up at him, her eyes like black, glistening pools in the moonlight.

"Hey, you gotta give me something here."

A petite tornado bowled him over. She launched herself at him and wrapped her arms around his neck. "Yes." Kiss.

"Yes." Kiss, kiss. "I want that." Kiss. "With you." She pulled back an inch. "More than that, though, I want you, Derek. You ruined me for any other man."

Another tornado burst on the scene, this one of the four-legged, furry kind. Whining with joy, Sadeé wormed her way between them.

HUMAN TRAFFICKING
IS ONE OF THE WORLD'S
MOST SHAMEFUL CRIMES!

<u>Facts Everyone Should Know</u>

- **Human Trafficking, a form of modern slavery, is a serious crime and a grave violation of basic human rights.**
- **There are 20-30 million victims each year.**
- **This worldwide criminal industry fetches profits of more than $32 billion annually.**
- **The average cost of a human slave in the global market is $90.**
- **Trafficking includes a long list of human rights violations: forcing a victim into prostitution, involuntary servitude, compelling a victim to commit sex acts for pornographic purposes, child adoption sales, organ harvesting, and ova removal.**
- **The U.S. State Department estimates 600,000 – 800,000 persons are trafficked across our international borders every year.**
  - **Of these, 80% are female; half of all transported are children.**
  - **Of these, 80% involve sexual exploitation, while 19% involve commercial labor.**
- **Almost every country in the world is affected by trafficking, whether as the country of origin or a destination for victims.**

Learn How to Protect Yourself and Your Children & How to Fight Against Human Trafficking

U.S. Department of State
15 Ways You Can Help Fight Human Trafficking
http://ow.ly/EyLw302Ayys

Department of Homeland Security
Human Trafficking Awareness
http://ow.ly/MH3c302Ayv2

Department of Homeland Security
Human Trafficking: 101
http://ow.ly/wW7O302Ayip

Human Trafficking Awareness Organization
Spreading Awareness to End Human Trafficking
http://humantraffickingawareness.org/

The National Human Trafficking Resources Center
HOTLINE: 1 (888) 373-7888
https://traffickingresourcecenter.org/type-trafficking/human-trafficking

Text HELP to 233733 (BEFREE)
To get help for victims and survivors of human trafficking, or to connect with local services.

The Polaris BEFREE Project
http://polarisproject.org/human-trafficking

About the Author

Elizabeth Noyes, adventure-loving author, dedicated dreamer, tireless traveler.

Author of *The Imperfect Series*, she sets this riveting saga in the majestic mountains and plains of rural Idaho. Here, the Cameron family deals with the same character flaws, hidden vulnerabilities, outlandish hopes, and desperate dreams we all know so well. Like iron filings to a magnet, though, crime and violence is drawn to the family, forcing each one to confront difficult moral dilemmas as they struggle with lines blurred by today's society. Strong family values, a belief in an Almighty Creator, and a commitment to those who finagle a way into their hearts gives them the strength to make the hard decisions in the age-old battle of good vs. evil.

Her full-length, nail-biting stories touch on many hot topics plaguing today's culture, themes such as drug dealing and human trafficking. Warning: You might encounter a bevy of hot alpha males who meet their matches!

Elizabeth also co-authored two multi-author novellas, *A Dozen Apologies* and *The Love Boat Bachelor*, which are included in The Heart Seekers Series, available in print and on Kindle.

Contact Information:
www.ElizabethNoyesWrites.com
www.facebook.com/Elizabeth.Noyes.54
www.twitter.com/ENoyes5246

Amazon Author Page:
http://amzn.to/1HdjwOF

Other Books by the Author

ELIZABETH NOYES

Imperfect Wings
Book One in the Imperfect Series

Evil stalks TJ McKendrick.

Three years after burying her father, TJ visits Honduras where he died. While there, she witnesses a murder and is forced to flee.

Don Castillo dreams of power. Funnel the drugs into the States and it's his. First though, he must kill the woman who dared spy on him.

The last thing Garrett Cameron needs is another woman interrupting his life, but when the feisty vixen that put a monkey wrench in his mission two years ago shows up at his ranch running for her life -- what's a man to do?

The attraction between TJ and Garrett bursts into flame in the midst of danger, a fierce desire that neither is prepared for. Her past is filled with betrayal. He's lived a life of violence, and love isn't for someone like him. Do they dare let go of past hurts and embrace a future together?

Only faith in God and trust in each other can overcome the deadly odds they face.

Available on Kindle and in print from Amazon
and from other booksellers by request.

ELIZABETH NOYES

Imperfect Trust
Book Two in the Imperfect Series

Scarred by childhood tragedy and then abandoned by a mother who couldn't handle a gifted child, Lucy Kiddron survived foster care to become a computer analyst for the government. Three years later, she's poised to leave the agency and launch her own video game … until her final assignment goes horribly wrong.

Wade Cameron understands betrayal. His ex-fiancé sold him out and now he's neck deep in computer code, trying to find the back door she inserted. Worse, a smart-mouthed computer hacker has just flipped his world upside down.

A terrorist wants Wade's computer program. A psycho killer wants Lucy's life. And then the stakes are raised when a sniper takes aim. But who's the target—Wade or Lucy? The two risk everything as they muddle through a minefield of danger, distrust, and a burgeoning attraction that won't be denied.

Available on Kindle and in print from Amazon
and from other booksellers by request.

The Heart Seekers Series

Three Books in One, Plus a Bonus!

A Dozen Apologies: Mara Adkins, a promising fashion designer, has fallen off the ladder of success, and she can't seem to get up. In college, Mara and her sorority sisters played an ugly game, and Mara was usually the winner. She'd date men she considered geeks, win their confidence, and then she'd dump them publicly. Now, Mara stumbles, bumbles, and humbles her way toward employment and toward possible reconciliation with the twelve men she humiliated.

The Love Boat Bachelor: What's a sworn bachelor to do on a Caribbean cruise full of romance and love? Brent will either have to jump ship or embrace the unforgettable romantic comedy headed his way.

Unlikely Merger: If her best friend has her way, Mercy will simply marry one of the single, available men she meets, but they overwhelm her. So handsome and kind. And so many. Even if she felt obliged, how could she ever choose?

We've also included updates for most of the characters, too.

BONUS:

The Christmas Tree Treasure Hunt: Grace takes delivery of a

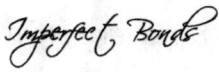
package and her life is turned upside down by nine sealed
mystery envelopes from her late grandmother. Grammie's
instructions require Grace to take the journey of her lifetime,
not only to far off places, but also into the deepest parts of her
heart. As she follows the trail laid out for her and uncovers her
family's darkest secrets, Grace is forced to confront the loss
and betrayal that has scarred her past and seek the greatest
Christmas Treasure of all.

Look for other books

published by

www.WriteIntegrity.com

and

Pix-N-Pens Publishing

www.PixNPens.com

www.ingramcontent.com/pod-product-compliance
Lightning Source LLC
Chambersburg PA
CBHW071640260626
47170CB00001B/176